America Loves
Johanna Lindsey

"First rate romance."
New York Daily News

"One of the most reliable authors around.
Her books are well-paced and well-written,
filled with strong characters, humor,
interesting plots—and, of course, romance."
Cincinnati Enquirer

"Johanna Lindsey has a sure touch
where historical romance is concerned."
Newport News Daily Press

"She manages to etch memorable characters
in every novel she writes."
Chicago Sun-Times

"The charm and appeal of her characters
are infectious."
Publishers Weekly

"Long may she continue to write."
CompuServe Romance Reviews

SCHUKRAFT BOOKS
2261 W. LELAND AVE.
CHICAGO IL 60625
(773) 283-3171

Also by Johanna Lindsey

ALL I NEED IS YOU • ANGEL • BRAVE THE WILD WIND
CAPTIVE BRIDE • DEFY NOT THE HEART
FIRES OF WINTER • A GENTLE FEUDING
GENTLE ROGUE • GLORIOUS ANGEL
HEART OF THUNDER • A HEART SO WILD
HEARTS AFLAME • THE HEIR
HOME FOR THE HOLIDAYS • JOINING
KEEPER OF THE HEART • LOVE ME FOREVER
LOVE ONLY ONCE • THE MAGIC OF YOU
MAN OF MY DREAMS • ONCE A PRINCESS
PARADISE WILD • A PIRATE'S LOVE
THE PRESENT • PRISONER OF MY DESIRE
SAVAGE THUNDER • SAY YOU LOVE ME • SECRET FIRE
SILVER ANGEL • SO SPEAKS THE HEART
SURRENDER MY LOVE
TENDER IS THE STORM • TENDER REBEL
UNTIL FOREVER • WARRIOR'S WOMAN
WHEN LOVE AWAITS • YOU BELONG TO ME

And in Hardcover

THE PURSUIT

ATTENTION: ORGANIZATIONS AND CORPORATIONS
Most Avon Books paperbacks are available at special quantity discounts for bulk purchases for sales promotions, premiums, or fund-raising. For information, please call or write:

Special Markets Department, HarperCollins Publishers, Inc., 10 East 53rd Street, New York, N.Y. 10022–5299.
Telephone: (212) 207–7528. Fax: (212) 207-7222.

JOHANNA LINDSEY

HEART of a WARRIOR

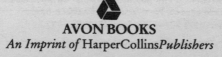

AVON BOOKS
An Imprint of HarperCollinsPublishers

This is a work of fiction. Names, characters, places, and incidents are products of the author's imagination or are used fictitiously. Any resemblance to actual events, locales, organizations, or persons, living or dead, is entirely coincidental.

AVON BOOKS
An Imprint of HarperCollins*Publishers*
10 East 53rd Street
New York, New York 10022-5299

Copyright © 2001 by Johanna Lindsey
Excerpt from *The Pursuit* copyright © 2002 by Johanna Lindsey
ISBN: 0-380-81479-X
www.avonromance.com

All rights reserved. No part of this book may be used or reproduced in any manner whatsoever without written permission, except in the case of brief quotations embodied in critical articles and reviews. For information address AvonBooks, an Imprint of HarperCollins Publishers.

First Avon Books paperback printing: March 2002
First William Morrow hardcover printing: May 2001

Avon Trademark Reg. U.S. Pat. Off. and in Other Countries, Marca Registrada, Hecho en U.S.A.
HarperCollins ® is a registered trademark of HarperCollins Publishers Inc.

Printed in the U.S.A.

10 9 8 7 6 5 4 3 2 1

If you purchased this book without a cover, you should be aware that this book is stolen property. It was reported as "unsold and destroyed" to the publisher, and neither the author nor the publisher has received any payment for this "stripped book."

For Dylan, a warrior at heart

HEART
of a
WARRIOR

Prologue

BRITTANY CALLAGHAN STARED IN THE MIRROR ABOVE her dresser, satisfied with the results. The blouse was sequined, fancy, but not too sexy. The jewelry was demure, nothing flashy. The long velvet skirt was elegant, slim, slit to the knee. It had taken her two hours to get ready, not that she needed that much time to look nice, but tonight was special, so she'd devoted more time than usual in her preparations.

Her makeup, applied just right, brought out the deep green of her eyes. Her roommate, Jan, had done her hair, managing to get the long mass of copper into a tight coiffure that would have earned Jan praise in her beautician's class. They made a great pair as roommates, swapping each other's skills as needed. Brittany could fix just about anything that went wrong in the apartment and kept Jan's car in top shape, while

Jan cooked most of the meals and did Brittany's hair for special events, since she never had time to get to a beauty shop herself.

They had been sharing an apartment in Seaview now for three years. It wasn't a big town by any means. Oddly, it wasn't by the sea either and the standard joke was that it was named in anticipation of "the big quake" that would show up one day, bringing the coast to them. A joke in poor taste, but if you lived in California, you either joked about earthquakes or you moved.

Seaview was one of the newer towns spread out inland away from the big cities, but within reasonable driving distance if you happened to work in the big city. The closest big one in their case was San Francisco. They were far enough away to not experience the chill weather and fogs off the Bay. They enjoyed such mild weather, in fact, that Sunnyview would have been a much more appropriate name for their town.

It was great having a roommate she got along so well with. Jan was petite, effervescent, always had a boyfriend on hand for anything she wanted to do, whether it was the same one or not, she didn't particularly care. She liked men, had a need to always have one around, even if she didn't take any of them seriously. Her only fault, if it could be termed one, was that she was a matchmaker at heart. She might not be able to settle on any one man in particular herself, but she saw no reason that her friends couldn't.

Brittany had proven to be a challenging subject for matchmaking though, and not for the usual reasons. She was beautiful, intelligent, responsible, had interesting careers, and admirable goals. She just happened to be six feet tall.

Height had always been a problem for Brittany, from childhood on. It put a serious restriction on the relationships she could develop, to the point where she had stopped putting any effort into developing one.

She had tried dating men shorter than her, but it never worked. The jokes would come out eventually about her height, or the man would get ribbed by his friends, or more often, their faces would accidently brush against her breasts—deliberately of course. She had decided, when she did marry, her husband would have to be at least as tall as she was. Taller would be nice, but she wouldn't hold her breath on getting that lucky, would settle for the same height.

Yet having such a problem did tend to make her notice tall men right off. Unfortunately, with a lot of really tall men, most of that height was naturally in their legs, and on some men, this tended to look a bit odd, particularly on the skinny ones. She'd take odd, though. She wasn't particular, just particular about not wanting to look down on her husband.

But a husband was a long way off for her, despite her age approaching thirty, or so she'd thought. Not that she hadn't wanted one eventually, but she was goal-oriented, and she had one major goal that all her efforts were put into these days, owning her own home that she built with her own hands.

To that end, she worked two jobs, part-time at the local health spa in the evenings and all day on Saturdays, where she kept herself in good shape while doing the same for others, regulating diets and exercise programs. Her full-time job through the week was with Arbor Construction.

Sunday was her only day off, and the only chance

she had to take care of the normal activities of life, like writing her family, balancing the checkbook, paying bills, house cleaning, laundry, shopping, repairing her car, etc. It was also the only day she had to simply relax, and she preferred to spend that free time catching up on sleep or working on designing her dream house, not working on a relationship. The two jobs gave her next to no time for socializing, which was why she had stopped trying—until she met Thomas Johnson.

She had tried seeing the same man more than once, every Sunday actually, tried it with more than a few men thanks to her roommate's persistence. But that never worked out well, because they soon resented that she wasn't available more often. She'd been waiting until after she had her house. She could quit the second job, then have the same free time that everyone else enjoyed. Then would be soon enough to start looking for a serious relationship.

Tom had changed her mind about that. She had begun to think she'd never find the right man for her, but Thomas Johnson filled the bill beyond her expectations. He was six foot six so he met her major criteria, but he was also exceptionally handsome and an established executive in advertising. She was blue-collar, he was white, but they still found common ground. He might make her feel self-conscious occasionally, but that was too minor a thing to counter her belief that he was the one for her. Stubborn certainty might better describe it, but then she *was* Irish.

Actually, her last name might give testament to that, but her family were Americans to the core. Her grandfather Callaghan had owned a farm in Kansas that he built from scratch and that her father inherited when he died. This is where she and her three brothers grew up. None of the Irish part of their history had been preserved, if anything was known about it, because her grandfather had been orphaned too young to have learned any of it.

But their first names, well, it wasn't hard to guess that her parents had been a bit flaky when they'd started having children. They denied being part of the hippy generation, called themselves "free-spirited," whatever that meant, and in fact, they had met while hiking cross-country, and had gone off to see the world together. They were hitchhiking through England when the first child came along, and had been so impressed with that country, that their sons got named York, Kent, and Devon, in that order.

As the only girl who showed up last, Brittany got named after the entire country. Her parents took offense when it was pointed out that Brittany was actually a province in France, and not the shortened version of Great Britain.

Brittany had a no-nonsense attitude about life. You lived it, and eventually, you might even enjoy living it. That was actually a joke or meant to be, yet it wasn't that far off the mark on her own life. She actually liked her jobs, got a lot of satisfaction out of them, she just missed having the time to do all the little things in life that everyone else took for granted. But then she was no stranger to hard work and having little time for simple pleasures. Growing up on a farm, you went to school, then came home to endless chores. She hadn't had much free time then, and when she left home, even less.

She had made time for Tom, though. They'd been

dating for four months now, went out every Saturday night, spent every Sunday together. As a busy executive who often worked late into the evenings during the week, his time was also somewhat restricted, so he never complained that he couldn't see her more often, was probably relieved that she had no such complaints either. He hadn't mentioned marriage yet, but she didn't doubt that he would soon, and her answer was going to be yes. Which was why she had finally made the decision to give up her virginity to him.

It was an odd thing to still have at her age, odd enough that it caused a good deal of embarrassment if she was forced to own up to it. That usually only happened when whoever she'd been dating started putting the pressure on to have sex. But the result of her confession would always be the same, laughter on their part—or disbelief.

Tom didn't know. He merely thought she was being cautious. It was more than that. Heavy necking was fine, could be fun or incredibly frustrating, but going all the way required more than just liking, at least for her. She needed feelings first, strong feelings, and she had those now. . . .

"Tonight's the night then?" Jan said from the doorway of Brittany's bedroom with a knowing grin.

"Yes," Brittany replied and managed not to blush about it.

"Hot damn!"

Brittany rolled her eyes. "Let's not discuss it, or I'll get cold feet."

"Cold? It's a wonder your feet haven't moldered, you've waited so long—"

"Which part of 'not discuss it' did you misunderstand?" Brittany cut in.

"Okay, okay," Jan conceded with a chuckle. "Just trying to alleviate some of that nervousness you're drowning in. You've been tense about this all day, when there's no need. You *are* sure about him, aren't you?"

"Yes, I—" Brittany started, then groaned. "Oh, God, you're going to make me have second thoughts!"

"Don't do that! Okay, I'm shutting up. Zipped lips. You're going to have a great time tonight. Stop worrying. This guy's right for you. Hell, he'd be right for anyone! He's almost too perfect to be believed—no, scratch that. I didn't say that. Didn't I say I was shutting up?"

Brittany smiled, grateful for Jan's silliness. She *had* been tense, when she shouldn't be. She'd made the decision, had been agonizing over it for weeks, but was satisfied that it was the right step for her at this point. She *was* sure about Tom. That was all that really mattered—wasn't it?

Chapter 1

THE LY-SAN-TERS WERE FINALLY GOING HOME. THIS VISIT to his mother's homeworld of Kystran had been a much longer journey than Dalden Ly-San-Ter had counted on. Still he was glad he had elected to go along. Unlike his sister, Shanelle, who had gone there to study for a while, he had never been to Kystran before. He'd heard much about it from his mother, had seen computer-simulated pictures of life there, but it simply wasn't the same as seeing it firsthand. It was also something he hoped to never have to experience again.

But it was where his mother came from, and he felt he understood her a little better by seeing firsthand the things that made her so different from the Sha-Ka'ani people whom she now lived among. He had always been torn, nearly literally, in two by his parents. His mother, Tedra, represented all that was modern and "civilized," while his father, Challen, represented old beliefs and what most worlds termed *barbaric*.

There was no compatibility between two social cultures of such complete and utter differences, and yet his parents had managed to become lifemates anyway. Not an easy thing for them, and not easy for their children, who grew up wanting to please them both.

Dalden had finally had to make a choice, and thankfully, his mother not only supported it, but had expected it. He was a Sha-Ka'ani warrior, after all. He could not *be* that warrior if he was going to slip every once in a while and talk as she did, or worry whether he would be displeasing her. So he had fully embraced his father's ways and never regretted it.

His sister, on the other hand, was comfortable with both cultures, could be a dutiful warrior's lifemate, as she now was, adhering to rules and laws that she knew were antiquated by most standards but worked well on Sha-Ka'an. Or she could go out and discover new worlds, as she had once planned to do.

Shanelle hadn't been the least surprised by her first visit to Kystran. Dalden had been nothing but surprised.

He had thought it would be fun. He had expected to be amazed. He even knew the language as well as his own, since, unlike learning it from a Sublim Tape, he already knew all the words that otherwise might not match up without explanations. But nothing could have prepared him for feeling so out of place, for being in a near-constant state of awe. His mother called it "culture shock."

Even after some of the awe died down, which it did

because they ended up staying longer than planned, he still couldn't be comfortable in a land where he wasn't just considered a giant, he *was* a giant by their standards.

Even during the short time they had stopped on the planet Sunder last year to collect Shanelle, his "runaway" sister, Dalden had felt he was dealing with children, those people had been so small.

The Kystrani weren't *that* small, but even their tallest was a good foot shorter than Dalden, and their average a lot shorter than that. It was distinctly uncomfortable to always be looking down on people, and to have those people always staring at you in fear or shock.

The fear was understandable. Some of the Kystrani still remembered all those years ago when warriors like Dalden had tried to take over their planet and had succeeded for a time, enslaving their women, taking away their rights, holding their leader hostage. It was Dalden's mother, with the help of his father, who had defeated those warriors and won Kystran its freedom again.

Tedra had become a national heroine in so doing, and that was the main reason their trip had been extended. They had gone because her longtime friend and old boss, Garr Ce Bernn, director of Kystran, was retiring and had requested their presence for the ceremony. Because it had been more than twenty years since she had been back to her homeworld, he had also arranged for her to be honored while she was there. This amounted to not one but many ceremonies, in many different cities.

Tedra De Arr Ly-San-Ter did not take honoring well. It embarrassed her. To her, she had just been doing her job as a Sec 1 back then, which was to rescue her boss and put him back in power—exactly what she'd done. She had then retired from her life of security enforcement to live with her lifemate on his planet of Sha-Ka'an and had never regretted it. All that honoring had put her in a testy mood that was still with her, even though it was over and they were nearing home.

The trouble was, as Dalden had heard Martha, his mother's Mock II computer, point out more than once, there had been no way to let his father know why they hadn't returned home two weeks ago when they were expected to. Long-distance communication did not include reaching across two star systems.

The distance had been shortened by the discovery of gaali stones on Sha-Ka'an as an energy source that far surpassed anything else known to either of their star systems, but communicating between those star systems was still only possible by the old-fashioned way of sending a ship within range. They would be home by then. So Tedra expected to be facing one very angry lifemate for the worry her longer absence would have caused him.

Dalden was merely amused, but his mother, who would hear no reassurances from him, was determined to fret and worry over the matter. He knew his father would be worried, extremely so. Challen didn't like it when he couldn't protect his lifemate himself, which was why he had "insisted" on Dalden's presence on this journey. But Challen would understand, once informed of what had kept them. No difficulties would come from it, as Tedra seemed to be anticipating.

Brock, Challen's Mock II computer, who was in control of Dalden's ship, offered yet another reason for Tedra's short temper. She simply missed her lifemate. This was the longest she had ever spent away from Challen since she had met him.

Fortunately for the rest of them, since they spent most of their time on Tedra's ship with her, Martha was managing to channel most of the explosive feelings onto herself. It was one of her main functions and she did it extremely well, keeping Tedra from hurting innocent bystanders either with her deadly physical skills or with angry words, which might cause her later grief. Mock IIs were super-modern, super-expensive, free-thinking computers created for one individual only.

These unique computers couldn't be acquired without the buyer undergoing extensive testing first for the final programming that would bond them to their owner. They were more like a companion than an actual computer, their sole purpose being to assure the health, well-being, and happiness of the one they were created for.

Not surprisingly, there weren't too many Mock IIs in existence. Because they were so powerful—a single Mock II could run an entire computerized world by itself—their cost was prohibitive, so only highly advanced, rich worlds could afford one. Kystran, a very rich trade world, actually owned two. That Tedra had acquired a third when she lived on Kystran was due only to Garr losing a wager to her, and Martha had been the payoff. That she had bought yet another for her lifemate was a minor point, due to Sha-Ka'an now being the richest planet in the two star systems because of the gaali stone mines there. Their family owned the largest of those mines.

Wealth meant very little to the Sha-Ka'ani, though. They were a simple people with simple needs. But when something specific was needed, it was nice to have the wherewithal to obtain it.

So, Challen had acquired a battleship to accompany his lifemate to Kystran. Her Transport Rover, while able to carry thousands, was a ship used for world discovery, not serious battle. Dalden and another fifty warriors had been sent to protect Tedra, but Challen had wanted her ship protected as well.

They had had no trouble from other ships, though; the trip had been completely uneventful in that regard. But they were all gathered in the Recreation Room six days from home when Martha announced she was picking up a distress call.

"From who?" was Tedra's first question.

"Sunder."

That answer caused major silence, for various reasons. They all knew the planet. All but Tedra had visited it last year, when Shanelle was trying to escape her father's choice of lifemate for her.

Tedra broke the silence first, wanting verification. "Isn't that the planet that Shanelle sought sanctuary on and didn't get it?"

"One and the same," Martha replied in one of her cheerful tones.

But Shanelle complained, "Mother, *must* you describe them like that?"

She had been sitting on an adjusticouch with her lifemate's arms wrapped around her. Falon Van'yer had been talked into letting his lifemate come on this trip, but not without him. And he hated space travel, really hated it. Yet Shanelle had wanted to come, and he would do anything to make her happy—within reason.

Shanelle now glanced back at him warily. He had good reason to despise the Sunderans and wouldn't like being reminded that they had tried to keep his lifemate from him, had even tried to make him completely forget about her. But Falon was looking absolutely inscrutable, though Ba-Har-ani warriors didn't usually hide their emotions. Kan-is-Tran warriors like Dalden and Challen didn't hide their emotions, either; they just had such unique control of their bodies that they seemed to lack any emotion of a strong nature, be it anger—or love.

But Tedra also had good reason to not like the Sunderans. Martha had given her a full account of all that had happened to her daughter while she was there, and if Tedra *had* been there, there would have been a lot of hurting Sunderans before she left.

She snorted now at Shanelle's complaint and turned her aquamarine eyes on Falon. "You know I love you to pieces and will, just as long as my daughter does," she told the *shodan* of Ka'al. "But she sought help from those people and they failed to supply it. It's a moot point that the help was needed against you in particular. And they want help from us now?"

Tedra's ending tone implied, *Fat chance they'll get it*. Falon merely nodded. Dalden knew better than to comment when his mother's dander was up. He left it to Martha to point out the obvious, which she did now.

"They want help from anyone. We just happen to be close enough to hear it. And having heard it, there is no option of ignoring it—or did you suddenly become an uncaring, callous individual when I wasn't looking?"

That got a baleful glare out of Tedra, directed at the intercom on the wall that Martha's purring voice was coming out of. "I didn't say we wouldn't help, but I don't have to like it, do I?"

"Shanelle doesn't hold grudges against them," Martha pointed out.

"They did *try* to help me," Shanelle explained. "They just weren't very good at it. But they were dealing with Sha-Ka'ani warriors, so it's hard to hold them at fault for their failure."

"Not hard at all," Tedra insisted. "Incompetents have never been high on my list of want-to-know people. The Sunderans *did* have a weapon in their Altering Rods that could have worked without hurting anyone—physically," she quickly added for Falon's benefit, since he was the one who would have suffered if he had been made to forget about Shanelle. "And don't get me wrong. I'm pleased with the way that whole fiasco turned out in the end, and so are you. But that doesn't alter the fact that if you had really needed help of a life-threatening sort, you definitely picked the wrong people to get it from."

"Exactly," Falon put in.

Shanelle turned around to her lifemate. "You *agree* with her?"

"Absolutely."

Shanelle threw up her hands in exasperation. "I give up."

The distinct sound of chuckling was coming out of the intercom unit. "Now can we get around to helping the 'incompetents'?"

"By all means," Tedra said with a smile.

Chapter 2

IMPATIENCE WAS SETTING IN. FEW ANSWERS HAD BEEN supplied after they had arrived on Sunder and been escorted to General Ferrill's office. The little general had immediately gotten on Tedra's bad side with his belligerence and condescending attitude, particularly since the Sunderans were the ones asking for help this time around.

Normally she would have ignored it, but in her present fretting mood, it very quickly had them shouting at each other. Which was when Shanelle suggested tactfully that Donilla Vand be summoned to deal with them.

Ferrill had acceded to that request gladly, obviously uncomfortable arguing with a woman he had to look up at, and had left them there alone in his office. He had neglected to mention, however, that Donilla would have to be fetched from prison. That information was volunteered by one of the military types standing guard at the door outside the office when asked what was taking so long.

When Shanelle had sought help from the Sunderans eight months earlier, Donilla Vand had been the general in command of Sunder's military forces. She was also the one who had explained how the women of Sunder had wrested control of the planet from their men, to keep them from going to war with their neighboring planet, Armoru.

It had been a global conspiracy made possible by the invention of what they called the Altering Rod. Sunder was, after all, quite advanced in the fields of science, having conquered all their known diseases. The rods had been created to control the minds of the mentally imbalanced, to make them useful citizens again. That they had been used by the women to take over all positions of power on the planet left many of them feeling quite guilty about it, Donilla included. So Shanelle wasn't really surprised that some of them had finally reversed the process to let their men take over again, though apparently the consequence was that those women had been sent to prison for what they'd done.

But there was no point in speculating about it until they knew for sure what had happened to put the men back in power. And they still didn't know what kind of help was needed or who had sent out a distress call, though that could be easily guessed at, now that the men were in power again. No doubt Sunder was in a state of war and possibly losing, now that their aggressive, war-minded men were ruling again.

Unfortunately for them, Tedra and her family were governed by the policies of the League of Confederated Planets, of which Kystran ranked twelfth, and by which the neighboring Niva star system also abided. Steps could be taken to prevent war, which had been done to keep more advanced planets from trying to take over Sha-Ka'an when it was discovered in the Niva system. But once war was declared, no help or hindrance could be offered, for the simple reason that some planets were too highly advanced for others to hope to compete with. For example, the battleship they had in their control could totally wipe out both Sunder and Armoru.

Nearly an hour had passed since the general had left them alone in his office. Tedra sat cross-legged in the center of his desk. The chairs in the room were too small to risk sitting in without breaking. Dalden, Falon, and Falon's brother, Jadell, were sitting on the floor, leaning against the walls. Shanelle was pacing the room, feeling the worst of their impatience, since she alone had any sympathies for the Sunderans, having gotten to know Donilla Vand during her short stay here and liking the women.

Not surprisingly, when Donilla finally arrived, Shanelle pounced on her with her first concern. *"Why have you been imprisoned?"*

Donilla smiled. She was a small woman, barely five feet in height, which was the norm on this planet. Their men only averaged half a foot more. To them, the Sha-Ka'ani really were giants, and Tedra and Shanelle, only a few inches short of six feet each, were close runners-up.

But Donilla showed none of the nervousness that

other Sunderans did in their presence. Her gray eyes warm in greeting, Donilla held out a welcoming hand to Shanelle.

"They didn't tell me it was you who answered our call for help," the ex-general said. "I can't tell you how often I worried about you, despite your assurance that you would be fine. But since *he* is with you, dare I hope that you are comfortable now with your father's choice for you?"

The word *comfortable* didn't come close to describing life with a warrior, but it did bring a smile to Shanelle as well. "Yes, I came here previously with foolish fears, all of which have been put to rest. Happiness beyond measure is what my lifemate gives me."

"My woman is being modest," Falon said as he rose from the floor to stand next to her.

The remark caused them all to laugh, even Tedra, which momentarily relieved the tension of not knowing what was going on. Shanelle then took a moment to introduce Donilla to her mother—she had met everyone else in the room the first time they were there.

Donilla, like most people who first met the Ly-San-Ters, couldn't hide her amazement that Tedra could be old enough to have children of twenty-one, when she looked no older than thirty herself. Nor did either of her twin children take after her in looks. Both Dalden and Shanelle were blond and amber-eyed, while Tedra's long hair was pitch black, her eyes a light aquamarine. A woman of strict physical disciplines all her life, she was aging very well.

Shanelle got back to the question that hadn't been answered yet. "How did you end up in prison, Donilla?"

Donilla replied, "Several months after you left us, I had an opportunity to meet with a large number of the women who, like me, had taken over key positions on Sunder with the use of Altering Rods. It wasn't hard to see that most of them weren't happy with the way things had turned out, any more than I was. Our original motive was sound, to keep Sunder from going to war. We just hadn't counted on the results leaving us with men who were barely recognizable from their former selves, or that we would feel so guilty about it. So, in effect, another conspiracy was begun. It wouldn't have worked unless enough of us were willing, because like the first instance, it had to be accomplished in a close time frame. One man back in power could do nothing if he had no support, after all. But we pulled it off again: we gave them back their identities and memories."

"And ended up in prison for it," Shanelle said indignantly. "I can't believe—"

"Yes, you can," Donilla cut in. "We took away their memories of who they were, took away their power, took away their aggression. They'll never trust us again."

"Sounds like you haven't stopped feeling guilty about it," Tedra remarked. "The way you went about it was underhanded, yes, but your motives were sound. And a few months' detention is long enough for trying to keep your planet from going to war, a noble effort in my book."

"Thank you—I think," Donilla replied, blushing slightly. "But if we didn't feel we deserved what we got, we would have made a fuss about it and been freed by now. Most of us see it as a vacation, one well needed after the stress and worry of trying to keep our men under our control for so long. And it's not a real prison they've detained us in. We have all the luxuries we could ask for. It's more like a resort, just one with locks on the doors."

Shanelle would have discussed it more, but Tedra was more interested in the immediate problem and asked Donilla, "You know why we're here?"

"Yes. I may be locked away, but I'm still the only one Ferrill feels comfortable talking out his problems with, so he's kept me informed about everything that has happened since he took over again."

"If you're now at war with Armoru, we can't—"

"No, it's nothing like that," Donilla interrupted, smiling. "There was one benefit of what we did. We didn't make our men forget about what had happened during the years of our rule, and five years of seeing that we could get along just fine without conquering any more people made them not jump back into the race of who could wipe out their neighbors first. They have in fact continued our plans of defense rather than attack. We just might be ready and fully prepared when Armoru finally makes its move."

Tedra grinned. "Congratulations and welcome to the concept of Life Appreciation. But what, then, is the problem here?"

"A crate of Altering Rods has been stolen," Donilla admitted with a sigh.

"That's an internal problem. Why would you ask for off-world help for it?"

"Because the rods have been taken off Sunder, and we have no means to leave Sunder ourselves to retrieve them."

The Sunderans might be highly advanced in most fields of science, but space travel wasn't one of them. They hadn't even known that worlds other than Armoru existed until they had been discovered by the Antury six years earlier. They had, in fact, been trying to build their first spaceship at the time, not for space travel, but to get them over to the neighboring planet of Armoru with the intent of global war, with Armoru doing exactly the same. It had been a race about who could invade first, a race that Sunder dropped out of during the few years the women had been in power.

"Do you know who took them?"

"Yes, we don't get many visitors here, since we have so little to offer in trade. But these people came with the sole intent of buying the Altering Rods from us. This was strange in itself, since very few people know of the rods on our own world, let alone on other worlds."

"Did the Antury who discovered you know?"

"Possible, but doubtful—unless they have some means of reading our minds. The rods weren't something we were proud of by then. Shanelle was told about them because she needed reassurance on how we could help her against giant warriors like these here."

The rods had been used on those warriors and had even worked on most of them, making them forget that they had come there to find Shanelle. The process had failed on Falon, however, because he had refused to learn the Sunderan language before coming down to their planet, and for the rods to work, it was necessary for the targets to understand what was being said to them.

The other warriors who had come down didn't have Falon's deep distrust of all things unnatural to Sha-Ka'an, and since almost any ship computer could analyze a new language and create a Sublim so that the language could be learned in just a few hours, the old universal language that was so frustrating had long since become obsolete. Sublims made it possible to communicate with newly discovered worlds with ease. There were a few glitches, like some words not having an immediate association and so needing a visual or verbal explanation to make sense. But basically, Sublims worked amazingly well and were used by all world traders and discoverers.

"So what happened?"

"The visitors were honored, given the royal treatment, actually, being who they were. But the rods are naturally a sore subject with Ferrill. He refused to discuss selling them, and said only that the rods were locked away in our strongest vault and would never see use again."

"Why weren't they just destroyed after you stopped using them?"

"Because the men realized the day might come when *they* would find a good use for them."

"As in Armoru knocking on your doors with weapons in hand?" Tedra guessed.

"Exactly," Donilla replied. "Besides, quite a few women know how to make them now, and since they don't work on women, those women can't be made to forget how to make them. So the men felt that locking them away was sufficient. After all, our strongest vault is guarded by the military night and day, impossible for anyone on *our* world to break into."

"But not for someone from another world, obviously."

"No, indeed. They used some kind of gas that put everyone to sleep and an explosive unknown to us that easily opened our vault. They left the planet immediately thereafter, and were gone before the theft was even discovered."

"When was this?"

"Yesterday."

Tedra sighed and pushed the button on her computer-link unit. "Martha, I know you've been listening. What's the worst-case scenario on these stolen rods?"

"If they were stolen for profit, they could end up distributed throughout the galaxies and well-established policies could suddenly end up changing with no one the wiser as to why or how. Entire economies could be destroyed, wars would result, the League of Confederated Planets could topple."

That got a low growl and the demand, "How high is that on your list of probables?"

"Not very," Martha replied in one of her bored tones. "Considering who stole them, it's more likely that a single planet will be a target for takeover, pretty much in the same way it was done here. Quiet, efficient, without bloodshed, and without most of the populace even aware that they have been taken over."

"Considering who?" Tedra frowned. "And how do you know who our culprit is, when that hasn't been mentioned yet? Probables doesn't come close to dissecting a simple phrase like 'they were honored.' "

That resulted in a bit of computer chuckling, a sound Martha had created to perfection. "That's debatable, but the fact that there is only one ship within a day's travel of here does manage to narrow things down."

Tedra rolled her eyes. "A known race I hope, so we at least know what we're dealing with?"

"Better than that, you know them personally. It's Jorran of Century III, the very same High King who tried to make mincemeat of our Falon in the competitions last year."

"*Farden* hell."

Shanelle noticed Donilla's blush over her mother's swearing and whispered to her, "That's just the Kystrani word for bloody, pretty mild when you consider mother has seventy-eight languages to draw on for serious cussing."

Donilla grinned, but Martha, who had no trouble picking up whispers, said, "She's in shock. Give her a moment, she'll get around to some serious swearing."

Since everyone there could hear Martha, including her mother who was raising an annoyed brow at her, Shanelle was now the one blushing.

Chapter 3

TEDRA WALKED OUTSIDE THE MILITARY COMPOUND where General Ferrill's office was located. Dalden was deeply distracted and not paying much attention to anything other than walking. Shanelle was waiting to hear what Tedra would decide.

As far as Shanelle was concerned, having been apprised of the situation, they couldn't do anything but help. And that had nothing to do with Sunder or her liking for the Sunderan Donilla Vand, nor even her strong dislike of the High King Jorran, who had wanted to make her his queen by underhanded means. No, her concern was that an entire planet of unsuspecting people could become the victims of Jorran's tyranny. But Tedra might not see it that way and being more familiar with the policies of the Centura League, otherwise known as the League of Confeder-

ated Planets which strived to keep peace among all
known planets, might be wrestling with good reasons
why they shouldn't get involved.

Martha was being unusually quiet, even though her
link was still open. But then, Martha only interfered
when she knew that something might adversely affect
Tedra. Otherwise, she let Tedra make her own decisions. That it often seemed otherwise was only because Martha covered all possibilities when she
dissected a problem, from the most obvious to the least
likely, and every variable in between.

Tedra finally stopped walking, and the frown she
was now wearing said she wasn't happy with her own
decision, but had made it nonetheless. "We need to get
back to the ship and be on our way."

"You aren't going to help?"

"I retired from 'saving planets' twenty-one years
ago," Tedra said matter-of-factly. "And the sooner we
get home, the sooner we can notify the proper authorities to deal with this problem."

"Even though that might be too late? Once war is
begun, the League won't get involved."

"I doubt Jorran's intention is to make war," Tedra
replied. "Is it, Martha?"

"Highly improbable." Martha was using her bored
tone again, which, unfortunately, usually precluded a
bomb, which she dropped now. "Subjugation and utter domination are what he'll be looking for."

Tedra made a face. *Subjugation* was a word she seriously disliked; it was what the Sha-Ka'ari had tried to
do to her own people. The Sha-Ka'ari were originally
from Sha-Ka'an, but had been taken some three hundred years ago to a mining colony in the Centura star

system to be used as slave labor. But they were still incredibly huge warriors, and it didn't take them long to take over that colony and subjugate those people and any others they happened to conquer. They had lost touch with most of their old beliefs, didn't even know where they originally came from, and had developed much differently than the Sha-Ka'ani on the mother planet.

They were still considered barbarians, though, were still sword-wielding, slave-holding warriors, just a smaller variety, having interbred with their slaves for hundreds of years. But unlike Challen and his people, also considered barbarians, who pretty much snubbed their collective noses at the wonder that could be had from advanced planets, the Sha-Ka'ari weren't averse to using whatever was obtainable if they could put it to good use, nor averse to space travel.

Jorran's people from Century III were much like the Sha-Ka'ari. They were still medieval in development themselves, yet having been discovered and dealing for many years with off-world visitors, they didn't deny themselves the benefits of modern technology. They had trade ambassadors on almost all of the known planets, and their kings enjoyed space travel as well, but not much was really known about them, since they weren't members of the Centura League.

The League of Confederated Planets wasn't just one solar system, but half a dozen neighboring star systems now comprising seventy-eight planets that abided by one set of rules and regulations to the benefit of all. The Niva star system, newly discovered, had yet to be brought into the fold, though no one doubted it would be one day. Century III was another system within traveling distance that, although it dealt well with the League, had yet to be invited to join.

And their own first dealings with the humanoids of Century III had been less than pleasant. The High King Jorran and his entourage had come to Sha-Ka'an the previous year, when the visitor restriction had been lifted for the competitions that Challen had opened to one and all in hopes of finding a lifemate for Shanelle among the winners. Shanelle hadn't known that was the purpose of the competitions, and the winner wasn't guaranteed to be chosen, but Jorran hadn't seen it that way.

He hadn't competed either, competition being much too undignified for his esteemed self. No, he had demanded to fight the winner who had gone through the process of elimination in the appropriate way, and Falon, being that winner, could have refused to fight him, should have refused, yet he didn't. No one suspected that Jorran's intention was to kill him, rather than just defeat him.

The competitions had been friendly matches of strength and skill, not the deadly fight Jorran tried to make of them. Falon didn't find that out until after he had accepted Jorran's challenge and Jorran used not a normal sword but a razor sword. This was a weapon so light and maneuverable that there was no way to avoid it by normal means, nor was Falon able to.

He would have died if a meditech unit hadn't been handy, he had been sliced up so badly. He would have lost the match as well if he hadn't given up using his own weapon and simply taken Jorran out with his fist instead, just before he passed out himself from loss of blood.

This was when Shanelle, fearful of having Falon for her lifemate, had run away. And Falon, determined to have her, overcame his own fears of space travel to follow her. Challen had already given her to him, and Falon wasn't going to let a mere thing like a universe keep him from her. Nor had the Sunderans been able to keep him away, despite their promises to the contrary.

"Shani, this is *not* our responsibility," Tedra said now. "Just because we know what those rods are capable of, and what a first-class jerk Jorran is, doesn't make this our problem. The League will be given all the information we have and will do what's appropriate with it. We are already late getting home, and I refuse to make Challen continue to worry."

"I will go after Jorran and see to the proper destruction of those rods."

Both women turned toward Dalden, his silence until now having made them forget he was with them. Shanelle was merely surprised that her brother would want to involve himself personally when matters outside of Sha-Ka'an had no interest for him. Tedra's own surprise was brief, her response less than diplomatic.

"No," she said.

Chapter 4

DALDEN SMILED AT TEDRA. SHE WAS HIS MOTHER, BUT HE was a Sha-Ka'an warrior full-grown, which made all decisions his own to make, and she knew that. She could make her objections known to him, but in the end the decision was still his.

"I have no choice in this matter," he told her. "You wondered how the High King could have had knowledge of the rods before he came here for them? That knowledge came directly from me."

"How?" she demanded, "and when? You weren't even home, had left with Falon to fetch Shani back. And Sha-Ka'an closed down to visitors again right after the competitions."

"All did return to their respective planets—except Jorran. He was still at the Visitors' Center when we returned. It was necessary that I go there as well, to negotiate with the Catrateri on Falon's behalf. They were still eager to trade for the gold from his country."

"But how did you end up having anything to do with Jorran, after what he tried to pull at the competitions? I would have thought you would have ignored him like the insect he proved to be."

"And I would have, but a man with such a high opinion of himself as Jorran has cannot comprehend that someone might dislike him or not want to be 'honored' by his attention. There was a dinner for a newly arrived ambassador. The Catrateri had been invited to it and insisted that we could continue our negotiations over fine food. Jorran invited himself, and of course the head of the Center would not think to insult him by asking him to leave."

"No, Mr. Rampon is the administrator there because he's about as diplomatic as they come. I doubt he even knows how to insult someone. It's just not in his genes."

"I could wish that it were not in mine."

This was said in such a tone that it brought an immediate blush to Tedra. Challen didn't insult people, after all, so Dalden certainly wasn't talking about the genes he had gotten from his father.

"Let's stick to specifics," she grumbled. "How did you happen to have words with Jorran? The dining hall at the Center is huge. You could have gone through the entire evening without getting within forty feet of that Centurian jerk."

"Except that he sought me out specifically, to question me about Falon. He did not pretend indifference, nor hide his underlying anger over the subject of his interest."

"Don't tell me his nose was bent out of shape figuratively, after Falon bent it out of shape literally? It's really too bad the meditech unit corrected that."

"I gathered the same, that he was still at the Center for no other reason than he had waited for Falon to return, with some sort of revenge in mind. Falon was unaware of this, or he might well have obliged him. But he had gone straight home to Ba-Har-an with Shanelle when we returned, and no visitors could get to his country, so the High King was forced to give up and go home, which he was scheduled to do the next rising."

"So mention of the rods occurred when he grilled you about Falon?"

Dalden shook his head, even sighed. "I would not speak of Falon with him, other than to give Jorran no doubt that Falon was beyond his reach. Speaking to him at all put a foul taste in my mouth that I tried to wash away with Mieda wine."

"You should have just left."

"I am aware of that."

"How did the rods get mentioned, then?"

"It was toward the end of the dinner. I spoke no more with Jorran, but I made sure I was close enough to hear anything he might say. He was talking with the people at his end of the table about the tedious process of mind control in Century III prisons, to rehabilitate their lawbreakers and make them useful members of their realm again. I mentioned that even a low-tech people like the Sunderans had mind control down to a fine art, and instantaneous, at that. It was a deliberate attempt at subtle insult of which I am ashamed."

That Dalden would have used phrases like *low-tech* and *fine art*, words he gained from having a "visitor" for a mother, not words a warrior would use, showed just how drunk he had been that night. And he probably didn't even realize that whatever means Jorran's people would use for mind control was probably gained from offworlders; they weren't even low-tech, they were no-tech at all. Not that any of that mattered when the damage had already been done.

"Martha, did you know what Dalden had done that night?" Tedra asked.

"Sure did. You kept me on the Rover at the time, if you'll remember, so I could keep tabs on Shanelle. And after what Jorran tried to pull during the competitions, he was on my personal list of 'keep under surveillance' as well."

"*Why* didn't you mention this sooner?"

"Because Jorran's intention was to return to his world, which he did. Despite the fact that he left us furious, he had few options that might cause you trouble. His learning about the Altering Rods did set off alarms in my circuits, but when he gave absolutely no indication that it was something he felt he could take advantage of, I crossed him off my 'endangered species' list."

Tedra rolled her eyes. Martha's "endangered species" crack was her way of describing anyone she saw as a threat to Tedra's well-being. She was programmed against killing things herself, though she was rather good at threatening to do so, and she could defend and render harmless as needed. Tedra, on the other hand, wouldn't think twice about demolishing someone who threatened her life or that of any of her family.

"But there's no reason for Dalden to get involved, is

there, aside from guilt? This *can* be handled by the League, right?"

"In time to stop Jorran, no," Martha replied. "In time to prevent him from taking over more than one planet, you betcha. But that won't help the people who get forced to worship him as their new king."

Since that wasn't what Tedra was hoping to hear, it wasn't surprising that she slammed her palm down angrily on the link-unit so she wouldn't have to hear any more of Martha's less than supportive commentary.

"That isn't going to work," Shanelle pointed out.

"No, but after nearly two weeks on the ship where there is no shutting her up, since she has complete control of the farden thing, being able to do so now is a luxury I won't deny myself," Tedra replied.

"She can still hear you."

"Of course she can, but she can't reply."

"Wanna bet?" boomed out of the heavens.

Shanelle blinked, noticed the complete look of shock on Tedra's face, and then started laughing. "Droda help us, half the people on this planet are going to think their God just spoke to them." She fell to the grass and held her stomach as another round of laughter ensued.

Tedra wasn't amused, slammed the button on the unit again and growled into it, "You misbegotten metal nightmare, you know better than to cause global panic! You're in meltdown, right? You've totally lost it?"

"Relax, doll." Martha's voice came through the unit again in purring mode. "General Ferrill doesn't take chances with visitors anymore; he makes worldwide announcements warning his people to expect the bizarre and unusual for the duration. And since we've been let inside their global shield this time, we're pretty hard to miss."

Tedra glared up at the two spaceships hovering in the sky above them. "Beside the point."

"Actually, that was the point," Martha said, using her tone that was laden with amusement. "Much as I might get a kick out of being mistaken for a god, that isn't going to happen here, when the Rover is in plain view for anyone who heard me on this side of the planet. And I have information that you require before you can make an informed decision, so shall we proceed?"

Tedra hated it when Martha dropped carrots like that. She would have preferred to tell her circuited friend to stuff it, but couldn't now.

"Proceed," she grumbled.

"I made a point of finding out all I could about Jorran when he became a contender for Shanelle. He's indeed a High King of Century III, but what isn't common knowledge is that he's a king without a kingdom. Probables tell me he had hoped to find a kingdom in Sha-Ka'an, through Shanelle. He's apparently been looking for one for quite a while now."

"Backtrack, old girl," Tedra said. "How'd he lose his kingdom?"

"He never had one."

"Then how does he hold the title?"

"That answer requires a bit of information about Century III."

"The brief version, if you don't mind."

"You got it. Century III isn't just the name of their main planet, but also of their star system. There are twelve planets in all, but only six are habitable, and only the main planet had developed to the point of intelligence and world governance, ruled by one family that give themselves the titles of High Kings. The current family possesses seven High Kings. The planet used to be divided among the family, but that wasn't working out well with this last crop of seven, probably because they didn't have enough countries to go around. When they were discovered by the League and learned of space travel, they decided to divide up the planets in their system just as they had previously done with the countries."

"But they still came up one short?"

"Exactly. Now, the rest of the family are perfectly willing to share with Jorran, to give him anything he wants, but it's just not the same as having an entire people revere you as their only king. It seems to be a serious disgruntlement for him, and one he is finally taking steps to correct. His first option was to marry into a ruling family that would offer complete takeover eventually. He doesn't command a large army after all, nothing of the sort needed to go in and take what he wants by force. So this was his only option—until he learned about the Altering Rods."

"He learned about them eight months ago. Did it take them that long to find Sunder?"

"No, my guess is it took that long for Jorran to call in favors to get his own ship. He didn't have one when he came to Sha-Ka'an. They came with the Century III ambassador, which is how they returned home as well."

"Call in favors? Does he lack wealth as well as a kingdom?"

"Not at all, but keep in mind they don't produce

their own ships, nor are their people trained to fly them, nor are they likely to possess a Mock II capable of making crews obsolete. And they don't get ambassadors arriving from every known planet like Sha-Ka'an does, since they don't possess anything remotely as in demand as gaali stones are. They're on a few trade routes, but they're more a tourist attraction than a stopover for necessities. I'm frankly surprised it didn't take longer for Jorran to acquire his own ship and crew for this expedition."

"What type of ship did he get?"

"Your basic run-of-the-mill Trader, large cargo space, a few weapons to ward off pirates, good speed to outrun bigger ships, designed for long hauls."

"What kind of speed are we talking about?"

"A bit faster than the Rover, but about the same as that overpowered war machine that accompanied us."

"I take it you're not talking about Brock?" Shanelle couldn't resist saying, which got the expected snort out of Martha.

Brock and Martha got along much better than they used to, but there were still times when their objectives clashed, and this could well be one of them if Tedra decided to head out after Jorran herself. Brock would side with Tedra's original insistence of wanting to get her home with all speed, since getting her home and back into Challen's arms would be his main concern, ultimately insuring Challen's peace of mind. Martha, however, would know that Tedra was torn at the moment, wanting to help, but too worried about Challen's worry to be able to devote her full attention to helping.

Dalden was actually offering an alternative that

both Mock IIs would be able to support. Tedra hadn't reached that point of acceptance yet, though, and was still in questioning mode.

"From their current course, any idea which planet they have in mind for takeover?" she asked Martha.

"They are heading into uncharted space."

This surprised all of them. "You mean they're hoping to find a new, undiscovered planet out there?" Tedra concluded. "That seems like a rather stupid plan."

"No, actually, it's rather smart of them. That sector of space is uncharted, but there *are* solar systems in it, and there are rumors of at least one planet that's inhabited. But one planet in an entire solar system isn't worth putting them on a trade route when their system is so far off the beaten track, so no official World Discoverer has bothered to head over that way to verify or discount the rumors. But Jorran would want a target that is very far out of the way. This would pretty much assure him that no other off-worlders would be coming around to mess up his plans."

"Just how far off the beaten track are we talking about?" Tedra asked.

"Unknown data."

That was too abrupt, even for Martha, reminding Tedra that Martha based her probables on known facts, and rumors didn't fall even remotely close into that category. Martha hated being wrong about anything, after all, and rumors could be proven false.

So Tedra rephrased her question. "What's the general speculation, based on the rumor?"

"Three months for a Trader, five months for a World Discoverer."

"Three months even under gaali speed? *One* way? No one travels that far anymore without several stops along the way. Fuel isn't needed, but world communication is. Wars can be fought and won in three months, entire worlds can disappear in three months. No one likes being gone so long that when they come back, nothing is as they left it."

"World Discoverers are a spoiled lot, Tedra, and you know it. The Centura League would never have been formed if the old school thought like that, because the old school didn't have such high speed available to them. A year, two years was nothing to them, if it meant discovering a new world. Three months away would have been considered a short trip. Of course, today's three months is equivalent to more than a few years of travel back when space was first explored, but there's no need for a history lesson you're already familiar with."

"Three months—*six* months round trip." Tedra was looking at Dalden now and shaking her head. "You realize that's just travel time, doesn't count the time it will take to stop Jorran, reverse any damage he does if he can't be stopped before doing any, and find and destroy all the rods? This could conceivably take a year or more. You *aren't* going, and that's my final word on the subject."

Chapter 5

BRITTANY DIDN'T GET TO THE SHOPPING MALL OFTEN. Parking wasn't usually a problem, though, since Seaview wasn't a big town. It had only just gotten their first enclosed mall last year. Today, however, parking was a problem, and Brittany found out why when she got inside. The mayor was using the large community stage in the center of the mall to make a campaign speech. It was an election year. Mayor Sullivan was running for his second term.

The town was only four years old, so Sullivan was the only mayor it had known so far. He'd done a good job as far as Brittany was concerned, so he'd get her vote again. The town was growing at a steady pace thanks to him, which meant job security for her in her field of construction, so he could be forgiven for campaigning on a Sunday, her only day off.

Brittany even stopped to listen to him for a few minutes, though from the sidelines. Crowds like the one gathered around the center stage were things she tended to avoid, hating that penned-in feeling where you couldn't move without bumping into someone. Such crowds made her stand out like a sore thumb with her height, and getting rudely stared at was guaranteed to put her in a foul mood.

Actually, she hadn't been in the best of moods since her break-up with Thomas Johnson. She'd even given some thought to moving. But she was well settled in Seaview now, had a roommate she got along well with, even though Jan still tried to fix her up with dates that she didn't want. And she was meeting her goals here, was on schedule, would be able to quit her jobs and build her dream house in two more years.

She lived and breathed for that day, counted every penny, begrudged every worn-out purse and dented hard hat, not just because they cost her extra money but because, unlike some women, she actually hated to go shopping. And she had put off today's shopping excursion for two weeks now. But having to wash her work jeans every other night because three pairs had finally reached the irreparable stage with their worn-out seats was a pure waste of time, and she hated wasting time more than she hated shopping.

She had expected to be in and out of the mall in under an hour. She hadn't counted on the mayor and his campaign staff being there to draw her interest briefly. But she wasn't hearing anything she hadn't already heard on the six o'clock news, which she tried to catch each day while she ate dinner. She did have a few hours between jobs to eat, shower, take care of the daily chores she shared with Jan, or whatever else couldn't wait until Sunday. Her spa job was from seven to ten at night, giving her no time for other than another quick shower and bed when she got home from it.

Brittany was just heading around the outer fringes of the crowd in the direction she needed to go for her favorite jeans shop when she saw *him* and did a double-take. Bumping into the person in front of her stopped her completely and she didn't even think to apologize, she was so amazed at the man's height. How had she missed seeing him work his way into the center of that crowd when her eyes were always drawn to tall men? You couldn't miss him. He stood more than a foot taller than everyone else there.

Had he been sitting down and only just stood up? There could be some chairs in the center of the crowd, she supposed. For that matter, he could be standing on one—no, she'd see a bit of waist if that were so, but all she was seeing was some incredibly wide shoulders and a golden mane of hair that reached them. And that wasn't nearly enough to satisfy her curiosity, which was why she quickly worked her way to the sidelines, to catch a glimpse of his face.

Brittany didn't realize that she'd been holding her breath, or was filled with anxiety, until she got that better look at the man and sighed long and loud in relief. The worry had been natural, because although her eyes were constantly drawn to tall men, they were usually disappointed as well. There had only been a few tall men over the years whom she had actually been seriously attracted to, and only one whom she had come close to losing her heart to.

Thomas Johnson she would never forget, because he'd crushed her thoroughly in proving just how hard it was going to be for her to ever find the right man. She'd really thought he was it. Her instincts had said so. She'd even been willing to go all the way with him, though she could be grateful now that their relationship hadn't progressed that far before she found out that even he had a problem with her height. She was a good half a foot shorter than Tom, but that was *still* too tall for him. Damn jerk must have a thing for midgets had been her unkind thought before she'd shown him the door.

But this guy, surrounded by a sea of shorter heads, was absolutely gorgeous. And despite her immediate attraction, that sent off alarms in her head. Anyone who looked that good couldn't *be* that good. There had to be something wrong with him. Her instincts might be saying otherwise, but she could no longer trust them after Tom.

He was too young for her, that was it. Actually, it wasn't that he looked young—it was hard to look young when you were that big. It was more that he just didn't look old enough. Of course, age didn't matter much these days, when people were smart enough to have figured out that compatibility and common interests were much more important for holding a relationship together.

Brittany could apply that concept to her height problem as well, if it wasn't such a big bone of contention with her. And if she was going to hold his age against him, then she ought to find somewhere to sit down and work on getting her pulse rate back to normal, because it was definitely leaping about in maximum attraction mode at the moment.

He wasn't listening to the mayor's speech, he was looking around as if he were lost, or didn't know what he was doing there. Brittany was still searching for something wrong about him when she realized that his expression had abruptly changed, was the very picture of a man about to panic. Claustrophobia bigtime was about to happen.

She didn't doubt it, nor did she think twice before she barged her way in through the crowd, grabbed his arm, and dragged him a good distance away. Her good deed for the day. It had nothing to do with the fact that she *wanted* to meet him, and her rescue was a perfect excuse to. But she should have read the Girl Scout manual more thoroughly, because she must have missed the section that warned that good deeds just might change your life forever.

Chapter 6

RESCUES DIDN'T ALWAYS WORK OUT AS PLANNED. SOME of them that you thought were rescues might not even be so, might turn out to be intrusions instead.

This was Brittany's first thought when she turned to face the man whom she assumed she had pulled out of the jaws of his own personal hell. She had expected at the very least some gratitude, but she got merely a curious once-over from him. How deflating. Not that it mattered, when she was struck dumb by her own amazement.

Up close and personal put her system into overdrive. She never thought she'd see the day when a man might be too tall for her. But goodness, seven feet tall *and* properly proportioned for it!

The rest of him that she could see now, from the shoulders down, defied description. She was used to bulging muscles after three years working in a spa, but the muscles on this guy seemed natural rather than a result of strenuous exercise. Everything about him was big, and yet a right kind of big. You couldn't create and mold that kind of physique, you had to be born with it.

He was also dressed in high fashion—heck, he was wearing what you might expect on a rock star, actually. A wraparound tunic with no buttons, belted at the waist, and a soft metallic blue in color. His black leather pants weren't the least baggy, nor did they have visible seams that she could find.

If she didn't know better, she'd think those pants had been poured on him, they were so skintight. Leather boots of the same color, with flat heels—no artificial height here—and just as soft-looking, went up to his knees. The fat medallion that was visible in the *very* deep V of his neckline, hanging from a thick gold chain, appeared mystic in design. It was plated to look like it was made of solid gold, which of course it wouldn't be, when it was the size of her fist in roundness and nearly as thick.

He had a fancy-looking little radio attached to his wide belt, with all kinds of buttons on it. At least she assumed it was a radio, since it had a thin cord plugged into it that ran up to one of his ears, one of those miniature earphones, she supposed.

Her thorough examination of him came to an abrupt end when he spoke to her. A deep rumble. Foreign. The accent was strong, distinctive; she just couldn't place what country it might be from.

"Do you require something of me?" he said.

She blushed, something she strived never to do, because pink cheeks just didn't go well with copper hair. "No," she answered, "and maybe I should apologize. You looked like you were having a claustrophobia attack." At his blank stare, she added, "You know, hemmed in by the crowd and panicking because you can't find your way out—never mind. I thought I was helping, but obviously not."

He seemed to pause to listen to the music coming out of his earphone for a moment before he replied, "Ah, you assisted me. Now I understand, and offer my gratitude."

He smiled at her. She wondered if fainting was allowed in the mall. *Good god in the morning, find something wrong with him, girl, before you fall instantly in love.*

Now that he had relaxed, with that incredible smile that almost doubled his appeal, his amber eyes said he liked what he was seeing, which thrilled her to the core. But then, as looks went, she had some nice ones—aside from her height. At least, constantly being hit on *despite* her height confirmed what her mirror said.

She had big breasts, dark green eyes that could turn murky or be crystal clear, and a thick mass of bright copper hair inherited from her grandfather that no beautician could quite match in color. Some nicely defined bones went with the package for a combination that was loosely termed a knockout. She wouldn't go that far in describing herself, but was glad she had a few nice features to make up for that last half a foot of height she could have done without.

They were staring at each other when they should be talking, or at least getting past all the standard first meeting info, like name, profession, number of children they planned to have, and so on. And since he wasn't making the effort, that left it to her to get the ball rolling on getting acquainted, not something she had much experience at, since American men had that sort of thing down pat. But it was either that or let him walk away and never see him again, which at the moment was out of the question.

So she started from the top, telling him, "I'm Brittany Callaghan, and you are?"

"Sha-Ka'ani."

"Excuse me?"

The volume must have gotten turned up by accident on his radio, because even she could hear the tinny-sounding screeching coming out of his earphone that made him wince. He yanked it off his ear, held it a moment while he glared at it, then attached it again.

"I understand now it was my name you requested. I am Dalden Ly-San-Ter."

Brittany grinned at that point. "Let me take a wild guess. That's not a radio, but some kind of language translation recording you're listening to?"

"It does indeed assist me in understanding this language of yours that I have just learned."

"Just learned? You speak it amazingly well for only just learning it."

"Yet do I not have a translation for all of your words. Some require an explanation."

"Yes, I can see where brand names and slang might throw you off, as well as first names sounding like countries, like mine does." She took another guess on the next subject. "So, did you just get signed up for pro basketball?" A blank look. "Uh-oh, if that didn't translate, then you can't be a professional player, though if you stay in this country long enough, the scouts will probably find you. Sorry for the assumption, but we don't see seven-footers every day, and those we do see tend to all be players—"

"I am not seven feet tall," he corrected her in a serious tone.

She chuckled. "So who's counting an inch or two when you're *that* tall? Not me."

"Is my height a problem?"

"Not a chance. Your height is absolutely perfect, just what the basketball scouts are always on the lookout for." Herself as well, though she didn't add that, and he didn't seem to be understanding anything she was saying again. "Never mind, I don't think I've got it straight yet in my head that you're not American. Heck, basketball might not even be a sport in your country. Where do you hail from, by the way?"

"Far from here."

She grinned. "That's obvious, but how far? Europe? The Middle East? I don't recognize your accent, and I'd thought television had done an admirable job of introducing us to the full range of foreign accents."

"My country would be unknown to you."

She sighed. "You're probably right. If Shaka-what-you-called-it is its name, I've never heard of it. But then, geography was never my strong point. Are you just visiting America, then, doing the tourist thing?"

"My time here will be brief, yes."

Another sigh. "Well, hell, so much for getting married." His blank stare this time brought on a chuckle from her. "Don't panic, that was just a joke to loosen you up. You don't say much, do you?"

She blushed as soon as she said it, because she hadn't been giving him much chance to say anything with her nervous, nonstop chatter. A foreigner. Of all the rotten luck. But if they were growing them like this overseas, perhaps she ought to add a trip around the world to her goal list.

Her disappointment was almost a physical ache. Just a visitor. He'd have to leave the country when his visa expired. She'd never see him again . . . but that wasn't confirmed yet. His "brief" might only refer to Seaview. Foreigners did still move to America and apply for citizenship these days. Marriage worked wonders in cutting through that red tape, as well. She wouldn't ask, didn't want it confirmed, that he was just passing through.

"I will have much to say to you when my task is done here," he said.

She blinked, having forgotten her question. And those words sounded so promising, they managed to push her disappointment to the side.

"No time for socializing? Man, does that sound familiar," she remarked. "What task?"

"I seek a man. His name is Jorran, though he may call himself by a different name here."

"Are you a foreign cop, or a detective?"

"Is that what is required to find him?"

"Wouldn't hurt." She grinned. "Detectives have that find-what's-missing thing down pat. I don't think we have any in Seaview, though. Plenty of lawyers and even a pawnshop, if you can believe it. But there wouldn't be much work for a professional detective in a nice quiet town like this. If this guy's a criminal, you can always ask the local police to help."

Screeching came from his earphone again, when his hand was nowhere near the unit to have adjusted the sound. What a strange translator—or was it? It seemed more like someone was actually talking to him through it, with the occasional yell thrown in, coaching him on what to say.

"Police would be more hindrance than assistance, when they would ask questions that would lead to many more questions, and have no understanding of the answers."

"That complicated, huh? Well, your best bet for finding a detective who won't ask too many questions is to head to San Francisco."

"There is no time for detours. Nor is the assistance I need of a complicated nature." His amber eyes seemed to glow for a moment before he added, "You could help me."

Brittany's pulse rate sped up rapidly. His tone *and* look implied something other than help. "I could?"

"An understanding of your people is needful, and help in determining if the one in power here begins to behave in an abnormal manner."

She frowned. The one in power here? Did he mean the mayor? She turned around to glance at the platform, to see that Sullivan was wrapping up his speech. Standard political jargon. Nothing unusual in that. Abnormal? What the heck did he mean by that?

Brittany turned back to ask him, and found herself alone. She turned in a full circle. He was nowhere to be seen. People passed her. Shops were nearby. He wasn't. That gorgeous hunk of foreign masculinity had pulled a perfect disappearing act on her.

Crushed, she fell into the foulest mood imaginable. She didn't buy any jeans that day. She went home and broke a few things.

Chapter 7

"WHY DID YOU REMOVE ME FROM THE FEMALE'S presence?" Dalden demanded the second he materialized in the control room on board the battleship *Androvia*.

The question was asked of Martha. Though Shanelle was there as well and might know how to work the Molecular Transfer that could move people from place to place instantly, since she had learned how to fly spaceships during her time in Kystran, Martha was in control of every aspect of their ship and wouldn't relinquish any part of it to human error.

"Just listen to yourself, warrior, and you might figure that out on your own." Martha's placid tone drifted up from the huge computer console in the center of the room. "Or is so much emotion coming out of you a normal occurrence?"

"Are you blushing, Dalden?" Shanelle asked with some surprise.

Most blushes wouldn't be noticed with their identical golden skin tone; they had to be severe to show up at all. But Sha-Ka'ani warriors, who rarely blushed in the first place, had such natural control of their emotions that they wouldn't allow something so mundane as a blush to reveal emotions they maintained they didn't possess. They *could* feel embarrassment; you just had to know a warrior really well to guess when they might be experiencing it. Shanelle, as Dalden's twin, qualified for knowing him well.

But Martha had a whole list of complaints on her own agenda, and wasn't waiting for Dalden to answer insignificant questions from his sister. "You were supposed to be giving me a tour, not taking one yourself," Martha reminded him. "You were supposed to make contact with their leader. *She* isn't their leader."

"I did not initiate contact with her."

"You didn't try to end it, either."

"She wanted me."

"Sooooo . . . *what!*" was stretched out about five times longer than the words would take to say normally, just to stress how little that mattered in the scheme of things to Martha. "Women want you all the time, Dalden. Since when do you go haywire over it? And don't try to deny it when I am monitoring your vital stats."

"You're blushing again, Dalden," Shanelle pointed out, trying to keep from grinning.

She'd been there all along, and had been listening to Martha rant and rave about everything Dalden was doing wrong on the planet before she lost patience completely and brought him back to the ship.

They had arrived yesterday. Since Dalden was determined to hold himself responsible for retrieving the Altering Rods, Tedra had finally given in and supported his decision. Her support meant that Martha had to go along, though, as well as all the warriors who had escorted them to Kystran. Brock could have handled it and was already in control of the *Androvia*, but with one of her "babies" going into deep space without her, Tedra would only trust Martha at the helm.

So the two Mock IIs had traded ships, with Brock taking Tedra home to Sha-Ka'an in the Rover, a short enough trip so Challen wouldn't complain too much that she'd made it alone. What hadn't been expected was that Falon would insist on going after Jorran as well, especially when he so disliked space travel.

Martha had expected it, though, pointing out that Falon hadn't gotten anywhere close to evening the score with Jorran after the High King tried to kill him. He had simply had more important things to deal with first, like chasing after his lifemate. But now he'd like to get his hands on Jorran to finish that long-ago fight more properly.

Of course, with Falon going along for the ride, Shanelle insisted on going, too, and although Tedra had objected most strenuously, Falon didn't, so that settled that. But understanding the Sha-Ka'ani way of life, as well as Martha's advanced and unique nature, Shanelle was the perfect buffer between Martha and the warriors aboard the ship. The warriors might get along well with Brock, who had been created for their *shodan* Challen, so he was one of them. That couldn't be said for Martha, who had a tendency to provoke a warrior's placid nature without even trying.

It had taken two months and twenty-three days to reach their destination, the no longer rumored planet in that sector of the universe a verified fact now. But because the humanoids on the planet were advanced enough to have equipment that could see their ship when it neared them, even disguised as it was to look like a common piece of space debris, albeit a big piece, they couldn't remain hovering over the planet for more than a few seconds.

This was gotten around by Martha taking the ship down to the surface of the planet at incredible speed, halting it just before impact, and lowering it into a large body of water where it wouldn't be discovered. If it had been seen, it would be assumed a meteor had fallen and disintegrated before reaching the surface.

This was the planet that Jorran had come to, though his ship didn't remain near it for very long. His first impression was that this planet wasn't suitable for his purpose, and he left to find another. Martha didn't deal just with first impressions, however, and as it turned out, Jorran's ship had merely moved to a place of concealment behind the planet's single moon.

It had been easy to track and keep up with Jorran's ship, and the *Androvia* was designed to avoid being tracked, so Jorran wouldn't know that he had been followed. Concealing his ship in the area was a clear indication that he had gone down to the planet himself. Scanning his ship proved it had fewer bodies on it than it had arrived with. And having sneaked the android Corth II onto it to install a one-way data probe was keeping Martha apprised of Jorran's men's positions on the planet, as well as giving her other pertinent information that Jorran was sending back to his ship.

Fortunately, the captain of Jorran's ship was proving to be a nosy sort who insisted on being kept apprised of the situation, and from a few choice words dropped during a communication, Martha was able to determine that the ship and crew were merely hired, and there was a time limit remaining on their employ, and most of that had been used up getting here. But Jorran wasn't going to dismiss them until the very end, in case things didn't go as he planned. It did, however, force him to make his move within a month, or give up and go home.

The rest of the time since their arrival yesterday had been spent gathering information about the planet and its people, and creating the Sublims necessary to speak the language. Corth II had come in handy for that as well, being sent to the planet's surface first to find an unused computer terminal that Martha could be connected to, and even Martha was impressed at the wealth of information she was finding.

"They might not be advanced to high-tech standards, but they are excellent recordkeepers and have at least mastered global computer connections, so that only one terminal is needed to access everything I require. But it's still in the primitive stages, which is why it's taking so long to access their vast stores of information."

That had been Martha's remark yesterday. By last night she had been complaining, "Did I say they were advanced? I have never encountered *anything* as slow as the machines those people call computers." She was still collecting data.

"Okay, we're going to take it from the top again," Martha said now. "And see if it sinks in this time. They are an aggressive, war-minded people up there on the surface. Their history is filled with violence from their very beginnings, and they think nothing of wholesale slaughter. And although the concept of life on other planets fascinates them, it also terrifies them, so Probables tell me that while there might be some of them who would greet off-worlders with open arms, most of them will go out of their way to destroy any visitors. They just aren't *ready* to be discovered yet. Have I made that clear enough yet?"

"The woman did not have war on her mind," Dalden pointed out stubbornly.

"We could hear perfectly well what she had on her mind, just as we know perfectly well what was on yours, all of which is redundant. I am stressing a point here, big guy, if you haven't figured that out yet, and if you don't get it by the time I finish, then you are *not* going back to the surface. Are you listening yet?"

"Is it possible not to, when in your presence?" Dalden replied stiffly.

A very good imitation of a sigh filled the control room, loud and prolonged. "We don't have time for bruised warrior egos, Dalden. My job is to get you back home in one piece and still breathing. If you can manage to recover the rods as well, then you're happy, Tedra's happy, and I'm happy. Which means I'll help you to do that. None of which means you have time for hanky-panky."

The third blush was immediate and quite vivid. Dalden had no trouble understanding the "ancients' language" that his mother and Martha both used, having grown up hearing its use. Tedra had always been fascinated by the ancient history of her people, when most Kystrani couldn't care less, and only recent history was still taught in their learning systems. *Hanky-panky*, one of those ancient words, equated to Sha-Ka'ani *fun*, or what was more universally known as sharing sex.

"Now, from the top once more, *no fraternizing with the local species*," Martha continued. "If even one of those humans figures out that you aren't one of them, you'd have billions of people trying to wipe you from their memories, and given their history, that means kill you on sight. They won't care that you're here to help them. They won't care about the wealth of advanced knowledge you could introduce them to. They would consider you a threat to their survival, not a benefit, and exterminate you accordingly."

Shanelle frowned at that point. "You said he'd have no trouble passing for one of them, Martha, as long as he left his sword on the ship."

"Nor will he, since they come in all sizes and shapes themselves, even Sha-Ka'ani warrior size. But that's *if* they aren't already looking for him."

"Why would they be?" Shanelle asked. "Didn't you say that they would have to conclude that we disintegrated, if they noticed us at all, because no disturbance of their water was caused by us?"

"Correct. They have viewing devices to see farther into space than the naked eye can, which means they could have seen us coming if battleships of this line weren't equipped with a wide selection of disguisers. It also means they probably *did* see Jorran's ship if it hovered long enough above them and if one of the operators of those viewers was paying close attention, which fortunately isn't a guarantee, since they are operated by humans, rather than by computers."

"So if they are looking for anyone, it would be Jorran, not Dalden."

"Yes. But that means that Dalden can make no mistakes to draw attention to himself, or they'll think they've found what they're looking for in him. And these people are in a constant state of readiness for war. Though most of them have reached a point of wanting global peace, they are too diverse in cultures to attain it completely."

"I wish you could just get a fix on Jorran and zap him to us," Shanelle mumbled. "Problem solved."

"Already tried it, kiddo, without success," Martha replied in a matching mumble. "Without a homing link attached to him, I can't get a perfect lock on him, even if I can pick up his voice. I'd have to transfer the entire area he's in to guarantee getting him as well, which is out of the question unless we know for certain that he's alone. Besides, he's wearing one of those old-fashioned personal Air Shields that prevent contamination when visiting suspect areas."

"Never heard of it."

"Didn't think so. Personal Air Shields have long been considered inferior devices, since a simple pill these days can destroy any contamination in seconds, if there isn't a meditech unit handy to do the same. The shield around him isn't visible to the naked eye, doesn't prevent access to him other than of the germ type, but it definitely interferes with Molecular Transfer."

"As in, can't be used with?"

"Right. He'd have to turn it off for me to get at him,

and he's not likely to do that, if he's paranoid enough to wear an old-style shield in the first place rather than trust a meditech to cleanse and purify or a pill to prevent. But chances are his ship isn't equipped with an expensive meditech. Nor are the pills standard issue on Traders like his that usually have only contamination-free planets on their scheduled routes, so they have no need for such devices to begin with."

"Why was it discontinued for use if it still serves its purpose?"

"It became obsolete when Molecular Transfer first came into use. It worked fine when the only way you could get down to a planet was in a landing ship, but because Transfers can't be made while using one, if you transfer without the shield activated, you get contaminated before you can turn it on."

"That would be rather pointless," Shanelle agreed. "But wouldn't there be a time when Jorran might need to turn it off, like for cleaning up or sleeping?"

"Yes, but without a homing link on him, I can't keep him on track. I can zero in on him only when he communicates with his ship, but once he goes silent again, I lose him in the crowd. Besides, as long as he keeps the shield control within five feet of him, the shield will remain on him, even when he removes the control unit from his person, so I'm not counting on getting lucky there."

Shanelle sighed. "So we have to physically get our hands on him and the rods."

"Exactly, but Dalden should be able to manage that just fine once he finds him—as long as he stops being distracted by the locals."

No blush this time; in fact, Dalden's expression had

turned warriorish, as in no expression at all. Martha usually took such opportunities to try to provoke a reaction, one of her small forms of amusement, but with a specific task at hand, she restrained herself.

"I haven't determined if Jorran did his homework first, or just picked a country at random," Martha continued. "But there are many different forms of government here in the different countries, and a hierarchy of government in the one he did pick. Head of a town, then head of a state that has hundreds of towns, then head of the whole country. They don't have a head of the whole planet yet, haven't progressed to that. But there are a few countries that are considered world leaders: their opinion counts big-time and they have the power to back it up, if you know what I mean. He's picked one of the big leaders, but it looks like he's going to start small and work his way up. Didn't think he'd be that smart."

"Why is this smart, when it's not what he really wants?" Shanelle asked.

"Because what their leaders do here is quickly made known to all the populace, especially what the big leaders do. Whereas the actions of the little leaders, the ones who only govern a single town, tend to only be made known to that town. In other words, the fewer eyes on him, the better.

"He probably wasn't expecting this planet to be so hugely populated, since most planets grown to this size begin dispersing their people to other planet colonies before they deplete the mother planet's resources. Century III is still in the baby stages itself, with a gross population under five hundred thousand. This planet has people in the billions. They have millions jammed into little cities. They don't spread out, they spread up. There's just too many people here. It's no wonder any ship that has come close enough to check them out has run the other way instead of making contact."

"On the other hand, Jorran might be delighted by the overabundance of population," Shanelle remarked. "The more people falling at his feet in worship, the better."

"True, though I doubt it will matter when Probables tell me it's not going to work the way he's hoping, on a big scale—though he seems to think it will, and can cause a lot of grief in the trying."

"Why not? It worked perfectly on Sunder."

"Yes, because Sunder was a global unity that shared power between the military and science departments, and they didn't have world communication systems like this one does, where everyone can be apprised of what's going on in their world by just turning on a box in their homes and listening. On Sunder, the leaders could step down and appoint anyone they wanted to take their place, and most of the planet's people never knew the difference. On this planet the leaders are either elected by the people, born into the position, or take power by might. The general populace knows what's going on and if they don't like it, they most definitely aren't quiet about it. And he's picked the elected form of government, so he can't just use the rods to have one of the leaders resign and appoint him in his place."

"But won't that approach take much longer?"

"You betcha." Martha switched to a smirking tone. "It would take years for him to work his way up through the hierarchy. And it's a good guess that Jorran won't figure that out before he runs out of time."

"Then couldn't we just sit back and wait for him to run out of time and go home? If he's back on Century III, we can file theft charges against him and get the rods back through normal diplomatic channels."

"We could," Martha replied. "But we won't, when he could decide to take the risk and strand himself here, the old do-or-die approach. And there is one other possibility we have to take into account."

"You mean you haven't told us everything yet?"

"It's those slow computers," Martha's new tone was thick with complaint. "I was concentrating on retrieving their history, military, science, and governmental records first, but I'm now getting information that introduces new options. Jorran doesn't have to get into a position of leadership to be in a position of power on this particular planet. Wealth is a highly motivating, highly powerful commodity here, so he could obtain his own empire in the field of finance instead. And in that case, those rods can do exactly what he needs."

"Have people shower him with their riches, without knowing why, and with nothing to prevent them from doing so?" Shanelle guessed.

"Exactly."

Chapter 8

❦

"Is ALL THAT SILENCE BROODING, DALDEN, OR BECAUSE you've been paying attention?" Martha asked.

They were alone in the control room. Shanelle had been informed that Falon was showing signs of impatience in wanting to search for Jorran himself. Sending fifty seven-foot Sha-Ka'ani warriors to the surface for a mass search for Jorran would have hastened the search, but was out of the question. There might be humans of an equivalent size on the planet, but they were a rarity, not the norm.

Sending down even two warriors would be pushing it for drawing unwanted notice, which was why Martha was insisting the search begin with just Dalden. Shanelle, being in agreement, had rushed off to remind her lifemate of that.

"I understand what worries you, Martha," Dalden

replied. "I would not let the woman know that I am what she would call a barbarian."

Chuckling floated about the room. "She wouldn't think that. No, her word for you would be an alien. It would have no meaning to her that other worlds consider your world a bit barbaric in nature. She'd recognize only one thing, that you aren't from *her* world, and that would shock the hell out of her, taking precedence over anything she might have been feeling about you. I'd then have to bring her aboard the ship, erase her memories of you, and hope that it works on these humanoids. And you know I don't deal well with 'hope it works.' So why don't we just avoid all that—"

"I need someone who will immediately recognize another visitor like me," he interrupted. "I will not be able to know the difference, since they all sound strange to me. Jorran I will recognize."

"Not guaranteed, when he could change his looks. Did we say your task was going to be easy?"

Dalden ignored the commentary to continue to make his point. "The rest of his people I would not know. But she would know. She knew immediately that I was not from her town. She already thinks I am part of her world, a foreigner, she called me."

"I was there, remember? I heard every word."

"Then you can agree that to have her help would be a benefit to us."

"Of course I agree, but that doesn't mean it can be allowed. Other factors have to be taken into account, Dalden, the main one being that the longer you deal with one of those humans, the greater the risk of giving yourself away. The woman Brittany isn't even in a position of authority, yet she asks the same questions you will run into from everyone. Those are a curious, bold people. Butting into others' business is a natural process for them. And she will continue to grill you with questions until you end up slipping and telling her something that you shouldn't."

"With most of those questions already dealt with, the risk has been lessened."

Martha chuckled. "I just love it when warriors prove they aren't all brawn."

"Does this mean—"

"Not so fast, kiddo." Martha did the interrupting this time. "I sent your sister out of here so I could speak plainly without embarrassing you. The woman Brittany does happen to be ideal for what you need, and you've passed with flying colors, making her think you're just someone from a different part of her world. I could wish you weren't attracted to her, so let me just stress: Jorran first, then rods, girl last on the agenda. If your reproductive instincts become a problem, get them out of the way. Too much trouble can be caused if that's all you're thinking about. So if it becomes a problem, take care of it, then get back to business. Can you do that?"

"Certainly."

"Why do I get the feeling that would have been your answer whether you believe it to be true or not? Never mind," was said with an accompanying sigh. "I know you wouldn't lie to me intentionally. I know you *think* you can do what needs doing. I've come to expect an abundance of confidence from any of you warriors, no matter the endeavor, and you and your father have proven time and again that your own confidence is rarely off the mark."

"Is the woman still in that place you sent me to?" Dalden questioned.

"No, but I have already accessed all pertinent information on her and have the location that she calls home. I've also launched a miniature viewer above her town so I can have visuals as needed and not have to depend solely on the viewers on the combo-unit."

A grid appeared on the computer monitor that enlarged and then enlarged several more times until it became more clear that it was an overhead view of a small section of the planet that included dwellings, foliage, and objects moving along the grids that looked similar to the flying vehicles of Kystran but without the capability of flying. A large red circle appeared on one section of the grid, another was drawn some distance away, then three more smaller circles.

Martha's voice was all business now as she explained, "Brittany Callaghan lives here." The first circle flashed brighter in color. "The leader called Mayor lives here." The second circle flashed. "The largest bank depositors live here." The three circles flashed together. "All three are corporations rather than individuals. I will monitor their accounts for any unusual withdrawals, but I am not overly concerned yet that Jorran might go the money route. His mentality is deeply set in being a titled ruler, rather than a wealthy despot, so he will at least make the attempt to become the mayor here."

"Can he succeed?"

"Sure, if he uses the rods on every male in town and waits to get elected by them through the normal process, but he doesn't have time for that. He'll more likely try something stupid instead like having the

mayor resign and appoint him as his replacement until
the election. He'll be using those rods a lot to do it this
way, and will have to have the support of the city
council and every other man in a position of authority,
as well as a full-blown history for himself to offer the
public, because these people won't accept a stranger
taking over, they will want to know *all* about him. But
the rods will work to make people think they've
known him forever and that he's a really great guy
who'd make a perfect mayor for them."

Dalden frowned. "Then he *can* accomplish what he
wants here."

Martha spared a moment to offer one of her more
smirking-type chuckles. "He could if it were only men
in the equation, but the women, at least in the country
he's picked, aren't of the silent, do-as-they're-told variety. Many of them hold positions of authority themselves. The rods worked fine on Sunder because it was
a conspiracy of women that took over there, so they
only had the men to worry about. Here, it's the women
who are going to throw a wrench in Jorran's plans."

"This is true on the whole planet?"

"No, he's just picked the wrong country to try to
take over. It's up to you to get your hands on him before he changes tactics and picks another country, or
goes after riches instead. The last thing we want is for
him to lose himself in one of their big cities. It's hard
enough trying to pinpoint his location in the small
town he's in. It'd be impossible in one of their major
cities."

"The amount of people in that place today cannot
be called small by any standards."

Another chuckle. "That was not a normal place,

Dalden, it was a place the entire town goes to for shopping and other forms of entertainment, their version of a Sha-Ka-Ra market. You wouldn't find crowds like that in the rest of the town, though in a large city you just might. But the local news of the town had the mayor scheduled to be there today, which is why you were placed there."

"But was Jorran there?"

"Undetermined. The mayor was there, and we have to assume that Jorran will be following the mayor until he makes his move, which is why you will need to keep close to him as well. But keep in mind, you can't just grab Jorran when you do find him and expect no one to interfere, and we do *not* want those people yelling for their security forces. You can't give him a chance to use a rod on you, either. You need to stun him, turn off his shield, then I can get you both back to the ship and we will have the leverage to have the rest of the rods turned over to us. But you need to get him alone before you go assaulting him with a stun."

"The stunning and the turning off of his shield can be accomplished in a matter of moments, as is Transfer. Why must such precaution be taken?"

"Because I don't take chances with one of Tedra's babies. You know that. And there are too many unknown variables involved on this planet, things I am unaware of yet because their computers aren't up to my speed and aren't giving me all their information fast enough. I shocked a good many people today by putting you down in the center of them. I shocked many more taking you back out of their midst, since the Brittany female wasn't the only woman down there who couldn't take her eyes off you, kiddo. A good many of them will now be visiting their eye doctors, which is okay, as long as we don't make a habit of shocking them. Had violence broken out in their midst, that whole crowd could have swarmed on you, and having you end up in what they call jail is *not* on the agenda."

"If I had my sword—"

"No, no, no, don't turn pure warrior on me, Dalden. I know what you're capable of, you know what you're capable of, but those people up there are not going to find that out for themselves. Swords are archaic here, used only by performers enacting their history. They are not worn in public without causing a great deal of curiosity. You have an excellent weapon in your phazor combounit: it covers all emergencies and gives me a six-sided view of the proceedings as well, and none of these humanoids will guess it is a weapon because they have nothing like it. It looks like what they call a portable radio, and Corth II even attached that wire to it so you can hear me without anyone near you hearing me."

"The woman could hear you."

"No, all she heard was noise, she didn't hear my words and wouldn't have understood them even if she did, which is beside the point. The communicator phazor unit has been made to look familiar to these people, so they won't question it. Now let's get back to the matter of the Brittany woman and using her to aid your task. The info I have gathered on her from all computer sources indicates that she has two places of employment that take up most of her time. You will need to tempt her away from these jobs to work for you. Just asking might do it, but let's not count on that. You will need to hire her."

"With what do I hire her? You can obtain their currency to do this?"

"Unnecessary," Martha replied. "Like the Catrateri, this is another planet that worships the metal gold, and that chunk you wear around your neck should be more than sufficient for the short-term employment you require. Now, are you ready to get back to business?"

"Indeed."

"Then hold on to your socks, kiddo, Transfer imminent."

Chapter 9

"IT CRACKS ME UP WHEN THIS JUNK MANAGES TO GET into the local paper. I mean, you expect it in the supermarket tabloids, but—"

"What junk?" Brittany asked as she closed the refrigerator, the cold soda she'd come for in hand.

Her roommate was sitting at their small kitchen table with a cup of coffee and a piece of coffee cake in front of her, even though it was midafternoon. Of course, Jan had only just gotten up an hour ago, having slept in later than usual today after a late night out with her current boyfriend. Several newspapers were there that she was catching up on reading, with one open in her hands.

"And on the second page, no less," Jan added as she glanced up at Brittany. "This is too funny."

Since Jan wasn't exactly laughing, Brittany took the funny part to be sarcasm. "What junk?" she asked again.

"Another UFO sighting."

Brittany rolled her eyes and headed out of the kitchen. Jan called after her, "No, really. Three people from Seaview swear they saw it. I wonder how long they stayed for happy hour."

Brittany came back and sat down across from Jan. "Some people actually take that stuff seriously, you know," she pointed out.

"We don't."

"No, but I can see why it would make the local paper, if three locals are claiming they saw something unusual. That's the first sighting in our area, which makes it newsworthy or at least of interest, even if it was just another weird-looking government plane being tested or a trick of the light. Besides, look at what those initials stand for, 'unidentified' being the word of note. I'm sure if the little green men ever do decide to pay us a visit, we'll have no trouble recognizing their transportation as a spaceship and calling it that."

Jan rolled her eyes now. "You are too kind, Britt. A flaky, delusional person is still a flake."

"No, actually, *those* sightings we probably never hear about, just as a known drunk isn't going to be taken seriously, either. The sightings that do make the news are usually from sober, respectable people who really do believe they saw what they claim to have seen."

"Or sensationalists who lie just to bask in the public spotlight," Jan countered as she continued to glance over the paper.

Brittany gave up with a chuckle. Her friend was one of those stubborn individuals who would adhere to an opinion to the bitter end, despite evidence that might suggest they have their facts wrong. She enjoyed such discussions, though, because she didn't let them frustrate her. She wasn't the type who had to be right all the time; she was perfectly happy to shrug and say we'll agree to disagree without getting hot under the collar about it, and go on to the next subject.

She'd still been in a rotten mood when she'd come into the kitchen, still furious that that gorgeous foreigner she'd met a few hours ago hadn't had the decency to at least say good-bye before disappearing on her. Trust Jan though to lighten her mood, however briefly.

They were three years apart in age, Jan the younger at twenty-five, but had hit it off immediately when Jan answered the roommate ad Brittany had run soon after she moved into the two-bedroom apartment. She could have afforded the place easily by herself, but her goals were already set, and having someone split the costs with her fit well into her plan. Besides, she wasn't a loner; she liked having people around, liked having someone there to talk to when she felt like it, or leave her alone when she felt like that, too.

But today she knew she wouldn't be good company. So she started to head back to her bedroom to lay on her bed and brood some more about all the things she should have said to that hunk to make him at least interested enough to ask for her phone number.

But again Jan arrested her attention, this time with a gasped, "Jeez!" and a moment later, "Oh, Jeez, I don't believe it!"

Brittany came back to stand in the doorway that separated the kitchen and tiny laundry room from the oversized living room. "What now?"

"We almost died yesterday and didn't even know it!" Jan exclaimed.

"Excuse me?"

Jan laid the paper down to stare up at Brittany wide-eyed. She was actually pale. "I thought meteors and comets got tracked coming toward us, like we had months' advance warning? Did *you* hear anything about this one?"

Brittany frowned. "A meteor passed by near us?"

"It didn't pass by, it was last tracked dropping into the Pacific, was already in the atmosphere when it was spotted, and then—gone."

"So there was no danger?"

"Are you kidding? It says here it was the size of a football field. If that thing had actually hit the water instead of disintegrating, the tidal wave would have been big enough to reach the next states over."

"But it obviously didn't hit."

"No, but that's beside the point. This one came in so fast that no one saw it coming."

"The size of a football field would be no more than a speck of dust in space, Jan. The observatories wouldn't pick up anything that small."

"I still don't like it that we hear about it *after* the fact," Jan grumbled.

Neither did Brittany, but she was pragmatic about things that she couldn't change. "If it came in as fast as you say, so it wasn't even noticed until it was already here, then nothing could have been done about it either way. Meteors flash through all the time, some hit, most disintegrate. We can be glad they aren't the size of comets, and chalk this one up to it wasn't our time to go."

"Is that farm philosophy?"

Brittany grinned. "No, just old-fashioned acceptance of fate."

Jan snorted. "I'd rather make my own fate, thank you very much, which includes at least having the option of trying to run for the hills."

Brittany might have suggested Jan go back to school and figure out how to build better telescopes, but she preferred to get back to her brooding, so she shrugged instead and once again headed toward her bedroom. But she'd no sooner closed the door when another shriek of astonishment was heard from the kitchen. Brittany shook her head. She *did* wonder what could possibly top the story of the meteor to upset Jan this time, but decided she could wait to find out.

But less than a minute later she was heading back to the kitchen despite her resolve. Curiosity could be a major pain sometimes, and she did occasionally have an overactive imagination that could go haywire if her own curiosity started acting up. She began to think of other things that had nothing to do with news articles that might have made Jan cry out, and she was actually running those last few steps to the kitchen door to make sure her friend was all right.

She wasn't. Jan was slumped across the table, the coffee cup spilled, the cake just missed by her head, the newspaper scattered on the floor next to her chair. Behind her stood—him. Unbelievable. That gorgeous hunk of foreign masculinity in *her* kitchen? And he looked annoyed and upset at the same time, if that was possible, as he stared down at Jan.

"What'd you do, scare the bejesus out of her?"

He hadn't seen Brittany yet in the doorway. He looked at her now and seemed to visibly relax, though he did sigh.

"She could not withstand the sight of me," he said by way of explanation.

"That's what I said—never mind. Help me get her to her bed."

There was no helping about it. He lifted Jan so easily that he could have been picking up the coffee cup, and simply waited for Brittany to lead him, which she did. A few moments later she stared down at Jan laying peacefully in her bed and had no idea what to do to bring her out of her faint. It wasn't as if she had any experience in the matter.

She sighed. "I really don't think we have anything in the medicine cabinet that covers fainting."

"I am told she will recover in due time."

"Told?" she said. "Or is that your way of stating your opinion? Oh, never mind," she added, realizing as she said it that she'd said it an awful lot to him in the brief span of their acquaintance.

She directed him out of Jan's room with a wave of her hand, followed him into the living room that adjoined both bedrooms, and pointed at the couch there. He took the hint, though he was very careful as he sat down on it, as if he were afraid he might break it. Come to think of it, some springs just might snap under his seven feet of solid man weight. He really was *big*. And although their living room was extra large in comparison to the rest of the apartment, it looked cut down to half its size with him in it.

Brittany was still in a bit of shock herself that he was there, when she had been sure she'd never see him again. And the fact that Jan had still been sitting at the kitchen table meant she hadn't let him in, so it was no wonder his sudden presence had scared the heck out of her. Some overdue annoyance that he had just barged in on them rose now.

"Is it normal etiquette in your country to just walk into someone's home without knocking?" she asked. "There are laws against doing that here, if no one has bothered to mention that to you."

He didn't answer immediately. She had changed into shorts and a loose T-shirt when she got home, but he was still dressed as he'd been at the mall, and still had that radio, or translator, or whatever it was, attached to his belt, the miniature earphone still firmly in ear.

"I knocked," he told her. "Yet no one opened the door."

She found that hard to believe. As big as his hand was, any knocking he did could probably be heard over on the next block.

So she raised a brow at him. "You didn't figure, then, that maybe no one was home?"

Another pause before he said, "I knew that not to be the case."

Okay, so he could have heard them talking through the door, but then how the heck hadn't they heard his knocking? She might not have heard him after she'd closed her bedroom door, but Jan should have. And why was she nitpicking when he was here? She still found that amazing. He'd actually tracked her down—but how had he?

She immediately asked, "How did you find me when my phone number is unlisted?"

Once again, a long pause before he answered, "I have excellent resources."

"No kidding," she agreed. "So much for thinking you needed a detective, when you've got the kind of access usually only law enforcement, government, or ambassadors—ahh, that's it, isn't it? Your embassy in this country is helping you cut through red tape?"

"For what reason would I cut tape of a certain color?" he replied.

Screeching out of the earphone. Well, he *had* answered immediately, without waiting for the coaching. Brittany almost laughed, but his wince restrained her. Poor baby. He was having a heck of a time coping with the new language he'd learned, and his translator was obviously of the impatient sort.

"How about we have a conversation without your hyperactive friend's help?" she suggested, staring pointedly at the radio on his hip.

He gave her a brilliant smile and removed the earphone, dropping the cord so it dangled over the couch by his feet, a good guess that was far enough for him not to hear anything else coming out of it. Brittany only vaguely noticed, though, that smile of his having dazzled her to the core.

"Be at ease," he said. "I will be fine."

"Was that for me or your friend there?" she managed to ask him.

"My friend. She worries overmuch about me."

The dazzling subsided completely, some unexpected bristling taking over. "She?"

"She is a computer."

Brittany blinked. "Was that a joke?"

"Why would you think so?"

She laughed. He was quite funny. "Probably because computers don't have emotions, so they can't worry. Now, what brings you here?"

"I need you."

Those words almost melted her on the spot. She had the greatest urge to hop across the coffee table between them, right into his lap. The butterflies in her belly had just gone absolutely wild. Never had she been so thoroughly turned on, and incredibly, just by words.

Chapter 10

IT TOOK BRITTANY NEARLY A MINUTE TO CONVINCE HERSELF that Dalden's definition of need was a far cry from hers. That he hadn't moved from his position on the couch sort of pushed her toward that conclusion sooner than her body was acknowledging. She *knew* she should have broken down and bought an air conditioner for the apartment; a blast of icy air would definitely be welcome at the moment.

She settled for sinking into the matching lounge chair next to the couch and inconspicuously fanning herself. Hearing his definition of need would probably help even more, so she asked, "What can I do for you that your embassy can't?"

"I must find the man Jorran in all haste," he told her. "Yet I am not assured of recognizing him if I see him, because he may have changed his appearance from when I last saw him. You would know him, though, as you did me, for someone not from your country."

"Well, that's debatable," she replied, pointing out, "It was only your accent—"

"He will speak differently, as do I."

She chuckled. "I hope you're not talking about having a chat with everyone in town, just to hear their accents."

"If such is needful—"

"Time out," she cut in. "I was joking. We're a small town, but we still have a population now exceeding twenty thousand residents. If even half of those are men, you're talking a heck of a lot of time to track them all down for a little chat. And I was under the impression that you don't have a lot of time."

"Nor do I. Nor will it be needful. Jorran will wish to make contact with the one you call Mayor, so he will most likely be found in the vicinity of this leader."

"What's he want with Mayor Sullivan?"

"His position."

"His position on what?"

He looked confused. Brittany *was* confused. He tried to clarify. "He will try to become mayor here. I must stop him before he succeeds."

"He's here to run against Sullivan? But I thought he was a foreigner like you?"

"He is."

"Then I don't get it. You have to be an American citizen to run for political office in this country. How could he not know that?"

Dalden grinned, showing signs of relief. "Because he is as ignorant of your traditions as I am."

She grinned back. "Well, there you go, your problem is solved."

He sighed now. "Actually, it is not. I still must find him and remove him from your country before he causes problems here."

"Ah, international incident of the big sort, huh?" It was pretty obvious when he glanced down at the earphone at his feet that he was in need of an explanation. Brittany tried. "A big ruckus that would make the papers in both our countries, to everyone's embarrassment?" When he still looked blank, she added, "Oh, go ahead, pick it up. I'm sure *she* can make you understand."

He nodded, did so, and after a very long moment of having the earphone attached again, said to Brittany, "Your analysis is appropriate. Will you help me?"

"I'd love to, really I would, but I don't see how I can. You need someone with more time on their hands than I have. But with two jobs tying me up for most of the week, the only time I could help you would be on Sundays, and that doesn't seem nearly enough when you've made it clear you're in a hurry to get this wrapped up."

"You misunderstand, Brittany Callaghan. I wish to pay for your time, for you to work only for me until my task here is accomplished."

He lifted the large medallion off his chest and off his neck, leaning over to hand it to her. Her hand actually dropped before she put some effort into holding it up. The medallion was really heavy, with the added weight of the chain, which was more the size of a bicycle chain than a piece of jewelry, probably weighing ten pounds itself.

She gave him a questioning look, to which he said, "That is a cheap metal where I come from, yet I am told it has high value here. Will it be sufficient to hire you?"

She glanced down at what was probably fifteen, maybe even twenty pounds of disk and chain. "How much gold plating are we talking about?"

"Plating?"

"The percentage of actual gold?"

"There is no percentage. It is only one metal. Are we misinformed, that you do not value pure gold?"

"You have *got* to be kidding."

She wasn't sure what gold was priced at by the ounce these days, but knew a chain not even a tenth the size of the one in her hand could cost upwards of six hundred dollars, and not even be pure gold at that. She did some quick calculations in her head and realized they were talking about a *lot* of money—if he wasn't pulling her leg about it being pure gold. And what was she even thinking about? It was way too much for what he was suggesting.

"Look, it probably wouldn't take more than a week to find your guy, even less if he really is going to be hanging out around the mayor. I can take a week off from my jobs, and you can pay me with the currency of your country the equivalent of a couple thousand American bucks. This," she added, handing him back the medallion, "is worth a small fortune, far too much for one week's work."

He pushed the medallion back at her. "It may require more than one week, and—it is all that I have to pay you with. I have not this currency that you speak of."

"No money, and here you are trying to dump a fortune in gold on me?" she rolled her eyes. "No offense, but you need a baby-sitter, big guy."

After a moment he grinned at her. "You have just endeared yourself to Martha."

"Who's Martha?"

"The voice in here." He tapped the earphone. "She suggests that 'baby-sitter' be added to the job you will do for me. What is baby-sitter?"

Brittany blushed. "You don't know? I mean, she didn't explain—? Never mind. I was just joking, really. But what happened to your money? Have you just run out, or were you robbed?"

"Neither. I had no requirement of currency until it became needful to hire assistance."

She stared at him long enough to draw her own conclusion and even thumped her head for not thinking of it sooner. "Credit cards, of course. And for some reason, you aren't equating them with money. Okay, no biggie. Your hotel might not advance you a couple grand, but the banks will tomorrow."

The look he was giving her said clearly that she was talking Greek to him again, but after the requisite pause while he attentively listened to Martha's explanations, he said simply, "I am reminded that I cannot return to my place of sleep until the new rising."

"Rising?"

He sighed after some brief coaching from the earphone and clarified, "Many call it a new day."

"Oh, tomorrow!" Brittany said, but then frowned. "Why not?"

He explained, "Because I was called back for an un-

needful consultation, I have exceeded my limit for returning there on this rising."

This was said with a degree of grouchiness. Not that
it mattered when she was completely baffled anyway.
She understood now how frustrating it must be for
him, needing translations for just about everything she
was saying. That must have been one heck of a lousy
language course he took, if such worldly things like
credit cards, hotels, and banks hadn't been included.
Talk about a simplistic definition for hotel—place of
sleep. She mentally rolled her eyes again.

The only other conclusion she could draw was that
he came from one of those countries that still got
around on camels, where most of their population had
never heard of such things. She hoped not.

And then it dawned on her and she asked, "Wait a
minute, are you saying you have nowhere to sleep
tonight, but tomorrow you will have?"

He nodded. She sighed, telling him, "I'm not even
going to try to figure out how that could be possible,
when it doesn't sound like you're referring to messed-
up hotel reservations. But you're welcome to sleep on
our couch, I suppose. My roommate Jan might object,
after the scare you gave her. Then again, after she gets
a good look at you, she might not. We eat around six.
The bathroom is through that middle door behind
you. In the meantime, how about telling me a little
more about yourself, so I can better understand what's
going on here and what's going to be expected of me
on this temporary job?

"And put this back on," she continued, tossing the
medallion at him so he couldn't push it back at her this

time. "Much as I could use what that thing will fetch, I'm not in the habit of taking advantage of foreigners. We'll find you a buyer for it tomorrow so you can pocket the bulk and just pay me the couple thousand I've asked for, to cover taking off from my regular jobs."

Brittany settled down into the chair to wait while the female on the other end of his earphone did her thing. Sooner than expected, though, Dalden smiled and said, "I am told you eat real food here. I look forward to sharing your meal."

Brittany burst out laughing. She couldn't help it, deciding it was probably his Martha who needed a translator, not him.

Chapter 11

THEY DIDN'T EXACTLY GET AROUND TO TALKING ABOUT him as Brittany had hoped they would. Somehow, the subject got turned in her direction instead, because Dalden's curiosity had been pricked earlier by one of her remarks that didn't get addressed immediately.

"What is the job you have here that ties you up?" he asked her.

Just by the way he said it, she knew immediately that he had taken the word literally and had envisioned ropes twined about her limbs. "Err, that was ties up as in restricts, as in, I don't have much time left in the day after I get home from work for anything other than sleep. Was that easier for you to understand?"

"Indeed," he acknowledged. "But I would still hear of your job."

She had no idea why she was suddenly embarrassed, had thought she had long since reached the immune stage where her job choice was concerned. And it had been a long haul getting there.

Because she worked in a field that most men considered exclusively theirs, she'd been called a libber and every other nasty name you could think of. She'd heard it all and learned to ignore it. She'd had whole crews refuse to work with her. She'd had architects turn down her contractor because she was on his crew.

It was a wonder she hadn't lost her quirky sense of humor, but she hadn't. It was, at times, the only thing that sustained her.

So why didn't she find a job where she didn't get so much grief?

She could have moved on to something else after she had learned all she needed to know about construction. But she was good at it, and she had yet to find anything she was as capable at that paid as well, and that was the bottom line for her when she had such an expensive goal. And one of the nice things about her profession was that she could quit for a few months, even years, and then get back into it and not feel that she'd missed anything, because it was what she would be doing when she quit to build her home. Not much changed in construction. Better tools were made, union reps came and went, dues were raised, benefits got better, but houses were still basically built the same.

Her delay in answering him brought the remark, "I am told you are defensive about your job. Why is that?"

Since that voice on the other end of the earphone couldn't possibly have guessed that just from her prolonged silence, she was beginning to think that his "I am told" was just his way of stating his own opinion, rather than something Martha was telling him. Besides, her hot cheeks had probably been a dead giveaway, and only he was seeing that. Martha might be able to hear them, but that was all she could do.

"I used to be," she admitted. "Hard not to be, when you get so much flak about an occupation from all sides. But I'm stubborn. I have a goal, to build my own home with my own hands. My grandfather did it, and the concept always fascinated me, which probably had a lot to do with finally making the decision myself. So everything I do now is done with that goal in mind, which includes my choice of work, so I could learn about all aspects of house construction from the ground up. Basically I'm a carpenter, though I can roof, lay drywall, and paint with the best of them."

"It is difficult here, the building of one's home?" he asked.

"Well, no, not if you have a well-paying job to afford it, or in my case, know how to build it yourself. I'm probably making it harder than necessary by wanting to have all the money up front first. I thought about taking out a home loan instead, but I really hate the idea of going that deep into debt. I know everyone does it, but that didn't mean I had to. And besides, I'm going to save tons of money by doing it myself, since it won't cost anywhere near what it would cost if I just went out and bought a house already built."

"You will build your home here in this town?"

"Yes, I've already bought the land. I could get started on it already, but that would be building it piecemeal in my spare time, which would take years. I prefer to have enough money to spare for all the materials and extra help I'll need when more than two hands are required, enough so I can quit both my jobs until it's done. And doing it myself, I'll make sure it's done right."

"I find it admirable that you know how to create a house from nothing."

She blushed profusely. That had to be the first time a man had ever complimented her about her job choice.

But then he spoiled it by adding, "And do not view it as a punishment."

"I think we need another time-out," she said. "Either things are done really weird in your country, or you've been given the wrong definition for punishment. The only work around here that can be considered punishment is forced labor in prisons. Now some folks might not like their jobs, some might even hate them, but doing them anyway isn't punishment, it's more a necessity until something better comes along. Punishment, on the other hand, is pretty much universally reserved for disciplinary measures. No one around here is going to punish someone by forcing them to build a house for them. Do you see the difference?"

He smiled at her in answer, but also added, "I see that you have a good understanding for what must be done when one breaks rules. And I am told 'chore' would have been a more appropriate word to express my thoughts in the matter of how you view your job."

She chuckled. "No, I don't see it as a chore; I actually like building things, whether it's cabinets, tables, or an entire house. I work mostly for Arbor Construction here. I like their foremen, get along really well with their crews due to long association, and they know I do good work, so I don't have to constantly prove myself like I did in San Francisco when I lived there."

"Prove yourself how? In challenge?"

She blinked, then grinned at him. "Another of those misdefined words? No, occasionally there'd be no work in the city, so I'd have to go to the union to get work, and those jobs were usually with small crews that I didn't know and I'd have to go through the whole proving process again each time, because not once did they ever accept me as one of them. So when Arbor relocated here and offered me a chance to move with them, I jumped at it. It meant steady work with the same crews, instead of being sent who-knew-where by the union. And I love it here. I come from a small town and prefer them small, where you actually get to know your neighbors and develop a real sense of community."

Something she had said surprised him, which he mentioned right off. "You have lived elsewhere than in this town? Marriage brought you here?"

"Good heavens, no, I've never been married," she replied, amused at how easily he'd gotten that information out of her without actually asking if she were married. His two questions combined, though, led her to guess, "I take it your countrymen tend to stay where they're born?"

"Indeed, only would marriage separate a woman

from the place of her protection." And then he sighed. "I am reminded that our cultures are very much different, that women here even live alone."

She matched his sigh with the conclusions that remark drew. "Just how antiquated *is* your country?"

He grinned. "Barbaric, you would call it."

The grin suggested that he was joking. She hoped he was joking. She decided to accept that conclusion and forget about getting it clarified. Unfortunately, a picture of men riding around on camels and locking their women up in tents was hard to shake. She tried shaking it by continuing the job discussion.

"I've tried other jobs, but haven't found any that give me as much satisfaction."

"What other jobs?" he asked with interest.

She started to just tell him when she realized that those other jobs were in that same "for men only" classification, or might as well be when so many people still viewed them that way. So a little explanation was required first, if she didn't want to start blushing again.

"I have three older brothers. With no sisters, I tended to follow along in their footsteps, and did in fact enjoy the same pursuits they did growing up, you know, fishing, hunting, sports. You could say tomboy was my middle name."

"Is it?"

She chuckled, because that had been a serious question, but rather than explain what a tomboy was, she just said, "No," and continued. "We lived on a farm. My oldest brother, York, was the tractor-fixer in the family, so it wasn't surprising that he became a master mechanic who now owns his own gas station back home. Learning what I did helping him on weekends, it wasn't surprising I became a mechanic's helper myself for a few years. I could have gotten certified, but I knew that wasn't a job that I wanted to stay with when getting the grease out from under my nails became a never-ending source of annoyance."

That was said to amuse him, but his expression didn't change, remained merely attentive. Too attentive, actually. It was hard to tell if he were really interested in what she was saying, or just wanted to hear her talk. For all she knew, he could just be dissecting her words to better his grasp of her language, using her to teach him, so to speak. Or his interest could be purely on a base level, because he might be attracted to her, but that was wishful thinking on her part better left unexplored for the moment.

She got back to the résumé explanations. "My middle brother, Kent, moved to this state quite a few years ago. He'd always wanted to see more of the country and figured he might as well get paid for it, so he drives the big-load trucks cross-country. Visiting him one summer convinced me to move here as well, and after accompanying Kent a few times on his longer hauls, I decided to try my own hand at it. That job only lasted about a year, though; it was just too boring for my tastes, and boring on the road can be real dangerous."

"How do you equate danger with boring?"

"As in falling asleep at the wheel."

For some reason, his blank look said even that needed an explanation for him. Brittany decided to let Coach Martha deal with that one, and she must have, since he nodded understanding after a moment.

"You did not want to do something different from your brothers?"

She grinned at him. "Why waste valuable knowledge already learned?"

She had thought about joining the military, actually, but didn't volunteer that information. She was rather well-suited for it with her size, after all, but had nixed that idea, preferring to follow her own strict regimen rather than one forced on her. And she liked building things, liked leaving her mark in such a way.

"I did finally go my own way. My youngest brother, Devon, is what you might call a born farmer. He really loves growing things. I don't. In fact, I couldn't wait to spread my wings and get away from the farm. But Devon is still there helping our father, and will probably take over after our parents pass on."

"One grows, one builds, one fixes, one transports. You have a family well-suited for trade."

"Diverse, I think you mean."

He shrugged, allowing her her own interpretation. Annoyed for a moment that he wasn't going to make the effort that she had in explaining things, she almost wished she could borrow his "coach."

"And the other job that ties you up?" he asked next.

"That one's a piece of cake, at the local spa in the evenings and on Saturdays. Just one person could handle it, but there's two of us, so there isn't all that much to do, other than man the desk and offer guidance when someone wants to start up a strict exercise regimen. My coworker, Lenny, and I get along pretty well, too. We have an understanding: he doesn't try to hit on me, and I won't drop weights on his feet every chance I get."

Again, that was said just to amuse him, and again, it didn't. Actually, he sat forward and said in a concise, somewhat ominous tone, "The man you share this job with hits you?"

Brittany rolled her eyes, explaining, " 'Hit on' has a completely different meaning from the 'hits you' that you're using. No, Lenny has never hit me. But he has tried a few times to get me to go out with him."

"Go out where?"

"Dating?" He wasn't the only one drawing a blank—his earphone was quiet, too. "Oh, come on, you have *got* to understand dating. You know, girl and guy getting together to get to know each other better."

"You speak of fun?" he said with a big grin.

It was that big grin that had her replying cautiously, "Well, sure, at least, it can be hoped a date will turn out to be fun, but that certainly isn't always the case, and some can turn out to be a real pain in the—"

She cut herself off. He was looking alarmed. And she heard the distinct sound of laughter coming out of his earphone. She gave up. She was either having her leg pulled halfway across the state, or whoever had taught him English didn't have a good grasp of it themselves.

She said, "We should probably stop at the library in the morning to get you a real English dictionary. It might take you a few weeks of studying it, but you definitely didn't learn all you should have the first time around."

"I am aware that we are having difficulty communicating, but I would not be able to read one of your books. I was taught in audio, not visual."

She sighed. "Was your teacher a complete idiot, or one of those rinky-dink language—?"

The screeching out of the earphone was seriously

loud this time, causing Dalden to yank it out of his ear before it did some real damage.

Brittany raised an eyebrow at him. "Let me guess. The gal on the other end of the line there was your teacher?"

He winced, but nodded. She chuckled, adding, "Okay, I'll assume, since you're still being taught by Miss Coach, that you haven't had a full language course yet, and you're actually doing pretty well, if we go with that assumption. It's not a major problem, just time-consuming, all this explaining stuff. No biggie."

The earphone had gone silent while she spoke, prompting him to risk putting it back on. It buzzed for a moment at a normal volume. The woman Martha was obviously temperamental, but able to recover swiftly and get back to business.

He said now, "I am told that your language is more familiar to us than was first realized. Taken from the computers, the language was basic. Hearing you speak it, the similarities are becoming noticeable."

"Similarities to what? Your own language?"

"No, to the ancient language of my mother's people, which I have full understanding of. If such continues apace, and other of your words have the same meanings, I will have the correct translations momentarily. Thus we will have no further difficulties in communicating."

"Huh?"

He held up a hand, silently asking her to wait on any further explanations. The noise coming out of his earphone now was a steady buzz, a nonstop low-volume sound like a high-speed acceleration on a tape recorder, much too fast to be understood. It was probably broken. Good. She didn't really mind explaining things to him. But she did mind third-wheel Martha continuously butting in. How were they supposed to find any time alone to get to know each other better with that ever-present eavesdropper connected to his ear?

Chapter 12

"CAN THAT BE TURNED OFF?"

Brittany blushed as she asked it. She shouldn't have asked. It smacked of her obvious preference to be alone with Dalden.

Yet he didn't seem to notice any ulterior motive to the question and simply answered, "Only partially can Martha be disabled. The unit can be made so she cannot, or will not, speak, but there is no way to keep her from hearing when she is already hearing."

Brittany assumed that something got lost there in the translation, because it almost sounded as if Martha had some other means out of his control for listening in on him, which conjured up an image of her apartment being bugged with a spying device, which was absurd. And she was *not* going to start looking under tables.

The subject went no further, though, because noises were finally heard from behind Jan's bedroom door, a bit of swearing, then the door opened and Jan stumbled groggily out, rubbing her eyes. Seeing Brittany first, she said, "I had the weirdest dream," then noticing Dalden on the coach, "okay, so maybe I didn't. Who the—"

She didn't go any further, was absorbing Dalden's looks by slow degrees, to the point that her eyes got wider and wider. If someone could be said to be drooling without actually drooling, Jan was doing it. At least, she was until Dalden pushed off of the couch to turn to face her, so he didn't have to crane his neck to look behind him.

His neck-craning was nothing compared to hers. Jan was on the petite side and had to look up at Brittany if they were standing too close, but Dalden's seven feet were a bit intimidating. She'd been amazed at his handsomeness, but his size had her literally backing up until she was almost back in her bedroom.

She stopped at the door and said, "Holy cow!" And then as an explanation occurred to her, "One of your brothers, right? You could have warned me he was coming."

Jan had never met any of Brittany's brothers, but for some reason she assumed they were all a *lot* taller than Brittany was. Which wasn't the case at all. York was six-six, but both Kent and Devon were a bit shorter than that.

Brittany replied, "I'm happy to say he's no relation."

"Oh?" Jan's eyes swung to Brittany and, seeing the

blush, added, "Ohhhh," which made the blush even brighter.

Brittany made introductions and offered a bit of explanation about why Dalden was there. She then escaped to the kitchen with the excuse of getting dinner started, and stayed there until her cheeks cooled off. It was appalling that she'd blushed more in this one day than she had in the last several years.

She didn't have to worry about leaving Jan alone with Dalden. That longer "oh" had been clear understanding on her part. Jan even managed to disappear for most of the evening. She was a compulsive matchmaker, after all, had been trying to fix Brittany up with one guy after another in the three years they'd shared the apartment, and wasn't about to be a third wheel tonight when it was so obvious that Brittany was attracted to their guest.

Brittany cooked one of the most lavish meals she'd ever prepared. She even broke out the cookbook for it, not wanting to make a single mistake. Realizing afterward what she'd done, going to so much anxious effort to impress Dalden, she was disgusted with herself. If he couldn't like her the way she was, then there was no point in even thinking that they might be able to form a relationship, even if only a brief one. She wasn't going to change for anyone, was very comfortable with her life and her goals.

He was impressed with the meal, though—at least, he cleaned his plate thrice over. She knew men his size could eat a lot at one sitting, her brothers being testament to that, but even she was amazed at the amount of food Dalden consumed. Fortunately, she had prepared enough side dishes that she didn't run short. Still, there were no leftovers, and thank goodness Jan had a sweet tooth, so there was half a chocolate cake available for dessert as well. With half of that and a full carton of milk, she was reasonably sure her guest was finally replete.

And then she got nervous.

It was natural, she supposed, with a few hours yet to kill before her usual bedtime, that she'd start thinking about sex. Not that it hadn't been in the back, or forefront, of her mind all day, when she'd never before met someone she was this powerfully attracted to. And since that attraction had seemed to be mutual, she was pretty much expecting Dalden to make a move on her at some point in the evening.

For an immediate distraction, she turned on the television. It wouldn't be the first time she had used it to ease awkward moments with new acquaintances. But Dalden didn't seem the least bit interested in it, was staring at her instead, which just increased her nervousness.

"What would you like to watch?" she asked him.

He chuckled. "Is that not apparent?"

Back came the pink cheeks. "I meant on the TV," she explained.

He finally glanced across the room toward where she nodded and, after a moment of visually examining the floor console sitting there, rather than what was on the screen, said, "It is a strange-looking computer."

"It's not a computer—" She paused with the incredulous thought. "Oh, come on, don't try to tell me you know about computers, but have never seen a television set before, when television has been around *long* before computers."

"I am told it is a means of entertainment."

"But you didn't know that until Martha just told you, did you? How is that possible?" she asked, then answered her own question. "Okay, so maybe you live out in the boonies somewhere, and maybe your village doesn't even have electricity. But, newsflash, most computers require electricity, too. So how can you know of one and not the other, when most households have a TV or two or three, long before they even think about buying a home computer?"

He didn't reply. He got to his feet, moved to stand in front of her, and pulled her to her feet as well. One hand came to her cheek, and tilted her head so she would meet the eyes looking down at her. That easily all thoughts of questioning him were gone. She'd wonder later if it were deliberate on his part, to avoid answering her, but at the moment she was knee-deep in anticipation and simply didn't care.

"I like your concept of dating, now that I understand it," he told her. "But I think you will like the concept of my fun even better. We each of us know what the other wants, thus would dating best be seen to after we first have fun."

She could barely think to decipher what he'd just said, but managed to get out, "I get the feeling you have a really odd definition for fun."

"Not odd at all," he countered. "Though you may call it making love, you must agree no matter what it is called, it is fun."

"I—I agree it's reputed to be, yes, but—are you

suggesting we forget about the getting to know each other better part and get right down to the bottom line?"

He smiled beautifully. "If that means you will take me to where you sleep, yes."

Chapter 13

BRITTANY'S STOMACH WAS DOING THE BUTTERFLY THING. Her heart was slamming in her chest. Her instinct was to drag Dalden straight to her bedroom, and yet she had twenty-eight years of strict upbringing rooting her feet to the spot there in her living room.

He hadn't even kissed her yet. They'd only just met, not even six hours ago. How could she possibly give in to these primitive urges she was feeling? How could she not, when she'd been waiting so long for the right man to come along?

It wasn't as if she had to wait for marriage. Very few women did anymore in this day and age of self-gratification. And she'd been willing to sleep with Tom before he made that tactless remark that killed her feelings for him. But there was the rub. She'd had feelings for him after their many months of dating, had felt she knew him really well. That might not have been the case in the end, but she'd *thought* it was. But she didn't know Dalden at all, and she was reacting to him in a purely physical way that had absolutely nothing to do with emotions.

She suspected she might be more old-fashioned than she'd thought when she heard herself saying, "I'm not sure I can relax my morals quite that much, Dalden, when I barely know you."

He didn't exactly look disappointed, but then he hadn't been told a flat-out no yet, either. "You require the dating first?"

"That's usually how it's done."

"Our finding each other cannot be considered usual, *kerima*. In all the universe, we have managed to meet. What is felt here, between us, is stronger than either of our cultures, stronger than any ideals."

Was it? She'd certainly never experienced anything like this herself before. Was he saying he hadn't, either? She was so thrilled with that thought, her knees actually got weak. But a small, rational part of her warned that some men would say just about anything they thought you wanted to hear if they sensed they were close to sexual victory.

She wished the rational part had kept quiet. She didn't want to think that Dalden might be one of those men. But she had to remind herself once again that she knew next to nothing about him. She'd told him practically her whole life history. He'd told her only that he was here to complete a pretty strange task and needed her help for it.

"Your uncertainty is felt," he remarked, his tone without inflection when there should have at least been some disappointment in it. "Very well, tonight we see to dating, tomorrow we see to having fun."

She started to laugh. She couldn't help it. He still didn't get it, and she just didn't feel like explaining it any further. Nor was she given a chance to. He was suddenly kissing her. For him, that was apparently allowed, part of dating. Nor could she possibly have objected in that precious moment of tasting him for the first time.

His other hand came up to cup her left cheek. Her face was warmly cocooned between his large palms, his lips amazingly soft. He was touching her in no other way, just holding her face while he gently kissed her, and yet she felt as if he was touching her all over. To have felt all of him just then would probably have been too much for her senses, already on a thin thread of control.

She found out she was right when a few minutes later, he sat down in the chair she'd been in and drew her onto his lap. Wearing shorts, her legs were mostly bare, and all of that bareness was now exposed to the buttery-soft leather of his pants. It was one of the most sensual sensations she'd ever felt, not even remotely similar to leather upholstery. But that wasn't even half of what she was able to feel of him, sitting sideways on his lap.

Against her hip was the power and strength of his desire, impossible to ignore. One breast was pressed hard to his side; the other rubbed against his chest as he wrapped her arm about his neck. One of his hands was then placed high on the back of her thigh to keep her from sliding, not that bare skin had much chance of sliding on leather. His other arm fully supported her back and drew her even closer to him as his mouth came down to hers again, this new kiss so different from before, deep, claiming, branding her his.

It was absolutely more than she could handle, the kiss along with touching him in so many places. The passion that overcame her was amazing. She had nothing to compare it with in her own experience. And it took her beyond thought, beyond anything except feeling and need.

She clung to him for all she was worth. She was kissing him back as if she meant to devour him. So she could hardly blame him for drawing the wrong conclusion.

"Have you changed your mind?" he asked. "You will show me where you sleep?"

She was gasping, while his tone was calmness itself. "No, no, I just . . . got a bit carried away."

"It was not my intention to punish you, yet does your dating seem to do that very thing."

"Huh?" Okay, so her thoughts weren't exactly coherent yet, but how could anyone equate punishment with kissing? "I thought you had the definition for 'punish' figured out. Need me to break out the dictionary?"

"Punishment may come in many forms."

Her thoughts were starting to clear, enough for her to realize he was probably talking about sexual punishment, the kind sometimes practiced when one half of a married partnership was annoyed with the other half.

"You mean like my telling you I've got a headache?" she said.

His frown was filled with sudden concern. "Your head hurts?"

She sighed. "No, that was just a comparison—never

mind. And you don't have to keep petting me. I've got it under control now."

From the moment he had mentioned punishment, he'd been caressing her in a very nonsexual way, soothing her to calmness like he might a child. Not that it did much good, when any touch from him at all was stimulating. But he didn't seem to need calming down himself. If she couldn't still feel that thick bulge against her hip, she'd swear he hadn't participated at all in the heavy kissing they'd just done. His composure was—unusual, to say the least, something else beyond her experience of men.

But then she noticed his eyes, and she was completely reassured that she wasn't the only one who'd gotten hot and bothered. He'd been affected, all right. His amber eyes were liquid gold, filled with enough passion for three men, the intensity unnerving in a man his size. And yet his control seemed almost superhuman. His breathing was normal. He hadn't broken a sweat. His tone was steady, his heartbeat probably the same.

But with that passion still there under the surface, just laying in wait, she figured it might be prudent to more fully distract them both. To that end, she asked, "What was that foreign name you called me?" His questioning frown added the prompt, "Cara something?"

"*Kerima*? It means little one."

She burst out laughing. "I know you're big, but I am, too. It's music to my ears, really, but it's kind of ridiculous to call me little."

"For your men, perhaps. For me, you are a perfect size. Any smaller, and I would fear to break you."

She grinned. "Let me guess. You've had the same

problem I have, of finding partners of an acceptable size."

He surprised her by shaking his head. "Size is of little matter. Frailty of body is of greater concern. But you are not frail, are you?"

"Wielding a hammer all day tends to build a sturdy frame, no pun intended."

"Pun—ah, you speak of house-building as well as body-building."

She blinked. "You got it without an explanation?"

"I have the proper translations now for all but what you call brand names."

"I don't get it. It just suddenly all clicked for you? A few hours ago you couldn't make head or tails out of some pretty common words, but now you can?"

"This is so."

"Then I think you'd better convince me that you haven't been pulling my leg all along, because what you're suggesting just isn't possible."

She had shot out of his lap, had her hands on her hips, was glaring down at him, so his remark wasn't really a question. "You are angry."

"Damn straight," she growled. "I don't like being made a fool of."

"Nor have you been," his calm tone continued. "The mistake was made because of the slowness of your computers. It has been corrected. I have been receiving the proper translations for several hours now."

"Language courses don't work that fast!"

"I am told you would understand 'new technology,'" he offered. "The means of teaching me is not known to all the universe yet."

"World," she mumbled, somewhat mollified, though

she was still incredulous that something had been invented that could speed along learning that fast. But apparently all the kinks hadn't been worked out of it yet, since he was still getting a few words wrong.

"Explain?"

"You keep using the word 'universe,' when you obviously mean *world*. Universe implies beyond this planet, but there's nothing out there in deep space, at least nothing alive, so 'world' is the better descriptive word for what you were talking about."

He smiled at her. "Are you certain?"

"That it's the better word?"

"That there is nothing out there?"

She made a soft snort, would have expounded on the concept that seeing is believing and so forth, but once again she got thoroughly distracted. She hadn't jumped very far away from the chair. He had sat forward, which narrowed the space between them even more, so he didn't have to even stretch his arms when his hands came to her hips to rein her back in.

"Ah . . . what are . . . you doing?" she asked a bit breathlessly.

He had circled her hips with one arm to put her in the position he wanted and keep her there. His other hand made a slow trip from the edge of her shorts down the back of her bare leg to nearly her ankle. His head was pressed squarely between her breasts.

He tilted his head up to answer her, a grin on his lips. "Dating you."

She would have laughed if her senses hadn't gone haywire again over what he was doing to her. Her breasts had seemed scalded by his breath. She had so much gooseflesh running down her legs, it was a wonder she wasn't sprouting feathers. And yet he looked so boyish with that grin, so pleased with his answer, so delighted by what he was doing, that she didn't have the heart to correct him. But she had to, because she was afraid he still hadn't grasped where she was coming from, with her objections to their having his kind of fun right off the bat.

"No, this isn't really dating, this is the stage beyond that. Perhaps a better definition of dating would help. The kind of date we're talking about is a social appointment made by two people of the opposite sex to meet, usually for a specific purpose, like going to a movie, out to dinner, on a picnic, things like that. And typically while they are out together they do a lot of talking, which lets them get to know each other better. Now, I've been doing a lot of talking, but you haven't been doing much of any."

That finally got a frown out of him. "It will be a hindrance, my inability to talk?"

She brushed the hair back from his forehead. "You talk just fine, Dalden, just not enough about yourself. Can you understand my need to get inside your head, to feel like I know all there is to know about you, before we do anything so intimate as making love?"

He released her, slowly. "I am reminded I have a specific task here, and my need to join with you cannot interfere with it. When the task is done, then may I speak of myself. Until then, I am warned to keep my true self from becoming known to your people."

"So there's a specific reason you don't say much about yourself? Because you can't?"

He nodded. He sighed as well. He leaned back in the chair and stared up at her, and there was such yearning in his eyes it made her catch her breath.

She couldn't imagine the reason behind his needing to be secretive, other than to not give that Jorran guy any warning that he was on his trail. The reason wasn't all that important, really. His hands were tied, so to speak. There was certainly nothing she could do about that, other than accept it. And he'd said he could talk freely when his task was done. There was hope in that.

Still, there was some definite disappointment in her own tone that she simply couldn't conceal when she said, "Then I guess we should concentrate on finishing your task. A good night's sleep and an early start in the morning will help for that."

"Will you sleep with me—here?"

It was amazing, what those simple words did to her. The urge to jump back in his lap and start kissing him again, and to hell with getting to know him better, was so strong that she had to take a step back to resist it. This kind of temptation was more than she'd ever experienced, more than she could reasonably be expected to handle. How could she say no when her body was thrumming with desire to say yes? But how could she throw caution to the winds and say yes?

Honestly, she told him, "I don't think I would be able to sleep, touching you."

"You will," he insisted with confidence as he held out a hand to her. "You will be soothed in my arms. The only thing that keeps you from me is these 'morals' you speak of. This is understood. But understand as well that having found you, I cannot bring myself now to let you go far from me. I will rest easier with you in my arms. And you will know that you have nothing to fear of me."

There was no way she could say no now, not to a simple request for closeness. She knew she wouldn't sleep, she was wound up with too much sexual tension, and getting close to him again was just going to increase it. But she gave him her hand anyway and let him pull her back into his lap, where he positioned her for maximum comfort.

For a moment she felt like a child again, curled up in the lap of one of her parents. The lights were still on, and the TV droned on at low volume. It was silly to try to sleep in a chair when there was a perfectly good bed nearby. She almost mentioned it, but caution prevailed and she said nothing.

He said nothing more either. But his hand pressed her head to the bare part of his chest, where his tunic spread wide. And she didn't know how she did it, but she fell asleep listening to the steady beat of his heart.

Chapter 14

BRITTANY WOKE AT DAWN WHEN THE BIRDS ON THE two trees in front of her apartment building began their morning greetings. She didn't stir immediately, just opened her eyes and absorbed the fact that she was laying sprawled across a very big body and was utterly content to be there.

Dalden had moved down in the chair at some point in the night, to where he wasn't actually sitting in it anymore, was spread at a near prone angle, which was why she wasn't sitting either. She was actually laying on top of him, one leg bent across his hip, the other lost with his somewhere under the table in front of the chair.

She wondered what Jan had thought when she had come home and found them like that. The lights and

TV were off now, showing that Jan had quietly passed through the room without waking them. And Brittany and Dalden would probably be gone before Jan got up to go to work, since her job started much later in the morning than Brittany's—which reminded her she had to call Arbor and the spa to let them know she was taking a short vacation.

"Did you sleep well, *kerima*?"

She lifted her head to find those lovely amber eyes on her. "The birds wake you, too?"

"No, it was the sound of your purring."

She gasped, sputtered, and chuckled all at once. "I did . . . no such thing!"

He smiled at her. "Perhaps it was myself, then. I believe I could wish for no other thing than to wake with you in my arms every rising."

Brittany was a little shocked—actually, a lot. Those words spoke of permanence, of forever after, of never being parted. They were something a woman might say or think, but a man? When men tended to go through a heck of a lot of agonizing before they even came close to thinking about commitment? But then he'd used the word "wish," which could put the statement back into perspective. He wasn't really saying, Let's get hitched. He was just being fanciful.

That conclusion annoyed Brittany somewhat, enough to have her pushing off of him. "Careful, big guy, or you might get your wish."

She didn't get very far in the pushing. His arms around her tightened, and she quickly found it pointless to try to squirm out of that. So she gave him a look that said release me or . . . actually, she couldn't think of an "or else" in his case, but she was sure he got the point. Not that it worked. He wasn't letting her move off of him yet, and that was all there was to that.

"What has annoyed you?" he asked.

"I'm not annoyed," she grouched.

"What has annoyed you?" he repeated, refusing to accept her evasion.

"Okay, you asked for it. I really dislike how men forever say things they don't mean."

"And women do not?"

"Not nearly as much, and besides—"

"Did you not *just* say something that you did not mean when you said you were not annoyed?"

"No. That was a flat-out lie. That isn't at all the same thing. I'm talking about things that get said between a man and a woman that can affect feelings, that can build hopes and dreams, that will finally shatter a relationship when it's realized that it's been nothing but BS."

"All this resentment over a wish I am inclined to grant?" There was suddenly a lot of screeching coming out of the earphone that was still attached to his ear, reminding Brittany that they weren't alone. "I am told you require asking, that I cannot decide the matter for you as I should."

"What are we talking about now?" she demanded.

"A difference in our cultures, one I find unacceptable. Asking can be done, but if the answer is not the right one, the question will be withdrawn and the matter seen to in the proper Sha-Ka'ani way."

She had the distinct feeling he wasn't talking to her just then, but to Martha. His own annoyance was sensed, rather than reflected in tone or expression, but it was still crystal-clear to her. He hadn't liked the interruption from Martha any more than she had.

She had to wonder why he hadn't spoken to Miss Coach earlier. If the woman could hear every word they said, and was speaking to him through that earphone, wouldn't it have been much easier for him to have simply asked Martha for clarification of the things he'd been having trouble with last night, rather than making her guess what he needed to know?

Brittany knew to the second when his attention was fully back on her. His eyes absorbed her. His body seemed to as well, and, oh my, that bulge was back. He even shifted her and pressed her against it in that very spot that nature had intended it to go.

Swirls of desire took flight in her belly, so it was like a dash of ice water when she heard from him, "What is the meaning of bee-ess?"

She managed to get off him this time. Thrusting an elbow into his belly for leverage helped.

"I know you can hear me, Martha. So why don't you explain that one to him," Brittany growled as she stomped off to the kitchen to make coffee and call Arbor. The spa would have to wait a few more hours until it opened.

She had that flare of passion under control again by the time she turned back toward the living room with the coffee cups in hand. She didn't get far. Dalden was blocking the doorway, a normal-sized bath towel around his neck that seemed more like a hand towel around *that* neck, his tunic removed. Not enough time had passed for him to have showered, nor did he look damp, he just looked good, too good, good enough for her to want to meld with that body of his.

She'd already seen a good portion of his chest through the gap his tunic made, but it was nothing like seeing it all. The man was simply too huge. She'd never seen anything like his size before, not even in pictures. Without the height, he'd look really weird; with it, he simply looked gigantic. A fantasy giant came to mind, wielding a club as big as he was. She would have smiled at her own fancy if she wasn't so mesmerized by all that bare, golden skin.

No stressed muscles or overly taut skin to accommodate them, just natural bulges in his relaxed pose, the difference being that everything was oversized to begin with. And those arms, bigger than anything she could have imagined when they'd been concealed by his loose sleeves. The kind of strength represented by them had to be amazing. She wondered if they were registered as lethal weapons. And yet they'd held her with tenderness through the night. Her gentle giant.

She did smile this time, but had it and her fanciful thoughts wiped clear away when Dalden remarked, "Martha says that as long as you have spoken to her directly, you may be allowed to hear her voice."

"Wow, lucky me," Brittany said sarcastically as she shoved a cup of instant coffee in his hand.

"You can shelve that jealousy, doll" came out of the box clearly, which nearly made Brittany drop the other cup she was holding. "I'm not what you've been thinking. Try this one on for size: I was there for his birth, even assisted in it. That help? Yes, I can see that it does."

Brittany's face was going up in mortified flames. God, she had been jealous of a name, a voice, a faceless woman, without even once thinking the lady could be a little old grandmotherly type.

To cover some of her embarrassment, she asked Martha, "How can you see?"

"There are six viewers on the combo-unit attached to Dalden's belt, one on every edge, so no matter which way he's facing, I'm bound to get a good shot of what's going on around him."

"So it's a camera, too?"

"You could say that. Actually, why don't we call it a new advanced model of what's known to you as a cellular phone, under experimentation, and obviously failing. I should have whipped him up an old model instead, since I am now aware that your men of business walk around with them attached to their ears, so he wouldn't have drawn much notice using one."

"Not drawn notice?" Brittany replied. "Him? You're kidding, right?"

The distinct sound of chuckling came out of the box. "Aside from his looks. He needs to keep a low profile. We don't want Jorran alerted to his presence and having a chance to disappear on us."

"If he wants a low profile, we should probably stop by the mall on the way to City Hall and buy him some normal clothes. His rock star get-up might be fine for L.A., where people expect to see stars in fancy outfits, but we don't get many celebrities passing through Seaview."

None of those camera angles could have seen Dalden's blank expression, yet Martha still knew to share with him. "She's talking about their entertainment industry, Dalden, the gist of it being, she's going to buy you some local clothing this morning."

Brittany blinked. "I am? Okay, I suppose I am, but while you're on the phone, how about telling me why he seems to be lacking any ready cash, or was he actually sent over to this country without any?"

"File that one under hard to explain, kiddo. There's a good reason for his lack, but not one that we can divulge at this time."

No other explanation came out of the box. Brittany wondered if Martha was waiting for her to fire off more questions, now that she could. But she didn't really have any more at the moment, at least none that she thought might get answered instead of being dumped into the "hard to explain" file. Well, there was one . . .

"I notice you don't have his accent. You don't come from his country?"

"No, my origins are very far from his. But the voice I use is irrelevant when I can simulate any tone, accent, or language imaginable. What you hear is only for your convenience."

Brittany was impressed. "A master linguist, then, or an impressionist?"

More chuckling. "You could say both, though just plain old master has a nice ring to it."

Whether Dalden was feeling neglected or not, he became Brittany's center of attention again when he asked, "Will you create a meal to sustain us for the day?"

Brittany grinned at him. "Why do I get the feeling that a bowl of cereal and milk won't do it for you? Never mind, I'll whip up some eggs and other breakfasty-type things while you take a shower."

"You will need first to show me how the water is acquired for it."

She raised a brow, though she shouldn't have been

surprised. A village without electricity was probably a village without proper sanitation.

Still, she'd rather not guess if she could get an answer, so she tried, "No showers where you come from?"

"We bathe in large pools."

She pictured big ponds with only a few trees and plants, an oasis, camels again—bah. She really was going to have to figure out just where his never-heard-of-before country was located. This imagining of primitive tents in a desert didn't say much for their ever being compatible. She and tents didn't get along well at all.

She headed to the tiny bathroom and leaned into the shower to adjust the single water control handle to get the water running at a comfortable temperature. The shower had been remodeled just last year by the landlord, and now had one of those newfangled spigots that concealed the shower turn-on valve under it. If you didn't know where it was, you'd never find it, so she could understand how Martha might not have been able to help him this time.

"My mother uses a different means, a solaray bath," he added while she was still leaning halfway into the shower, waiting for the hot water to show up.

"You mean a solar bath? Now that's a bit modern, and cost-effective, too. I plan to put up a few solar panels on the house I build, for the water heater at least. And I plan a really large bathroom, probably the same size as the bedroom attached to it. I've been dreaming of big ever since I first walked into this cubbyhole."

"I am accustomed to the bath being in the room of sleeping," he volunteered.

A pool in a bedroom? Now she was picturing a palace, or an incredibly large mansion.

She turned around to ask him once again just where the heck his country was, but found him towering over her, barely an inch separating them. Not surprising, since it was a really tiny bathroom. She couldn't turn around in it without banging elbows herself. With him in it, too, there was absolutely no space to maneuver without them bumping into each other.

It was hard to concentrate with him that close, but she managed to get out, "You can at least tell me the continent that your country sits in, can't you? So I can have something to relate to when you drop these little tidbits like pools instead of bathtubs and . . ."

That was as far as she got. Being lifted off her feet and deeply kissed worked pretty well to put an end to any kind of concentration. She was surrounded by his body, by his scent, by his taste. Her senses began rioting with her morals and were coming out ahead. And then she was set down and pushed toward the door.

"Be gone from my sight quickly, *kerima*, unless you wish to share the water and more with me now."

That was about as plain as could be, that he'd reached his limit of sexual forbearance. Caution prevailed and got her out of there real quick.

Chapter 15

"YOU CAN'T GO KISSING ME TO DISTRACTION EVERY time I ask you something that you don't want to answer. If it's secret, just say so. If I get fed up with hearing that, *I'll* say so. Okay?"

They were in Brittany's car on the way to City Hall. It was much later than they'd planned on getting there. She'd fed Dalden before they left, and was definitely going to have to stop for some groceries on the way home after that mammoth meal.

And there'd been an amusing moment when they left the apartment and she told him not to mind the rust-bucket look of her car, that she kept it in tiptop shape so it purred. He, of course, misinterpreted that and started looking around for buckets and *fembairs*, the latter being what she figured he called cats.

It was now almost noon, since their brief stop at the mall had turned into hitting every shop with men's clothing, after it had been apparent from the first shop that they were going to have trouble finding something to fit Dalden. In fact, they never did. There had been a few extra-extra-large T-shirts he could have worn, but they just didn't look right on him, and besides, leaving those arms of his bare would draw as much notice as his fancy tunic.

There was hope, though, at least for tomorrow. An on-duty seamstress in one of the larger clothing stores had felt challenged upon seeing Dalden, and after taking some quick measurements, had promised to have some jeans and a plain cotton shirt ready for him by the end of the day.

Brittany had expected Dalden to draw some notice, but experiencing it firsthand in the mall that morning went beyond even her own expectations. She hadn't noticed yesterday because she'd been unable to take her eyes off him herself. But he managed to affect everyone that way. No matter where she looked, people were staring at him open-mouthed, boggle-eyed; he was causing traffic pile-ups of the pedestrian kind. One young kid even asked him for his autograph and refused to believe he wasn't a celebrity. Keep a low profile? Yeah, right.

There hadn't been much time between her apartment and the mall for talk, and besides, she'd been too busy watching Dalden examining everything on the dashboard, as if he'd never been in a car before. Yet she'd wanted to wait until they were in the car, where he wouldn't dare try to kiss her again, to bring up the subject of his unique way of distracting her.

She wasn't expecting an argument. Her suggestion had been so reasonable that it didn't leave room for arguing. But he put a new twist to it.

"Yet is it much more enjoyable, for both of us, to kiss you to distraction," he said.

Undeniable, but beside the point. "Remember 'getting to know each other'? Part of that is answering questions, not avoiding them."

"When I make you mine, Brittany Callaghan, you may have all the answers you seek. I am told, however, that you will not be happy with the answers."

Thank God the traffic light in front of them was red, because Brittany temporarily forgot how to drive. When he made her his? Again, that had such a ring of permanence to it, coming from him. Not when they made love. Not when her job was done. When he made her his. The effect that had on her was swift and primitive.

Driving down the boulevard was not the place for this discussion after all. She tried zeroing in on his second remark to get her mind out of fantasyland. Unhappiness. Answers she wouldn't like. Okay, that worked.

She gave him a quick glance, then glanced a bit longer at the box on his hip, trusting that Martha's camera views were working. "Are these 'I am tolds' his opinion, or what you've been telling him, Martha?"

"You really don't want to hear his opinions, doll," Martha replied.

There was clear amusement in the older woman's tone, which rubbed against Brittany's nerves. "Actually, I do," she said stubbornly.

"Really, you don't," Martha countered, then elaborated. "From the information I've assimilated so far, your culture and his are so far on opposite ends of the spectrum, the distance could be described in light-years."

"Bah, I know an exaggeration when I hear it," Brittany replied.

Some chuckling drifted up from the box before Martha said, "If it means anything to you, and Probables is starting to lean toward it will, his mother's and father's cultures were also light-years apart, yet they've managed to adjust—or maybe I should say, she's managed to adjust. There's not much budging with a Sha-Ka'ani male."

"Was that supposed to be a warning?"

"You betcha."

Brittany snorted. She was beginning to think that Martha was toying with her, and getting a kick out of doing so. But it did worry her that Dalden wasn't trying to correct the impression Martha was trying to give her. In fact, he didn't look too happy. Actually, he looked a bit green.

"Are you all right?" she asked him.

"I am familiar with transportation that moves on other than legs, but I am not accustomed to the many stops and starts of your rust bucket."

She ignored the name he'd given her car and asked with a bit of amazement, "You're getting carsick? We *have* hit a bit more traffic than usual, the lunch-hour crowd, I suppose. But we're almost to our destination. Another minute or so. Can you last that long?"

"Last?"

"Without dumping your breakfast all over the car?" she clarified.

His expression turned a bit indignant over that remark, pretty hard to do when he'd been cringing with nausea. "A warrior has more control over his body than to reject an excellent meal."

"Delete that" came out of the box in an exasperated voice. "What he means—"

"I got the idea, Martha, but let's not delete that warrior part just yet. He's in the military?"

"You could say that."

"I could, but you wouldn't? What's it called, then, in his country?"

"The men of Sha-Ka'an merely keep themselves in a constant state of readiness, sort of what you might term the national guard, or the national militia, or—"

"I get it," Brittany cut in. "Not military, but available if needed."

"Exactly!"

"And where is this country?"

Not just a little chuckling, but nearly thirty seconds of assorted humor sounds came out of the box before Martha said, "Tenacious, aren't you? But you've heard of classified info, haven't you? Yes, of course you have."

"Oh, come on, you've told me the name of it. I can go find an atlas and look it up myself."

"You can, but you'd be wasting your time. You won't find it in any atlas."

"A country so newly formed it's not on the maps yet?" Brittany said incredulously.

"Not new," Martha corrected. "But then, new is subjective. What would be new to you wouldn't be to him, and vice versa, of course."

Brittany could allow that there might be places in

the world still unexplored. But to have an entire country tucked away in one of them? OK, so it was possible. Actually, Dalden and his people were proof of that.

"*How* have they managed to remain undiscovered?" Brittany asked.

"You could say their—borders—are closed to visitors. No one gets in without permission, and permission is rarely if ever given."

"Are we even talking about a country? Maybe you've got town and country mixed up?"

"Actually, you're working on assumptions," Martha told her. "You're the one who called Sha-Ka'an a country. Dalden never confirmed or denied that. *Sometimes* he actually follows my directives."

The last was meant for Dalden, but it got no reaction out of him. He didn't look like he was paying attention to the conversation at all. His eyes were closed, his skin still off-color, his forehead damp. Brittany didn't doubt that his full concentration was still on keeping his breakfast where it resided.

But she knew she'd get no answers out of him, anyway. And as long as Martha was spilling some beans, even if dried-up useless ones, she'd rather keep trying to get at least one whole kernel out of her.

She tried a different tack. "I'm not asking for any great secrets. All I want to know is who I'm helping. There happen to be factions in this world that I'd be completely opposed to, and I don't want to find out later that I've helped one of them."

"Okay, listen up, because I'm going to break my own rules, but only this once. Sha-Ka'an isn't a country. Let's call it a place, and where his people as a whole get their name. His actual country is Kan-is-

Tra, and no, you won't find that on one of your maps either. His town is Sha-Ka-Ra. And none of the above have politics opposed to your people, so rest easy on that score. Now with no other information forthcoming about any of these locations, you'll agree what you've just heard has no meaning for you. Leave it at—"

"Damnit upside and down!" Brittany gave her exasperation free rein. "You can at least give me a region to relate to. Desert, arctic, tropics? Igloos, tents, *what*?"

"Ah, so it's the carpenter that's going nuts with curiosity? Very well, their architecture is pretty impressive, some of it ranking right up there with a sultan's palace, and no, you won't find any Sha-Ka'ani in that part of the world," was added with a chuckle. "Now give it up, doll. If he chooses to enlighten you when this is over, it would be info you can't be allowed to keep, so all of this is pointless. Whatever he tells you, I'll have to erase before we go home."

"Erase?" Brittany gasped. "Are you talking about making me forget somehow?"

"Necessary."

Brittany was outraged. "Is that how they've remained unknown? Anyone who finds out about them gets their memory tampered with?"

"Are we getting disturbed by the concept of self-preservation?"

Brittany hissed, "Messing around with someone's memories is a dangerous—"

"Not even close," Martha cut in this time. "Meticulous, exact, no guesswork involved. Only what needs to be removed gets removed. Everything else remains intact."

"Are you talking about hypnosis?" Brittany asked, her tone only slightly calmer.

"Something like that. That relieve your mind?"

It did—and it didn't. "You aren't planning on erasing my memories of him, are you?" was asked in a small voice.

"Lucky for me, I don't possess a single sentimental circuit. You'd be better off not remembering him, kiddo, believe me—"

"You need have no fear that you will be allowed to forget me, *kerima*" came from a new quarter.

"Not another word, warrior, until we go over the facts of Sha-Ka'ani life again," Martha warned in a seriously annoyed tone.

"What Martha has to say will be listened to, but it will make no difference when the decision has already been made," Dalden replied.

"You can't do that."

"It is too late for denials."

"I swear, you're getting more and more like your father every day."

The disgust in that remark was thick enough to cut, yet Dalden replied with some pride in his own tone, "I am pleased to hear you say so."

"Where is the common sense you inherited from your mother? Never mind," came out in a low growl. "We'll discuss this later. Her rust bucket has stopped moving. Finish the task at hand, and *then* we'll talk about decisions that don't have a chance in hell of working."

Chapter 16

"SLOUCH DOWN. SOME MORE." A SIGH. "I SUPPOSE that will have to do. Now stay there and let me do what you're paying me for."

Dalden watched Brittany walk away from him, a smile in his mind. He was aware that she had no doubt whatsoever that he would obey her and stay on the bench where she had told him to sit. She had no understanding yet that it was against a warrior's nature to take directives of any sort from a woman. But a woman could be humored. And special allowances had to be made when dealing with females from planets other than Sha-Ka'an. He understood that, for the most part. He didn't like it, but he understood.

But he continued to watch her as she moved about

the atrium in the place she called City Hall, stopping one person after another to speak a few words with each of them. It was, in fact, becoming increasingly difficult to do anything but watch her, when she was in the same area as him.

He wondered if it was the influence of his mother's Kystrani blood that was making him have unwarriorlike reactions around her, or simply because Brittany reminded him in many ways of his mother. Or it could be no other thing than the instinct he had been warned would take over when he found his true lifemate.

Whatever it was, it seemed to be beyond his control. Some *dhaya* juice could be wished for to eliminate the constant urge he had to carry her to some quiet place and make her his, but the abundant supply that had been brought along, which would have been more than sufficient for the original trip, hadn't lasted for this extended journey and had been exhausted the previous month. He had to wonder if even that would have been sufficient, when what he was feeling was beyond his experience.

She fascinated him in myriad ways. She spoke like a Kystrani Ancient. She was very much like his mother, taking matters in hand and issuing orders. She was bold, stubborn, creative. She took pride in a craft that a Sha-Ka'ani viewed as slave labor. She was independent. She felt she needed no other protection than what the laws of her country supplied her. She cooked and worked like a Darash servant and saw that as a normal thing to do. She was fulfilling the roles of both male and female and doing so happily. Her culture was so different from his that indeed there seemed no point where the two could meet and coexist.

He suspected that Martha would point out all of this. He was prepared for it with a simple answer that even Martha couldn't dispute.

"Tedra's going to wish she had come along on this trip," came out of the combo-unit in Sha-Ka'ani, so anyone passing near wouldn't understand it.

"Why?" Dalden asked in kind.

"Because these people so resemble her Ancients, you might wonder if they didn't evolve from one of the original colony ships."

"Would they not be more advanced if that were so?" Dalden asked.

"Not if they lost all data and had to start over from scratch. Unlikely, though. And it's possible for two planets to evolve in exactly the same way, which would account for the similarities."

"You like Brittany," Dalden remarked. "This I have sensed."

A chuckle. "What you meant to say was that Tedra would like her. But let's not be tepid. Your mother would love the heck out of her. She'd be like a never-ending Ancients tape for her to listen to. Probables say they'd become great good friends."

"When your goals always center around my mother's ultimate happiness, how then can you object to bringing Brittany home with us?"

"Because unlike you, I can see down the road, and Tedra won't be happy if two people she loves are making themselves miserable."

"Such *would* not happen."

A sigh, prolonged, exaggerated; then in a no-nonsense tone, "Let's spend a moment to open your eyes beyond a squint, shall we? You and this female have the hots for each other. This is fine, even healthy. No one's objecting to you having a bit of pleasure while you're here, time permitting. But you have got to start looking at this thing realistically, Dalden."

"Why do you think I am not?"

"The fact that we're having this conversation was a good clue" came out sarcastically. Then, "A man can be and often is blinded by his sexual drive, and yes, that includes warriors. Take away that driving force, and a completely different perspective is open to them. If they still feel the same afterward, well, then, they're hooked. But half the time, and I do mean at least half, they find that it was no more than those primitive urges, and once satisfied, nothing is left, at least not enough to base permanent double occupancy on."

Double occupancy was the Kystrani term for two people wishing to share their lives together. They used to call it marriage, as they did here. The Sha-Ka'ani had no specific term for it, though even there it differed per country, what the partners called each other. In Kan-is-Tra, a warrior would choose the woman to be the mother of his children, and this was how she would be referred to. Generally, they called each other lifemates.

"In all your years on Sha-Ka'an, Martha, have you not learned that a warrior has a special instinct in the matter of his true lifemate? Many become impatient of experiencing this instinct and settle for a lifemate of indifference."

A snort came out of the box. "Careful, kiddo, or I might think you're talking about love—you know, that silly emotion that warriors insist they *don't* feel."

Dalden growled, "There is no similarity between instinct and that female emotion."

"I'm drawing a picture of rolling eyes. I've got eyes rolling on every monitor in the Control Room. You should see all these rolling eyes—"

"You cannot change the way a warrior is."

"Do I look stupid enough to try? But you've just hit it on the nose yourself, kiddo. It's because of that very thing that you and the carpenter will never see eye to eye on any subject. And without some common ground, of which you two don't have any, you simply can't coexist compatibly."

"We will."

"Stubbornness won't make it so. But I can see it's going to take more than just telling you it won't work. Okay, let's delve into a few of the specifics that my Probables are based on. The woman can accept being 'taken care of.' That isn't the problem, was the norm around here a few centuries ago, considered old-fashioned now, but not so long ago that she wouldn't know how it works. She'll be bored silly, just staying home and not working herself, but like Tedra, she could find other things to occupy her."

"I am pleased to hear you say so."

"You won't be after I've finished, because what she'll never get used to is the warrior's right to control all aspects of Sha-Ka'ani life, with the woman stuck in a role of subservient silence. They used to be like that, but the women here have crawled out of that hole, and having done so, they'll never crawl back in.

"Do you see what I'm getting at? It's against her nature to let a man make all decisions for her. It's against her nature to accept a situation she doesn't like without trying to change it. And she'd never accept that it can't be changed. The rules that warriors have made for the protection of their women are so contrary to the way she was raised, she'd laugh in your face if you try to enforce them on her. You'd have one fight after another on your hands, kiddo, never ending. That's how incompatible you and she are."

"Was I not to realize that you are describing life between my parents?"

A chuckle. "Must be the air up there."

Dalden didn't miss the jibe. "I do not lack intelligence, Martha."

"I know you don't, kiddo, but the warrior mentality gets in the way of it sometimes, which is why your people are still called barbarians. But we digress. I pointed out how it has worked for your parents, but you know me well enough to know there's a catch coming."

"Which is?"

"There's one big, and I mean really big, difference between your parents' case and yours. Tedra knows how to compromise. She also grew up with full knowledge of a universe filled with a diversity of races and cultures. Her schooling in World Discovery prepared her to deal with that diversity and taught her the basic premises of the Confederation, that each planet is unique, each culture to be respected, not changed. Discovered races aren't to be tampered with, aren't to be 'taught a better way,' are to be left alone to evolve at their own pace in the natural order of things. So as much as she has wanted to change some of the things she really doesn't like about Sha-Ka'an, and you know exactly what I'm talking about, she wouldn't dream of seriously tampering with the way things are."

"She has assisted many of the women."

"Of course she has. But she hasn't tried to change the rules, she's merely helped some of the women to be removed from those rules."

"By sending them off-planet."

A shrug entered Martha's tone. "Whatever works, kiddo, is one of Tedra's mottoes. And besides, she usually gets anything she wants—in the long run. It might take a challenge loss or two first, but eventually, your father gives her what she wants. She just knows better than to go after the impossible, like trying to bring a planet classed as barbaric up a notch or two on the civilized scale, or trying to change the way a warrior views things. And now we get to why it would be a completely different scenario for your Brittany."

"But she is just like my mother."

"I hate to break it to you, warrior, but the way she talks is about all they really have in common. They were raised differently, with completely different cultures and beliefs. They probably have the same outlook on what rights a woman should have, because they both grew up in cultures of equality of the sexes. But it pretty much ends there. Yet this is only half the problem."

"I do not see what you have said so far to be a problem," Dalden insisted.

"And *that* is the other half. You *think* you'll manage to overcome her objections, but you're basing that assumption on your father's success with Tedra. But you've overlooked a very simple fact. Because of your mother's blood, which is in many cases held against you, you've spent most of your life trying to be the ideal warrior. This included embracing and obeying to the letter the laws and rules of your people, even when you might have disagreed with them. You've strived not to be different. You are constantly trying to prove that Tedra's blood has had no influence on you. You *are* different, but you refuse to accept that. And we're talking years and years of struggle here, Dalden. Do you think you can set all that aside and finally *be* different?"

"There is no reason for me to change or be different from what I am."

"I rest my case. *That's* why it won't work. You won't compromise, and neither will she."

Chapter 17

BRITTANY HAD TO LAUGH AT HERSELF FOR THINKING that leaving Dalden on a bench under a slightly overhanging tree would keep him from notice, even slouched down to detract from his height. Her experience at the mall with him should have told her otherwise, and every time she glanced back his way, she noticed the stares, people stopped in groups of two or three to covertly look his way.

It wasn't just his size and handsomeness. There was a confidence about him that went beyond the norm, a unique presence that commanded attention and speculation. People who knew their own worth, or felt capable of accomplishing anything, carried that kind of confidence. Politicians, celebrities, billionaires came to mind—and perhaps specially trained military types, too, which was the only thing she could think of to explain it in Dalden's case.

Of course, that was just her take on it. She felt his confidence, his utter lack of the common worries that plagued normal individuals. Other people just might be simply agog at his looks.

The end of lunch hour had not been the ideal time to start her job of finding Jorran, when most of the people passing through the hall just then were city workers on their way back to their offices. It meant there were too many people to talk to all at once, and that she was going to miss speaking to most of them.

The easiest and most common question to stop people with was to ask for directions. Usually she could move on to the next person within seconds, unless she ran into someone who simply liked to talk and could take five minutes to say three words, but that only happened once.

The mayor was on the premises. She'd ascertained that first, and briefly spoke with everyone in his waiting room, which was only three testy people who had missed their own lunches to try and get in to see the mayor instead, and apparently were wasting their time. She stayed out in the main hall after that, just kept her eye on the door to the mayor's inner offices for anyone new coming along.

After close to an hour, she finally had a reason to return to Dalden and, sitting down next to him, whispered to him, "Don't look immediately, but that guy over there to the left of us with the curly brown hair and the pasty white skin is pretty weird."

Dalden did look immediately, and frowned in the

direction where she had tilted her head. "Weird in what way?"

"He not only talks somewhat like you, but he also told me that I didn't see him, like he thinks he's invisible or something. And that silly stick he's carrying around like a wand—"

Brittany didn't get to finish. Dalden shot off the bench with such amazing speed that she was left with her mouth hanging open. She didn't think it was possible that someone his size could move that fast, yet within seconds, he was across the hall behind the weird fellow and putting an arm around his shoulder like they were friends. They weren't, of course, and there was a moment of grappling that seriously alarmed her, considering that the entire hall was probably watching them. But it didn't last long, and a few words were quietly said, then the weird fellow was following behind Dalden as docilely as you please, back to the bench.

Brittany's alarm was gone. It now seemed like it had merely been two friends doing the weird wrestling-type greeting thing. What was left was pure incredulity that had her simply staring at them as they reached her. What the hell had just happened?

"You did not predict this was a possibility?" Dalden was saying to Martha, still in Sha-Ka'ani. "That Jorran would not know to keep the rods off of women?"

"You didn't tell him," Martha replied. "And Ferrill wouldn't discuss the rods at all with him, so no, he didn't know they only work on males. I knew that, but I gave him more credit. I figured he'd be smart enough to test the rods before putting them to use.

He probably did, he just wasn't smart enough to include women in the testing, likely because he envisioned his new home to be like his old home, where women are only slightly up on the scale from slavery. Speaking of which, that was quick thinking on your part, kiddo, to use the rod on him and have him think he's your slave. They have them where he comes from, so this peon knows exactly how to imitate their behavior."

"Do you two know just how rude that is, to be talking that gibberish when someone is standing here who doesn't understand a word of it?" Brittany growled finally, her impatience turning to pure vexation.

"Didn't it occur to you that that was the point, doll?" Martha purred back at her. "Classified info, remember?"

That was hardly pacifying, and Brittany said as much. "If you think you're going to get away without telling me what just happened, you're crazy. And why is this man looking like he's about to bow down and kiss Dalden's feet?"

"Probably because he is," Martha replied dryly. Then, "Send him off to a safe distance, Dalden, so he doesn't get confused by what he hears."

Brittany watched as Dalden told the man to go stand in a corner and await him there, and he did just that. She guessed aloud, "He's not a stranger to you after all, is he? He's on your payroll or something like that?"

Martha shot that premise right down. "We've never seen him before."

"Then why is he doing what you tell him to do?" Brittany demanded.

Martha sighed, not once, but three times to stress the point that she felt her arm was being twisted. "All right, considering the matter is going to either be redundant or erased, I can divulge this much. A lot of amazing things have been invented where we come from, things that would defy belief. That rod Dalden just confiscated is one of those things. It was stolen, a whole crate of them, actually, and we have been tasked with retrieving them."

"What's it do?"

"You wondered how Jorran thought he could just waltz in here and become your mayor? Well, he thinks these rods will let him do just that."

"You haven't answered my question," Brittany pointed out, her impatience rising again.

"Oh, you wanted *de*tails?" Martha said with a big dose of innocence.

"What happens if I break your box?" Brittany snarled, glaring at it.

"Dalden gets another one" was answered in placid if somewhat smirking tones.

"Figures," Brittany mumbled.

Ten seconds of laughter followed before Martha continued, "Who would think a man's mind could be altered instantly with the power of suggestion and a mere touch of a rod? But someone figured out how to do just that. Call it hypnosis revolutionized, if you like. But someone who doesn't know the first thing about mind control can use one of these rods and completely alter a male subject's thoughts to anything they want. Example being, Dalden used the rod on this fellow and told him he's his slave, and voilà, the man fully believes he's Dalden's slave. So until he's told otherwise, he will obey any directive Dalden gives him."

Brittany gritted her teeth, even counted to ten before she said, "Do you really expect me to believe that?"

"Did I not say inventions that defy belief? And weren't you subject to it yourself, when the fellow tried to convince you that you didn't see him?"

"Which just proves it doesn't do what you say it does. I still saw him perfectly."

"Lucky for you, doll, it doesn't work on women," Martha replied. "And lucky for us, Jorran and his people obviously don't know that yet."

"His people? You mean that wasn't Jorran that Dalden just took control of?"

"No, he can alter his looks, but not his height. Jorran's about as tall as you are. But we knew we'd have a lot of peons to deal with as well. Jorran travels with a full entourage, and the Altering Rods have likely been passed out to the lot of them. Getting our hands on Jorran will gather them all in, though."

"So that's what this is all about? Retrieving stolen property? Why haven't you just gone to the police about it?"

"Don't you realize the kind of mass paranoia that can be caused if word spreads about these rods and that there are people running around using them? Have you even realized yet what's possible with their use? A perfect stranger can be asked for all his worldly goods and he'll turn them over happily, then go off and never know what happened to pauperize him. A man can be told to quit his job and do so, and never figure out why he did. People can be made to do things totally against their nature. Is it sinking in yet, why the fewer people who know about them, the better?"

"No. The police have the manpower to find them more quickly—"

"Brittany, Brittany," Martha cut in with a sigh. "You are missing the point. First you'd have to convince your law enforcement that the rods are real; then you'd have to swear them to secrecy. We now have one of the rods to do the first, but human nature will counter the second. Word *would* spread, and you'd have your whole town suspicious of everyone they see. Mass hysteria, paranoia, and panic. Is that what you're suggesting?"

"What *you're* suggesting is next to impossible, if there are a lot more people involved than you first led me to believe. How are we supposed to find them all?"

"We don't need to find them all, we only need to find Jorran. The rest will come voluntarily to us if we have him, and we'll take the lot of them back to where they belong. We happen to have a lot more manpower available to send in, but they would just alert Jorran to our presence, which we *don't* want to happen. If he suspects at all that we're here looking for him, he'll relocate and then we'll be reduced to zero chance of finding him."

"Won't he suspect something is wrong when the guy you entranced doesn't report in?"

"Not to worry, doll. You'll find I'm always one step ahead in any situation. Now, we really don't want to send any more people rushing off to visit their eye doctors, so point the big guy to a place where he can be assured of some privacy to deal with our 'slave.'"

"Deal with him how?"

A chuckle came out of the box. "That's rich. You don't really think we're here to kill anyone, do you?"

Brittany blushed profusely. She *had* sounded a bit horrified there, and *had* been thinking the worst. But what else did they suddenly need privacy for, if not to dispose of this fellow they'd managed to capture?

"Interrogation," Martha continued, as if she'd been able to read Brittany's mind. "And then he'll be sent back to the enemy camp with no memory of us, but minus his rod, of course, which he'll assume he lost. But he'll be given a link to me, and once a day I'll get a report in about Jorran's progress—an added bonus for our side."

"You make it sound so easy."

"That *is* the easy part," Martha told her. "The hard part is still in your court. We'd like to stop Jorran before he alters too many personalities or causes too much irreparable grief."

"You don't think you'll find out from this fellow where Jorran is now?"

"Highly improbable. Jorran will surround himself with only a select few. The rest of his people will have been turned loose to do his bidding without question. They'll have means of communication in case directives get changed, but not with Jorran himself. It would be beneath him to speak directly with mere underlings."

"Like a crime boss?"

"Like an autocratic king."

"Not much difference there."

"An excellent observation, though the two might disagree—just on principle, of course. Now if we're done with the jokes, that place of privacy?"

Brittany sighed. She would have preferred to continue the discussion. The new piece of the puzzle was still missing some of its edges. But she supposed it was pointless to keep at it, once Martha was done with a subject.

"The bathroom around the corner over there would afford some brief privacy, but being public, that won't last long. My car would probably work," and she tossed the keys at Dalden. "Just turn on the air conditioner and keep the windows rolled up, and no one should be able to hear you."

"I was more concerned with sight," Martha said. "But I suppose that will do. And how about having a chat with your mayor while we're gone? We *do* need to make sure he hasn't been tampered with yet."

"You don't just get to have 'chats' with the mayor around here. I need an appointment first, then a good reason for it. He's a busy man. His secretary would object to taking up his time just shooting the breeze."

"His secretary a woman?"

"No, a man, actually."

"Dalden, get the little gal an immediate appointment before we adjourn to the parking lot with your slave."

Brittany's mouth dropped open when Dalden nodded, left to enter the mayor's inner realm with the Altering Rod, came back out moments later, collected the "slave," then left the building completely. She stared at the door leading to Mayor Sullivan's offices. Dalden

hadn't really managed to get her an appointment with
him, just like that. She'd make a fool of herself, telling
the secretary she had one. Yet wouldn't Dalden have
come back to tell her it was a no go?

Chapter 18

BEFORE BRITTANY COULD TALK HERSELF OUT OF IT, SHE marched into the mayor's waiting room. She was expecting the worst, still not really believing what that Altering Rod was capable of. Yet the worst that might happen would be her getting laughed at and pointed to the door.

"Brittany Callaghan to see the mayor."

"Go right in, miss," the secretary said, barely even looking up at her. "He's expecting you."

He wasn't, of course. Dalden hadn't included in his suggestion to the secretary warning the mayor of his next visitor, which was probably standard procedure. A mayor would want to know who he would be dealing with, so he'd know which political face to wear. And Sullivan was quite upset that she just waltzed unannounced into his office while he was eating a quick lunch there between appointments.

Security was about to be called. Brittany was about to panic. A double-talker she was not. And while there were a number of excuses she could have come up with for being there which she thought of later, nothing came to mind in that moment of staring at a very annoyed mayor.

And then Dalden was there, back much sooner than expected, and merely remarked as he passed her on the way to Sullivan, "It did not require a return to your rust bucket. The Centurian has been sent to Martha, who has pointed out that I may not have cleared a proper path for you here."

The mayor was so surprised by this new presence barging into his office that Dalden was able to reach him before he managed to get out, "Who—?"

The rod touched him, and Dalden's voice was calmness itself. "You were expecting the woman," he told the politician. "You will answer her questions truthfully and forget them when she leaves. You will ignore me."

He then dropped into a chair on the side, which broke. He growled, tried the one next to it more cautiously, and, settling there, grinned at her. The mayor didn't give him another glance, even when the chair broke, and Brittany had just enough time to pick her jaw up off the floor before Sullivan came around his desk, hand extended in greeting, all smiles now, and asked what he could do for her.

It was now alarmingly clear to her just how powerful those rods were and how much damage they could cause in the wrong hands. Which was probably why she was a bit ruthless in her "interrogation" of the mayor. Backed with the assurance that he probably wouldn't remember her and certainly not what they talked about, there was no need for dancing around a subject or leading into it.

Directly, she asked Sullivan if he'd noticed an influx of foreigners in their town, if he had made any recent policy changes, if there were any differences in his routines that he'd found strange for any reason. She covered every subject she could think of, and a few others that Dalden thought to mention.

By the time they left him, it was pretty obvious that Jorran's people had started tampering with Sullivan, though not to any alarming extent yet. Yes, he knew Jorran. They were best friends. No, he couldn't recall where they'd met; no, he had no idea what Jorran looked like and didn't find that strange. He'd apparently been prepped for a meeting between them soon, but it hadn't actually happened yet.

But Dalden put a monkey wrench in Jorran's immediate plans by leaving Sullivan with some opposing facts, including that Jorran was his enemy and to be avoided at all costs. It was a temporary measure and could be got around with new suggestions. But it should buy them a little time, which hopefully was all they needed.

"Jorran will want the entire building neutralized before he involves himself, to minimize his own risk," Martha explained when they were out in the hall again. "But that could already have been done."

"Then where does that leave us?"

"Sticking around to make sure we spot him *before* he gets near the mayor. And continuing to pick up his men and send them to me."

Brittany assumed that the fellow they had found earlier had been put in a taxi, since Dalden had returned so quickly without him, and while under the influence of the rod he would go exactly where he was told. Which had to be to Martha. But that meant Martha had to be close by.

"How about having dinner with us tonight, Martha?" Laughter greeted that suggestion, which had Brittany demanding, "Now why is that amusing?"

Martha wasn't going to answer her, if the prolonged silence was any indication, so Dalden did. "She does not eat."

"What he *means* is, I don't socialize," Martha put in now, exasperation clear. "But you know how that is, don'tcha, doll. Never enough time to see to all that needs seeing to, et cetera, et cetera."

Brittany sighed. "Yes, indeed. Perhaps, then, when this is over?"

"No," Martha replied curtly.

"Yes," Dalden countered, and Brittany's face was lifted in his hand, his eyes consuming her. "When this is over, *kerima*, I will take you home with me. It will mean leaving all that is known to you behind. But in return, I give to you my life, yours to keep until the day I die."

"You call *that* asking?" came Martha's complaint in bitter tones.

Dalden's smile was brilliant, unrepentant. "It was decided when she slept in my arms without fear."

Chapter 19

I T WAS DECIDED? *"WHAT WAS DECIDED?"*
Brittany was asking Dalden to explain his cryptic
remark, but it was Martha who answered in derisive
tones, "The big guy just joined you at the hip. He was
supposed to ask your permission first, said he understood that's how it's done around here, but he arbi-
trarily went ahead and did it his way rather than
yours."

"Did what? I still don't get it."

"Does shackled ring a bell? Ball and chain? Hooked
up? No? How about married?"

Brittany started chuckling. "Get real. It takes more
than a few words to perform a marriage."

"Wanna bet?"

Brittany stared at Dalden, but he wasn't laughing.
He was looking back at her as if he'd just bought her

and was quite pleased with the purchase price. She started to get annoyed.

She'd tried to go along with their joke and treat it as such, but it wasn't the least bit amusing when her feelings for this man were so new and fragile. She couldn't deny that the thought of being able to keep him was thrilling, but it was also unrealistic. For crying out loud, she'd just met him yesterday and still knew next to nothing about him. So for him to want to, or even think about, marrying her at this stage was so farfetched, it was beyond imagining.

"Okay, chuckle-time is over," she said tersely, making no attempt to hide her annoyance. "Shall we get back to business, or do we go off on a honeymoon first?"

For an answer, Dalden took her hand and started to drag her out of the building. She heard Martha's alarmed voice from some distance away, since there was over six feet of stretched arms between them now.

"Stop right there, warrior. She was kidding! She didn't mean it. And you are *not* going to run off and have some fun now just because you gave yourself permission to do so—not when Jorran could walk in here at any moment."

Dalden stopped. He looked utterly chagrined until his gaze fell on Brittany, then he just looked inflamed. She caught her breath. Dalden in the throes of passion was an incredible turn-on. And he must have sensed that she felt so, because he closed the space between them, clasped her face in both hands, and kissed her right there in the center of City Hall.

Nothing like being taken out of mind and place. They could have been up on a cloud for all she knew, she was so consumed with him and nothing but him.

But it wasn't Martha's voice that brought her jarringly back to earth this time, it was one she could have wished to never hear again.

"Into exhibitionism these days, Britt?"

It was absolutely the worst interruption Brittany could think of. Thomas Johnson, ex-boyfriend, the one guy she'd actually thought about marrying—and having sex with—because she'd mistakenly thought there was more between them than there was.

They hadn't exactly parted amicably, after she'd kicked him out of her apartment that night and told him to drop dead on the way out. It was a small town and she'd known they would run into each other eventually, but she'd managed to avoid doing so up till now.

"Still breathing, Tom?" she said, hoping he'd take the hint and just leave. "What a shame."

"Aren't we bitchy these days."

She smiled tightly. "Only around you."

He chuckled, though it was forced. They both knew she wasn't kidding around, that her animosity was quite real. She'd invested three months of emotions in this guy. Then for him to admit he had a problem with her height after all that time, even though she was a good half a foot shorter than him. Not short enough for him to feel like a giant, apparently, which had to be what he was looking for.

Dressed in a well-tailored pinstriped business suit today, Thomas made her feel tacky in her blue jeans, white T-shirt, and sneakers, which she'd felt adequate for playing the tourist in City Hall. Come to think of it, though, he'd always made her feel inferior in one way or another. Blue eyes, wavy black hair, sexy, extremely handsome—at least she'd thought so until she met Dalden.

"I tried to call you a number of times," Thomas informed her, like she might actually believe it when he knew her schedule, knew exactly when he could find her at home to receive any calls.

She let that pass, though, and attacked his motive instead. "Whatever for? Wasn't I clear enough that I didn't want to see you again?"

"Because you misunderstood that remark I made about your height. I wanted to explain."

"Oh, really? So you don't really think I'm too tall for you?"

"Well, for anything permanent, yes, but not for—"

"Get lost," she cut in, feeling some of the same acute embarrassment she'd felt that night. "I swear, you should get JERK tattooed to your forehead, just in case some poor fool doesn't figure it out right off."

"Britt—"

"My woman has suggested you leave her presence. Do so now before I assist you in the doing."

Thomas stared up at Dalden for a moment. He'd only glanced briefly at him before, then dismissed him as some dim-witted jock who got unevenly divided— lots of body, little mind. And even now, Dalden didn't seem all that threatening, standing behind Brittany with his hands on her shoulders, his expression calm despite what he'd just said.

Which prompted Thomas to remark snidely to Brittany, "Where'd you find this Neanderthal?"

"You can consider yourself really fortunate that he probably doesn't have a translation for that word," Brittany guessed aloud. "He's new to our country and doesn't have a full grasp of the language yet. Should I translate for him? You think he might appreciate derision coming from a shrimp like you?"

Tom finally got the point that his physical well-being might be in danger. There was a smidgen of alarm, but it was quickly dismissed. They were in a public place, after all, and one that usually had a few policemen roaming around it. So he felt absolutely safe in the assumption that Dalden wouldn't start anything there.

Brittany was sure of that as well; she'd just hoped Tom wouldn't be and would back off. So they were both somewhat surprised when Dalden set Brittany to the side of him, then completely behind him, where she didn't have a chance of seeing what he was going to do.

What he did was pointless, though, when Martha was in interfering mode. Dalden had no sooner wrapped his large hand around the man's neck than his fingers were grasping thin air instead.

A low rumble of annoyance came out of him while Martha was saying in Sha-Ka'ani, "So the eye doctors around here are really going to make a killing this week, but better that than you splattering his blood all over this pretty white floor."

"Where did you put him?" Dalden demanded in the same language.

"Back outside. He'll think he was so scared of you, he ran *really* fast. And lucky for you. Starting a physical brawl in a building devoted to politicians is a sure trip to a local jail. Remember our discussion of their jails? Places to be avoided at all costs?"

Brittany had heard enough that she didn't understand. "You guys are doing it again," she complained as she moved back around Dalden to find the space in front of him empty now. "And where did Tom go?"

"Who cares?" Martha countered. "We've had too many distractions as it is, when you're both *supposed* to be working toward our common goal of Jorran-hunting. Our friendly Centurian has volunteered that there are two more of his good buddies in there doing what he was doing, which was prepping everyone in the building for Jorran's arrival so that he's greeted by one and all with open arms. Find the other two and send them to me for new programming. *Then* we can get back to discussing Dalden's lack of warrior restraint in his dealings with foes and lifemates."

"Huh?"

Brittany didn't get any further explanation, which was becoming an annoying habit with these two. She almost preferred hearing the no-make-sense stuff that fell into the "classified info" realm than these cryptic remarks she thought she might understand if she could get past the disbelief stage. And this "warrior" label? Once mentioned—and Martha hadn't wanted it mentioned—it was now being mentioned much too often. Hardly indicative of a national guard type of part-time soldiers; more like a full-time career.

Well, he had the body for it, and he certainly had the reflexes. So he was a soldier, and they called themselves warriors where he came from. She could deal with that. Why did they try to fluff it off and downplay the fact that he was a military man?

Just more of the little oddities that didn't add up. And the main source of answers went off on Dalden's hip as he began covering all the offices in the building, getting to ask questions now without worry of causing alarm, because he took that rod with him. While Brittany was left with the foot-traffic crowd again and two hours remaining before City Hall closed shop for the day.

But she *would* get some answers, and pretty soon. She was working for them, helping them to round up this ring of thieves. Though *lunatics* might be a better word for people who thought they could just pop in and become an instant politician. She deserved better than double-talk, tasteless jokes, and when that failed, simply being ignored.

Chapter 20

BRITTANY HAD NEVER REALIZED HOW EROTIC A MAN could be in tight jeans until she saw Dalden in the pair that had been made especially for him. Or maybe it was just him. Actually, it probably *was* just him, because the sight of him when he came out of the dressing room, with the long-sleeved white cotton shirt tucked into those dark blue jeans was such a turn-on that she almost dragged him back into the dressing room.

Of course, helping him to look normal didn't help to keep eyes off of him. His amazing height and size couldn't be disguised. But at least he didn't look like a rock star now, though Brittany cracked up when the seamstress who'd supplied the new clothes hadn't wanted payment for them, but had blushingly asked for a picture of Dalden instead. She figured if he wasn't a celebrity now, he would be one day, and she wanted proof that she'd sewn for him.

Night was approaching by the time they left the mall. Her first day working for Dalden had been pretty successful. Even though Jorran hadn't been found yet, three of his people had been rounded up and sent off to Martha for interrogation. With night just around the corner, her job was over for the day. And as much as she hated the thought of losing his company even for a little while, she supposed she ought to offer to get him back to his own lodgings.

So as she was driving out of the mall parking lot, she remarked, "I know you said you couldn't get to your hotel yesterday for some reason, but you implied you could today. Shall I drop you off?"

"My place is now with you."

She spared him a glance. "You want to sleep on my couch again?"

He smiled at her. "What we sleep on may be of your choosing."

The chair and laying there in his arms all night again flashed through her mind and brought on a blush, even though he was probably using the "we" in a singular sense, rather than meaning him and her together.

But if he was going to spend the night again, she'd have to feed him, and she really didn't feel like a trip to the grocery with him in tow. Besides, she could just picture shopping carts banging into each other in the aisles, cans and boxes spilling all over the place, if he walked into the local food store.

With quite a few hours before bedtime ahead of them, and since they didn't have to get up as early tomorrow as she was accustomed to, she suggested, "Want to go out to dinner? Catch a movie? Go dancing maybe?" Then she grinned. "You know, a date?"

"Dancing?"

She rolled her eyes at him. "Why are you looking like that's another new word to you?"

Martha, quiet since they'd left City Hall, decided to explain, "There's no equivalent for it on Sha-Ka'an. It's a form of exercise that requires music, but music hasn't been embraced yet by the Sha-Ka'ani."

"No television, no music, but he's familiar with computers. Do you realize how bizarre that is?"

"Do you realize how diverse this world is in cultures?" Martha shot back.

Brittany sighed, allowing the point. "All right, dinner first, then we'll play it by ear. And since we're not exactly dressed for fine dining, how about a pizza? Or two." She chuckled, giving him another glance. "Or three."

"What is—?"

"Food! Just plain old Amer—well, it's an Italian dish, but I hear we've Americanized it so much, the original tastes nothing like what we serve up here. And there's a nice little parlor on the next block."

The pizza parlor was surprisingly crowded for that early in the evening, or for anytime, actually, considering it offered delivery service, which most people took advantage of. The crowd consisted of a children's soccer team celebrating a victory with a lot of the parents in tow. Which meant service was slow and they ended up being there for a couple of hours, rather than in and quickly out as was usually the case.

Dalden flipped out over the pizza, which made the

wait well worth it. But then Martha got interested in the ingredients for making it, which resulted in a long and detailed discussion, because she didn't just want to know the shopping list required, she wanted to know the process for making the ingredients from scratch. Raised on a farm, Brittany was able to answer most of her questions.

And then there were the interruptions, which she was getting used to by now. Dalden got asked for his autograph again, and two men stopped by wanting to know what team he played for. Brittany was amused that she wasn't the only one who immediately assumed he would be a basketball player. And she didn't know how it happened, but she came back from the bathroom at one point to find the entire soccer team piled up on his shoulders for a group picture with the "giant."

He seemed to be enjoying himself, and three large pizzas later, it was actually late enough to hit Seaview's one nightclub. Ordinarily she wouldn't have considered going dancing on a weeknight but since Dalden had no experience of dancing at all, she wanted to find out if it was something else he might enjoy.

The weekend would have been a better time for it, when the nightclub was hopping, but she had a feeling he'd be gone by the time the weekend rolled in again. They had made a lot of progress today, and Jorran's people had as well, supposedly, so the wanna-be mayor could well make his appearance tomorrow. Then Dalden would take control of him with that rod as easily as he had his lackeys, and he'd have no further reason to stick around. Task done, he'd be going home—and Brittany refused to think of how much she was going to miss him.

She'd foolishly let herself get too attached too quickly. She still barely knew anything about him, yet even that didn't matter. It was going to be heartbreak, big-time.

She'd already been assured that she wouldn't be opposed to his factions, which left nothing else that she could think of that she might find objectionable about him. Martha seemed to think otherwise, that their cultural differences couldn't be bridged. But what did culture have to do with feelings, especially when her every instinct was telling her that he was the man of her dreams, her ideal mate? Even the fact that he might be younger than her had no relevance. Nothing mattered compared to the emotions he stirred in her.

So tonight was for fun, and for memories. But the thin crowd in the club was daunting. Only four other couples were there, and only one of them seemed inclined to dance. And contrary to Tom's snide remark today, Brittany wasn't an exhibitionist. So it took three and a half drinks before she was ready to get out on that nearly empty dance floor.

Dalden was fascinated with the place. The lighting was old-style disco, the music was typically blaring, and the one couple who pretty much stayed out on the floor were giving him a decent how-to demonstration. Martha continued to call it exercise, and an obsolete form of it banned in many places. Brittany would have asked for a definition of "banned" if she wouldn't have had to shout it, because their "banned" had to be something other than "not allowed."

"Are you ready to try it?" she finally asked him.

"I will try anything with you, *kerima*."

She was just tipsy enough to be really moved by how sweet that answer was. She gave him her hand, and led him out on the floor. A fast song was playing, not a hopping beat, but a steady tempo that could accommodate just about any style. She danced the way she'd learned to in high school, a bit on the sexy side, but the only way she was familiar with. He seemed to be swinging some kind of invisible weapon himself, his movements precise, and she almost laughed when she realized he wasn't dancing, he was doing exactly what Martha had called it, exercising. They were still having fun, and his eyes, which he never took off of her, said he was enjoying watching her dance more than anything else.

And then the music segued into a slow song, the first one played since they'd arrived. Dalden hadn't seen slow dancing yet; she had to show him how. He took the closeness a step further, though, and within moments, he was kissing her instead. And that quickly was she taken out of place and time, just like that afternoon, everything around her fading to nothing. All that was left was the man and his touch, consuming her.

"Martha, please!"

Brittany seemed to hear it from a distance, his voice. She didn't know what he was asking for, but it didn't stop what he was doing for more than a second. She was still being kissed, still being held so closely she could feel all of him. There was a tingling that had nothing to do with the drinks she'd consumed. And then there was softness under her, and a very big man above her, and it simply didn't dawn on her yet that she was in a bed with him, or to wonder how she got there.

Chapter 21

Brittany had begun the evening wanting to store up memories, because she was certain that was all she would have left of Dalden soon. She hadn't thought of lovemaking as an added possibility, but what better memory to retain of him than one of the most profound intimacy?

It was no longer a matter of her wanting some kind of commitment from him first, or needing to know him better. That previous reasoning seemed very old now, in the matter of importance. Her feelings had taken a big step forward even from just yesterday, yet despite that, there was the simple fact that she wanted him, and could no longer think of a logical reason to deny that need.

There was some small confusion left, that the matter was already at hand, that they were in her bed, in her apartment, and already deeply involved in the mating ritual. She simply couldn't remember how they had gotten there, when her last memory of them was on the dance floor in that nightclub.

She was forced to assume that her drinks had gotten double shots without her knowing and the result had snuck up on her without warning. She'd heard of bartenders doing that, a male-helping-a-male-score type of thing they ought to be shot for. And although she was sobering up quickly now, she must have been quite bombed to have gotten them home without remembering it. Incredible as that was, there was simply no other explanation for it.

Her clothes were gone. She did recall them being stripped away with amazing speed. His were as well. And Dalden naked was a marvel to behold.

She didn't think it was possible for a man to fit her ideal specifications, yet Dalden did in every way imaginable. She hadn't thought it was possible for her to ever feel small, either, but laying next to him, she felt that, too. He was just so big, every part of him, so much power and strength on visual display. A normal-sized woman might have been scared senseless by it, but Brittany was delighted instead.

That urgent desperation she'd heard in his voice earlier was only slightly modified now. It was still there, the strength of his passion unleashed, but that didn't frighten her, either, because he seemed to have absolute control of it, now that he had her where he wanted her: naked, clasped to him, her body his to possess.

And explore. He did that. He molded her, moved her this way and that, positioned her exactly to his preference, and explored every inch of her with his hands, his mouth, his golden eyes.

One of them had turned the light on in her room and left it on. She should have experienced some embarrassment because of it, but there was none at all, probably because she was too busy being fascinated by his body. She did feel almost dominated, but even that was all right, because she knew she could have control back if she chose to. She didn't. It wasn't as if she was confident yet in making love, having never done so before. So his guidance, or command of what they were doing, was welcome and left her more open to just feelings, and those were numerous and intense.

She was thrilled to a level hard to contain. What he was making her feel was exciting. That she was finally going to "do it" was exciting. That it was with *him* was exciting. It was a spiral upward, senses heightened, each new sensation a step closer to the pinnacle . . .

And then she remembered Martha, with her prying ears and six-sided viewers, and panicked, thinking they weren't alone. "Where is it? Martha's box?" There was no answer, at least not from Martha. "She's gone?"

"She would not intrude here."

That didn't mean she was gone, but it was good enough. At least the panic subsided, only to be replaced soon after with a different form. He had mounted her, was about to breach her. She scrunched her eyes closed, tensed to the max, but assured him, or rather herself, "I'm in good shape, I'm ready for this, go for it."

He stared at her tightly closed eyes. A bass rumble of laughter came out of him.

"You are in no way ready, *kerima*. You have not done this before?"

Brittany opened her eyes just a crack so she could squint up at him. "If I had, do you *really* think I would have put you off yesterday?"

He seemed so very pleased by her answer that she was immensely glad that she'd been able to say that. She'd waited a long time for the right man to come along, and he was the right man. Instinct told her that even if circumstances didn't, and even though Martha seemed to think there was no chance of their different cultures mixing. None of which mattered. This was something she had to do for herself. If she only had some hope that this wasn't going to be a onetime thing, it would be perfect.

That moment of sadness made her wrap her arms around his neck and squeeze. "Make me believe in happy endings, Dalden, even if we're not going to have one. Tell me this won't be the only time we love each other."

He leaned back so he could look into her eyes. "I cannot fathom your confusion. You are my lifemate. And until I have you in a place familiar to me, where I can be assured of not losing you, you will not be parted from me. Is this the assurance you need?"

Relief flowed out of her, made her glow with happiness. "Was it ever."

He smiled at her, kissed her cheek gently, nuzzled her neck. He was restraining himself now, for her, because she had interrupted her state of readiness with her worries. He was apparently willing to start over, which filled her with such a wealth of gratitude and warmth that her feelings for him escalated yet again.

His own state of need hadn't lessened. Hers was brought back to match his with amazing speed. Not that he rushed her; she just wanted this to happen so much, her body was cooperating perfectly with her mind. And it didn't even hurt that much. She probably had the liquor to thank for that—or Dalden's restraint and expertise. He entered her so slowly, so very carefully, distracting her with his kisses, that by the time she felt the uncomfortable pressure of him pushing against the virginal blockage, it popped open, causing no more than a minor gasp of surprise.

He went no further than that, though. He was practicing that amazing restraint of his again. Unbelievable, the control he had over his emotions and his body. It wasn't normal. It wasn't necessary, either, when her own heightened senses were clamoring for more of him.

Without words she tried to tell him, grasping his backside with both hands, trying to push him forward into her. That didn't work, of course. She couldn't budge him if he didn't want to be budged. She felt a moment of resentment, that he could so easily move her body exactly as he wanted, but she couldn't do the same with his. It didn't last, though, because he was smiling down at her, amused by her efforts, but obviously pleased, too.

He kissed her gently, then caught her gasp in his mouth as he slid the rest of the way into her. It was exquisite, more thrilling than she could ever have imagined, having him so deep inside her. And his restraint was still in full force—no swift pummeling, now that he could, but a slow, exacting ritual.

He was letting her experience every aspect of his

taking possession of her. She couldn't complain, not when the pleasure was immediately there and gradually increased, so that she could enjoy it longer—or would have, if her body didn't like what was happening too much!

There was no delaying her climax when it came; it washed over her in powerful waves, the pinnacle of sensations so intense she nearly fainted. He joined her in that, prolonging that unique pleasure, until it really was too much ecstasy all at once.

She awoke sometime in the middle of the night. She was wrapped around Dalden, covering him like a blanket. She tried to move, to turn off the light that was still on, but his arm tightened around her, refusing to let her leave his side even in sleep. She smiled and put her cheek to his chest again. He made a lumpy mattress, a hard pillow, but that was okay. Her contentment couldn't be measured in comfort.

Chapter 22

"BRITT, YOU AWAKE YET?" JAN CALLED FROM THE LIVING room. "You've got company."

Brittany knew she had company. She opened her eyes to see that her company was still sleeping, his feet hanging over the end of her bed quite a bit. It was an extra-length model and fit her just fine, but they really didn't make beds for seven-footers.

"Britt?" It was shouted this time.

Okay, so she wasn't quite awake yet, or she would have realized Jan wasn't talking about Dalden, that her friend likely didn't know yet that he'd spent the night.

"Coming!" she shouted back.

She leapt out of bed, yanked her bulky white terry robe out of the closet, wrapped it on, and stepped out

into the living room. She vaguely heard Dalden stir-
ring behind her, but didn't dare look back at him, or
she'd be really rude to whoever was there and simply
tell them to get lost. She had a mind to anyway, up until she got a look at the man standing just inside their
front door.

Jan was staring at him as if she were starving and he
was six feet of chocolate cake. Brittany couldn't blame
her. The man was unbelievably handsome; actually, way,
way too handsome. She'd never seen anyone who
looked that perfect, like he was created to someone's
ideal specifications. He even fit her own specifications,
was at least as tall as her if not taller. She wasn't sure she
wanted to get close enough to see if he might top her by
a few inches, when she was still doubting her eyes. He
was even more handsome than Dalden, if that was possible, though in a different way, less masculine—*beautiful*
was the word that came to mind.

He wore a one-piece jumpsuit that looked like some
kind of uniform. His eyes were so green that the color
was clear even from across the room. His hair was coal
black, cut short, though not excessively short. And he
carried some sort of large plastic container that Brittany did a double-take on when she realized it was
filled with groceries.

She finally asked, "You sure you have the right
apartment?"

He smiled at her. "Martha doesn't make mistakes.
She sent me with some necessities for the big guy."

"Ohhhh, you're a friend of Dalden's."

That didn't get confirmed. Instead she heard behind
her, "Corth II, Martha? Is that wise?"

"Just saving time, kiddo, since you depleted the little gal's cupboards yesterday," Martha's voice chimed in.

Poor Jan was staring wide-eyed now at Dalden's bare chest. He'd donned only the jeans before appearing in the doorway to the bedroom, and was hooking Martha's box over the denim. The female voice she'd just heard, with no body to go along with it, was probably confusing the hell out of her. She was also undoubtedly shocked to find Dalden coming out of Brittany's bedroom.

Tactfully, though, all Jan said was, "I think I need a cup of coffee," and disappeared into the kitchen.

Brittany wanted one as well, but decided some clothes might be a better idea first. "I'll just get dressed while you chat with your friend."

She'd still been staring at their visitor while she said it, which was possibly why there was some annoyance in Dalden's voice when he replied, "Corth II is not staying."

"It sounds like I'm not staying," Corth II said with a cheeky grin. "Nice to meet you, Brittany Callaghan, however briefly. Perhaps—"

"Be gone!" Dalden growled.

The man obeyed, though he seemed quite amused as he left. Martha was chuckling some as well.

"My, my, that was interesting," came purring out of the little box. "Losing some of that renowned Sha-Ka'ani control there, warrior? 'Course, I shouldn't be surprised, after you totally lost it last night."

Brittany frowned at the box on his hip. "Why are you picking on him, Martha?"

If a shrug could be heard in a voice, it was heard now in Martha's. "Just setting the stage for my explanation, doll, before Dalden starts to fret over natural inclinations that he's convinced he doesn't possess. A fretting warrior is like a time bomb, which we don't need at this stage of the game."

"Martha has said too much already," Dalden said in grumbling tones.

"Martha hasn't said nearly enough yet," Martha countered. "But you can relax over some of those inclinations, warrior. Last night, you were provoked big-time. What you witnessed has been a form of sexual enticement for centuries. It's known to easily incite passions. Some cultures have managed to get rid of it, the thinking being that their people have enough stress to deal with, that sexual stress in that form only compounds the problem."

"Good grief," Brittany said incredulously. "You're talking about our dancing last night?"

"Watching you dance pushed him over the edge, doll, if you didn't notice at the time. You might want to make sure there is no more of that nonsense until after we've finished our task here."

"Some people consider dancing to be fun," Brittany pointed out.

"Some people are used to it," Martha shot back. "Dalden isn't one of them."

Brittany stared at Dalden and then blushed profusely. "I hope you don't think it was my intention to—to—"

He quickly closed the space between them, clasped her face in his hands, smiled at her. "I would change no part of last night, *kerima*."

She wouldn't, either—well, she wished she could recall getting back here. Black holes in the memory were a bit frightening, in not knowing what you might have done during the missing time frame. But she supposed if she had done anything more stupid than driving under severe influence, he would have mentioned it by now.

Everything else she remembered clearly, including his assurance that she was his lifemate, that they wouldn't be parted until he had her in a place familiar to him. She would like to get "familiar" defined. Tacking "home" to it was unrealistic, when he could have just meant back to wherever his base of operations was for this assignment he was on. *Lifemate* was another word she needed his interpretation of. She knew the definition she'd like to put to it, but in some cultures, mate just meant friend, so she wasn't going to assume what it meant for him.

But she wasn't quite up to an interrogation yet, and what she suspected might be some considerable disappointment on her part as a result. She'd rather savor the contentment she'd felt last night awhile longer.

So she wrapped her arms around him, squeezed a bit, and said, "I'll endeavor to keep you out of any more disco-type establishments, but I'm sure we can manage to have fun without the dancing part."

Martha was chuckling. Dalden's smile widened considerably. And Brittany remembered too late that he referred to lovemaking as "fun."

She stepped back and snorted at the both of them. "That's not what I meant—bah, never mind. While I get dressed, why don't you unload the groceries your friend was nice enough to drop off."

"Corth II is not a friend."

"Fine. Enemy then."

"Nor that," he replied. "My mother considers him part of the family."

"She does? Which implies you don't?"

"Like my father, I have little tolerance for those of Corth II's ilk."

"Ohh—kay," she said, stretching out the word. "I suppose that made perfect sense—to you. And come to think of it, I'd just as soon *not* know what you mean by 'ilk.' I do find it odd, however, his having a number for a last name. Is that common in your country?"

"It is not a last name. He is the second in his line, an advanced model of Martha's creation, similar to the original Corth."

"Martha's son?" she said with surprise.

"Something like that."

"Something like—?" She frowned now. "Okay, I know I'm missing something here, and now I'd like that explanation. Martha, want to fill me in?"

"Not a chance, doll. I just love watching warriors dig holes they can't get out of."

Brittany made a face, but turned her questions back in Dalden's direction. "So why didn't this Corth get an original name?"

"Martha is a Mock II. It follows that anything that improves on the original, as she was, would get the same classification from her."

"I give up. You're talking like he's a machine, an android or something like that, when that's impossible."

"Why impossible?"

"Because we might be making strides with robotic gadgets, but nothing even remotely like what just walked in here. That was a man. I've got eyes. There was nothing mechanical about him."

He reminded her, "Inventions that defy belief, you were told."

She blinked at him, but then she chuckled. "I'm glad you've got a sense of humor, Dalden, I really am. It's an odd one, but none the less amusing."

"Woman—"

"This might be a really good time to drop the subject, children," Martha interjected dryly at that point. "You've overslept this morning. The big guy still needs to be fed. I was hoping we'd get to City Hall when it first opens, but now you'll have to backtrack again, to make sure no mischief gets caused before your arrival. Waste of time that could have been prevented if someone's alarm had been set."

Brittany blushed, mumbled something about grumpy old women, and went back to the bedroom to get dressed.

Chapter 23

"IT'S AS I SUSPECTED," MARTHA WAS SAYING AS THEY walked into the central lobby at City Hall. "Jorran's people were all turned loose on your fair town. The three that I have links to each abided the night in different locations, harmless for the most part. But *they* showed up here bright and early, unlike some—"

"There are times when you may ignore Martha," Dalden told Brittany, his arm around her waist. "Were it important for us to be here sooner, she would have woken us herself."

A snort first, then, "Actually, waking you myself, without any other distractions there to get you out of bed, would have guaranteed a *lot* more wasted time. Both blushing? I see you understand why I didn't do the waking, but sent Corth II over instead."

"Is there going to be a time when you can turn her off?" was Brittany's mumbled response.

"Indeed, but not for several more months."

Brittany frowned. "You don't really think it's going to take that long to find Jorran, do you?"

"No," he replied. "But Martha cannot be gotten rid of until I return home, and she is returned to being only my mother's nuisance."

"Tedra does *not* consider me a nuisance," Martha interjected in hurt tones.

"Can my father say the same?"

"'Course not" came out with a chuckle that belied there'd been any real hurt in the last comment.

Brittany ignored the banter, was stuck on that "several months" remark. "Then you're not going straight home after you're done here?"

"Indeed we are."

Her eyes widened. "So it's going to take you a couple of months just to travel? Wow, I didn't think anything still took that long to cross the ocean. You must have a really old, slow ship lined up for the trip."

Martha wasn't the only one chuckling this time, and feeling herself the butt of yet another joke she couldn't possibly decipher, Brittany added, "Wrong guess? Maybe you plan to swim home?"

The sarcasm was clear to her ears, but Dalden didn't hear it, and said only, "Such would not be possible."

Martha was more perceptive, and replied, "No need to get bent out of shape, doll. You'll understand all too soon and probably wish you'd been left in the realm of 'unknowing' instead. In the meantime, how about you two getting to work? Same agenda as yesterday. Start with the mayor first and work your way out from there, Brittany, while Dalden makes the rounds of the rest of the offices."

With a sigh, Brittany nodded and headed toward the mayor's reception room. With three rods confiscated yesterday, she now had one for her own use and Sullivan's secretary got to be her first test subject with it.

It still amazed her, the total hypnotic control those rods gave the user. She was sent right in to the mayor's office, had herself announced first this time so as not to startle the man again. And didn't once think that he might be in the middle of a meeting already, which happened to be the case.

Where was her mind today? Still savoring last night, of course, and not attending to current business. But that was no excuse to blunder like this. . . .

There were four other people gathered around the mayor's desk. They weren't talking, were merely relaxing in the plush chairs for the most part, looking bored. And Sullivan did stand up, all smiles, to greet her as if she weren't intruding on a meeting already in progress.

Was he still under the same influence from yesterday, ready to answer any questions she put forth and then forget about them? But she couldn't exactly grill him with these other people present. Nor could she use the rod on the lot of them without one or two realizing what she was doing before she reached them, and bolting to raise an alarm.

A hasty retreat was in order, and before she started blushing over this blunder, she jumped right in with, "Someone get their appointment times mixed up? If you'd like me to wait outside a few more minutes until you're done here, Mayor Sullivan, I—"

"Done with what?" he asked with a curious frown. "I was expecting you, wasn't I?"

"Yes, but—"

"Then sit, sit," he told her, wearing his public smile again. "What can I do for you today?"

The blush was coming up anyway. The four men must be members of his staff. And they still weren't saying anything, just watching the proceedings in a bored manner. Which really put her on the spot. Was she supposed to conduct her business with them present? Was that normal around here, for the mayor to be surrounded by his people during private appointments? She *had* caught him on his lunch break last time, after all. And if this was standard procedure, why hadn't they at least introduced themselves to put her at ease?

Annoyed that she wasn't going to accomplish her mission with them there, she pointed out their rudeness with some of her own by asking one of them directly, "Who are you?"

"An observer."

Fat lot that told her, so she held out her hand to shake his and even though he ignored it, she still said, "I'm Brittany Callaghan, and you are?"

"An observer" was repeated, but then, "Commence your meeting, woman, then begone."

She caught the accent this time. Like Dalden's but not quite the same, still very foreign-sounding. Alarms went off in her head. She needed to get the hell out of there and warn Dalden that they'd most likely hit the jackpot, and used that last comment to take offense over.

"Excuse me, I can tell when I'm not wanted," she

said tersely, and to Sullivan, "I'll reschedule, Mayor, when you're not being—observed."

She turned and started to march out of there on her high horse, only to be drawn up short because one of them had moved to block the exit. Nor was he little enough that she might have been able to push her way past him. He was her height, but with the physique of a nightclub bouncer, all brawn and happy to show it off. The price tag dangling from the lapel of his new suit was a bizarre touch, but not enough to detract from his seriously threatening demeanor.

And she heard behind her, "It is difficult to hide fear beneath other emotions. Most people cannot manage it. You fall into that group. Then the question becomes, What was said here to cause you fear?"

She swung back around. It was the same fellow she'd spoken to who had sensed her fear. The observer. He'd looked more important than the other three bored interlopers, which was why she'd addressed him. Jorran himself?

He was standing now, with that aura of command even more prominent, wrapped around him like a cloak. Tall, lean, with light blond hair and emerald green eyes, he held himself like royalty, was lacking only a crown to make the impression complete. But then the price tag hanging from his sleeve ruined the impression and threw her off again.

She noticed it as he crossed his arms. A brief, nervous glance at the other two men showed that their suits also sported them. Fashionable where they came from? Or was their country so backward that they simply didn't know that if you left the store wearing new clothes you just bought, you were supposed to remove the evidence? And that they were all wearing brand-new suits for this appearance made her wonder why they had felt it was necessary. To replace desert robes, perhaps?

She was doing it again, making assumptions, when she should just deal with known facts. Trouble was, there were so few of those. And such blatant ignorance of the modern world was making it easy for her to put her fear aside. How was she supposed to take this plot seriously when these people knew absolutely nothing about the country and politics they were trying to gain control of?

He was waiting for her answer. She kept it simple. "I don't know what you're talking about."

A slight annoyance showed in his expression. "Of course you do. And you can own up to the truth, or I can have you arrested for attempting to assassinate Mr. Sullivan. He will, of course, swear that you did indeed try to kill him."

He was bluffing. He had to be bluffing. Send her to prison, and that's what that particular charge would do if the rods were used to support it, just because she wouldn't answer his question?

Panic mixed with indignation had her demanding, "Are you listening to this, Mayor?"

Sullivan was frowning at her. "All I hear is you talking nonsense to yourself."

That produced a sigh from Jorran, drawing her eyes back to him. "It is really too bad that he mentioned that. I was merely curious about what caused you to be suddenly afraid. Now we will have to detain you."

So it had been a bluff. Of course he wouldn't want to cause such a big to-do, which would only draw more attention to himself. But detaining was just as bad in her book.

"And do not ask why he does not hear or see me, woman," he added disdainfully as he sat back down. "Your curiosity is unimportant."

That easily she was dismissed. And that was what made her angry. She was inconsequential, a nuisance to be brushed under the rug. She posed absolutely no threat to their carefully laid plans.

"Ask? I don't need to ask," she said with an equal amount of disdain. "I know exactly why he doesn't hear or see you."

Chapter 24

BRITTANY COULD CLAIM THE DEVIL MADE HER SAY THAT, but it was a known fact that anger was its own worst enemy, and she was no exception to that rule. She should have kept her mouth shut. She should have pretended that she was just what she seemed to be, just another appointment on the mayor's busy schedule. Now she had to admit that she knew more than they had counted on anyone knowing, and offer a reason for that without implicating Dalden.

He might be bigger than the lot of them, though the two bouncer types might cost him a bit more effort. He could still probably take them all down by normal means. But if all four of them were equipped with those rods, there'd be nothing normal about it. Dalden could be rendered harmless within seconds, and the only end to that would be Jorran wins, Dalden and company lose. So it was imperative that they not know he was in the building looking for them.

Jorran was standing up again, and there was no "slight" to his annoyance this time. A short, rotund fellow had also moved behind the mayor and was whispering in his ear. It looked like she had just been made invisible as well, since the mayor proceeded to ignore her as he started browsing through some papers on his desk.

"Explain yourself, woman," brought her eyes back to the regal-looking Jorran.

She decided on the most plausible lie out of the few options she had. "I'm a news reporter assigned to City Hall. It's my job to ferret out anything of interest going on around here, and your crew and those sticks they've been waving around the last couple of days were most definitely interesting. I followed, I listened. A child could have put two and two together here, when your people haven't exactly been trying to hide what they were doing."

The last wasn't exactly true either, but he didn't address it, merely pointed out, "We have been following your town news. No mention of what you say has appeared in it, which means you lie."

"No, that just means I haven't finished writing the article yet."

"Then you have told no one else of your findings?"

Dilemma time. Cover her own butt and claim others knew, put the fear of imminent discovery into them, or keep them from panicking so Dalden could do his thing and round them up? Actually, there was no dilemma, when Martha had mentioned that if they went into hiding, it would be impossible to find them again. No panic—well, aside from her own.

So she took an accusatory tack, complaining, "You're kidding, right? And get labeled as writing science fiction? I need more proof before I put my name to an article as unbelievable as this one is so far. I mean, what it seems those sticks of yours can do is just not possible. Maybe you'd care to explain what exactly it is they *do* do?"

"What is your conclusion?"

"I'm not paid to draw conclusions, merely to report what's newsworthy," she said. "But it's pretty obvious you want to be mayor."

"What is obvious is often proven irrelevant," he replied, then nodded toward the mayor as he added, "He does not do much that impresses me. He decides no matters of great import. I am not sure now that I want his title. I am taking a few days to observe and decide."

She almost laughed. The man wanted the mayor's job when he had absolutely no idea what it entailed. Or was he trying to throw her off the track?

"The position of mayor can't be encompassed in just a few days," she told him, "when the projects he undertakes can take months, even years to finish. A mayor's greatness or failure is seen at the end of his term, in what he has accomplished during that term. It's not a title, it's a job. He works for the people, for the betterment of the town, not for the betterment of himself."

A hand was waved to dismiss that reasoning. "The position will be what I make of it, not what the townspeople have come to expect. Not that it matters. This is merely a stepping-stone to true rulership."

So much for the misleading theory. Sounded more like he was going into bragging mode now, which didn't hold much hope for her being released when they were done talking. She might as well hear it all, then . . .

"Rulership, huh? Don'tcha mean leadership? But just out of curiosity, how did you think you could manage to jump into an elected position of prominence in this country when you're not a citizen of it, or known to the populace?"

"I am known. The people in this building already think I am their mayor. He will make a speech today to the thing called media that he has been merely my puppet, that I have been making all decisions for him from the start."

It was on the tip of her tongue to tell him that such a speech would cause outrage—to say that the people had been duped—not have the desired effect he seemed to think it would give him. But just in case they couldn't stop him before then, why give him warning that he'd be digging his own grave with that course of action?

So she said instead, "Aren't you forgetting the other candidates running for the job?"

"If I decide to continue on this stepping path to the presidency, I will be the only candidate running for mayor during the thing you call election. The others will concede to the better man."

"You plan to use those rods to force them to drop out at the last minute, don't you?"

He smiled. It was such a confident, I-can't-lose sort

of smile. But that wasn't what had her belly rolling with dread, it was the realization that the man could do exactly what he planned to do, and what he planned to do was much worse than she'd been told.

The presidency? He was out of his flipping mind, and yet those rods could get him there. Men could be told how to vote. The media could be given false information about him and make it nationally known. Women who might suspect what was going on and try to prevent it could be warned off by their bosses and men in their families, or railroaded into jail as they had threatened to do to her.

There were countless ways they could get around any opposition, just with the touch of a hypnotic stick and a few whispered words. Judges, other politicians, top law enforcement positions, hell, even the high brass in the military, all could be made puppets in Jorran's camp.

"Why bother with small potatoes, why not go straight for the big seat?" she asked, trying to understand his reasoning. "Plastic surgery could make you look like the current president." Hadn't Dalden been worried that he had changed his appearance? "You could just take over that way—"

"And assume his name?" was said indignantly. "Never. I share no glory. It is my name that will be revered, as it should be."

She forced herself to remember he'd said "if" earlier, that he wasn't fully committed on this path yet. There was nothing standing in his way from his point of view, since he didn't know about Dalden and Martha yet. So what else was making him have second thoughts?

"You've gone to a lot of trouble here, to be undecided in the matter. Perhaps you've realized that it's not going to work in the long run?"

The curious look he gave her wasn't doubt; it was laced with amusement. "Why would it not?"

"Because you're always going to have someone questioning who you are, where you came from. Everywhere you turn there will be reporters hounding you, demanding answers. You can fool a few people, but this country is comprised of millions, and every one of those millions is concerned with who leads them. And every time you open your mouth, you will generate even more questions."

"How so?"

"Because your accent points out that you're not one of us, so you have no business governing us. Now if you plan to have someone else do all the talking for you, you might get by for a while. But you strike me as a man who doesn't want to take second place to anyone."

He actually chuckled. "Your suppositions are based on what has been, not what will be. Do you understand that your governing foundation will be changed to *my* foundation? A king is not questioned. A king's word is law."

"And you would be king?" she said derisively.

"I am already king. I merely require a new country to rule. My indecision is in regard to your particular country. I have more information about your world now. I must weigh immediate power of a lesser degree against a greater, true power that requires much time and effort. I lean toward great power, but I abhor being made to wait for it."

Was he just hatched yesterday? How could he not know the different forms of government to be had, and that the one he'd picked was the least suited for what he had in mind?

She didn't get a chance to ask. The rotund fellow who'd put the mayor into complete ignore-mode said peevishly to Jorran, "You need waste no more time on this female, Eminence. I will see that she is disposed of."

Jorran gave that a moment's consideration before he replied, "No . . . no, I have enjoyed the discourse, Alrid, and wish to continue it later."

"She knows too much—"

"Get real," Brittany interrupted, afraid she knew where that line of reasoning was going to go. "I could have screamed my head off already, and had the cavalry arriving to bash down the mayor's door by now. But I'm a reporter, remember? I'd rather get an exclusive interview after the mayor makes his speech to the cameras. Everyone and their mother is going to want to know about the brains behind the puppet after that speech. Work with me, and I'll give you the best news coverage you could ask for."

"Why would you do this?" Jorran asked.

"Because it would be a *huge* boost to my career, which means more money for me. I've got a mortgage to pay, kids to feed." Bah, she was laying it on too thick. "Look, the fact is, I was getting nowhere with the article I'd planned to write, so I'd just as soon forget about that one for the real story. Fact two, you're going to need some good press coverage that you have some control over. The average reporter is going to write what they want to write about you, not what you want to be known."

"And you would write what I want known?"

"Exactly—for a price."

Jorran threw back his head and laughed. "Greed. This I understand perfectly. I was beginning to wonder if your species was capable of corruption. My faith is restored. You will remain with us to our mutual benefit."

He had bought it. She'd be put on the payroll. Amazing. She certainly wouldn't have believed that hogwash she'd tossed his way. It had to be the greed part, right up his alley, something he was comfortable dealing with. Not that it mattered, when it was probably going to be her shortest job ever—because she was fully expecting Dalden to take this guy out of commission before the mayor started spouting his rod-induced lies.

Chapter 25

"WE'VE GOT PROBLEMS." MARTHA'S VOICE CAME through the phazor combo-unit a bit erratically.

"Your impaired speech?" Dalden said as they returned to the main lobby.

"Not just that. Something has moved into the area that is causing major interference that makes Transfer too dangerous to consider. Do you notice anything unusual?"

A quick glance around the central hall had Dalden saying, "Other than Brittany is not here?"

"Yes, other than that. Strange equipment? Electrical storms?"

"Your viewers are not working, either?"

"Only sporadically, which is unacceptable. Corth II

is on his way with a few emergency essentials. He'll be a few minutes getting here, since I had to set him down out of the range frequency of that interference. It's imperative that it be located and disabled, whatever it is."

"It is more imperative that you tell me where Brittany is," Dalden countered.

A sigh. "She's still in the mayor's office."

"Why?"

"Probably because Jorran is in there, too. Hold it right there! If you go barging in, she's liable to get hurt. At the moment, she's fine."

"I will not leave her in there, Martha."

It was said so emphatically that only a fool would try to argue—or a computer. "She's fine, kiddo, *really* she is. I'm not getting full conversations with this interference, but from the bits and pieces I am getting, it sounds like she's got them believing that she's joined their camp and will be a benefit to them. Besides, he's not going to hurt her when he finds her interesting."

"I find these trees growing indoors interesting. That does not mean I would not cut them down."

"I meant interested as in bedtime fun—hold it right there! You don't chop someone up for what they are thinking, and that's as far as his interest has gone. She doesn't know he finds her attractive. He's the type who won't reveal emotions to anyone if they could be perceived as a weakness that could be used against him."

"You have had chains on me too long, Martha."

"Dalden, sweetie," she cajoled in syrupy tones. "We are almost done here. The end of this rising should see us on our way home. Don't blow it now because you're impatient to get your hands around his neck. If it sounds like she's in the slightest trouble, you get the green light. But at the moment, we want him to think he's got the upper hand, so he'll leave here and you can then deal with him under less public scrutiny. Here, there are a good forty people or more who will jump to his defense."

"He has that many with him?"

"No, but you keep forgetting what I told you about the people in this country. They are an aggressive lot. They will interfere just because they can."

"Not if I stun them all."

Another sigh, much longer and riddled with static. "Tedra could pull that off, but you haven't had any practice with that phazor combo-unit. With calm, slow use and sightline up, you'd have no trouble with it, but Probables say that in your rush to stun them all before they can get to you, you'll end up missing one or two and risk the chance of the beam reflecting off something and coming right back at you. But in case you haven't realized it yet, Transfer isn't the only thing currently being affected by that local interference. Your weapon is out of order as well."

"Then what do you propose?"

"Let him get beyond the interference, or get rid of it first. And *please* keep in mind that you can't kill Jorran, much as you might be currently relishing the thought, or we lose the leverage for a recall on *all* of the rods. So the original plan still holds: disable his shield so I can Transfer him to the ship, but do it in the least crowded place so you won't be jumped by locals who think you're accosting an innocent party. The advantage is still ours, since he still doesn't suspect that we're here.

Ah, that's better." A sigh filled with relief, and minus any static.

"What?"

"Corth II has arrived and turned off the interference, though not very diplomatically," Martha complained. "I'll have to talk to him about threatening to break people who don't want to cooperate with him, and leaving stunned bodies all over the place. We're going to have to wrap this up, kiddo. We've got about an hour before those stuns wear off and all hell breaks loose around here."

Dalden grinned. "I will have to thank him for releasing me from your restraints."

"If I don't fry his circuits first," Martha mumbled. "But all systems are back in full operation—on our end. And those cameramen coming into the building haven't realized yet that they've been disconnected from making a live broadcast. So it was the media transmission equipment causing—Jorran is coming out. Show time."

"Show time?"

"Time for you to do your thing, warrior."

Quite a few people were coming out of the mayor's reception room. Dalden saw none of them until he saw Brittany and that she was all right. Jorran followed her. He looked harmless wearing local clothes, rather than his royal garb, but Dalden knew just how dangerous he could be, especially if he had a razor sword tucked into the pocket of his suit. Would he feel the need for a weapon here, or assume that the Altering Rod was all the weapon he needed?

At least a dozen people had come out, including the mayor. "How many are Jorran's people?" Dalden asked.

"Three of them," Martha replied. "The others with them are on the mayor's staff, though Probables say they've all been altered. *Your* main concern will be avoiding any rods pointed your way."

"I will have you to counter any suggestions that halt me, as Brock did for us on Sunder when we were told to forget my sister."

"That will work, but it requires time for the correcting speech to be said, time in which weapons can be used against you. *Avoid the damn rods!*"

"This might help," Corth II said as he sauntered up to join them. "The emergency essentials Martha called for, just in case the interference didn't get turned off. Not exactly needed now—except for the confidence gained in having the right equipment at hand."

The right equipment in this case was Dalden's own sword and his intricately carved arm shields. Martha was mumbling about creating spectacles, but Dalden had gone into ignore-Martha mode as he stripped off his shirt and strapped on the *Toreno* steel arm shields that wrapped about his forearms from elbow to wrist. They were his only protection, but then not much more was needed with a four-foot sword in hand. *Droda*, it felt good clasping his fingers around that hilt again.

"I owe you," Dalden told the android.

"Yes, you do, big-time." Corth II grinned at him. "Just keep that in mind the next time I flirt with your beautiful lifemate."

That got him a scowl, but Martha wasn't done, and suggested in reasonable tones, "You could at least make an effort to conceal that ridiculously long instrument of death until you get close enough to Jorran to use it."

"Martha is too cautious where her owner's children are concerned," Corth II pointed out, more as a reminder for Martha, since Dalden already knew it from firsthand experience. "She cannot be faulted for that. It is against her basic programming to allow anything to cause Tedra distress if she can prevent it. But now that the target has been located, there is no reason not to capture him with no holds barred. I'll keep others from interfering."

"No more stunning unless absolutely necessary," Martha warned Corth II.

He just grinned cheekily and replied, "I have the third confiscated rod."

"Then why didn't you use it on those broadcast people outside?"

"Because we needed a guaranteed time frame, which the stunning has given us. Rod suggestions could have been countered, the machines fixed that I disabled, the interference turned on again—"

"All right already, I get the *farden* point. Let's wrap this up, children."

Chapter 26

B RITTANY WAS NERVOUS AS ALL HELL, AND BEING AFRAID
that it was obvious only increased it. She'd worn a
pullover sweater today with her jeans, so she could
conceal the Altering Rod up her sleeve for easy access.
Since City Hall was air-conditioned, she'd figured
she'd be okay in the thick winter sweater and had been
comfortable—until she came face-to-face with Jorran.
She was sweating now.

How did she get herself into this mess? This was no
longer just helping a man she'd flipped over locate a
wacko foreign thief. That had seemed easy, something
anyone could have done, adventurous even. These
people were dangerous. She had little doubt that the
fat man's "dispose of" was of the permanent sort. This
was a play for power, serious power. With that kind of

stake involved, they wouldn't care who got hurt—or died—in the process.

And where the hell was Dalden? One of the news-people had told the mayor they were having camera trouble, that someone had pulled the plug on their connection, so it would be a few more minutes before they were ready for his speech. That speech was going to turn this town upside down if Dalden didn't do something before Sullivan had a chance to speak.

Or if she didn't.

What would be the chance of her using the rod she had up her sleeve on Jorran before one of his two bruiser bodyguards put her out of commission? She wouldn't have to say much, just tell him to call this off, well, maybe also mention that he didn't want to be mayor—or president, maybe even suggest that he should go home.

She was standing close enough to him to do it. He'd moved in front of her, was so close that the few extra inches he had on her was blocking a good portion of the room from her view. But then the rotund fellow named Alrid was standing just as close to her at her back . . .

God, should she take the chance, or wait and see if Dalden was in the crowd gathering behind the camera-people? She peered over Jorran's shoulder to get a better view of the room, hoping to spot the big guy, and caught her breath when she did. He was there and marching purposely toward the gathering in front of the mayor's offices. But half naked and with a sword in his hand? A *sword*, for crying out loud?

Jorran had seen him, too. Jorran was smiling, not at

all confused by what he was seeing the way she was. They knew each other. That was apparent. Perhaps Jorran hadn't noticed the sword yet.

He turned to tell his men, "A Sha-Ka'ani warrior among us, how interesting. Do not interfere. This is going to be my pleasure."

"Jorran, if there is one, there will be more." There was distinct worry in Alrid's voice, in his expression as well. "We should—"

"Enjoy the diversion," Jorran cut in. "They are men, subject to the rods just like any other, and will make excellent bodyguards for me after my empire is established. But this one's family thwarted my plans. This one dies. The rest that we find, we will tame."

Such confidence went beyond mere bravery, it was certain knowledge of having a *huge* advantage. Brittany couldn't see what that advantage might be. Jorran lacked the muscle, the height, the brawn to compete with someone of Dalden's immense stature physically in close combat, which the sword Dalden held seemed to suggest he had in mind to do. How, then, did Jorran think to win without a gun or other long-distance-type weapon that could stop him before he was within arms' reach? And he had no weapon of that sort . . .

He had something. It was taken from the pocket of his coat before he shrugged out of it and tossed it at Alrid. A tube of some sort, it looked like, no more than six inches in length, grasped in his right hand. But it wasn't pointed at Dalden, it was squeezed, which caused an extension to shoot out of it, a little more than three feet of shining metal that was so thin, it could barely be seen if viewed from the side.

"What the hell is that?"

She said it aloud. Alrid heard her and answered, "A razor sword, capable of slicing a man in half with little effort. The Sha-Ka'ani is about to find that out."

Brittany blanched, and was rendered nearly immobile by the accompanying weakness that spread through her limbs. Jorran had said it. Alrid had just confirmed it. The plan was to kill Dalden, not just stop him or use the rod on him.

It was so utterly bizarre, that scene in the middle of City Hall. A bare-chested giant in tight jeans and knee-high boots with what looked like an old-fashioned transistor radio hooked to his belt, a mammoth sword in hand. And what appeared to be no more than a simple businessman in tailored slacks, silk shirt, and tie, with something hooked to his belt as well, a round disk flat on the side facing him, the size of an orange—and a sword so thin it couldn't really be called a sword, was more like an exaggerated razor blade.

It was no wonder everyone there was staring open-mouthed, disbelieving. People just didn't come into City Hall carrying swords and looking like they intended to use them. But then she noticed that one man was ignoring the two facing off in the center of the room. Corth II was there, and working his way around the side toward Jorran's bodyguards.

She came to life herself then, figured the tall though lean fellow was going to need help with the two bruisers, and she was the least likely to raise their suspicions. She started with Alrid, whom she needed to get past to reach the other two, touched his arm and told him he couldn't move or speak. She did the same with one of the bodyguards, but wasn't quick enough to reach the other before Corth II did.

The bodyguard might look the stupid sort, but apparently he wasn't. He recognized the threat to himself immediately and used his own rod on Corth II. Brittany was close enough to hear Martha's son say, "Sorry, big guy, but those don't work on me," before he grasped the offending hand touching him and, with absolutely no effort, broke it.

She didn't stop to wonder why Corth II was immune to the rods when no other man seemed to be. She was in active mode herself, and went ahead and used her rod on the bodyguard, telling him the same thing she had the other two, though she added for him, "You feel no pain."

Corth II chuckled at that, and told her, "You're too soft, beautiful."

"No, I'm just having a nervous breakdown," she answered in an agitated tone, "since nothing going on here right now makes any sense."

Others were beginning to be of the same opinion. The immobilizing initial shock had worn off, and now gasps, shouts, a general sense of panic were going on—and the loud clash of metal. Brittany turned to see that Dalden and Jorran had engaged in combat, and the audience, not having believed it could possibly have come to that, was reacting normally, some backing away intent on getting the hell out of there, some calling for the police, the newspeople avidly watching, those with cameras shooting the fight.

The people trying to leave the building were in for yet another surprise, no less equal to Brittany's, though, when she noticed the exits to the building were presently blocked. The several men standing there keeping anyone from entering or leaving were just as tall as Dalden, just as brawny, just as bare-chested, golden-skinned, golden-haired—actually, identical to Dalden except for their facial features, and with sword belts strapped to their hips.

It was the identical part that gave her a clue. She didn't know how they'd done it, but it had to be an illusion, those extra bodies, to make Jorran and his people think the odds had just been upped in favor of the Sha-Ka'anis.

She did what she could to alleviate some of the panic, working her way quickly through the crowd, repeating over and over, "It's a local theater troupe, enjoy the performance, nothing to be alarmed about."

The spectators could now discount any blood they saw as fake. She wished she could as well. She had been deliberately avoiding looking out in the center of the room herself. She still heard the clash of metal on metal, knew they were still at it, but couldn't bear to watch.

She stopped by Corth to demand, "Why don't you help him disarm Jorran and get it over with?"

"He would dismantle me if I presumed to interfere in his personal fight," Corth II replied. "Warriors are touchy about such things."

"Dismantle?" she growled. "I'll dismantle you myself if he gets hurt."

A smile. "As long as there is life, he can be fully repaired."

What an odd way to say doctors could patch you up, if the wounds weren't mortal. His lack of worry should have reassured her. It didn't. And she finally looked toward the center of the room—and wished she hadn't. It was impossible to turn her eyes away now.

Blood *was* splattered on the white floor, though not too much of it, and apparently just Jorran's so far. There was a minor gash on his upper left arm that had cut the silk sleeve and left a red path in the material to his elbow. But most of the blood was coming from his nose and a cut on his cheek, which indicated that the flat of Dalden's sword might have smashed against his face.

Neither injury stopped the whirlwind motion of Jorran's other arm, which held his weapon. It was non-stop, his efforts to slice into Dalden, and with such speed, it was fairly obvious the razor sword weighed next to nothing. But he was having no success yet, because Dalden's arm shields, rather than his own sword, were constantly there to meet the razor blade and slide it off harmlessly to the side.

Dalden was also using his own weapon, just not as one might expect. When Jorran extended his reach too far in his impatience to inflict damage, Dalden grasped Jorran's right wrist to prevent another swing and slammed his own sword against a vulnerable spot, but with the flat of his blade, not the edge. He could have disarmed him. He could have killed him. He cracked ribs and broke noses instead.

"He's just playing with him," Brittany said aloud, some annoyance now mixed in with her worry.

"Yes," Corth II agreed.

"But Jorran isn't."

"No, indeed."

"Then why take the chance that Jorran will get lucky?" she demanded.

"Because he's a warrior."

"So instead of getting the job done by the easiest

and quickest means possible, he's got to do the macho thing instead? That's positively medieval."

"Actually, barbaric would better describe it" was Corth II's reply.

It was said with that cheeky grin of his, as if it were some kind of inside joke she should have grasped. She didn't, and it made Brittany want to hit him, a barbaric impulse of her own. Was she the only one who could see the difference, that macho grandstanding was misplaced when life hung in the balance?

Chapter 27

THEY CAUTIOUSLY CIRCLED EACH OTHER FOR A FEW MO-
ments. Dalden allowed the break, which was what
it was. Jorran was breathing heavily. Sweat beaded his
brow, soaked the silk shirt under his armpits, down
the center of his back and chest. It was hard work, trying to slice someone to bits. Dalden's exertion so far
had been minimal in comparison.

"Surrender is an option you may want to consider,"
Dalden remarked casually.

"Are you offering to do so?" Jorran replied.

"I am not the one losing."

"Nor am I."

"Are you not? Warriors learn from witnessing mistakes. Having seen the effectiveness of your razor
sword, Falon and I both have trained to deflect it."

"Practice does not equate to a razor intent on your life," Jorran smirked.

"True. But nor does your own experience prepare you for a Sha-Ka'ani warrior intent on yours."

Jorran wasn't expecting an aggressive move, when Dalden had shown him only defense thus far. Nor were his reflexes quick enough to avoid being lifted and tossed a dozen feet across the room.

Dalden added when he came to stand over Jorran, "Your fight with Falon was not to the death, from his perspective. Have you realized yet, there is a difference?"

This fight wasn't going to be to the death either, if Dalden could help it, but Jorran didn't need to know that—yet. And he was furious now. The toss had rattled him. It was not something one did to High Kings, tossing them about like so much refuse. The resulting anger was yet another point in Dalden's favor.

Jorran rolled away from him, went immediately on the offensive again. It was nearly a blur, the movement of that razor sword now.

It was finally an effort to keep up with the raging razor. Good. The fight had been too easy up till then. And he didn't want Falon, who was sure to be furious that it was not he facing Jorran here, to feel less able, because his previous fight with Jorran had not been as easy. Of course, Jorran's advantage then was that Falon had tried to use his heavy sword, while Jorran's weighed next to nothing. They knew now how to defeat a razor sword.

The anger was Jorran's downfall. The furious burst of energy it had produced brought him quickly to exhaustion. And the moment his swings slowed down, Dalden made his move to end it.

Instead of just deflecting the next swing, he thrust it away from him, throwing Jorran off balance. In quick succession, he then smashed Jorran's kneecap with the flat of his own sword, further unbalancing him, and while Jorran was absorbing the shock of that, Dalden disabled him completely by twisting his right arm behind his back until it broke.

It was overkill. At almost anytime during the fight, he could have snatched the contamination shield and let Martha take over. There would have been no punishment in that, though, merely defeat. Jorran deserved more than that. Dalden now ripped the shield from Jorran's belt and tossed it to Corth II, who smashed the metal in his hands as if it were a wad of paper. Only then did he let Jorran drop at his feet.

"He is yours, Martha."

"N—!" Jorran began to shout, but was gone before he could finish.

"And no meditech for him," Dalden instructed, ignoring the collective gasp that went up in the crowd when Jorran disappeared before their eyes.

"Wasn't planning on it," Martha agreed. "The slap on the wrist he'll get when we take him home isn't nearly enough for what he's done."

"Your silence was appreciated," Dalden felt the need to add, after spending several days with Martha's constant input, wanted or not.

"I know when not to distract, warrior," Martha said in unmistakably smirking tones. "And now you need to gather up all remaining evidence of our presence here, before we depart for our sector of the universe."

"What of the mayor? Is he still under Jorran's control?" Dalden asked.

"He was moved safely back into his office soon after the fight began, but Corth II got to him first with the forget-Jorran suggestions, as well as a few others. Amusing that some of the people present actually thought their mayor was pulling a publicity stunt, since they'd been rod-told that Jorran was the mayor already. Corth II will do a little more clean-up in that regard later today, while we're collecting the rest of the rods from Jorran's people."

"What other evidence, then, do you speak of?"

"Unfortunately, your entire fight was recorded by the news crews. We can't leave these people anything that's beyond their own technology to understand. Those here will discount what they've seen as illusion, like a disappearing act in a magic show, but any experts who could study those tapes would know better. So get rid of the tapes before I take you out of there. There are two of them, from the two shoulder-held cameras. The big television camera you don't need to worry about, it's still inoperative."

Dalden glanced toward the newspeople, but first saw Brittany, standing behind them. She was staring at him as if he weren't real.

"Is my lifemate all right?" Dalden asked Martha, his concern rising.

"She's fine, just a bit amazed over the violence she just watched you dish out. She'll get over it."

"Take her to the ship now, in case I need to get violent again in the recovery of evidence."

"I *really* don't think you're going to have any more trouble, kiddo. These locals are pretty much in awe of you at the moment. But you're right, the rest of Jorran's crew is going to disappear in seconds, and with her standing among them, she won't be able to help but notice. Better just one nervous breakdown than a bunch of little ones."

"You *will* explain and calm her, yes?"

"Sure I will. Don't give it another thought. She'll be waiting for you in your quarters."

Martha's glib reply, for some reason, was not very reassuring. But the sooner he finished here, the sooner he could see to Brittany himself.

He watched her Transfer, along with Jorran's remaining people. Corth II and the half-dozen warriors at the exits remained, in case they were still needed. He then turned toward the newspeople.

Their cameras were still pointed at him. They tried to back up as he approached them, but there wasn't much room for that. And they were still recording, even when he stopped in front of them.

One of them, though obviously nervous, said, "Man, that's about the best special effects I've ever seen. Want to clean up some?"

A cloth was tossed at him. He looked down at his torso to find what might need cleaning up. He hadn't felt the cut that ran from his upper left side across his abdomen to his right hip until he saw it now. He patted the cloth along the line. It did no good. More blood immediately oozed out to flow down and soak into his jeans.

The cameraman, however, had expected the line and blood to be gone, was staring wide-eyed at the new flow. "That's—real, isn't it?"

Dalden looked back at him, and said only, "I require

the evidence you have recorded. If it can be removed from your camera and given to me, then I will not need to destroy the camera."

"Ah, sure, whatever you want, guy. No problem."

The man couldn't get the film out of his camera and into Dalden's hands fast enough. The other camera holder was still backing away, though not in nervousness. He was apparently looking for an exit. He had no intention of giving up his evidence.

Corth II became a solid, immovable wall at his back. "The big guy requires your film, bud. His option was to not destroy your camera to get it. My option is to not destroy you to get it. Which of us do you wish to deal with?"

"Okay, okay," the man tried, stalling until he could turn around to take a swing at Corth II. Big mistake, that. He ended up with broken knuckles that hadn't budged the face they struck, and wailed, "What the hell is that, a steel plate in your jaw?"

"*Toreno* steel to be exact, and not just the jaw, but the whole body. Welcome to your worst nightmare, friend," Corth II said as he prepared to flatten the guy.

"Enough with the showing off, children." Martha's voice rang out loudly with distinct displeasure. "Must I do *everything* myself?"

Not surprisingly, the heavy video camera disappeared from the man's hand, Corth II disappeared next, then Dalden and the remaining warriors followed. Martha was, after all, capable of doing almost everything herself.

A shocked silence remained in City Hall. It was finally broken by a chuckle from the fellow who still possessed his own camera, minus any film. "I'd sure like to be there when you try to explain what just happened," he told his friend. "And why you shouldn't have to replace that camera yourself."

"I'm not the only one who saw things poof around here," the other man snarled.

"What you saw was one hell of a performance that you shouldn't have gotten involved in. But if you're lucky, those magic people will return your . . ." There was a pause due to the camera reappearing on the floor between them. "Wanna bet the film's not in it?"

Chapter 28

H E FOUND BRITTANY WRAPPED IN A TIGHT LITTLE BALL
on the floor of his quarters aboard the *Androvia*,
her back against the padded wall, her face tucked
against her raised knees, her long copper hair spread
like a cape around her. She didn't look up when the
door slid open and then closed behind him. She was
rocking slightly, and making sounds of angst.

Dalden felt a constriction in his chest. Her pain was
not physical, it was mental, and he wasn't sure how he
could help that.

Martha had warned him that the shock from the
Transfer had put Brittany into a refusing-to-believe-
anything mode. Most people had warning beforehand,
knew what Molecular Transfer was, knew it was going
to happen prior to it happening. And even if they
didn't know it was going to happen, at least they could

guess what had happened to them if they suddenly ended up in a place other than where they had been. That required knowledge of Transfer, which most of the known universe had, all except undiscovered planets like hers.

"Brittany."

She looked up instantly, her dark green eyes wide, full of fear and confusion. But then she shot to her feet, flew at him, clung to his chest. And in a small voice that steadily grew louder, said, "I was beginning to think you weren't real, that I'd dreamed you, too. You are real, aren't you? Tell me you're real!"

"Very real, *kerima*."

"You aren't going to disappear on me again?" she demanded sharply.

"You will never be far from me, not ever. I would not allow it."

She relaxed somewhat, leaned back to stare into his eyes, as if she might find all her answers there. She found none, but she did seem to find the reassurance she'd been in need of. She stepped away from him, agitation now taking the place of her fear, though the confusion was still rampant.

"You've got some explaining to do."

"I know," he agreed.

"You can start by telling me how I got here, and where *here* is."

"Martha has already told you—"

"Don't even think of feeding me that same line of bullshit that she did! It's all been a dream, and I've just woken up from it, right? I can buy that. But how did I get here to begin with, and when? Last night? So everything that happened in City Hall today didn't really happen, you didn't fight Jorran with swords, didn't get wounded—no, of course you didn't. There's no cut on your chest."

She was staring at his chest triumphantly, thinking she'd just managed to confirm everything she'd just said. "The cut was there, but is now gone," he was forced to tell her. "Such is the amazing ability of a meditech, which I was Transferred into upon arrival here."

"Dalden, are you okay—mentally? You don't really believe that nonsense, do you?"

He smiled at her concern for him. "You were told that all would be revealed to you after our task was completed. The time for answers is now."

"Then start telling me the truth, because this science fiction crap just doesn't wash. And you can start with where we are."

"In my quarters aboard the *Androvia*."

"Aboard as in—on a ship? Quarters without a bed or bathroom? Sure."

In this case, it was much easier to show her than convince her. He took her hand, pulled her over to the Sanitary wall, and pressed a button there. Walls immediately enclosed them in a small area, a toilet and sink slid out, the circular shower rose up from the floor to fill the corner, and a ledge dropped down with other amenities, including access to the dial-up closet. He took a moment to dial a light blue tunic. It was delivered in less time than it took to don it.

While she was staring incredulously at everything that had been revealed, he pressed the button to send it all back into concealment and dragged her over to the other corner of the room. Pressing the button there slid out new walls, and a section of the floor flipped over, leaving a narrow bed in its place that would adjust in size once someone laid down on it.

These, too, he sent back before he said, "I feel confined here, which is why I do not leave these things out, but send them away until they are needed. I am told it is designed to make these rooms seem bigger than they are."

"I get it," she said, finally looking at him again. "This is a movie studio, right? Props, make-believe stuff that isn't really real."

He sighed. He had known this would not be easy, but he hadn't thought it would be impossible.

"You search for any answer but the truth," he told her.

"Show me *proof*!" She was getting agitated again. "If this isn't a studio made to look like a ship, show me what's outside of it."

"This room has no windows."

"Correction." Martha's voice came through on the audiovisual ship's intercom on the wall, proving she was in standby assistance mode. "Knowing how much you hate being reminded of what you're traveling in, Dalden, the windows were never revealed to you."

The walls began to move again, in Martha's control this time, opening up a long bank of windows made of something other than glass that revealed nothing but water and a lone fish swimming past.

"A submarine?" Brittany said in surprise, but then she frowned and added skeptically, "Or a large tank of water. You call this proof?"

Dalden growled in exasperation. Martha chuckled. "Give it up, kiddo. She doesn't require proof. She already knows what she's dealing with, she just refuses to accept it, and no amount of words will change that."

"Because aliens are a myth, perpetrated by the UFO craze!" Brittany shouted for Martha's benefit, but then she rounded on Dalden and slapped her palm against his chest. "Look at you, you're flesh and blood, you've got all the right parts in the right numbers, even if you are a bit big. There's nothing alien about you!"

"It pleases me to hear you say so," he replied. "This name you have for off-worlders is only slightly more tolerable than what I am usually called."

"He's referring to the name *barbarian*," Martha supplied. "It's how the rest of the civilized universe views his world, not because of the way his people look, dress, or even that they still fight with swords. It's their overall outlook, their primitive laws, their stubborn adherence to tradition that's outlived its time."

"You are *not* helping, Martha," Dalden said.

"Just telling it like it is, warrior. Why go through this stonewall disbelief twice? Besides, her idea of an alien is something bizarre-looking that isn't humanoid—another reason why she's having trouble grasping reality here. If you looked like the Morrilians with their oversized heads that accommodate their magnificent brains, she'd have no problem pointing at you and saying you're an alien."

Brittany wasn't listening. She was gripping the hair on both sides of her temples and saying to herself, "There has to be a logical explanation for this. There has to be."

Dalden moved to put his arms around her. "*Kerima*, your distress pains me. What must I do to ease it?"

She leaned into him, trying to accept the comfort he

offered. "Just tell me there's a really good reason for lying to me."

"Talk about a double-edged request," Martha said in one of her more distinct you've-annoyed-me tones.

Brittany swung around, searching for Martha's voice, since Dalden was no longer wearing his communicator. "The audiovisual monitor on the wall," he pointed out with a sigh. "She controls the ship, thus she has eyes and ears in every room."

Brittany marched to the monitor on the wall, which was presently blank. "Show yourself to me. I want to see the woman who has the gall to try to convince me I'm on an alien spaceship."

"I'll do better than that," Martha purred.

Dalden stiffened, but before he could warn Martha off, Brittany was Transferred out of the room. He swore, knowing where she'd been taken, and that he couldn't get there in time to prevent Brittany from further shock.

Chapter 29

BRITTANY *WAS* IN SHOCK. IT HAD HAPPENED AGAIN, THAT moment of tingling, then waking in a completely new location. Waking? No, she was standing up. Even if they'd been able to put her to sleep somehow to move her somewhere else, she wouldn't wake up on her feet.

It had to be illusions, or perhaps rotating walls. She'd seen enough moving walls since she got here to know they had that process down pat and in high speed, so she could be in the same room, just with new walls and—and a really big computer console in the center.

"This is the command center." Martha's voice seemed to come at her from all sides. "If I weren't here, this room would be filled with the specialists needed to run a ship this size, all made obsolete with a Mock II on board. I'm the Mock II, by the way."

"What is a Mock II?" Brittany demanded. "And where are you hiding this time?"

"I'm currently housed in the console you're looking at. That's right, doll, I'm a computer, one of the most highly advanced computers ever created. Dalden let that slip the other day, but fortunately you decided he was just pulling your leg. Not an unrealistic conclusion on your part, since the computers you have on your planet are prehistoric dinosaurs compared to me, and those are all you've had for comparison—until now."

"More bullshit?"

"Your disbelief is wearing thin, child," Martha said with a sigh. "I'm going to make this brief before Dalden barges in here to retrieve you. He's not too pleased with me at the moment. You're causing yourself, and him, a lot of grief over nothing. He did good today. He should be celebrating his victory instead of having to deal with a hysterical woman who can't get past one simple little fact."

"A simple fact!?"

"Why don't you try using the logic you were crying for a few minutes ago? It's rather egotistical of your people to think that your insignificant planet, tucked away in this sector of the universe, is the only planet that supports life. Look at it this way: your solar system has moved into a well-established neighborhood, sorta like the new kid on the block. But there were other systems on the block first so much older than yours that the species in them were exploring far into space while you still had dinosaurs roaming."

"You don't get it. I'd have to be dreaming for this to

be real, but I'm not dreaming. I know I'm not, because I pinched myself and it damn well hurt. So stop trying to mess with my mind."

"We'd have to be pretty cold-blooded to try to pull what you're accusing us of trying to pull. Is that really how you see Dalden?"

Of course she didn't, which was why none of this made sense. There had to be a reason for these lies, but she couldn't hope to guess what it was and was driving herself crazy trying to find a plausible explanation.

"Just take me home already," she said wearily. "My job is done. You've captured your thief. You don't need me anymore. I want to go home."

"It's too late for that. It became too late when Dalden made you his lifemate."

"What the hell does that *mean*?"

"You were already told what it means. You chose to see that as a joke, too. It wasn't. And you're still not taking it seriously yet, but for him, it's about as serious as you can get. You're now his to protect, his to have and to hold, for life. There's no getting out of it, like you people do around here. There's no breaking it. It's a done deal, and it's permanent. So you go where he goes, doll, no ifs, ands, or buts. And where he's going is home to Sha-Ka'an, a planet in the Niva star system, light-years away from here."

"You just slipped up," Brittany said, pouncing on it, and pointing out triumphantly. "Light-years would take more than one lifetime to travel."

In response, chuckling filled the room. "With anything your planet can currently produce, yes, but the rest of the universe runs on different sources of power. This spaceship is powered by gaali stones, the newest and most impressive known source, so it will only take us a couple of months to get home. But even crysillium, the last, now obsolete power source, was capable of similar speed, as well as the one before that. Your planet hasn't come close to knowing what real power is yet."

"You have an answer for everything, don't you?" Brittany said bitterly.

"'Course I do, I'm a Mock II. We don't stagnate, we grow with age."

"You mean upgrade," Brittany corrected.

"No, my parts can't be replaced, but nor will they ever need to be," Martha recorrected and made a brief attempt at explaining. "Imagine a simulated brain, superpowerful at birth, yet like any brain, capable of maturing. Yes, that means I'm capable of thoughts and decisions just like you, even though I am man-made."

"That's not possible."

"Doll, anything is possible for the Morrilians who created me. They are a *very* old species whose intelligence can be likened to godlike, if you need a comparison. I'm talking genius beyond anything you can imagine, beyond anything most worlds can imagine, even high-tech worlds far more advanced than yours. Ironically, they are a very simple people with few needs other than intellectual, and very nonaggressive, which is fortunate for the rest of the universe. That nonaggression is made part of all Mock IIs before they are sold."

"Sold? You're actually owned by someone?"

"It might help if you stop thinking of me as a person. While that's great for my ego, it's not very factual.

Mock IIs are designed to be compatible with one and only one owner, so all programming is geared to that one individual, and his or her happiness and well-being are our number-one priority.

"My individual is Tedra, Dalden's mother," Martha added. "And her happiness includes her family's, which is why I was sent along on this retrieval trip, not just to recover the Altering Rods but to make sure her son returns home in one piece. Remember her son, the Sha-Ka'ani who has decided that you're the only woman he wants to spend the rest of his life with? Do you *really* think that he would intentionally hurt you by messing with your mind?"

"I'm trying not to think. Thinking right now is going to lead to a nervous breakdown."

"I wouldn't allow that."

"You wouldn't be able to prevent it."

"Sure I would. Or have you forgotten the option I was going to use if Dalden had just had his fun with you and left you behind? You can be made to forget us and everything we've revealed to you. Is that what you want? To never see Dalden again, to have him leave you behind?"

"And the alternative is? To be taken off into deep space? To never return here, never see my family again? That *is* what the bottom line is here, right?"

Martha made a *tsk*ing sound. "One thing that hasn't been mentioned yet is that in the universal scope of things, Dalden's family is about as rich as rich can ever get, for the simple reason that they own the largest gaali stone mine in existence—power that the entire universe is in need of and is willing to pay just about anything for. So with the right inducement, I'm sure you could convince your lifemate to bring you back occasionally to visit your family."

"I didn't get asked if I want to be his lifemate," Brittany said in a small, resentful voice.

"Warriors never ask. On Sha-Ka'an, it's a male decision that females have no say in. But just out of curiosity, what would your answer have been if you were asked?"

"Before all the rest of this was revealed to me, or right now?"

"Never mind. I'll ask that question again someday, but right now, you'll just say something emotional that has no bearing on your real feelings. Humans tend to do that a lot. Silly of them, and half the time those wrong answers cause even more hurt feelings, all of which could have been avoided with a little honesty up front."

"You have *no* idea what I'm feeling. You couldn't even begin to—"

"Now there's where you're wrong," Martha interrupted in a purring I'm-ready-to-impress-you tone. "You're not used to a computer of my caliber yet, but you'll find that it's pointless to argue or disagree with me, simply because my forte is probabilities. So even if I don't have all available facts to work with, I can still come up with the answers. Let's take yourself for an example."

"Let's not—"

"Too late. I'm proving a point, and I'm a bit hardnosed when points need to be proven. You flipped over the warrior when you first saw him. There was no getting around it, you were hooked. Even thinking him 'foreign,' which was probably at the bottom of your list for acceptable mates, couldn't detract from the kind of attraction you were in the grips of. You threw up all the standard roadblocks your people favor for stalling the inevitable, but it took no more than a couple of intoxicants for you to break down all barriers and jump in with both feet to a full commitment. And you *did* commit yourself, by the way, which was all the 'yes' he needed to make his own decision to bind you to him for life."

"I'm not *agreeing* with you," Brittany said stiffly and with deliberate emphasis. "But what has any of that to do with now, with this ship, with your ridiculous assertion that you're aliens from outer space?"

"It's off-worlders, doll. That's what we're called. We're no different from your own people from Asia or India. You wouldn't understand their language until you learned it. You wouldn't take to their culture because it's not yours and you naturally prefer your own. But you can visit them and get along with them and might even like their countries and peoples well enough that you want to stay. The only difference between them and us is, instead of hopping over an ocean for a visit, it takes a spaceship for us to do so and vice versa. Besides, it's not that you don't believe any of this, it's that you don't want it to be true. And it's time for the final proof, so you can get around to relaxing and seeing this as an adventure rather than your worst nightmare."

"You want to rip my life to shreds and I'm supposed to find it adventurous?" Brittany snorted.

"You're going to be the first from your world to travel into deep space. You're going to see things that

will astound you. You should be excited by the
prospect, not crying that you want it to all go away.
The facts I have assimilated from your planet show
your species to be much more bold than what you're
showing me."

It was said in a derogatory tone. If the intention had
been to insult, it worked wonders. "What final proof?"
she bit out.

"You might want to have a seat," Martha said, and
one of the chairs in the room that were bound to the
floor turned in Brittany's direction. "And keep an eye
on that wall of observation screens that I'm going to
turn on with brief explanations for each. Biggest and
center is our frontal view. I've been raising us from the
ocean floor while we spoke. No point in hanging
around down there anymore when we have business
to complete on the other side of your moon. We'll be
on the surface in a moment, and then high-speeded
out of visual range of the planet's surface, so *sit*."

Brittany bolted toward the indicated chair and
dropped into it, gripped the arms for dear life.
"There's no seat belt!" she pointed out in a panic.

"What am I, an amateur?" Martha's tone turned aggrieved. "There isn't a pilot born who has a hope of
flying these things better than I. Don't worry about the
speed, doll, I adjust gravity within to accommodate for
it. You'll only feel a slight pull and shift in weight."

The screen had turned on to reveal mostly a torrent
of small bubbles in the water outside. Martha's voice
was heard vaguely echoing distantly in other parts of
the ship, warning anyone else on it that flight was imminent. Another screen lit up, but with a large dark
mass in it that looked like a misshapen rock.

"This ship is capable of disguise, and that's our current one. Nice rendition of a meteor, eh? I believe we even made some of your local newspapers when we arrived."

Brittany's eyes rounded on the computer as she recalled Jan telling her about the meteor that disintegrated just before it would have caused widespread disaster. "There were other UFO sightings last week. You didn't hide yourself in the ocean immediately?"

"That wasn't us. That was Jorran's captain being stupid. Watch the screens, I'm switching to a cloud disguise for the takeoff. Less conspicuous, since rocks are known to drop out of space to the surface of the planet, but not the reverse. And you'll be able to see through it, while anyone else will merely see a dense cloud—for a millisecond, just long enough for them to discount it."

The middle, larger screen revealed the break to the surface of the water, while the smaller screen showed a cloud hovering over the ocean. Another screen came on, showing a bottom view, and the ocean quickly became an entire view of the planet from the sky that steadily shrunk in size as it was surrounded by black space. The main screen now showed the moon steadily growing larger.

Brittany was beyond speech at that point. Had she just been taken off the planet with no hope of being returned to it? Or were these screens she was viewing mere computer-simulated special effects, made to look real?

Chapter 30

"DON'T BACKTRACK ON ME, GIRL," MARTHA SAID IN A sharply annoyed tone, somehow reading Brittany's mind just from her expression. "I've delayed Dalden getting here with the takeoff. He hates takeoffs, hates spaceships, hates space travel, and will be glued to a chair right now just as tightly as you are. His planet is not high-tech, if you haven't gathered that by now, but since they've been discovered, they've been forced to deal with the rest of the universe, which wants one of their resources. Now, you were accepting everything you've been told for a moment. Don't revert back to thinking we're trying to pull one over on you."

"I've seen space movies, Martha, *and* seen how they do the special effects to make them look real."

"And I thought Tedra wrote the book on being stubborn," Martha mumbled, then, in a more perky voice, asked, "How would you like to walk on the moon?"

"Are you out of your mind?"

A chuckle. "There you go mistaking me for a person again. The more apt comment would be 'out of your motherboard.'" Another chuckle. "No, it won't take but a moment to land—there, we've landed. And we just happen to have an emergency exit here in the Control Room that I'm opening—"

"Wait! Don't do that! Don't I need a spacesuit? The atmosphere isn't breathable—"

"Not to worry, kiddo. This battleship is capable of landing on any planet, no matter what it's made of, and creating its own air. I've released a domed shield around the ship and filled it with a breathable substance. Go ahead, the platform extending out from the door works like an elevator to lower you to the surface, currently in single-person length. It can be further extended to accommodate up to thirty people comfortably. The enclosing handrails will retract as soon as it touches ground, so you can get off."

Brittany stepped to the doorway. She didn't step on the short platform. Some twenty or thirty feet below was the surface—of the moon. She began to laugh, and only half hysterically. The moon, and she was within mere feet of it. A few rocky bumps, a few dents, but otherwise a flat gray surface lit almost white by the overhead lights on the dome. Beyond was infinite black space—the sun didn't reach this side of the moon. But inside, the dome was well-lit. It was a large dome, mammoth. It encompassed a really big ship.

"You're not going outside?"

"No, I'd rather our astronauts hold that distinction. They went through hell to get up here, while you make it seem like mere child's play."

"Sweetie, you're comparing apples and oranges. This battleship, which makes this seem like child's play to you, was designed by a people that have been in existence for more than twelve million years. How many years have your people been evolving? Look at your own age of inventions. In just a few hundred years, just about all the known improvements of your world came into being: electricity, flight, mass communication, convenient travel, and so forth. Look at your history and what you had available prior to these inventions. And imagine what you will create a thousand years from now. Your people are progressing normally; they are just still young compared to some of the worlds in other solar systems. If it's any consolation, there are other worlds out there younger than yours that haven't advanced nearly as far as yours has."

Brittany glanced back at the console. "Really?"

"Most definitely. Take Jorran's planet, Century III, for instance. Medieval in government, advancement, and mentality. They've been discovered, could buy modernization, but prefer their feudal way of life and a government that favors only a select few, the ruling house. And until those High Kings get toppled in revolution, nothing will change there. Another thousand years could pass and they'd still be medieval.

"Jorran is one of those High Kings of Century III, but the only one without his own kingdom," Martha continued. "It was his intention, with the rods he stole from the planet Sunder, to make your country his kingdom first, then your entire world. He might have succeeded. The Sunderans haven't reached the space age yet, either, so they couldn't track Jorran down to retrieve their rods. We just happened to be passing by on our way home and picked up their distress call— and knew Jorran for the jerk he is, so we decided to put *canceled* to his plans. Our good deed for the century, you could call it."

"So you didn't have to come after him?"

"No, indeed. But by the time the proper authorities could have been notified to pursue him, he would have been long gone. And even if they could have found him eventually, the damage would have been done. We already had him on tracking, were able to follow him, were the only ones who had a chance of stopping him before he ruined too many lives."

"And Sha-Ka'an?" Brittany said. "How does it fit in the age of development?"

"Sha-Ka'an is unique. It's not really barbaric, that's just a convenient name the modern worlds give it. It's perfected some crafts beyond manufactured quality without the pollution of factories, has an ancient formula for making the strongest steel ever created that even a laser can't penetrate, has palatial-like architecture in some of its cities, regulates birth control as well as sexual aggression, treats gold like you would common metals—"

"How can they regulate sexual aggression?"

Martha chuckled. "With another thing unique to their planet, the *dhaya* plant. The juice made from it will put even the strongest sex drive on temporary hold, and no amount of stimulation can break through its effect until it wears off naturally. In wine form it will prevent pregnancy."

Brittany frowned. "Why would they want to do away with sexual aggression?"

"Hold up, you've gotten the wrong impression. *Dhaya* juice is only taken in certain situations, when the warriors go off to hunt alone—and when they raid."

Brittany made a face. "Are we getting to the part that gives them their 'barbarian' label?"

"You betcha—at least, part of it. There's a difference, though, from what you're thinking. You hear the word *raid* and associate it with killing, pillage, mayhem. That's not what Sha-Ka'ani warriors are about. They don't go to war with each other. There are a lot of countries, each with their own leaders, but all in all, they consider themselves one. Raiding for them is sport, something fun to do. They'll go in, take something from their neighbor, try to keep it, but if the neighbor raids and retrieves it, they'll shrug and say well done."

"So it's just a game to them?"

"That's one way to put it. As for the other reasons for the label they wear, I've already mentioned it's a cultural thing, the way they view things and view themselves, the antiquated laws they uphold. These things differ slightly per country, yet one thing is universal on the planet. Warriors treat each other as equals, but treat their women like children."

"Excuse me?"

"You have enough to assimilate for now without getting into the things that still drive my Tedra nuts.

And Dalden will be here in about five seconds. He'll be glad to know you no longer think you're dreaming."

"Like children?" Brittany persisted. "You were joking, right?"

No answer, and the main door to the Control Room slid open to reveal seven feet of very annoyed male.

Chapter 31

DALDEN WAS REALLY ANGRY, THOUGH BRITTANY WAS A bit surprised that she could actually tell that, since it wasn't revealed in his expression. It was more that she sensed it, or maybe just that she was expecting it, after Martha had warned that he was annoyed.

He walked into the room, took her hand, and started walking out, dragging her with him. He didn't pause as he told the computer, "You have interfered with a warrior and his lifemate. You know that is unacceptable, Martha."

"Beneficial interference is acceptable," Martha disagreed. "Besides, since when do I ask permission when something needs doing? It's not as if there's a way to stop me, or that anyone using *common sense* would want to, when my actions calculate all Probables beforehand."

"Is there not?"

"Not what?"

"A way to stop you."

"Tedra would never agree to pull my plug," Martha replied in smirking tones.

"My mother is still answerable to my father. Would he hesitate?"

"Now just a minute . . . Dalden, come back here!"

He didn't, nor was it necessary for him to even stop, since Martha's voice followed them down a wide corridor and into an elevatorlike cubicle whose door closed, then immediately opened again to reveal a different corridor, this one with a slight curve to it. There had been no movement of the cubicle; at least, Brittany had felt no movement of the thing, yet it had apparently transported them elsewhere on the ship . . . oh, God, she really was starting to believe—everything.

"It's a good thing, actually, that it's going to take us nearly three months to get home." Martha's voice continued to follow them from each wall monitor they passed, every twelve feet or so along the corridor. "Plenty of time for you to settle into your commitment and possibly even get over some of the anticipated hurdles."

Mentioning expected problems didn't work to stir Dalden's curiosity, though it sure did Brittany's. He said merely, "Warriors have long memories."

"More's the pity," Martha mumbled, and then said, "It worked, by the way, which is the bottom line, if you haven't figured that out yet. *You* certainly weren't getting anywhere in the convincing department. And what's more important: that she accept what you are and where you come from, or that she continue to think you were lying to her, which was going to put a big dent in the recent bonding you did?"

He stopped at that point to look down at Brittany, wanting confirmation. "Do you?"

She knew what he was asking her, and although she would have liked to relieve his mind, since he did seem to be worried about whether she believed them or not, she had to consider her own peace of mind first. And there *were* other explanations, albeit elaborate, incredibly expensive ones, yet ones much more palatable than that she was traveling into deep space. When she thought of what it must have cost to create a studio big enough to give her the impression that she was looking out at the surface of the moon when she'd looked through that door . . . it simply boggled the mind, the effort these people were going to in order to fool her.

Or maybe it wasn't just her; maybe there were other people being put through the same program. She'd hate to think all this trouble was being wasted on just one person, such subtle details, a new view behind every door, out every window. Was she a test subject? Had Dalden blown it by getting involved with her when he shouldn't have? Martha had certainly made enough complaints about that involvement, and enough predictions that it just wouldn't work, to stop it before it got started. But Dalden got involved anyway. . . .

"No," Brittany said, causing Martha to make a snorting sound of disgust, and Dalden to frown in confusion. She added tonelessly, "That's not to say I don't think that the reason for this elaborate deception isn't for my own good, which is why I'm going to accept it for now and trust that at least your emotions are real—"

"What emotions?" Martha cut in. "Don't tell me you haven't noticed yet that he doesn't have any."

"Excuse me? Everyone has emotions. You told me yourself that he was annoyed."

"Actually, that was an understatement on my part. He was furious, still is, but you'll never see a Sha-Ka'ani warrior stomping around mad to prove it. A Ba-Har-ani warrior, maybe. The ones from his country pride themselves on absolute calm under any circumstances, which means they've done away with the more common emotions that might interfere with that calm."

"Sure, if you say so," Brittany replied.

That got a chuckle out of Martha, but Dalden was more concerned with her "no." "I fail to understand. How can you not believe, yet be accepting?"

"It's called humoring, Dalden," Martha put in. "In other words, while she's not going to give any credit to what she sees or hears, she's going to smile and go along with it all. She's decided it doesn't matter. Actually, she *does* know better; she'd just prefer to decide it doesn't matter."

It was absolutely uncanny, the way Martha could analyze and dissect someone's thoughts and motives from just a few spoken words, like a psychiatrist guessing right the first time around. Brittany had to keep in mind that these people had probably done this before, knew just what to expect, and so had answers for everything already prepared. But given enough thought, she could come up with answers for everything as well, from a different, more believable slant.

She just couldn't come up with a good reason why she was being put through this program. Some not so good reasons, yes, but not a really good one. If she were a scientist or someone in a position of power, then yes, it might be for national security reasons or something similar, to see if she could be tricked into revealing secrets or joining their cause or whatever. But she was just an average person, so why would they need to mess with *her* mind? What, after all, could she do for them or tell them, if they did manage to get her to believe what they were trying to?

"You do not dispute what Martha said," Dalden finally remarked. "Is it true?"

"That I'm humoring you?" Brittany replied uncomfortably. "I prefer to think of it as keeping my sanity, so how 'bout we give it a rest for today, okay? I've been fed enough for one sitting, more than I can stomach. I'm here, I'll listen, I'll probably even ask questions. And I'll ooh and aah when I should. But—no more today. I'm mentally exhausted, and stressed beyond coping."

"She's only slightly exaggerating, Dalden, but she *could* use some form of relaxant—either a round or two of lovemaking, or a visit to the massager unit in the ship's gym. My Tedra swore by the latter, until she got introduced to the former. In our Brittany's case, though, I'd say the latter for the time being would be more appropriate. No point in testing her resolve at the moment on what she's going to believe or not. And since you are part and parcel of what gets believed or not, you'll avoid any hurt pride on your end by practicing hands-off for now."

The blush that had started with that "round or two

of lovemaking" was gone by the time Martha finished. Brittany groaned inwardly. She had already considered how Dalden would feel about her disbelief if *he* believed all this, but she hadn't given it any in-depth thought, really—until now. He'd see it as a lack of trust, obviously, which could cause a really big breach between them, and one that wouldn't be crossable unless one of them changed opinions.

She didn't want to lose him, but damn it all, had she even had him to begin with, or was that just part of the program, too? It was beyond comprehensible that she might have been seduced, her emotions deliberately tied up in knots, all as part of the program or whatever the hell it was these people were trying to accomplish.

"I'm reading higher levels of upset, Dalden. Take her to the massager unit *now*."

Chapter 32

Brittany had never experienced anything quite like it. She'd splurged and treated herself to a fifty-dollar massage once, after the completion of one of the more grueling jobs she'd worked on. She'd had the kinks worked out of her body in a most painful manner and had come away from that experience thinking that massages sucked, that causing more pain to forget about current pain just didn't work for her. Yet by the next day, all those kinks had been gone. This was nothing like that. This was total, 100 percent relaxation, an absolute pleasure, and she was sorry when the lid finally opened, asking her silently to get out.

She'd been afraid to get into it. It reminded her of a coffin, or more precisely, a sarcophagus, since it was shaped like a body. There were quite a few of them in the large gym, and dozens of other exercise machines that she'd never seen the like of before either. She knew all the current best-of-the-best equipment available, yet nothing in this gym was familiar.

As for the massager, Dalden had assured her that she would enjoy the experience. He also complained that he couldn't demonstrate it for her, since they didn't make them in models long enough to fit him. Last, he assured her that if she wanted out of it before it was finished with her, she need only press up on the lid to have it open.

She'd had no trouble breathing after the top had closed on her, sealing her inside the box. That had really been her main hesitation about getting in. And then hundreds of little rollers and skin-pressers moved over her body from head to toe, above and below her, in a gentle, thorough massage. She had felt the tension leaving her body, the stress flowing out with it, felt so utterly loose and relaxed that she wasn't sure she'd be able to stand up.

When she got out she found that Dalden hadn't stuck around for a well-deserved "I told you so." But standing there apparently waiting on her was one of the loveliest women she'd ever encountered in person, the stuff models were made of, a face meant for the front page of magazines. Blonde, amber-eyed, golden-skinned and not quite as tall as Brittany, but taller than average. She was wearing a white one-piece jumpsuit that looked like a uniform and fit like a second skin, in a thin, stretchy material. She was also wearing a very friendly smile, even though her eyes were avidly curious.

Brittany was just as curious, and asked, "Who are you?"

The smile got wider. "My name is Shanelle Van'yer. Dalden didn't mention me?"

Brittany stiffened, ruining a good portion of the work that the massager had just done on her. "No, he didn't. Should he have?"

"I suppose not. I've been dying to meet you, though. I could not be*lieve* it when Martha told me that Dalden had chosen his lifemate. And after knowing you for only two days! Such impulsiveness just isn't in his genes."

"You know him well, then?"

"Shanelle, sweetie." Martha's voice interjected from one of the wall monitors across the room. "You might want to take a precautionary step or two back before she socks you one, because she's about as livid with jealousy as a humanoid can get at the moment."

Shanelle merely frowned. "Jealous? Why?"

Martha was quick to answer in one of her drier tones, "Possibly because you didn't make clear that you're a relation of Dalden's rather than a fun-sharing companion."

It was an utter exaggeration that she was livid with jealousy, but it still had Brittany blushing profusely, because she had just experienced some serious, but apparently unwarranted, negative emotion.

"A relation?" she asked.

"His sister, or to be more exact, his twin."

"Sister?" Brittany said hollowly, and her blush got ten times worse.

The beautiful Shanelle gave her a beautiful smile. "His only sibling, for that matter. Our father decided two of us were enough after our mother went through hell having us. Not that it was a really difficult delivery for her, just that they don't deliver babies where she comes from, so it was an experience she couldn't really relate to on any level."

Brittany stared at her. It was on the tip of her tongue to ask for a detailed explanation, but she decided there was no way an explanation was going to make sense.

Instead she said, "I think I'll have another round in this massager."

"The machine knows when you've had enough, can sense it by the looseness of your muscles, in the same way it senses the tightness, to know which areas need the most work. It won't operate on you again until you need it to work on you. It doesn't operate on 'want.' In that respect, it's like a meditech unit."

"What's that, a doctor in a box?"

"I know you were being sarcastic there, but that's pretty much exactly what a meditech unit is. It's one of the crowning achievements of Kystrani scientists. They're pretty expensive, so they haven't made the medical profession completely obsolete, since not all planets can afford them. Those that can tend to have one or more units in each town. Most ships also have a unit on them, except for the smaller traders. A battleship like this one would of course have quite a few."

"What exactly are we—you—talking about?" Brittany demanded.

Shanelle frowned. "Martha gave me a Sublim tape on your language. I thought I had it down pat. Wasn't I making sense to you?"

"I understood every word. I just don't know what you're talking about."

"The doctor in a box, that ring a bell?"

"That's ridiculous."

"No, it's called a meditech unit."

"Okay, I'll bite for the moment," Brittany said with a sigh. "What's it do?"

"Everything except bring life back—and deliver babies. It does everything a doctor can do, just a whole lot quicker. It accelerates the healing process to such an extent that it's almost instantaneous. It cures disease, mends bones and ripped skin and muscle, is so thorough in fixing anything that's abnormal that even old scar tissue gets erased."

"Do you realize what you're describing is nothing short of miraculous?"

Shanelle shrugged. "If it helps, a lot of worlds agree with you—or rather, disbelieve, just like you. Sha-Ka'an was the same, but it's kinda hard to dispute when you actually see someone injured beyond repair, about to die, and then after a Transfer to a meditech they are back to perfect health. It's so miraculous that the Sha-Ka'ani, who want absolutely nothing to do with off-world inventions and high technology, ordered at least one meditech unit for each of their towns. If something can save your life when nothing else can, that's worth having around, isn't it?"

"Sure," Brittany agreed. "If something like that really exists."

Shanelle grinned at her. "Let's hope you never need to find out."

"No, why don't we prove it to me instead."

Shanelle blinked. "You want to get injured just to experience something firsthand? I *really* don't think Dalden would allow that."

"You said it erases scars, didn't you? Well, I'm

loaded with them—no biggies, but lots of little ones, a hazard of my profession."

"She's got you there, kiddo," Martha's voice purred from across the room. "Take her to Medical. This ought to be interesting."

Brittany wasn't sure she wanted to go now. If Martha was all for it, then there must be some new trick awaiting her there. The massager had been nice, but she wouldn't be surprised if something like that had been invented already but just wasn't on the market yet for the general public. But this so-called meditech was about as believable as a spaceship was.

She followed Shanelle anyway. Curiosity was human nature, as well as walking eyes-open into traps because of it. So what would they tell her when she still had her scars afterward? That the machine was currently malfunctioning, or that the scars were too old to be erased?

There was a row of them in the pristine white room called Medical, but no technicians around to operate them. They were longer than the massager, wider, deeper, and really did resemble oversized coffins. Brittany almost balked at getting into one of them. This was ridiculous. The thing *couldn't* do what they said it could. Yet this was her idea; she couldn't back down from it now. Well, she could, but she preferred to not give a cowardly impression if she could help it.

The lid on the closest one opened automatically as soon as she got near it. The unit was low to the floor, the bottom about the height of a couch, easy to sit down and stretch out in. It was padded on all sides, and not as deep as its size seemed to indicate. Considering that there wasn't much depth to the lid either, they would probably only accommodate lean people, which was pretty silly when you considered people came in all sizes and shapes.

"What happens when people with a weight problem need to use one of these?" she asked as she cautiously laid down on the one that had opened for her.

"I mentioned they aren't designed to deal with pregnancies, didn't I?"

"I mean just your average person who likes to eat too much."

"Ohhh, well, I suppose they would need to lose some weight first."

"And die in the meantime?"

Shanelle smiled. "The world that created these is a world that no longer uses its animal resources, the few it has left anyway, for food purposes. They subsist on food that has the texture, taste, and look of the real stuff, but it's not real, and it's virtually impossible to become overweight on such a regulated, nutritious diet."

"But you also said these get sold to other worlds—have they all conquered obesity?"

"No, indeed, but can you imagine a better incentive to keep your body healthy? I'm sorry, that was a rather tasteless bit of humor. Actually, most of the higher advanced worlds have 'conquered,' as you put it, such health problems, if not through government regulation then with simple intelligence and an appreciation of a healthy environment. Then, too, you have militaristic worlds that keep fit for other than health reasons. Either way, once a world has been discovered, they can opt to advance their way of life, or continue to progress normally. The League of Confederated Planets has a strict policy of noninterference if a planet opts for the latter."

"But why would anyone refuse such—miracles—if they were offered?"

"For any number of reasons, including ingrained culture, ignorance, natural distrust of off-worlders—" Laughter circled, echoed about the room from the many wall monitors, causing Shanelle to make a face before adding, "Okay, and warrior stubbornness."

"I think she was being amused by *my* distrust," Brittany said, making a face of her own.

Shanelle just grinned. "Don't kid yourself, kiddo. The Sha-Ka'ani have other worlds beat hands down when it comes to *not* liking off-worlders and off-world inventions."

Shanelle stepped back then, and the lid closed on Brittany. Panic flared, but didn't last long. Once again she was completely encased in one of their machines, but this one was simply like a soft heat that moved around her, passing over all her limbs, a tingle here and there, and then the lid popped open again.

Brittany frowned as she sat back up. No more than a few seconds had passed, barely enough time to hear the low hum on the machine as it came to life and to feel that gentle heat surrounding her. Just as she'd figured. They were going to claim the thing had malfunctioned.

She beat them to it. "Not working, huh?"

Shanelle frowned at her. "Why? You still have some scars left?"

Expecting excuses, Brittany hadn't even thought to look down for proof. She glanced at her left hand, the one that had suffered the most injuries during the years she'd been learning her craft. She looked at both sides of it. Then she brought it up in front of her face for closer examination.

Her expression must have mirrored her incredulity, because Martha, viewing the room from the wall unit across from her, complained, "Oh, sure, I offer her a walk on the moon and she's still skeptical, but one little visit to a meditech and she enters 'have to believe it' mode."

Brittany snapped her jaw shut and gritted her teeth. "It's hypnosis, isn't it? The scars are still there, you've just convinced my mind not to see them."

"Hey, I'm impressed," Shanelle said with a chuckle. "That's a really good logical deduction if you're determined to doubt. But let's hope we don't need the meditech to prove any more points. Shall we adjourn to the Rec Room now? Dalden's probably done with Jorran by now and wondering why you're not where he left you."

Brittany had forgotten all about Jorran. "That egomaniac is behind lock and key, I hope?"

"Better than that, he's in a containing cell. It doesn't have doors, windows, or any other means to get out of it without Transfer. A very luxurious suite, actually, which in *my* opinion he doesn't deserve. But we don't mistreat prisoners, we just make sure those needing isolation get it. Though Martha has been Transferring his people aboard—they've all elected to travel with Jorran, rather than return home on their ship—they aren't going to be allowed to speak with him during the journey and are being delivered to an unused portion of the ship where they'll be kept happy but out of the way. Putting him with them would just be asking for trouble. How's the collection going anyway, Martha?"

"Two rods left unaccounted for," Martha replied. "But two of Jorran's people haven't checked in yet to know he's been captured. Current estimate is another three hours before we can depart."

"The captain of Jorran's ship is being very cooperative," Shanelle explained as they headed out of Medical. "Once he got a look at the battleship hovering over him, he gave the exact coordinates for the remaining Centurians on his ship, wanting them all *off* it immediately, and he's making every effort to find the remaining two still down on the planet."

"Then he's not a Centurian himself?"

"No, it's just a simple trader with a full crew that Jorran hired to transport him to his new 'kingdom.'"

They had arrived at the Rec Room. It was a really big room, designed to entertain the ship's crew in their off-duty hours. This ship had Martha, rather than a crew, but the Rec Room was filled with men anyway—nearly fifty of them, and all huge like Dalden.

"You aren't going into shock again, are you?" Shanelle asked with concern. "Weren't you told that there were other Sha-Ka'ani here?"

"I don't—recall."

"These are my father's warriors, sent along to protect my mother on her trip to Kystran. We were on our way home from that planet when we got the distress call from Sunder. Mother insisted the warriors accompany us, and went home alone." Shanelle's voice rose to reach Martha amid the noise in the room, even though there was a wall monitor right behind them.

"Assure me again, Martha, that the Probables say she *didn't* get punished for that?"

"Stop fretting, doll," Martha replied. "You know your father is more understanding than that."

"Except when it comes to the protection of his lifemate," Shanelle said in rising agitation.

"Punished?" Brittany choked out.

"You don't want to know," Shanelle replied before she stomped off, really upset now.

"*Martha?*" Brittany demanded, her own upset getting out of hand.

But Martha just purred, "She was right, you don't want to know. Besides, Shanelle typically overreacts whenever she thinks her mother has earned her father's displeasure. In this case she's dead wrong, but there'll be no convincing her of that till she gets home and sees for herself." And then Martha added, "But why get into the oddities and peculiarities of a people you don't believe exist?"

Brittany opened her mouth to protest, then snapped it shut. She *did* want to know what they'd meant by punishment, but she'd be damned if she'd ask now. The Sha-Ka'ani didn't exist, she wasn't in a spaceship, none of this was the least bit real. But where the hell did they find *fifty* giants to participate in this bizarre scam?

Chapter 33

"TEDRA ISN'T FROM SHA-KA'AN?"

"No indeed, she was hatched on the planet Kystran in the Centura star system, which is fortunate for you, doll. I'm sure she'll set you up with all the modern conveniences from other worlds that she enjoys, which most Sha-Ka'ani refuse to introduce to their daily lives. Kystran is a major exporter of luxuries, a member of the Centura League of Confederated Planets."

Brittany had settled into a chair near the entrance to the Rec Room, with a monitor on the wall behind her. She wasn't about to proceed any farther into that room with all those giants lounging about, and Dalden not among them. She had felt the chair move under her when she sat on it, shrinking somewhat, but wasn't going to comment on it.

Martha was less reticent, had remarked nonchalantly, "The beds here adjust to size as well, just so you know. When you're ready to crawl into one usually isn't the time for such explanations."

Brittany hadn't thanked her for the warning. She'd been too busy trying to keep down her unease of being in a room with so many huge men. Those men were ignoring her for the most part, but that didn't reassure her one bit. Some were watching what looked like war movies on really big screens. Others were involved in wrestling matches. Still others were exercising on mats. Actually, most of them were doing things that should have been done in the gym instead. . . .

"They hate the gym," Martha said, back to reading minds. "It's filled with things that are foreign to them, and like Dalden, none of them really like things that are unnatural to their own world. They'll play the war games on the ship's entertainment system, because they understand they are just games, but when it comes to workouts, they'll do it their own way. They'd be practicing with swords like they do at home if I hadn't forbid it."

Swords—warriors. Brittany still found it incredulous that they'd found this many huge men for this convince-at-no-expense project. All of them were over six and a half feet; one looked even taller than seven!

She had mentioned Dalden's mother to get her mind off what she was viewing. And much as she didn't want to appear curious, she couldn't let that "hatched" comment pass.

"Are you going to try to convince me now that your Tedra isn't human?"

"Put the brakes on," Martha said, injecting surprise in her tone. "Where'd you get that from?"

"Your 'hatched' instead of born. Either you don't know that 'hatched' implies a hard-shelled egg, which I doubt, or you were being cute to confuse the issue."

A good bit of soft chuckling floated about Brittany. "Can't deny I do have my 'cute' moments." More chuckling. "But I was just calling it like it is in this case. Kystrani are a species so far advanced that they long ago did away with natural childbirth as you know it."

"They couldn't have. They'd be extinct, yet you don't talk of them in the past tense."

"They did almost come to extinction during the Great Water Shortage many years ago. They lost most of their plant and animal life, but didn't abandon the planet. They are one of many colony planets founded by the original Ancients more than two thousand years ago, so they got a lot of help from their sister planets. They adapted because of the shortage, created water-less baths, new food sources, oxygen, liquid, and with the bad comes the good. They now have the technology to populate barren, resource-deprived planets."

"You get an A-plus in distraction, Martha."

"Now who's being cute? And I wasn't avoiding the subject, merely supplying a little history. They've done away with natural childbirth for the simple reason that it's painful and dangerous. It also isn't selective breeding, and Kystrani prefer to cultivate intelligence that can better their way of life."

"But how?"

"Give it a little thought," Martha replied, "and your

best guess would probably be right, since your own planet is starting to experiment in the same area."

"Cloning?"

"Close. You call it artificial insemination. The Kystrani took that one step further by eliminating the female from being the holding tank, using man-made artificial wombs instead. Add to that worldwide birth control that's not left to individual choice, but administered in all food and drink on the planet, and donors from only the most intelligent. The whole process is monitored by Population Control. The children are then raised in Child Centers, where they are tested to determine their best match for life careers."

"It sounds very—cold."

"Tedra would agree with you. Child Centers teach everything a child needs, they just don't supply what only a child's parents could. Tedra had to go to Sha-Ka'an for that missing ingredient."

"You're talking about love, right?"

"You betcha."

"Then you're contradicting yourself," Brittany was quick to point out. "Or didn't you just try to convince me awhile ago that the Sha-Ka'ani have their emotions mastered to near nonexistence?"

"The males do, not the females," Martha clarified. "But I'm going to let you in on a little secret. Warriors truly are convinced that they can't love. Caring, yes, but not the deeper emotion of love. But my Tedra upset that notion all to hell with her lifemate, Challen. He loves her to pieces even though he tried to deny it to begin with. It was what she was missing in her life, so you don't think that I would have let her stay there with him if he wasn't going to supply it in big doses, do you? But she had to almost die before he owned up to it. So expect a lot of frustration if you're going to try to make your warrior admit it."

"Thanks tons," Brittany said. "Just what I needed to hear."

"Now, don't get discouraged, doll. I like you. I'm not going to steer you wrong. And I've just given you a major advantage where your warrior is concerned: he might try to convince you that it's impossible for warriors to love, but you now know that isn't so. Just don't push it, would be my advice. He's Tedra's son, after all, which makes him quite a bit different from other Sha-Ka'ani, so he's likely to figure it out on his own, whereas most pure Sha-Ka'ani never do. Their own women don't buck the way things are. It takes off-worlders to stir things up and show them that ingrained beliefs aren't always what's real."

"So my role is to be teacher?"

Martha laughed. "That's a good one, and not even close. These men don't take to learning new ways, they think their way is the best way. I said show, not teach, and I meant *your* lifemate, not the whole planet. Tedra has tried to change things there, with little luck. Believe me, she hates their rules and laws just as much as you will. But you're stuck with them because *their* women don't mind them—yet. Your own people have followed the same path, subject to a male-dominated society up until they finally got tired of being treated like children and did something to change it. Sha-Ka'ani women just haven't reached that point yet."

"Talking to you, Martha, can be really depressing. God, I'm glad none of this is really real."

Martha sighed. "If it's any consolation, Tedra has been *very* happy with her warrior all these years. She wouldn't want to live anywhere but with him."

"In other words, she got converted to their ways rather than them learning from hers."

"No way. She just knows when to ignore things she can't change—and help where she can. She's gotten quite a few of their women off-planet and living where they can feel useful and needed."

"Which is the wrong thing to do. It takes dissatisfaction to want change. If she's shipping off the ones who aren't happy there, nothing will ever get changed."

Martha was back to chuckling. "I know that, and obviously you know that, but my Tedra needs to feel that she's doing something for those people, so *we* aren't going to point that out to her."

"To coin a phrase of yours, wanna bet?"

"So you're going to stir the pot?"

"You could always return me to my home instead," Brittany suggested.

Martha chuckled. "Blackmail?"

"Bargaining."

"You keep forgetting that you're dealing with a computer who can tell you exactly the end of that scenario. I send you home, I even take Dalden back to Sha-Ka'an without you, since there's no choice in the matter of who flies this ship. But then we have one very angry warrior, and one very angry Challen who will agree I overstepped my bounds. So I probably get unplugged, and Dalden gets another ship and comes to collect you, because there *is* no getting away from your lifemate. So at the most you've saved yourself from this horrid new life you're imagining for six months, then get taken to Sha-Ka'an anyway, but with an angry lifemate rather than one who is presently going to go out of his way to please you. Now I ask you, which option is going to be more to your benefit?"

"Oh, shut up and go away."

"I can't go away. The best I can do is offer silence. But then you'll just sit there and brood about everything you *don't* believe, and since arguing with me is more healthy than brooding, guess which you get?"

"I'm not Tedra," Brittany nearly snarled. "I'm *not* your responsibility."

" 'Course you are. When Dalden made you his lifemate you became part of Tedra's family, and I think we've already covered this ground. Her family, every member of it, falls into my sphere of responsibility. She's a very caring woman. She gets upset when her personal people aren't happy. She feels their pain."

"So who gets priority when two of her 'people' are unhappy with each other?"

"Priority is given to the best-choice conclusion with all variables involved," Martha replied. "That may mean someone will have to bend a little, but compromise is necessary in many disagreements."

"Why do I get the feeling that I'll be the someone who has to bend?"

"Not even close, doll. I've known Dalden all his life and you not even a week, but keep in mind I said best-choice conclusion. Dalden has been due for some bending. He strives to follow only the one path, ignor-

ing half of his nature. This has caused him a lot of unnecessary grief that I'd like to see end. He'll be happier
with himself, with who he is, once he accepts that he's
not just a Sha-Ka'ani warrior."

Chapter 34

BRITTANY DID GET TO BROOD SOME, FOR ALL OF TEN MIN-utes. That was about all she could stomach of try-ing to assimilate all the fantastical information Martha had thrown at her. There was simply too much of it, too many bizarre inventions, too many advanced con-cepts mixed in with the barbaric. And even that didn't make sense. If there were such advanced, godlike worlds such as Morrilia, why weren't they educating the primitive worlds? Why leave them to struggle in ignorance?

But none of it was true. Whoever had designed this program she'd been unlucky enough to get picked for had a really strange imagination. Or maybe it was just Martha, instructed to improvise as needed, who had the overactive imagination. And where did that leave her? Imprisoned on this so-called ship for nearly three months? Then what? Taken to some remote area that they had set up to convince her she was on another planet?

Somehow she doubted they planned to invest three full months on just one test subject. There was probably a time limit, a couple of weeks, a month at the most, to either convince her or admit it was all a farce and send her home—without Dalden.

Her heart constricted. He was one of them, part of the program. Work on the heart as well as the mind? God, she hoped not. She'd rather think their involvement hadn't been counted on, that at least *that* part of it was real.

But she still wasn't going to get to keep him when this was over. And she had to decide whether to cut that string to her heart now, before it got any stronger—or enjoy him while she had him. But hadn't she already decided to savor their time left, to stockpile the memories, anticipating that their time together *would* end? Of course, that was a decision made before their program went into full gear.

"Where is Dalden?"

"Done brooding already?" was Martha's reply.

Brittany sighed. "Tired of the headache already. Where's Dalden?"

"He's calmly assumed the role of ambassador and is presently explaining to Jorran why his demands aren't going to be met. I'm amazed he hasn't lost patience yet. Jorran's overwhelming arrogance is hard to stomach by any species."

"I suppose you've been listening in on them?" Brittany remarked.

"I'm capable of following *and* participating in every

conversation going on in this ship at any given moment," Martha boasted. "Computers aren't single-tasked like you humans, you know."

Brittany allowed herself a satisfying snort before suggesting, "How about directing me to him? I'd prefer not to stay—here."

"These warriors aren't going to bother you, doll." Martha went back to reading minds. "You're off-limits to them because they know who you belong to."

"I don't belong to anyone. Must you make it sound like slavery?" And then the thought struck her. "*Is* there slavery there?"

"Yes, in a few of the more distant countries. But before you go getting bent out of shape over that, kindly remember that there's still slavery in some of the far corners of your own world, and it was widely accepted just a couple of hundred years ago in your own country."

Brittany thumped her head mentally for even asking. Barbaric in the eyes of "most of the universe" would of course include things like slavery. A logical deduction. And much easier to convince the nonbeliever if the tall tale followed a logical path.

But Brittany proved just how single-minded humans were by repeating, "Directions? Or is there some reason I must stay here?"

"Out the door and right to the lift at the end of the hall. It's voice activated—or controlled by me." And then a chuckle. "Dalden doesn't even know that. He just assumes it's always going to take him exactly where he wants to go in the ship, because I always know where he wants to go and control it for him."

"Why not just tell him?"

"Weren't you listening when I mentioned that he doesn't like spaceships? The less he has to personally deal with the ship, the better."

"Will I get to explore this ship?"

"Sure, why not?"

Brittany could have thought of one major reason why not. If their ship was as big as it was being represented by them, then the size of the studio that had created this illusion would have to be mammoth to show her all of it. It would be much easier to restrict her to just a few rooms. Of course, when she got around to asking for that tour, they would probably come up with excuses to not allow it.

"Alone?"

Martha chuckled at that addition. "Doll, there's no such thing as being alone on a ship controlled by me. There are visual monitors in every single room that can't be turned off if I don't want them turned off."

"What about broken? Smashed? Demolished?"

"Are we getting hot under the collar? You could try, but they're made of unbreakable material. And why does that upset you?"

"Maybe I'm used to the concept of privacy?" Brittany growled. "Maybe I don't like the fact that there will *always be eyes on me*."

"I'm not intrusive, Brittany. I view when I need to view, I don't view just for the hell of it."

"I'm not impressed by that hurt-feelings tone. If you're a computer, you don't have feelings."

Another chuckle. "'Course not, but *you* don't think I'm a computer, remember?"

Before Brittany's blush got really bright, the door to the lift slid silently open. Dalden turned toward her immediately. So did Jorran. It was a circular room in the middle of which was another circular room enclosed by see-through walls. Those curved, seamless walls extended from floor to ceiling. As Martha had mentioned, there were no doors, no openings of any kind. There had to be a trapdoor in the floor, though, that she just couldn't see, because their only way in or out, called Transfer, was stretching the limits of even their imagination, much less hers.

"Why is she here?" Dalden wanted to know.

"Shanelle took her to the Rec Room, where she thought you'd be, then abandoned her there when she got emotional again over what she assumed happened to Tedra on her return home. Nothing we haven't seen her do a dozen times since parting from Tedra, but you know how your sister is, and how poorly she deals with *that* subject."

"Why is she here?" Dalden repeated, showing that barbarians could be single-minded, too.

"Didn't care for my subtle warning about what *you* can expect to be grilled about later? Forgetting that the Rec Room is where your good buddies prefer to hang out? Brittany got intimidated."

The blush that Brittany had gotten under control immediately returned. And Dalden's expression softened now as he put an arm around her and said, "You need have no fear of Kan-is-tran warriors."

"I wasn't afraid," she insisted. "Martha embellishes. I was merely uncomfortable. And she said you were playing the ambassador here. I wanted to see how one plays at being an ambassador."

He made a face now. "As you say, she embellishes. I have not the diplomacy needed for such a role. But I am capable of turning down Jorran's demands and making sure he understands why."

"Satisfaction in saying no?"

"Indeed."

"I suppose he's demanding that you let him go?" Brittany guessed.

Dalden shook his head. "He understands we are returning him to Century III and that he will be contained here for the journey. He has no difficulty accepting that as the consequence of losing the fight with me. But he remembers that a meditech fully healed him after his fight with my sister's lifemate, Falon. He demands that we heal him."

She was surprised. "You aren't going to?"

"We have decided that he is to have no more treatment than his own world would be capable of giving him, which is next to none. They have not yet progressed to the age of science or medicine."

She wasn't sure she understood that reasoning—and then it occurred to her that she didn't need to. She realized they hadn't just been telling her things. Telling was easy. They'd also been enacting their story, following their own scripts, and Jorran had been a major acting part.

He was one of them, of course. They'd actually had her believing what those rods could do, when in fact they did nothing, had been used on other members of the project who had merely pretended they'd been hypnotized. The mayor? His secretary? Either tricked into going along with the pretense or really hypnotized ahead of time. Jorran had just been their "reason" for coming here. So he had to be a continuing part of the script.

The damage done to him? Faked, of course, but damn, they sure did a good job of faking. His nose really did look crooked above the cloth he was holding below it to stem the fake blood. His broken arm was hanging rather limp at his side. He stood lopsided, to keep the weight off his supposedly broken kneecap.

Impressed, Brittany remarked casually, "You know, if I really thought Jorran was injured, rather than pretending to be, I'd tell you it's cruel to make him suffer like that when he could be mended."

Dalden frowned, but Martha chose to answer this time. "The man deserves some suffering. He's a member of the ruling family of his world. All they're going to do when we take him home is slap his wrist and tell him to not get caught next time. But even if he hadn't tried to take over your world, he's still on our endangered species list because he deliberately tried to kill Tedra's son-in-law so he could hook up with her daughter, for the sole purpose of taking over their world. He's *never* suffered any consequences for his merciless actions. Someone needs to show him that the way he does things just isn't acceptable to the rest of the universe."

"Why isn't he reacting to what you just said?" Brittany asked curiously.

"He didn't hear it. I turned off the communication speaker when you entered."

"Turn it back on. I'd like to hear what he has to say."

"You're too emotional to stomach it, doll. Make up your mind. You're either going to believe he's for real, in which case you have to believe everything else, or you're not. And if you're not, then what's it matter what he has to say?"

Touché. "Is he in pain?"

"No. Even medieval worlds have figured out painkillers of one kind or another, and he'll be given regulated doses in the air he's breathing for as long as needed. We're not out to torture him, merely to teach him a lesson, and even that will only be temporary."

"Why only temporary?"

"His bones will mend by the time he gets home, they just won't mend perfectly, so he'll probably leave us with a slight limp and not liking his pretty new nose job. But I have little doubt that he will find himself a meditech eventually that will put him back together perfectly. Even if he never leaves home again, his planet gets a lot of off-world tourists fascinated with their old-world culture, and most modern ships come equipped with a meditech or two."

Brittany stared at Jorran through the see-through wall. He was staring back at her, an abject appeal in his eyes. He wanted her to help him, was willing it, trying to play on her sympathies. He was a good actor, really good, was well-suited for the role of villain. He'd get no help from her, though, either way. Real or not, her only concern was whether Dalden could be cruel. He wasn't, though; he was just trying to administer some justice that he felt wouldn't be forthcoming from any other quarter. The logical path, something the good guys might do.

She tipped an imaginary hat to Jorran, turned to Dalden with a smile. "I can't wait to see the finale. When do we leave for Sha-Ka'an?"

Chapter 35

THEY DID LEAVE FOR SHA-KA'AN. AT LEAST, THEY wanted her to believe that. The announcement had been made. Everyone had heard it.

Brittany had been in Dalden's quarters when she heard it, staring out the long bank of windows. Those windows had shown her water before. When she had returned to Dalden's quarters, they were filled with black space and stars. After the announcement, some of those stars began to move. An amazing depiction of a ship moving swiftly through space—or an elongated computer screen giving that illusion.

So much to think about, way too much. She didn't want to deal with it anymore. It was depressing her. Even though she didn't really believe she was leaving Earth, she was somehow experiencing the same feelings as if it were so. And it wasn't the same as leaving home for the first time. She might not get back to Kansas to see the folks very often since she moved out, but she *could* just hop in her car and go anytime she felt like it. There was security in having that choice. No such choice here.

The door slid quietly open behind her. She heard it, just didn't turn to see if it was Dalden or not. The depression that had settled in as soon as she was alone, was weighing her down. Too many emotions, doubts, fears, and so much of it centered on *him*.

He stood in front of her. He looked concerned, probably because she was on the verge of tears and looked it. Was he for real? How could he be? A barbarian from another world just wasn't acceptable. But did he believe it? As they could make her forget, could they make him have memories that weren't real, a whole lifetime of memories inserted in his mind to make him think he was other than what he was? She really wanted to believe that, rather than he was just another actor in this "play."

"So you are not as accepting as you claimed you would be?" he said.

"I know this isn't real," she replied tonelessly. "You say it is. One of us doesn't have our facts straight."

His hands came to her shoulders, pulled her close enough so they were just touching. She had to tilt her head back now to still meet his gaze. Those lovely amber eyes were filled with sadness.

"I cannot make it all go away for you," he told her. "I would not want to. That would mean giving you up, and I will never do that."

"You mean Martha's means of making people forget what has passed?"

"Yes."

"No, I wouldn't want that either." She laid her head on his chest, wrapped her arms tight around him. "But it's occurred to me that to accept this is to accept that I'll never see my family again. Can you understand why that thought is abhorrent to me?"

"Certainly, yet is it in error? Your star system is farther than most from mine, yet is it still reachable. You will see your family again if that is your wish."

She looked up at him again. "You mean that?"

"I am not breaking your ties with all that you know, merely loosening them for now," he replied. "You have a new family. You have me."

He was doing it again, amazing her at how easily he could adjust her emotions. He was reputed to have none, but he sure knew how to mold hers. A few words and half the burden had been lifted from her shoulders.

It wasn't the first time. Actually, it seemed to be a constant with him. The way he looked at her, touched her as if he cherished her above all things, said just what she needed to hear . . . it was no wonder she fell for him so hard and so fast. He might not love her, might not even be capable of it, but he sure knew how to make her feel loved. And every time he did, he bound her heart more firmly to his.

Was it by design? Deliberate? Part of the plan? Brittany shoved those doubts away, savoring the relief he just gave her. She hugged him tighter, thanking him without words. He might be too good to be true, but he was one fantasy she could live with for the rest of her days.

"You're amazing."

"It pleases me that you think so."

"Don't get conceited," she said as she leaned back to grin at him. "I didn't say you were perfect. Close, but no cigar."

His hands continued to caress her in a gentle, soothing manner, rather than sexual. Was he still worried that she was falling apart at the seams? Or was he keeping Martha's "practice hands-off" warning in mind? She really hoped it wasn't the latter.

"What else—pleases you?" she tested, trying not to sound sexy, merely curious.

But that easily, his golden eyes filled with heat, and that quickly, he was kissing her. Martha wasn't always right. As a stress reliever, Dalden's lovemaking beat a massager, even their unique one, hands down. Just his kisses alone could do that, and for the simple reason that as usual, all thoughts, worries, fears, flew right out of her mind the moment his lips touched hers.

He lifted her, carried her to the bed, positioned her carefully on top of him as he laid back on it, so she wouldn't be distracted by any adjusting it did. As if anything could distract her just then. He took her into that realm of ecstasy again, so new to her, yet already addicting. His heat surrounded her, the strength of his passion thrilled her.

His lovemaking was all the answer she'd needed, yet he still said awhile later, "It pleases me when you want me. It pleases me to hold you close to my heart.

Everything about you, woman, pleases me. And it pleases me most to know that you are mine."

Tears came to her eyes. "Did I say you weren't perfect? You can have that cigar now."

He laughed, gathered her close. If she was dreaming, she really didn't want to wake up.

Chapter 36

IF BRITTANY DIDN'T HAVE SPECIFIC MEMORIES OF EACH and every day, she could almost think she'd slept through most of that trip, time flew by so quickly. She'd marked the days to begin with, but after two weeks and then a month passed, she had to give up the notion that they had a short time limit for convincing her. She was forced to conclude that the time involved was part of the project, to determine just how long it would take for her to crack. She was obviously just a test subject, after all. When they got around to doing this to their real objectives, they'd want to have a good idea of a time frame for it.

So much time spent on just her? Maybe not. The "ship" was certainly big enough that there could be dozens of others just like her there at the same time, and they just managed to keep her from running into them.

She *had* gotten that tour of the "ship" she'd asked for. And she had ended the day being even more impressed by the immense scope of this project, and the immense expense involved. Even if that lift wasn't really taking her to different levels of the ship, was just taking her back to the same floor where walls had been changed to make her think she was seeing different rooms, it was still a mind-boggling expense, the creation of all this. And she wondered if she was the only test subject who had yet to be convinced even partially, let alone fully.

They never lost patience with her disbelief, never tried to double their efforts to change her thinking. She was grateful for that, because it let her enjoy her time with them. It was almost like reading a book. Once she looked at it in that light, she found it an amusing pastime, to make them flesh out their story, to ask all kinds of questions about their part of the universe.

She learned that Dalden's mother was a heroine on her own planet, that she was also the one to first discover Sha-Ka'an and bring it to the attention of the rest of the universe. She knew that his planet was closed down to off-world visitors, that anyone arriving there had to stay in the Visitors' Center and conduct their business from there, that few exceptions were made to this rule. That wasn't always the case, but "tourists" had caused too much trouble in the early days of discovery, apparently, enough to make themselves unwelcome.

She spent a lot of time with Shanelle and learned that it was Falon's family that was ultimately responsible for ousting the visitors from their world. After his sister had been raped by one of them, they'd been ready to go to war if the planet wasn't made off-limits to off-worlders. Brittany figured this was a very good excuse to not show her very much of Sha-Ka'an, but Shanelle had assured her that exceptions got made for lifemates, that she was a Ly-San-Ter now and so one of them.

From Shanelle she also learned that like her own world, each country in Sha-Ka'an was somewhat different from the next, some with different rules and regulations, some with different philosophies, and in some the people looked different as well, though the amazing height and brawn were apparently a planet-wide thing.

Shanelle's lifemate and his brother were examples of that. From a far distant town, they were black-haired and blue-eyed, while everyone from Dalden's town fell into the golden to light-brown hair and eyes category. The women from Falon's town apparently weren't quite as restricted, either, as they were in Sha-Ka-Ra, but that was one aspect of Sha-Ka'ani life that Brittany did *not* want to learn about yet.

She became friends with Shanelle. At least, the feeling was there that they were friends, even if it was all pretense on the younger girl's part. She even became friends with Martha, amazing as that was, when she had yet to meet the real Martha, and had to wonder if she ever would. But Martha had a dry sense of humor that Brittany took to—after she stopped allowing it to annoy her. And Martha was still her main source of information. Because she was faceless, Brittany could ask her things that she wouldn't ask the others.

One of those things was their differences in speech, which had confused her from the beginning. Several weeks into the journey she finally got around to asking

Martha, "Why do you and Shanelle talk—I guess normally is the word I'm looking for? While Dalden, and Jorran's people as well, for that matter, sound foreign? If Shanelle is his sister, why doesn't she talk like him?"

"Dalden speaks pure Sha-Ka'ani. What you hear is his translation of your language. The same with Jorran, who speaks pure Centurian. Shanelle and I, however, speak Kystrani, and not pure Kystrani, but their Ancient dialect, which includes slang. We speak it because Tedra has a fascination with her Ancients, to include using their slang, and my main dialect is set to be identical to her preference."

"But why would that be different, if you're using a translation as well?"

"Because of the similarities that we've found between the Kystrani Ancients and your people. Your history has closely followed theirs, so closely that even your slang is mostly the same. So in effect my language, the one Tedra prefers, is already the same as yours in basic content, as in same meanings, same slang, even same phrases. If I tell you that you got your socks knocked off when you met Dalden, you know exactly what I mean, don't you? A normal Sha-Ka'ani wouldn't have a clue, however, since they don't have a similar phrase in their language."

"Why didn't you say Dalden wouldn't have a clue?" Brittany had asked.

"Because he would. I told you Dalden is unique, a product of two cultures, though he'd prefer it were only one. Both of Tedra's children received a major part of their education from me, but only up to a point. Shanelle wanted to know everything and continued to learn, Dalden didn't. After he made the decision to follow his father's path exclusively, he wanted no more teaching from me, and he's tried to forget everything he'd already learned about the rest of the universe. He *can* talk just like Tedra, he just won't."

"So he took after his father, and she took after her mother?"

"In speech, yes, but women tend to be better at adapting, and Shani is a shining example of that. She can be the absolute perfect Sha-Ka'ani daughter, obedient in every way but one, or she could move to Kystran and take up the life career of flying ships for trade or world discovery—she spent a year there learning those careers."

"Back up. Every way but one?"

"Come on, kiddo, common sense would tell you that since she's been educated on how things are elsewhere, she's not going to like every aspect of how they are at home. Ignorance is bliss, as the saying goes, and she's not ignorant, which is why she learned to fly. She had every intention of leaving home to find a lifemate on some other world—until she met Falon and got her socks knocked off just like you did."

"And she's happy to stay at home with him now?"

"Oh, yes." Martha spared a condescending chuckle. "There's something about that love emotion you people have that makes you perfectly willing to be where your mate is, whether you like where that is or not."

"Is this finally my preparation for not liking Sha-Ka'an?" Brittany said suspiciously.

"Not at all. You may love the heck out of it, once you get used to it. No crime as you know it, no fear as you know it, no worries about war, disease, sickness, jobs, or anything else you're used to worrying about."

"Utopia with a catch?"

More chuckling. "If everything was absolutely perfect, doll, you'd get bored real quick. Now back to Shani. She'd make an ideal ambassador for Sha-Ka'an, actually, because like Tedra, she's well versed in every known language in the universe, and respects each species for its own uniqueness. They both fully support the League's hands-off policy on underdeveloped planets, even though they might wish it were otherwise for Sha-Ka'an. They agree that a species must be left to develop at its own pace, for good or bad, that its full potential won't be reached otherwise. It's been proven by low-tech worlds that once they start trading with more advanced cultures, their own development stagnates, setting them back centuries in the way of personal growth."

"Why?"

"Because their creative people will naturally feel that anything that they could envision has already been created, so why bother."

"How is that avoided?"

"It's not, it's happened time and again. So now when the League discovers a new high-tech world, they rejoice, but when they discover a primitive world, they step very carefully. Trade gets restricted to the mundane, space travel isn't offered, educating the primitives on what's out there is minimal. A few non-League planets and rogue traders might break this policy, but for the most part, it's abided by."

"That doesn't sound like what happened with Sha-Ka'an," Brittany pointed out.

"They were an exception, because one of their natural resources is so greatly needed by the rest of the universe. But that's worked out well because they finally restricted off-world involvement themselves, so they get to progress at their own pace, while the League protects them from invasion by advanced worlds. And the League has a good representative there in Tedra. She's the perfect go-between, because she wants what's good for both sides."

In a contained environment like the *Androvia*, Brittany had expected to get bored pretty quickly, but she never did. She learned to play some of the games in the Rec Room, which really amazed her. She wasn't up to date by any means on computer-type games, never having owned a computer herself, but being able to control what seemed like real people in simulated wars and watch the action on movie-size screens was impressive. It was like watching a movie, but you were the director of it, or the master puppeteer in control of the actors.

And she had discovered a crafts room and ended up spending a lot of time there. It was for the crew, which the *Androvia* currently didn't have, or for people who might have personal hobbies they didn't want to give up just because they had elected space travel careers. Most of the stuff in the room made no sense to her, but the small section with stored wood and tools certainly did.

She cluttered up Dalden's quarters with her creations: a new table and chairs, and a nightstand—and she insisted the bed remain out at all times for it. She made a double-seated rocker that he'd never seen the like of and was sturdy enough for him to sit in with her. They used it each evening, sitting in front of the bank of windows, staring at the stars and the occasional streaking comet, and once, another ship that freaked her out until Martha's soothing tones assured her it was just a passing trader.

No, she was never bored. Corth II amused her a lot, too. He had a keen sense of humor and often used it to try and annoy Dalden, successfully. Martha explained that while Dalden had never experienced jealousy before and would discount it as being an emotion he wasn't capable of, he wouldn't experience it where other warriors were involved because he fully trusted them, while Corth II was a different matter, and unpredictable.

Which was why Dalden didn't mind her making friends with one of the young warriors who had an interest in woodworking. Kodos had always had a desire to make things with his hands, but had never come across anyone who could teach him how—until her. That was his story, anyway, and one she chose to accept, because teaching him was something else to keep her busy and her mind occupied on other than the end of the project.

No, Dalden didn't mind at all her counting Kodos as a friend, but he did mind any time she spent with Corth II, who was an outrageous flirt. His flirting she didn't take seriously. And Martha's insistence that he wasn't a real man but an android that she and her good buddy Brock, another Mock II, had mutually created, Brittany filed away with another mental "yeah, right." If Dalden knew he wasn't a real man, why would he be jealous?

Martha, of course, had an answer for that, too: because an entertainment unit had been used for the android's body, he was fully capable of sex-sharing like a normal entertainment unit, and Dalden knew that. But Corth II was anything but normal, was apparently a free-thinking computer that wasn't restricted to stationary housing, and answerable only to Martha and Brock.

Brittany had wanted to know why Martha hadn't given herself legs, since that was possible. Martha's reply was that you didn't tamper with perfection. Brittany had a good laugh over that.

She had made a point of not asking about things that she figured were going to upset her. Why rock an unsteady boat, after all? The rules and laws she'd been warned she would hate fell into that category. But the journey was coming to an end, so she was forced to finally put the matter to Martha.

"Isn't it time for me to learn their laws?"

"Not really." Martha used a bored tone, which was actually reassuring in this case. "As long as you're with Dalden, he's not going to let anything go wrong. When you're left to your own devices, *then* you'll need to know what you can and can't do alone."

"I am going to be told before I break any, right?" Brittany persisted.

"Tedra wasn't, but then Challen was just like you, convinced that she had to be from his planet and so already knew everything about his planet, including all laws. He refused to believe in off-worlders—actually, he knew she was telling the truth about who she was, he just didn't *want* to believe it. Sound familiar?"

That had annoyed her. They'd shown her some pretty fantastic things, or they would be fantastic if they were real. She just didn't believe anything was real.

So she wasn't the least bit apprehensive about arriving on Sha-Ka'an. If she thought she would be meeting Dalden's real parents instead of actors representing them, she'd probably be a nervous wreck, worried about all the normal things one worried about when meeting the family of the man she had committed to.

And she *was* fully committed. After spending nearly three months with Dalden, there was no doubt that her heart wouldn't be whole now without him. The thought of losing him when this was over and she was rejected as unconvinced, was so painful that she couldn't face it. Nor had she been able to seek reassurance or ask what was going to become of them when this was over, because he would just insist there was never going to be an "over" for them.

She sometimes thought that Dalden was actually as brainwashed as they were trying to make her, that he really did believe everything that had been told to her. She preferred to think that was the case, rather than that he was deliberately lying to her for whatever "good" reason. Lying would mean an end when the truth was finally admitted. And what would that end be? Go home, we're done with you? Or stay with me and be part of the program? Could she agree to put other people through what she was undergoing? She didn't think so, because bottom line, it was cruel to tamper with emotions to this extent.

But the journey was over; the announcement had already been broadcast that they'd be home in a few hours. And now she'd find out how they could possibly depict an entire planet—that was, if they were going to try. No studio could be that big. She'd have to be contained in a small part of it. But how would that be convincing? And they'd made the mistake of telling her that there was plant and animal life unique to Sha-Ka'an, that even the air was different, edenlike, it was so pure and pollutant-free. Hard things to fake.

So was this going to be the end, then? When she stepped off the "ship," would they tell her, "You failed, you can go home now"?

Chapter 37

"IT IS TIME."

Brittany was staring out the bank of windows in Dalden's quarters at a very large planet that didn't come close to resembling hers. Hers was two-thirds ocean. This one had a lot of green, but very little blue. A nice computer simulation, like everything else she'd seen out those windows. And yet it looked so real it gave her chills.

"We aren't close enough to land yet," she pointed out.

"We are. For a ship of this speed, it is a matter of moments."

Dalden's massive arms came around her from behind to draw her back against his chest. It was comforting and frightening at the same time, because he could be preparing her for their last moments together. The thought brought tears to her eyes, and she swung around to hug him tightly.

"Tell me this isn't going to be the end of us," she said in a voice that was as close as she could get to pleading.

Dalden lifted her face in his hands. His thumbs gently smoothed away the wetness on her cheeks. His own expression was intense.

"I feel your pain. What causes it cannot be allowed to continue. After today, there will be nothing else for you to fear."

"I hate to break it to you, warrior." Martha's voice suddenly floated about the room. "But you are *not* reassuring her."

He turned a chagrined look at the wall monitor. "What must I do to ease her distress?"

"Take her home, to her *new* home. Get her settled in. Introduce her to the family pets." Some positively wicked-sounding chuckling was inserted over that last suggestion before Martha continued. "It's really too bad this ship didn't come equipped with solaray baths. Three months of squeaky-clean without a speck of water might have done some convincing. But she's only had inanimate *things* to go by here, which she has discounted as being 'tricks' or things her own people could have invented. Fifty giant-sized warriors didn't impress her, when men *can* reach that height on her world. She thinks she's been on a simulated ship, thinks she's going to step off it and still be on *her* world. But you have things to show her now, live things. Living, breathing, unique, can't-be-shoved-into-the-'trick'-category things."

Brittany stepped back, bristling a bit with indignation. She really hated it when she got talked about while she was standing right there listening.

"I hate to break it to *you*, Martha, but you aren't reassuring me, either," she said testily.

"Wasn't trying to, kiddo. I'm just telling the warrior what it's going to take to end your delusional state. But then I did toss you a bone; you just didn't catch it."

"Excuse me?"

"'New home.' 'Settled.' Sounds like a beginning rather than an end, don't it?"

It did, but words could be deceiving, or outright lies. She glanced at Dalden again, her skepticism plain. His own look turned determined, and she figured out why when he took her hand and marched her out of the room.

"You're taking me off the ship?"

"Indeed."

"Why not take me off the same way I was brought on?" Brittany asked.

Martha chose to answer, from the comm-link Brittany had been given a few days ago. She'd been warned to keep it with her at all times until she ran out of questions.

"Transfer can't be done here until we've actually landed," Martha said. "Sha-Ka'an is surrounded by a global shield that prevents access by ships without permission. A hole in the shield is opened above the Visitors' Center if permission is given, but even that opening contains a contamination shield. There is at least one meditech in each town, but that isn't nearly enough to help if disease gets introduced to the planet by visitors. The second shield the ship passes through scans for contamination and, in the process, interferes with Molecular Transfer."

"But aren't we about to pass through it?"

"Yes, and I could send you straight to the palace once below the shield, but do you really want to miss out on seeing the sights on the way home? Your first ride on an airobus and then an *hataar*? The architecture in the countryside? Your first view of Sha-Ka-Ra from afar?"

"Things you think are going to make me a believer?" Brittany guessed.

"You betcha," Martha said in smirking tones.

Brittany snorted for Martha's benefit, but she was starting to feel some excitement. A beginning—that implied a life shared with Dalden. And she had reached a point of not caring where they shared it, as long as they shared it. She simply couldn't bear the thought of losing him now. But on another world? How could she accept that as being real?

Martha seemed to think she'd have no choice but to believe it by the end of the day. Dalden had pretty much said the same thing, that she'd have nothing else to fear after today. But where did that leave her? With Dalden, surely, but also with the fantastical concept of living on another world—and meeting his *real* parents. Oh, jeez.

Chapter 38

S HE COULDN'T HAVE IMAGINED IT IF SHE'D TRIED.
Brittany had been expecting a lot of spaceships laying around, nice, easy visual illusions. It was supposed to be a spaceport, after all. But none, zip, *nada*. Even the one she had just left wasn't visible by the time she was on the ground. They'd stepped out of it into some kind of tramlike thing that whisked them along for about a minute, then stepped out of that into a long tubelike tunnel that ended inside a large round building. Looking back, all she saw was the tunnel opening and a lot of wall surrounding it.

The building was immense, she'd give them that. It wasn't often that you saw a ceiling about ten stories high. There weren't very many people in it, though, for its size, and the few that were there were dressed strangely.

"It's just the disembarking terminal." Martha's voice started explaining from the comm-link on Brittany's hip. "For all arrivals. Ships don't land unless they need repairs. It's not good for them to shut down."

"So they just hover up in space depleting their fuel? Sure."

Martha didn't remark on her skeptical tone, said merely, "Fuel as you know it is obsolete. A ship can run forever on one inexhaustible gaali stone. And no, once inside the shield, they aren't let out of it until they're ready to leave. They connect to this hub to drop off passengers, then to the supply hub to restock, then return to this hub and float in standby above the center. It'd be a pretty impressive sight if seen from afar, but it was built to not be an eyesore to a people who don't want reminding that it's here, so it's a *very* long way away from any towns, even Sha-Ka-Ra."

A really good excuse to not show her the Visitors' Center from a distance. Their illusions must only be short-range.

She noticed the other tunnels then, like the one they'd come out of, ten in all, enough to accommodate a lot of passengers arriving at once, but no others were arriving except the people from their ship at the moment. There was a large open exit that they were heading toward, just a wide corridor that connected to yet another big building. No windows anywhere, to see what was outside. Now why didn't that surprise her?

"This Center is like a small city, at least what you would consider a small city—Sha-Ka'ani towns don't come this big," Martha said, continuing the role of tour guide. "It covers two square miles, the port taking up half of that, the trade goods warehouses taking up another big chunk. The rest is devoted to housing for the Trade Ambassadors, security, personnel, and visitors who don't get to stay long. Then you have the areas for maintenance, supplies, repair, and anything else needed to make it a self-contained area."

"The planet doesn't sustain it?"

"No indeed, most of the planet refuses to acknowledge that it's here. It's run by the League for the benefit of League planets. Dalden's father is the only *shodan* who has to deal with it on a regular basis; all the other *shodani* go through him if needed."

She'd already learned that a *shodan* was like a mayor of his town, or to be more exact, a medieval lord ruling over his small kingdom. But even that didn't describe it perfectly. Problems got brought to him, decisions affecting the town were made by him, widows and orphans got full protection from him, yet any warrior could challenge him for the position and take it over if he won. It wasn't a hereditary position in Kan-is-Tra, though it was in some countries like Ba-Har-an where Falon came from. Even then, the son wanting to take over still had to take on all challengers for the privilege.

"Heads up, doll, you're about to meet the new in-laws," Martha said next.

"Huh?"

Brittany stopped short, forcing Dalden, who'd been leading her along by the hand, to turn to see what was wrong. He smiled reassuringly. He'd seen the couple up ahead also, standing at the end of the wide corridor.

The man was huge, as big as Dalden and just as golden, just as handsome, too, for that matter. And after spending three months with fifty warriors, she'd already figured out that they all preferred those leather pants they called *bracs* and the wraparound tunics. The woman was nearly as tall as Brittany, with long black hair pulled up into a high ponytail, and wearing a strange outfit that seemed to be made of sheer green scarves, a lot of them not actually see-through, the points reaching her sandaled feet, with a white cloak attached at the shoulders. She was beautiful, no doubt about it. And young, too young to be a grown man's mother.

Dalden did some explaining now. "Be at ease, *kerima*. Martha has been in contact with Brock since the last rising. So my parents expected us and due to our long absence, could not wait until we reached home. She would have told them all about you, is that not right, Martha?"

"You betcha."

Shanelle had already run forward, was embracing the couple. The warriors with them were filing past and continuing on, leaving the family to their reunion.

"Go ahead. Give me a moment to compose myself," Brittany told Dalden.

She smiled for his benefit, though it was an effort. He seemed somewhat nervous, too, a normal reaction, to worry if his parents would like her—if this was for real. Damn, he was good, sneaking in those little subtleties that she might have missed if she weren't already so attuned to him.

But the moment he was out of hearing she hissed at Martha, "You could have at least gotten someone old enough to play the part of his mother. If you're going to try to convince me that *she* is Dalden's mother, don't bother. She's not much older than I am. Neither is he, for that matter."

A short round of chuckles. "Tedra has aged very well in comparison to average humanoids. The Sha-Ka'ani do also, due to their healthy environment, but Tedra has the added benefit of her Sec 1 training that she keeps up, grueling exercises that have honed her body into a lethal weapon—well, considered lethal on other worlds. But she's forty-four. I should know, she belongs to me."

"I thought that was the other way around and you belong to her?"

"Matter of opinion," Martha muttered.

Brittany didn't believe the handsome couple up ahead were Dalden's real parents, so what was she suddenly nervous about? Because the second phase of "convince at no expense" had begun, apparently. A spaceship hadn't done it. So now new actors and a make-believe whole planet were supposed to. She should be relieved. Her greatest fear before leaving the ship had been that she'd be back in her own bed by tonight, with the space next to her empty. But that wasn't on the agenda yet.

"Showtime," Martha said as the group up ahead stopped waiting for her to join them and approached her instead.

Martha was being cute, but that was too close to how Brittany viewed all of this. A show for her exclusive benefit, just actors following a basic script and improvising where needed.

"Welcome to Sha-Ka'an, Brittany Callaghan, and welcome to my family."

Oh, God, that sounded really nice. Her own family

had grown apart and rarely saw each other anymore. They kept in touch, but she missed that closeness of when they'd all lived together. One of her lessons on the journey had included that Sha-Ka'ani families usually stayed together, that when children reached adulthood they stayed in the same town, some in the same house. A few females might end up with a lifemate in another town or country, but that was a rare exception, since warriors tended to pick their mates from women known to them in their own town.

Following Tedra's welcome, she got a tight hug and a whisper by her ear. "Relax, kiddo, we don't judge here. When a warrior makes his choice there's no reversing it, so he gets wished happy. Some take a long time to decide, some know instantly. Either way, it's something they *know*. Too bad women never gain that kind of certainty."

Was that a joke? Tedra was grinning when she stepped back. Yet what she'd just said was kind of the reverse of the way Brittany knew things to be. Women knew right off when they were in love. It usually took the recipient of that love a heck of a long time to figure the same thing out. There were exceptions, surely, but on the average, women won hands-down in the instant-decision-making category.

Seeing her close up, Brittany still couldn't believe that Tedra was forty-four years old. "Aged well" was a definite understatement. She'd probably make a really cool mother-in-law, though. Brittany wasn't so sure about Challen, who was very intimidating with his size and his look that seemed to be analyzing, but was otherwise inscrutable.

Tedra now turned a stern expression on Dalden.

"Six months' absence, never again, Dalden. Contrary to the Ancients' adage, absence does *not* make the heart grow fonder, it's *farden* well painful. Never again. And your father agrees with me—for once."

"Do not give the impression that I never agree with you, woman," Challen rumbled curtly. "That would be an untruth of the size you call whopper."

Tedra snorted. "You only agree when it suits you, never when it suits me."

That caused a grin from the big guy. A yank to him that had to have hurt when Tedra collided with that big body. A slap on the backside that had to hurt even more.

"We will agree to discuss the matter of disagreeing later," Challen warned.

"Wanna bet?" Tedra shot back.

She then pushed away from him, grabbed Shanelle's arm, and marched off toward the front of the building. Challen and Falon followed more slowly. Dalden took Brittany's hand again to bring up the rear.

At her hip, Martha suggested in a cheerful tone, "Don't mind them, kiddo. Their way of joking around takes getting used to."

"Joking, huh? Sure."

Dalden gave her a glance. "Martha is correct, but it is my mother who will take getting used to. She does not behave as a Sha-Ka'ani woman should."

Brittany stopped, demanded, "And just how would a Sha-Ka'ani woman have acted? Smiled and thanked her lifemate for banging her around?"

Dalden looked confused, but Martha wasn't, and said instantly, "Put the brakes on, girl. Tedra's body is conditioned to take damage and not feel it. She wasn't hurt; if she even felt that love tap, I'd be surprised.

Challen would cut off his hand before he'd actually hurt her. Most warriors feel the same way about their women."

"Do you?" Brittany asked Dalden.

"Certainly," he replied, somewhat indignant that she'd needed that reassurance.

Certainly, she repeated dryly in her mind. But he was talking about physical pain, not the mental kind that could sometimes be just as excruciating. What would a warrior's philosophy be about that? As long as it didn't leave a bruise, it couldn't hurt?

She got the sneaky suspicion that phase two was going to be more emotional than visual. Bog her down with anxieties and uncertainties so she didn't notice when she started believing it all?

Chapter 39

Brittany began to relax on the short ride to Sha-Ka-Ra, Dalden's hometown. They weren't showing her things anymore, had perhaps finally concluded that it was a waste of their time and effort. She got flimsy excuses for this new tack, but she didn't really care.

There had been nothing outside the building to see except the front of the building they just left, and a hill on the other side was close enough to kill any views. It could have been an illusion; she wasn't allowed close enough to it to check it out. There were three vehicles there to transport the lot of them, and they all piled in.

Airobuses, they called them. They could have been remodeled normal buses. Remove the wheels, make the front streamlined instead of flat, extend the length to twice normal size, and voilà, a space-age weird-looking vehicle.

There were cushy chairs in the first section behind the pilot's pit, but most of the vehicle was just a cargo bay. They were supposedly used to collect and deliver trade goods to the outer reaches of the planet, but they had to remain more or less invisible, so they had preset routes that took them high enough above the clouds to not be visible from the ground. They required pilots, even though there was nothing for the pilot to see other than a large monitor. No windows, even up front, the excuse being that if a warrior had to be brought to the Center on one for some reason, they made it as painless as possible for him by giving him no visible reminder that he was flying while he was in the air. There was no sound, either, no feeling of lift-off, no feeling of any movement at all, for that matter, just a low, steady hum barely heard.

The landing points for these buses were called stations, all of them located far enough from the major towns, again, to keep the people from being reminded of their existence. It didn't dawn on Brittany until they arrived at their station just what that was going to mean.

Views. Incredible, far-reaching views of the majestic sort. The station sat at the base of a mountain they called Mount Raik, a mass so tall its point was capped with ice even though the climate was tropical. Mostly flat land spread before it, some cultivated with grains and vegetables. Forests were in the distance, with multi-colored trees, reds, greens, yellows, blues—blue?—and every shade in between. She saw long purple shadows on the horizon that could have been other mountain ranges, too far distant to define. She saw what might be a small lake in a field of wildflowers.

No telephone poles, no roads other than dirt paths, no buildings yet, no airplanes flying overhead to blow it for this look of Eden. And the air *was* clean, no smoke or pollutants floating on any of the horizons. Where on earth had they found such a place?

And then she saw the three airobuses, sitting on a paved landing pad, and what looked like a winding road leading up the mountain. They were too close to the mountain to see the town of Sha-Ka-Ra, which sat halfway up it, or so she was told.

"Are we going to walk up it?" she asked.

"My father has arranged transportation."

"Where?"

He took her hand and led her around the airobus that had been blocking a bit of the view. A small herd of *hataari* were now visible, about forty of them standing placidly off to the side of the pad. Some of the warriors were already mounting them; others standing there showed her just how big the beasts were, when their heads were barely a foot above the animals' backs, which meant those backs had to be as high off the ground as Brittany was tall. They were shaggy-haired, most of them black, a few brown, one tan, but all with white manes and tails that nearly reached the ground. Thin legs, extra-wide bodies, too wide to be horses—perhaps what prehistoric horses might have looked like? But even that was pushing it. They were like horses, but nothing like horses.

They were so funny-looking with their long shaggy coats, she started to laugh. They had to be made-up, Clydesdale horses probably—didn't they get that tall?

But someone's imagination had really gone wild in the creation of their costumes. The padding for the extra-wide trunks was a weird touch; it just made them look silly.

"What amuses you?" Dalden asked as he led her to one of the *hataar* and tossed her up on its back.

The suddenness of being on top of one of those things ended her amusement. There was no saddle, just a blanket covering its back and a harness contraption with reins and a post for gripping, which she did now while Dalden mounted behind her.

"Sure," she said, disgruntled. "Don't give me a chance to find the zipper on this costume."

His arms came around her, pulled her back against him. That easily did she relax and put aside her brief annoyance. He didn't ask her to explain, though if he were for real, he wouldn't have understood her remark. Martha did.

"I'm disappointed in you, doll," came the voice at her hip. "You know you're reaching now, grabbing at crumbs to explain away the obvious."

"Your obvious is so far-fetched, it's gone beyond silly now. If anyone's disappointed, I am. I expected better after such meticulous details on your spaceship."

"Hasn't it occurred to you that there's no choice in the matter of what's real? Yes, they are visually silly-looking. I've seen the animals you have in comparison that are sleek and beautiful. Not every world is so lucky in their beasts of burden. Believe it or not, some worlds have *hataar*-like creatures even more silly-looking than these."

"Sure, and I own a fantastic bridge I'll be glad to sell you."

"This habit you have of saying things you do not mean must end, *kerima*."

Brittany stiffened at Dalden's serious tone, but she caught her breath when Martha said, "Heads up, girl. He's home now and starting to sound like a warrior."

Brittany swung around to give Dalden a hard look. "What'd she mean by that?" No answer from him. "Martha, why'd you make warrior sound like a bad name?" No answer from that quarter, either, which caused her temper to erupt. "Damnit upside and down, don't you people *dare* spring any surprises on me at this late date! Have I fallen in love with a man who's only shown me half of himself? Is the other half some monster I'm going to hate?"

Dalden's expression softened, probably because she'd just admitted she loved him for the first time. She hadn't meant to own up to that yet. She didn't want it laid on the table if the end of the "project" wasn't going to be to her liking. But it was too late to take it back. She did love him—at least, she loved the man she'd come to know. But who was that? A man pretending to be an alien? A man so brainwashed he really believed he was an alien? Or a real alien who'd restrained his alien tendencies up until now, but now that he was home was going to release them? Just why *were* these people called barbarians?

Her barbarian put his hand to her cheek to draw her mouth to his. His kiss was soft, so tender. One of the things she loved so much about him was that despite his incredible size and strength, he was always so gentle with her. He wasn't a barbarian. No way in hell.

Chapter 40

IT HAD BEEN A LONG TIME SINCE BRITTANY HAD BEEN SO embarrassed that all she wanted to do was hide her face. Dalden was almost purring with satisfaction. He'd managed to distract her so thoroughly she forgot what they'd been arguing about, forgot that she should be watching things around her, forgot she was on the back of an animal and other people were riding along beside them.

He was proud that he could do that to her. He'd turned that sweet kiss into a raging inferno of passion—at least on her part. She'd turned all the way around to face him, her legs spread and laying over his, clinging to him, devouring him, lost in the moment. . . .

Until Martha's voice intruded dryly, "I could have sworn you were interested in architecture."

Kodos, riding next to them, was chuckling at Brit-

tany. Shanelle, on the other side riding double with
Falon, rolled her eyes at her. Thank heavens their parents were sharing an *hataar* up ahead and hadn't noticed, or her mortification would have been absolute.

She hissed at Dalden, "If I thought that was deliberate, you'd be in big trouble."

He was seriously amused, if his grin was an indication. "Define big trouble."

"For starters," she said, stabbing a finger against his
wide chest, "never speaking to you again."

"That would not be allowed," he said simply.

"Would not—!" she choked, unable to finish. "To
paraphrase Martha, wanna bet? And don't think you
can tease your way around it. They don't come much
more stubborn than an Irish American, which I happen to be. Stubborn is often our middle name."

"I thought your middle name was Tomboy."

"Oh, cute, real cute. Pretend you don't know what
the hell I'm talking about."

He disagreed. "You are telling me it is your nature
to be stubborn. This is the nature of most women, so
warriors expect it and find it amusing."

"Why amusing?"

"Because it is not a thing women succeed at very
well—here."

"You might want to readjust that statement a little
bit to include, until now."

He chuckled, then hugged her, then explained why
he was suddenly so pleased with her responses.
"You—and Martha—insist that you are different because you were not born here, but truly, *kerima*, your
reaction to an unwanted lesson is no different from
that of a Sha-Ka'ani woman."

She pushed out of his arms, narrowed her eyes on him. "Lesson? Just what were you trying to teach me there? That if I do or say something you don't like, you'll embarrass the hell out of me?"

"It was not meant to embarrass you."

"Then what was I meant to feel?"

"Exactly what you did feel."

What she'd felt was raw passion and a desire to make love with him right then and there. "I don't get it."

He didn't respond, which managed to infuriate her enough to say, "Martha, you and I are going to have a long talk before the end of the day, and you're coming clean this time."

But Dalden objected to Martha enlightening her, insisting, "Lessons are better learned by example than in the telling."

Brittany bristled, but before she could reply, Martha lit into the warrior. "Dalden, did that Sha-Ka'ani pure air muddle your brain all of a sudden? You've done fine until now, keeping it in mind that she's not Sha-Ka'ani. Don't blow it just because you're home, and don't make some assumptions based on one reaction when she's capable of reactions you've never seen before. Some of the things that you see as natural and right and your responsibility, she just isn't going to tolerate. That cultural difference I warned you about better be ringing a big bell, because it's real, it's huge, and it will cause problems of the like no warrior, even your father in dealing with Tedra, has ever faced before."

Brittany stiffened, feeling an ominous dread that frightened her. Dalden stiffened as well, though for different reasons. She didn't like hearing that she, specifically, was going to be the cause of trouble between them. He didn't like hearing that Martha was so certain he wouldn't be equipped to deal with it.

Brittany clutched him suddenly, the fear getting to her. "Whatever happens, we can work it out. Whatever it is she thinks I'm going to hate, I'll—I'll try to understand, I'll try not to hate it. We *will* work it out, Dalden."

He hugged her back, squeezing a bit harder than usual. "I am grateful, yet do you not need to make promises based on the unknown. We will indeed 'work it out.' I will allow no other thing to be."

His indomitable will managed to truly amaze her sometimes. They'd be fine because he said so. No matter what, no matter the obstacles, no matter anything. He'd have it no other way, wouldn't *allow* it. She wished she could grab hold of that certainty and take it to heart. But it was reassuring and took the edge off her fear.

"Did I mention architecture?" Martha's voice intruded in another really dry tone.

Brittany burst out laughing, the rest of her tension fading away.

Chapter 41

BRITTANY HADN'T MISSED TOO MUCH OF THE TOWN, just the approach. And Sha-Ka-Ra was bigger than she'd expected after Martha's remark that their towns didn't come in sizes she was used to—not so much in head count, but in the buildings being spread out with plenty of breathing space between each one. It was perched on a flat plateau, so nothing was built on the slopes of the mountain.

The main street was very wide, lined at regular intervals with trees of different colors—none that she actually recognized, though a horticulturist she was not—and lampposts. The posts were similar to what was used in the nineteenth century, when someone came by each night and lit the candles in them, but these used gaali stones that supposedly didn't need lighting, just uncovering, to reveal their soft glow.

She was looking forward to seeing one of these gaali stones she'd been told about up close and personal, a small one, though, since she'd been warned that large chunks were so bright they could blind. Yeah, right, something they couldn't prove to her, but she'd like to see how they were going to hide the seams of a battery compartment on the smaller stones.

Just now, though, she was experiencing some disappointment in finding that none of the buildings in the town were built of wood. Everything was light tan in color, either plaster or stone, she wasn't close enough yet to tell which. Mostly one-story houses, a few two-story, many with lovely arches, windows in all kinds of different shapes, each with its own yard and stable, its own garden. There were even some with balconies on their flat roofs, like sun decks. And clean. There wasn't a single piece of rubbish on the ground anywhere.

It was an even mix of old and new. The buildings were modern-looking, but the people weren't, and plenty had turned out to view the homecoming. Fifty men from this town had been absent for a long time, so their families were on hand to welcome them home. The procession started breaking up as each warrior was met by two or more members of his family. Oddly, never just one member, or more specifically, a lifemate. Even more oddly, now that it was noticed, there wasn't a single woman on the street standing alone.

Each woman there had a man with her. Each one was wearing one of those scarfy outfits they called *chauri*, each with a cloak draped behind them. They came in a wide range of colors, but all solid colors. There wasn't a single garment on anyone that was a mix of colors.

She found out later that the only reason she hadn't been given a cloak the color of the house she now belonged to was because her white T-shirt and blue jeans were already the two colors representing Dalden's house. That he'd let her wear her jeans, when the women of his town weren't allowed to wear pants of any kind, had been an exception made just for her because she wasn't Sha-Ka'ani and he'd wanted his people to see that plainly. It wasn't such a strict rule anymore though, now that his country knew that other countries like Falon's didn't even follow that rule, so exceptions for visitors did get made now, when that didn't used to be the case. It *was* still their rule though, which was why she was going to be supplied with a full new wardrobe and was expected to wear it.

She didn't mind. She was definitely tired of jeans after wearing hers for three months, even though they'd been cleaned and returned to her each day by that thing Dalden called dial-a-closet. She'd been offered ship's uniforms but had declined. She had never felt that her height looked good in one-piece jumpsuits of the clingy sort.

Old-style again were the marketplaces—they looked like something out of a medieval fair, with small tents with tables in front of them, or goods laid out on rugs. Then a beautiful park with a pond in it and children playing, that could have been in any American hometown.

The streets were laid out in even, straight lines.

Turning one brought the biggest building in the town into view, a towering white stone castle. Brittany's jaw dropped. It wasn't a castle as she knew them; it looked more like something that could be found in a fantasy picture book. It wasn't one big building, either, but built in sections, some round, some square or rectangular. All of the sections were in different heights and shapes so that none of them were the same, yet they grew in height pyramid fashion, the shorter towers on the outside, the tallest at the center. There were conical roofs on some, spiral roofs, normal roofs, and flat roofs on others, even crenellated walkways on top of some of the towers.

Tall white walls surrounded the castle, with a wide-open archway spanning the street to enter the inner castle yard. And they were heading to it. This was where Dalden and his family lived.

It was too much. They couldn't have built something like that just for this project; it had to be something they'd found and were going to make use of. The whole town, for that matter. Maybe somewhere in Russia or that part of the world. Didn't they have strange-looking buildings like this? And beautiful untouched countrysides? And towns so different-looking from anything she was used to?

She felt better with that conclusion, on firm ground again, and ready to be impressed as they rode through the archway into the castle yard. There was a long rectangular building right in front, with steps spanning the length of it, and at the center, a tall pair of steel-looking doors flanked by two warriors guarding it.

There was a stable for the *hataari* out front, and she got her first sight of small men that worked in it. They weren't really small, just not giant-sized like the warriors, and they dressed differently, too, in thin white pants and shirts. *Darash* males of the servant class apparently, whom she'd been told about. They were descended from a people conquered so long ago that no one had the date of it anymore.

They weren't slaves, but were more like a mix between a medieval serf and someone from the servant class of eighteenth-century England. They were the working class, the ones who did all the menial labor warriors snubbed their noses at, though they didn't get paid for it. There were laws to govern them, they had some rights, but they couldn't just pick up and move like normal working-class people. For the most part, she'd been told, they were a happy lot who knew their worth in as much as the warrior society would probably collapse without them.

Dalden's parents led the way inside. Shanelle would be staying a few more days, but then would be leaving for Ba-Har-an, a country that used to take a good three months to reach by *hataar*, but now was just a few minutes away by airobus. The distance, or prior travel time, was why not much had been known about Ba-Har-an before Challen had been asked to contact them for trade with the League, plentiful deposits of gold having been scanned in that region that other planets were interested in.

But it wasn't really the distance that had kept the two countries virtual strangers for so long, but that the Sha-Ka'ani were a sedentary warrior species. They might differ here and there in each separate country, but they pretty much universally weren't explorers. By nature, they preferred to stay, grow, and prosper in familiar surroundings.

Chapter 42

BRITTANY MIGHT HAVE BEEN PICKING HER JAW UP OFF the floor again after walking through the mammoth steel doors of the castle if she hadn't had prior warning—pools in bedrooms had been a clue—that inside wasn't going to look like a castle, but more like a palace. Even so, the bright, open airiness of the place made it unique: high ceilings, huge rooms, everything predominantly white, even the floors, which were marblelike granite.

Potted plants and flowering trees added greenery and other colors, and a blue carpet runner about twelve feet wide extended down the center of the hall where they entered. Two big rooms on each side of it were divided by arches, but arches so wide they were barely divisions, so that standing at the end of one room you could see clearly across to the end of the other. Tall open windows at the ends of these rooms let in soft breezes that kept the place cool, as well as so much daylight they might as well have been still outside. More trees in great urns were in the two rooms, along with backless couches, tables. . . .

Brittany's interest perked yet again. Tables meant carpentry, but her kind or—bah, there was only one kind. Yet Kodos had said there was no one around here who could teach him how to work with wood, that most of the buildings in town had been built by the Darash so long ago that the knowledge of how to do so had been lost. A challenge loser could be made to build a building in punishment, but it tended to be of such poor quality that it would never be used.

"You expect to lose some challenges?" she'd teased her young friend.

He'd replied a bit indignantly, "I want to show a challenge loser how to build something properly so it can be useful, rather than task the next challenge loser with tearing it down, as is usually the case."

She hadn't asked much about these challenges, figured they were just another warrior sport. But that conversation had illuminated the early one she'd had with Dalden when he equated her job with punishment. Warriors apparently could be merchants, could direct Darash in farming, but the only thing they did with their own hands was sword-wielding. Amazing how these people managed to connect and combine their stories into a whole tale without loose ends.

The party divided then, with plans to gather again for dinner: Challen off to attend to *shodan* business, Tedra off for a catch-up session with Martha, Shanelle and Falon off to her old room, and Dalden pulling Brittany along to his: down one hallway, then another, through a tower, then a garden outside with a covered walk that passed down the middle of it, into the next building, a few more hallways, some stairs, some more stairs. She was absolutely lost by the time they reached his room, which was so far away from the main sections of the castle that it might as well not be considered part of it.

The room covered the whole upper floor of the building it was in, so the balcony that surrounded it surrounded all of it. And yes, there really was a sunken pool in it, about eight feet round, like a miniature oasis with potted trees around it and a stone bench next to it. An extra-big bed was against the only wall that didn't have those open, arched windows. Not a normal bed as she knew it, it seemed to be a thick, stuffed mattress that fit into a full boxlike frame with no springs. Although it was very old-fashioned looking, the bedding appeared soft and comfortable.

There were a few more of those backless couches around a long, low table. Did they eat lying down? Carved chests sat between arches—detailed woodworking! The floors were again white marblelike stones but lightly veined with blue. Sheer light-blue curtains stirred at the windows, their only covering. There were no windowpanes or shutters.

"Tell me something, how do you keep out the flies and mosquitoes?" she asked Dalden.

"The what?"

"Insects, bugs, you know, tiny things that fly around in the air and make a habit of biting people."

"You will find such things in the lowlands, not up on a mountain."

"Ah."

"What think you of your new home?"

She knew he'd been eagerly awaiting that answer, though his expression was guarded. It was truly beautiful, his room, uncluttered yet lavish. But the whole place made her think of a sultan's harem. It brought home clearly that she was nowhere near her own home.

"It's big," she allowed.

"Indeed, a warrior has need of space to not feel confined," he agreed.

"I suppose."

"You do not like it," he remarked, clear disappointment in his tone now.

"I didn't say that," she said quickly. "It will just take getting used to."

"What do you not like about it?"

"Dalden, stop it. It's beautiful, really."

"You are mine, thus do I know you well, *kerima*, and you are not pleased with where you will live."

She held out her hand to him. When he clasped it, she brought his fingers to her mouth and bit one of his knuckles, hard. He raised a golden brow at her, though he barely felt any pain. He then grinned at her and pulled her to him. She pushed away.

"Bah, that wasn't an invitation. I was just proving you'll never know me as well as you think you do, which is a good thing. Surprises add spice to life, after all. As for these quarters, I *will* get used to them. But you saw where I lived. The house I had planned to build for myself would have been four times as big, but it still wouldn't be a castle. This place is like a—a fairy tale to me. Fairy tales are nice, but they are to be enjoyed temporarily, not permanently. I can't see staying here forever."

"You wish to live elsewhere?"

Instead of answering that, she asked him, "Did you plan to always live here, even after you took a lifemate and started your own family?"

"There is ample room here for more than one family," he stated.

"Yes, but you're missing my point. You have no desire to spread your wings? To have a place that's exclusively yours, rather than your parents'? Where I come from, people tend to leave home as soon as they're done with their schooling, to get out and start their own lives. Parents nurture up to a point, then turn their creations loose and hope they become productive adults. You *are* an adult, right?"

That got her a scowl that she couldn't help chuckling over. It was so rare of him to display frowns of any sort, other than in confusion.

"Sorry," she said. "But I had to ask, when nothing else around here is what I'm accustomed to. Do women even work on your planet, you know, make things, build, create? Do they have occupations?"

"Not in the way you mean."

"Take me home."

"Yet they do have hobbies."

"Doesn't suffice for a working woman," she mumbled. "And yet you *do* have industry here, craftsmen, woodmills. Evidence is all over your town. Where do you hide it?"

"Kan-is-Tra has not these things. We do not tamper with nature above the surface of the ground, other than to add to it in the growing of food."

"And below the surface?"

"The gold metal is extracted in many areas of the world, including here in Kan-is-Tra. Usually Darash who live near each mine have the knowledge of crafting and shaping the metal into useful objects."

"And the furniture I've seen?"

"It is made in countries to the south. Twice a year we get huge caravans of merchants who bring these things to us. There are potters in the north. Most all Darash are skilled in weaving, sewing, and dyeing. Glassmaking is known in the east, but is generally not transported by caravan because it rarely survives the trip."

"I guess that's something," she said with some relief. "How hard is it going to be for me to commute to one of these craft countries to get a job?"

No answer and a really blank look. Brittany sighed, but recalled that there was a better information source attached to her hip.

"Martha, what wasn't to understand about that question?" she asked.

"He understood it, doll, he just didn't *understand* it, if you get my drift. Sha-Ka'ani women have simply never had a need to work. They go from one protector to another all their lives, so they never lack for support—which doesn't mean they don't have responsibilities. If you need an example, think of them as the medieval lady of the keep who keeps everything running smoothly, supervises the servants, and makes sure things get done and done right."

"That isn't work, that's home chores."

Martha chuckled. "The culture you came from had evolved in leaps and bounds in just the last hundred

years, and took giant leaps where women are concerned in just the last fifty years. So I know your
women didn't always have this 'gotta work' attitude.
You have it because you were born when it was already starting, and by the time you reached adulthood
it was already fully in place. You expected to support
yourself, expected to continue doing so even after you
married, because your people have let their economy
go bonkers, forcing them to hook up to combine in-
comes in order to get anywhere."

"And your point?"

"Look back just fifty years ago, when your culture
expected women to stay home and be housewives as
soon as they married, and work in only menial, unimportant jobs until then, and your women were *happy* in
this role. Like the medieval women before them, they
didn't bring home the bacon, but they worked: they
ran the home front, which was often harder work than
their mates were doing elsewhere. Now look what you
have here: a lot of 'housewives' comfortable with that
position just as your women were a few decades ago,
something you *can* adapt to because it's not so far off
the mark from your own history."

"Inactivity is going to drive me up a wall," Brittany
insisted.

"That's a distinct possibility, and one that Dalden
will have to think hard to rectify," Martha said. "Paying attention, big guy?"

He was, and replied stubbornly, "Hobbies will occupy her as they have my mother."

Martha all but snorted, "Don't kid yourself. Tedra's
job had been in security. There was strenuous exercise
to keep fit, and the occasional head-bashing to do, but

for the most part it was a boring job because Kystran was a peaceful planet. So she's happy to putter about with a few crafts here, but she doesn't spend much time at it. She spends more time involving herself with people, and to a degree, security at the Visitors' Center. In other words, Dalden, she's active in things she enjoys. Everyone needs *that* kind of activity."

"My lifemate will have it."

"But not enough, if I know you, and I do," Martha warned. "She needs to build things, *useful* things. It's what she enjoys doing and she does it damn well. Her craft could also be a benefit to your people, since she can create things unknown here. Like this, for instance."

Brittany had been really impressed with Martha's speech, so it was a bit of a shock to have the double rocker that she had built on the ship suddenly appear before them. No one had carried it in. It was just—there.

"By the way, Brittany, my girl," Martha said now in smirking tones, "if that's an illusion, then you probably won't want to try sitting on it or moving it out to the balcony where it would be ideal for enjoying the view. On the other hand, if you would like to sit on it, you'll probably have to accept that I just Transferred it to you, huh? Just like I did with all your belongings, now piled into Dalden's closet."

"What belongings?" Brittany said resentfully. "You people didn't exactly give me time to pack."

"Your things weren't needed aboard the ship. But Corth II collected all of what was yours, with your roommate's help—all except your rust bucket. There was no point in bringing that here when its fuel source is unique to your world."

"All of my things?"

"Yes, not that you'll get much use out of your own clothing, though you can probably convince the big guy to let you wear some of it in private."

Brittany didn't remark on that demeaning "convince." She noted the two doors on the wall without windows. The larger one led to the stairs they had mounted to get to the bedroom. The other she moved to now, and saw that it was a room a bit bigger than her bedroom at home, filled with standing racks that had local clothing draped over them, so just about everything was seen at a glance. And there piled on the other side was her own suitcase stuffed to the brim, and some boxes she and Jan had been storing in case they were needed come Christmastime, filled with what hadn't fit in the suitcase. Even her tools!

The room had no windows in it, yet it was well lit. She had to visually search for a moment to find the source of the light, a small wooden box high up on one of the shelves where Dalden's boots and belts were laid out. For that matter, there had been short ledges in his room between the windows with identical boxes on them. This one was open on top, light pouring out of it.

She was able to reach it and lowered it until she could see inside. A small blue rock was in it, about the size of a silver dollar, a single stone, the rough edges smoothed, but not perfectly round. She brought her other hand close to it, but there was no heat coming off of it as there should have been, considering this was what the light was coming from. Closer still and still no heat.

It took a moment for her to gather the nerve to actually touch it, then clasp it in her hand. Cool it was, and almost weightless.

She was fascinated, wanted to examine it closer in daylight to find the seams she couldn't manage to see just by turning it around. There had to be some. There had to be a battery inside it, making it a light.

She brought it with her back into the bedroom. The rocker was gone, but a glance around showed that the sheer curtains had been opened on one wall, revealing an archway out onto the balcony where Dalden had moved the rocker. He was out there, too, sitting in the rocker. She gritted her teeth. Obviously, the real thing had been there before they got there, transported ahead of them along with her belongings. *Transfer my ass*, she thought to herself.

She'd figure out later where they had the cameras hidden that could project illusions. Just now she was too interested in the gaali stone in her hand.

She started toward the balcony to join Dalden where it was brightest. She was maybe ten feet away from the large arch when a cat landed on the balcony from somewhere but couldn't stop from the momentum of its jump. It slid into the bedroom, coming to rest at her feet, whereby she promptly fainted. Understandable, considering that it was as big as she was.

Chapter 43

DALDEN'S SIGH WAS NOT A STRENUOUS ONE AS HE LAID Brittany down on his bed. He sat down beside her and carefully smoothed her hair back from her face. Such a glorious color her hair was, unknown on his world.

"Did she hurt herself in the fall, Martha?" he asked, concern thick in his voice.

"Like intoxication that deadens natural reflexes, fainters drop without trying to break their fall, so they tend to suffer less bruising and breaking in the falling than someone who was fully alert."

"You did not answer my question."

"Oh, you wanted specifics?" Martha's voice turned dry. "She's fine, really."

He could be grateful for that, if nothing else. It was

everything else that was frustrating him to barely tolerable levels.

Martha had asked him to not follow his warrior instincts with his lifemate until she finally accepted him for who he was. But when would she? She was to have opened her eyes and accepted the truth when they arrived home, but still she wouldn't. Even the *hataar* she had discounted, claiming it an animal from her world in disguise. And the *fembair* had frightened her so badly she fainted, yet which animal would she claim *it* was from her world?

He was beginning to think his sister had truly cursed him all those months ago, when he'd helped to put her in Falon's control where she didn't want to be. She had been too furious to fully consider her words when she had shouted at him, *Stars, I hope the female you finally want for yourself isn't Sha-Ka'ani, and that she never gives you any peace!* It had been the worst thing she could wish for him, and it had already come half-true.

His woman wasn't Sha-Ka'ani. And her own stubbornness was going to keep an insurmountable wall between them. She loved him, yes, but not completely, nor would she as long as she continued to doubt who he was. This was already disturbing his peace. He had bided his time, though, had taken Martha at her word that Brittany would accept the truth once he got her home. That hadn't happened.

"Martha, have Shanelle come and collect her pet," he ordered.

"Not a chance," Martha declined. "The arrival of that furball was a good thing. I couldn't have planned it better myself."

"I will not allow her to be frightened again," Dalden said adamantly.

"She wasn't frightened, she just got a dose of shock too big for her to handle, no pun intended," Martha added, though she chuckled a bit. "But if you take Shank out of there before she wakes up, she'll just chock him up to another illusion. Let her get to know him, and there's no way she can deny him. Done deal."

"Our arrival here was to have been the 'done deal,'" he reminded her with clear annoyance.

Martha injected a sigh. "So I was a bit off on my estimate on the extent of her stubbornness. But she's borderline. She's clutching at straws now, and far-fetched ones at that, to maintain her disbelief. As soon as she realizes that the excuses she's coming up with to keep the wool over her eyes are more ridiculous than the truth, she'll open her eyes."

"How long?" he demanded.

"Practice some of that warrior patience that you men are renowned for. Give her one more week. Her 'project' scenario is like a security blanket to her. She clings to it because the truth frightens her."

"There is no *reason* for it to frighten her," he replied in frustration.

"Yes, we know that," Martha agreed. "But she can't see that far ahead."

"I happen to have perfect vision," Brittany mumbled in a groggy, testy voice as she came awake. "Which is a good thing, since this culture probably doesn't have eye doctors or glasses, does it?"

"Welcome back," Martha said cheerfully.

"I'm not sure I want to be back."

"Do you even think before you say things designed to inflict pain on the warrior?"

Brittany's eyes flew open in horror as that question sank in. She located Dalden next to her. She sat up immediately, and wrapped her arms around him.

"Martha is way off base," she assured him. "That wasn't said for you, but for her."

"Yet is it obvious that you do not like being here," he pointed out.

"No, if we're going to stay here, then I'll get used to it. I don't *have* to like it—really. What is important is that I *do* like being with you. Where doesn't matter. I'll be happy as long as we don't get parted when this is over."

He set her back from him, said sternly, "I have told you there can be no 'over' for us. You are mine for life, as I am yours. Such is the meaning of a lifemate. When will you accept this?"

"I—I think I do. It's just that everything else keeps getting in the way."

"Everything, as in your persistent belief that I am not a Kan-is-Tran warrior from Sha-Ka'an as I have told you I am? What, then, am I?"

"You're confusing me."

"You confuse yourself, woman."

Martha interjected, "I warned you the warrior was asserting himself, now that he's home."

"Be quiet, Martha!" they both said almost at once.

He had stood up in his agitation. Brittany's eyes flared as she finally noticed the *fembair* still in the room, spread out on the floor near the bed. Dalden had been blocking it from her view until he stood up. She didn't faint again, but the fear was back.

"Martha, get rid of that one!" she said in a high, squeaky voice, "that one" being yet another illusion, to her way of thinking.

"Contrary to *your* popular belief, I don't have any control over the local population, animal or humanoid. You can pet Shank, by the way. He won't bite."

That didn't reassure her. In this case, however, Dalden could not fault her disbelief. A *fembair* was a predator, the most vicious flesh-eater on the planet, something he would refrain from mentioning. Those that lived in the castle were tame, yet anyone who visited there and didn't know that would have the same reaction as Brittany.

It wasn't easy to tell these creatures apart. They were a non-interbreeding animal, so there was very little deviation in their looks. They all sported short white coats of an exceptional softness, long sleek bodies, and large round heads with great blue eyes. And fangs. He'd never taken one for a pet himself because they liked to sleep in beds and he didn't like sharing his—until now.

Explanations usually sufficed—for a Sha-Ka'ani who would not discount the existence of a *fembair*, merely that one could be found in a town, inside someone's house. They could make their home in any region of the planet, since the climates didn't vary greatly, they just preferred the wilds, far from people and cities.

The people of Sha-Ka-Ra were used to them wandering in and out of their town, and found it amusing that their *shodan* had managed to domesticate such a wild breed. All of which wouldn't matter to his lifemate, whose disbelief stemmed from a different reason. He still had to try.

"Shank belongs to my sister," he told Brittany. "She raised him from a baby when she was but a child herself, so he is completely tame."

"If he's hers, what's he doing here?"

"It was a game from when we were young. I would lure him here with treats so she could not find him. It became a habit with him. He still comes here expecting treats."

"I—I hope you had some on hand to give him," she said, her voice still apprehensive.

"He is content with petting instead."

He sat down cross-legged on the floor next to the *fembair*. It immediately curled its large, supple body around him. He scratched behind its ears, under its chin. Purring began immediately.

"Come here," he told Brittany. A glance at her showed that she was adamantly shaking her head. "Come *here*," he repeated in a tone that would have made any Sha-Ka'ani woman jump to obey, but not his lifemate. "We are going to remove your fear of this feline," he explained more calmly.

"Just remove the cat instead," she suggested.

Martha scoffed at her. "You think it's an illusion. Since when can illusions hurt?"

That caused Brittany to frown. Dalden took advantage of her confusion to point out, "Can you not hear the sound of his contentment?"

She couldn't help but hear it purring so loudly it rumbled about the room. She abruptly left the bed, marched determinedly toward him, and squatted down next to Dalden, though still several feet from

Shanelle's pet. He unbalanced her, and tugged her into his lap to bring her closer to Shank. She still didn't take her eyes from the *fembair*, not once, and her body was stiff with fear despite her determination. Courage his woman had, to charge ahead, fear or not.

He took her hand, guided it to the top of Shank's head, and left it there. She didn't pull it away. And having touched the animal, she now wanted to examine it fully. She lifted the heavy head, stared into the big blue eyes, measured the length of the two four-inch fangs.

"Sabertooths are extinct," she finally said in an awe-filled voice.

He knew not what she was talking about. Martha did and merely replied, "On your planet they are."

"Nor did they ever grow this big," Brittany said.

"Careful, doll, or you might convince yourself you're in a new world."

Brittany made a low growl and shot to her feet. "I know what you've done. You found this place and have somehow kept the rest of the world from hearing about it. What is it, something in the water here that makes the people and animals grow exceptionally large? Or genetic engineering? Have you actually tampered with nature here?"

Whether he could have answered her or not, Dalden knew those questions weren't for him. Whenever she came up with a new nonreality, it was Martha she accused with it. Never him. To accuse him would mean she would have to discuss *with* him her disbelief.

They had both been reluctant to do that, to "rock the boat," as Martha would put it. But perhaps it was time for that boat to sink. It was becoming painful, knowing that although she wanted to be with him, she wanted to be with who *she* insisted he was, not who he really was.

He needed advice from someone who had long dealt with an off-worlder.

He went to find his father.

Chapter 44

"WHERE'S HE GOING?" BRITTANY ASKED MARTHA when Dalden abruptly left the room.

"Probably off to kill something. Warriors tend to do that when they get frustrated."

"Something?"

"Don't sound so horrified, I was joking. But you, my girl, are going to have to start looking at this from his point of view. Every time you scoff at something we show you, you are scoffing at him. Every time you come up with one of your excuses, you're saying he isn't real. How do you think that makes him feel?"

"If he's brainwashed into believing all this, then it probably upsets him, but that's your fault, not mine. If he's just a really good actor playing his part, then I'll allow he might be frustrated that he's not convincing enough. But if you people would just figure out already that I'm never going to be convinced that you've brought me to another world in another star system, then he and I can both stop suffering with feelings we don't need to be feeling."

A big sigh. "Do you really want to be taken home and never see him again? Not that he'd allow it, but is that how you see this ending?"

"Why does that have to separate us? You admit the truth, I hopefully agree it's a necessary project for some greater good, and he and I can still be together—can't we?"

"The females in this society live with the males, not the other way around. For you to have him, you have to live here, in his world."

"Oh, I get it. Nothing else has worked, so now you're going to try using him specifically? The emotional angle? If I don't fall in line I lose him?"

"Your blood pressure is rising, kiddo."

"I have normal blood pressure!"

"Amazing how you humanoids can work yourselves into a snit without even half trying, and all on your lonesome. It makes my heart bleed, watching the way you struggle with so many conflicting emotions."

"According to you, you don't have a heart to bleed."

"Sector burn then, same thing."

Brittany made a sound of disgust and turned away from the door Dalden had left through. She didn't know why she continued to talk, or rather argue, with Martha, a faceless voice. The woman put new meaning into single-mindedness. Either that, or she was the head honcho in charge of the whole project, and everyone else was just window dressing.

Come to think of it, Dalden had never really tried

to convince her. He was just there, to comfort and soothe, to distract, to keep her mind off chaotic thoughts, to give her some peace. And if that was going to change now, she imagined she would go nuts within a month.

She finally noticed that the "prehistoric monster" was still in the room. God, it was *too* huge, as big as a horse. But she knew that genetic engineering could double the size of a creature. Could it be done again? And again? Until the result was something monstrous like this? Yet it was beautiful, sleek, well-proportioned, and probably graceful if it didn't have slippery floors to deal with.

Ironically, she really liked cats. She'd had several as pets when she was a child, and had one in the apartment when she first moved in, until it escaped out the door one day and never returned. That Jan turned out to be allergic to them was the only reason she hadn't gotten another yet. But she had planned to get a whole menagerie of them when she built her own home and had more room. But this one wasn't natural: it was a freak of experiments—or nature. And those fangs . . .

"Now you're being silly," Martha said, monitoring Brittany's edging backward away from the cat. "If that animal was the least bit dangerous to you, Dalden wouldn't have left you alone with it."

That was likely very true. He did seem to put great importance in protecting her. She decided she could safely ignore the beast. However it was created, it probably *was* a pet like they claimed.

But then Martha added, "There are more than just this one roaming the castle. Tedra and Challen both keep them as pets as well, so you'll come across more of them. Try not to run the other way when you see one coming."

"Why?" Brittany asked in new alarm. "Will that make it attack?"

Martha chuckled. "No, you just strike me as someone who doesn't want it to become common knowledge what a coward you are."

Brittany became very still. "Are we resorting to insults now?"

"Well, aren't you?" Martha persisted. "You're terrified to face the truth, which is pretty silly in my book. This is a nice world. Barbaric, yes, but it's got its upside to compensate for that."

Brittany relaxed. It was typical of Martha to toss out an eye-opener like an insult just to lead into what she wanted to discuss. She should be used to it by now.

"Name one—and don't mention the air again, when clean air can be found in most mountainous regions like this."

"How about a temperate climate planetwide? There are no seasons like you have. The climate remains the same year-round in each country, a bit hotter up north, a bit cooler down south, but nothing extreme."

"Like there aren't temperate zones at home," Brittany snorted.

"Disease is unknown here. Must be that clean air you didn't want me to mention," Martha said dryly.

She would be amazed—if it were actually true. "Is it the air?"

"I don't know," Martha admitted. "It's never been analyzed. It could just as easily be the Sha-Ka'ani constitution. But there's no need for you to worry. There's a meditech in the castle in case you catch something you shouldn't."

"I know damn well that thing isn't real. It's too bad I haven't caught a cold or the flu, to disprove your so-called meditech once and for all."

"I could probably order a virus for you. It might take a few weeks to get here, though."

"Cute, real cute. So far you're wasting your breath, Martha."

"What breath? Computers don't breathe."

"You know what I meant."

"Okay, let's try on faithfulness."

"Excuse me?"

"You'll find this interesting: a warrior who takes a lifemate will remain faithful to that lifemate for the rest of his life. I find that rather unique myself, since most cultures can't say the same, yours included."

"They love that deeply?"

A round of laughter. "You're forgetting they claim they don't experience love."

"You said some do."

"Some, yet all warriors with lifemates are faithful to them. It's more part and parcel with the protecting thing. It's a duty they take beyond serious, so it includes not only protecting from harm but also from emotional stress. And from fear. How many times now have you heard Dalden say he won't *allow* you to be afraid?"

"As if it's something he can control," Brittany scoffed.

"Don't kid yourself. He can and will assist you in conquering your fears, in one way or another. His methods might not be considered normal, but they'll be effective. Warriors are firm believers in teaching by example. Lasting impressions are gained in that way that mere words can't hope to duplicate. Which is why the old crime and punishment philosophy goes over so well here."

"Are we *finally* getting around to discussing the laws around here?"

"No, I've concluded that the extra information I've been feeding you isn't helping and could be part of the problem. You haven't been given time to assimilate what you're learning. Besides, you know the basics, enough to stay out of trouble. No more pants for you; they offend warriors. Never leave home without an escort at your side, or without wearing a cloak of this house, so anyone who doesn't know you will see that you're protected. Be respectful of other warriors, obey your own. See? Very simple."

"Bah, you call those laws?"

"Well, actually." Martha began another round of laughing. "I don't, but they do. Rules might be a more appropriate term. They don't have the kind of laws you're used to, because they don't have the kind of crimes that require strict laws. Theft here is more a sport, a back-and-forth kind of thing. If something or someone gets stolen, they merely buy it back, steal it back—or be glad it's gone."

"Then nothing gets stolen with the expectation to keep it? Why does anyone bother?"

"Like I said, it's more a sport, something done for fun. There's also no such thing as murder; the warrior ethic simply doesn't allow it. Challenge can cause death, but rarely; it's more desirable to humiliate an enemy with challenge loss service. They have their own rules that govern their behavior. Any disputes are brought to the *shodan* to decide. But you've let me get sidetracked."

"Is that even possible? For you?"

"My, aren't we feeling sarcastic today."

"I have a good teacher."

"I don't have an ego to bolster, doll, though I appreciate the effort. Now back to the subject, which was women. Women are the sole responsibility of their protector, be he father, lifemate, or *shodan*. Without a protector, they become claimable by any warrior who wants them, and a claimed woman isn't quite as desirable a position as a free one—for the women, that is."

Brittany stiffened, hearing that addition. "Why? And why haven't I heard about *this* before now?"

Martha injected a shrug into her tone. "It wasn't mentioned because it's never something you're going to need to worry about, as long as you obey those few simple rules we just discussed. As for why it's not a 'wanna-be' status, probably because it draws many parallels to slavery. A claimed woman can't be sold or mistreated, but they have so few rights, they might as well be considered slaves. Most women around here would rather enjoy the luxury of freedom."

"Free? When they can't go out without being led by the hand like a child?"

"Are we feeling aggrieved?"

"Damned right we are. You know I'm not going to be able to accept that when I come from total freedom of choice."

"So did Tedra, and she adjusted just fine. So will you. It just takes rearranging certain thinking and seeing the logic behind the protection that's offered. And I could swear I said I was done feeding you information. Start asking Dalden your questions. The answers he gives you will give you a better understanding of him. Signing off, doll."

"Wait! Martha?" No answer, but the *fembair* was still there, watching her with those big blue eyes. "Go away, cat. Go on, shoo."

It didn't, but then it perked up and glanced behind him, as if it heard someone calling. She heard nothing, but animals had better hearing than humans. It then rose so fast it lost its footing on the shiny floor, regained it, ran toward the balcony, and leapt off it the same way it had arrived.

Brittany sighed in relief. Martha signed back on long enough to laugh.

Chapter 45

BRITTANY DID START STORING UP SOME QUESTIONS FOR Dalden, but he didn't return to his room. A Darash female servant showed up instead, to help her dress for dinner. And she did need help in figuring out how to get into a *chauri*.

The outfit really was just a bunch of scarves, thin, almost transparent squares of material. A bunch of them were sewn together at the tips. These were placed at the shoulders, sections then draped just so to cover what should be covered, the lot then belted about the waist to hold it all in place. The skirt was separate but put together just about the same way, a bunch of scarves sewn to a waistband and just left to fall as they would about the legs, the tips floating halfway down her calves.

Other than walking fast or encountering a brisk wind, the outfits probably remained quite decent. They were soft, feminine, cool, sleeveless, V-necked, shapely with the belt, and actually very pretty in the way they draped. Sandals that tied on her feet were provided as well, kind of weird-looking, but serviceable.

The only thing that looked out of place now was the link attached to her belt. She almost considered leaving it behind, but didn't quite dare yet, even though Martha was being conspicuously silent.

The girl, Talana, who brought the white *chauri,* said more were being made for her and would be delivered on the new rising. Her much smaller height and dark hair and eyes marked her clearly as a Darash, if her simple sleeveless tunic and long skirt didn't. Brittany wasn't used to servants, but Talana didn't seem at all servile. She was perky, full of smiles, and seemed to have a sweet nature. Other than calling her "mistress," she was merely being helpful.

Talana was also tasked with leading her to dinner. They were passing through that little outdoor garden when Brittany stopped abruptly, it finally dawning on her that she'd had no trouble understanding Talana, nor Tedra and Challen earlier, nor anyone else she'd heard speak since their arrival that morning.

She couldn't believe something that simple would have been overlooked, and her tone reflected her incredulity when she said, "You people finally blew it, didn't you?"

"Mistress?"

"How are you going to explain the fact that the people here can understand me, if they are supposed to be a different race and language than mine?"

Talana was staring at her blankly, too confused to answer, but Martha proved she'd been eavesdropping all along when she said, "Took you long enough to notice, girl. But you got it a little backward. They aren't speaking your language; you're speaking theirs."

"Huh?"

"It really only takes one night of sleeping on a Sublim tape of a new language to have the basics of that language planted in the subconscious. Your world has started using a similar process, just not one as advanced as we have. And instead of just one session for you, I overdosed you a full week before arrival, to make the transition as painless as possible for you. Which is why it's taken you so long to notice that you have two completely different languages in your head now."

"Martha, why do you bother?" Brittany said with a sigh. "You *know* I'm not gonna buy this."

Martha's laughter had the distinct sound of triumph in it this time. "For once, kiddo, I don't have to convince you. You'll do that yourself with just a little thought. Take the word *chemar*. You know what it means, don'tcha?"

"Of course, it's—"

Brittany didn't finish. Martha had switched back to her own language with that last question, and she had answered in kind, naturally, without thought—just as she had been speaking the new language from the moment she first heard it spoken to her. Because she knew it so well, it had been automatic to respond with what she was hearing.

"It's too bad we gave you a simple communicator to

keep in touch with me, rather than a combo unit with viewers," Martha remarked. "I'd get a kick out of seeing just how white your face is about now."

Hot color suffused immediately. "Bright pink, if you must know."

"Finally amazed you, did we? With something you can't shrug off as being faked?"

Brittany ground her teeth. "Bull. Subliminal tapes are reputed to be a great learning tool, and you had three months to run one without my knowing about it while I slept. One day, my ass."

"If computers had patience to lose, I'd be losing mine about now."

That managed to surprise her. "You're giving up? It's over, then?"

"If you're never going to believe anything else, you should believe this. There isn't going to be an 'over.' There is never going to be a 'done.' The here and now is it. So get used to it. Start making the transition. You have a new life to live here; make the best of it."

"Just like that? 'Gee, how could I have been so wrong?' Is that what you expect me to say now?"

"Is it hereditary, this stubbornness of yours? Did your parents get along?"

"My parents got along fine. When they weren't fighting, they were kissing and making up."

"You said they were free-spirited."

"They grew up."

"Ah, finally the equation I've been missing. Okay, listen up, doll, because Probables did tell me what your problem is, and lucky for you, I'm still in a sharing mood. Your first fears were of the unknown. You equated aliens with weird-looking creatures. Those fears should have been alleviated by now. The Sha-Ka'ani aren't exactly what you're used to in humanoids, but they're close enough. Your next fear is more personal and still with you."

Brittany did not want to hear this. "This isn't going to—"

But Martha couldn't be interrupted. "You're afraid to accept the happiness that Dalden offers because deep down, you see him as too good to be true. He's everything you want in a mate, everything, so you figure something must be wrong. In your mind, no one gets that lucky. Your emotions are revving up. Did I hit a nerve?"

"Go to hell."

"I'll decline that, thank you," Martha said with a chuckle. "But your warrior is about to arrive and collect you. He's had a nice little talk with his father, and has concluded that you and he need some time off to yourselves where you won't be disturbed. Which means I'll be left behind. Good luck, doll. You're going to need it."

That last didn't sound promising, so she was rather apprehensive when Dalden appeared. He was wearing one of those determined looks again. And when he took her hand and started leading her off without a word about where they were going, her apprehension escalated.

Chapter 46

"YOU KNOW, DALDEN, WHEN TWO PEOPLE DECIDE TO
go on an excursion together, they usually discuss it fully beforehand, to make sure they both agree
that it sounds like a good plan. That way, one or the
other doesn't bring along any disgruntlement, and
they both can enjoy the outing."

He didn't reply. In fact, she'd made a number of remarks since they'd left Sha-Ka-Ra, and he hadn't
replied to them, either. He'd yet to say one word to her
since he dragged her out of the castle.

Two *hataari* had been waiting out front for them.
She had been alarmed, thinking she was to ride one of
them by herself, but she wasn't. The extra mount was
loaded down with stuff Dalden was taking with them,
and it merely followed along behind them.

It was full night by the time they reached the bottom of the mountain. Very dark, no moon yet, but normal-looking stars. She wasn't disturbed that there were no constellations that she might recognize. She'd already figured that they'd had to take her to some far-off country she wasn't familiar with for their project to have any hope of working, and the stars she was used to obviously didn't show up on this side of the world.

She was sitting in front of him on the *hataar*. He had one arm locked firmly around her waist, so she had no fear of slipping. The other controlled the animal. They were traveling slowly, which was probably a good thing. Everything was in shadow, without much distinction. She could barely see the dirt road they followed, if it was even a road. But he obviously could.

She was still wearing the thin *chauri*, which felt rather odd—riding sitting forward with one leg dangling on each side of the animal, the scarf pieces of the skirt split, exposing her limbs halfway up her thighs. She wasn't cold, though. The weather didn't seem to change much come nighttime, was just as balmy warm as the day had been. And Martha's link *had* been left behind as she'd predicted, taken from her waist and tossed into the foliage back in that garden.

Dalden was wearing a little less than usual. He was bare-chested, except for his medallion. A sword belt had been added, along with the weapon it was designed to carry. Long, wicked-looking daggers were also strapped to each of his boots. He was wearing those arm shields again, too, that had been donned for his fight with Jorran that day in City Hall. He looked positively primitive in that getup, which probably should have given her a clue that he wasn't the same Dalden she'd become used to.

When they passed into some woods that were so dark she gave up trying to see anything in front of her, she tried once again to get some answers. "How come you won't tell me where we're going?"

"When you say something that needs a reply, I will reply. Until then, my attention remains on the path, to assure it is safe."

Something that *needs* a reply? In other words, where they were going was none of her business?

"I don't know if I like the sound of that," she said with distinct unease.

"Your opinion was not requested, *kerima*."

She began to bristle indignantly. She couldn't help it. He was suddenly acting way too...too barbaric for her taste. It must be the clothes he was now wearing. Look primitive, become primitive?

"Martha was right. You—"

"Martha has been a hindrance," he cut in. "You may forget everything she has told you."

"Are we finally getting to the truth?"

"What truth would that be?"

"About where I am."

"Where you are is with me," he said simply.

"O—kay, then where are you?"

"With you." His chin came to rest on her shoulder. "I will always be with you."

That had a nice, secure ring to it, enough to mollify her somewhat for the moment. She supposed that if she tried, she could read between the lines of what little he'd just said. Martha had only been interested in convincing her to believe the whole fantasy. Dalden apparently had a different agenda. He *was* the fantasy, or at least, a very big part of it. And for him, it wasn't important that she accept where she was, only that she accept who she was with.

Martha had said she'd convinced him to be patient, which pretty much meant that he'd held back up until now from showing her what he was really like. Was that what this was about, then? They were going off to be alone somewhere so she could meet the real Dalden—the barbarian she'd only seen little glimpses of so far?

She suddenly felt a very real fear. What if she didn't like the barbarian side of him? What if, as the word *barbarian* implied, he was so insufferable that she simply couldn't tolerate living with him?

They continued to ride through the wooded region, seemingly without direction. If there was a path, she no longer saw it. Miles passed with nothing to see because of the intense dark. As they got close to a clearing, it actually appeared brightly lit by the starlight.

"We will make camp here," Dalden said, dismounting and then lifting her down to the ground next to him.

Brittany had been falling asleep, and hadn't noticed the small clearing they finally entered and stopped in. A stream was nearby. She could hear it, just didn't see it yet. And a moon had risen when she wasn't looking, a great yellow ball seen through the trees.

"Is this our final destination, or do we move on in the morning?" she asked.

"We will stay here."

"And the purpose?"

"We are here to learn."

"Let me guess. I'll be doing all the learning, you all the teaching."

He had moved to unload the other animal. He glanced her way now with a raised brow.

"Your tone suggests you have brought some of that mentioned disgruntlement along with you. Have you not stressed, more than once, that you would be happy as long as you are with me? Was that not the truth? Does the place then make a difference to you?"

She sighed. "You're right. I don't know why I'm on edge—actually, I do know, but I'll get over it now that we're communicating again. We *are* communicating again, right? No more of that ridiculous silent treatment?"

"There is always a reason for what I do," he told her. "Wild animals make their home in these woods. Hunters come here to hunt them. Travelers pass through them between towns, as do raiding parties. My full concentration was needed to keep our journey safe. It was also my intention to be assured that Martha could not follow us with her short-range scanning, which she could have done from our speech. You do not need her protection any longer. You are *mine* to protect. Lastly, you have learned that there will be decisions that I will make that are not open to discussion."

"Wow, that was a great explanation—up to the end," she said drily.

He went back to the unpacking, but remarked in a tone without inflection, "You are determined to find fault with me. Why is that?"

"Martha warned—"

"Martha again?" he cut in. "Did I not say you should forget what she has told you?"

"You know that isn't possible."

"When most of what she has told you, you do not believe anyway?"

She blushed clear to the roots of her hair. Fortunately, Dalden wasn't looking and probably wouldn't have noticed those hot cheeks in the dark if he was. She *had* been expecting the worst after Martha's warning, had been expecting all kinds of unacceptable traits from him now. He said they were there to learn, and that *did* go both ways. What was wrong with that? She wanted to know him better, to know every single thing there was to know about him, didn't she?

"I'm sorry," she offered. "I did bring along some preconceived notions, but I'm putting them to rest now. Would you like some help with that? I was a Girl Scout as a kid, so I know how to erect tents, get fires started, gather food, and otherwise survive in the wild."

That gained his complete attention for a moment. "Truly? Such things are taught the females in your world?"

"Well, not the whole world," she was forced to admit. "It's a program offered in my particular country, with similar programs in a few others. It's not mandatory, and actually, very few girls join it these days with so many other activities to interest them instead. That's a shame, since it teaches some really good qualities, as well as useful things to learn. Enjoying camping with my brothers, I personally found it very beneficial."

He nodded, even grinned at her. "I am pleased you enjoy camping. Most of our women would complain mightily at being taken away from the comfort of their homes. They fear the 'wild' as you call this."

She hoped their fear was without good reason, and at least he didn't say *Your wilds are different from our wilds.* As to her suggestion, he seemed to be ignoring it, probably because the tent turned out to be too big and heavy for her to handle, no thin nylon or army canvas, but a seriously thick material designed to keep out whatever might come snooping around. There were a lot of things to carry inside, though, after it was erected, and he let her help with that.

When they were done, a large fur rug had been unrolled in the middle of the tent as their bed. Numerous sacks were brought in, as well as a gaali stone box that provided tons of light, making a campfire obsolete except for cooking. That wasn't needed tonight, since he'd brought along their dinner, already cooked.

They shared the meal. Dalden insisted on feeding it to her, which she didn't mind. Actually, he made it an erotic experience, whether intentional or not, that she thoroughly enjoyed. So she couldn't be faulted in thinking they were going to be making love soon after the meal.

"Come here."

Replete and mellow now, and having decided this camping trip just might turn out to be a lot of fun, Brittany didn't hesitate. She settled down on his lap, felt his strong arms come around her, and expected him to kiss her. He didn't.

He tilted her head in the right position for kissing, but there were other things on his mind. "Was that difficult, to obey me?"

It was the word *obey* that set off alarm signals really

loudly this time. Brittany stiffened and tried to move off him to a distance more appropriate for a discussion she didn't think she was going to like. But she was held firmly in place. A subtle reminder that if someone refused to obey, she could be forced to?

Chapter 47

BRITTANY TRIED TO GIVE DALDEN THE BENEFIT OF THE doubt, she really did. She allowed that she was overreacting to one simple word. Granted, it was a word that went against the grain for an independent woman who'd been making all her own decisions since she left home. But all she had to do, really, was give the word a less offensive meaning. After all, she hadn't been "obeying," and said so to answer his question.

"I didn't see it as an order, but a suggestion."

"Had it been an order?"

"Then it would have required thought on my part," she replied.

"Why?"

"Because I don't like orders. They are demeaning, suggesting I lack intelligence. That's why I didn't join the military. I wouldn't have been able to handle hearing nothing but orders. And don't look so surprised; women can be soldiers where I come from. Wasn't it the same where your mother comes from?"

"I will allow that the technology of these other worlds make such possible, if you will allow that in a society where the weapons are only swords and strength, a woman cannot hope to compete."

That caused an image in her mind of her trying to wield a four-foot sword that she could barely lift against one of these barbarian giants. It was an absurd image that caused her to grin, then chuckle.

"Good point," she said.

Again he looked surprised, probably because he'd expected an argument. "You agree?"

"Sure, but that still doesn't mean I'm going to jump when you say jump."

"Even if an order is given for your own good?" Dalden persisted.

She gave that some thought, then allowed, "Some orders are acceptable, certainly, but you aren't my boss with power over my job, or my government, or the law. You're the man I live with in a mutual relationship. Why would you even want to order me around?"

"It is not a matter of want, but of necessity," he told her. "It is my right to protect you. No one else has this right more than I—even you. This is not something that normally needs explaining. Our women are taught from birth what they can and cannot do, and who they must obey in all things—and why. A warrior needs the assurance that if he finds his woman in danger, and must instruct her to remove her from that danger, she will not stop to argue about it. If he cannot have this assurance, then he would restrict her more than is needful, and neither would be pleased."

"Okay, I see where you're coming from. If your women have been trained from birth to literally jump when you say jump, then you men probably take it for granted that they'll do just that. But you have to take into account that I wasn't trained that way, so instead of getting an old horse to follow new tricks, how about just keeping in mind that I'm not one of your women and so need to be treated differently?"

"Do you tell me you did not follow the rules of your father?" he said.

She frowned. "Not just my father, my parents. Both. Rules mutually decided on. Yes, when I lived with them I obeyed their rules, but it was with full knowledge that when I left home I'd be living by my own rules. Do you see the difference? Those were temporary rules, the rules for a child. Our children grow up knowing that eventually they'll be on their own, with no one but government and laws telling them what they can and can't do. You, on the other hand, are telling me that your people continue to treat your women like children even after they're adults. I'm twenty-eight years old, Dalden, in case that hasn't been mentioned yet. I am *not* a child."

His hands suddenly cupped her breasts fully, heat searing through the thin material of the *chauri*. "I do not see you as a child."

She blushed. He couldn't miss it this time with the gaali stone lighting the inside of the tent with daylight brightness. He smiled. She scowled.

"Don't sidestep the issue," she said. "I wasn't talking about sex, but general overall treatment. I've heard the ridiculous rules you place on your women, that they have to dress a certain way, that they can't walk out their front door without having their hand held by some man. Has it even occurred to you how demeaning I would find such rules?"

Now he frowned. "You were told the rules but not why there are such rules?"

"Martha didn't want to discuss them at all, probably because she finds them as offensive as I do."

"They are not meant to offend, but to protect."

"If your town was a civilized town, then I could walk its streets without fear of being bothered. Are you going to tell me it's not civilized?"

"How many times were you told that Sha-Ka'an is viewed by modern worlds as a barbaric world? Did you truly think you would find equality between men and women here?"

The blush was back. She *had* been forgetting that. Not that it meant much when this was all make-believe anyway, but if she was going to go along with the program—or at least accept the possibility that Dalden really did believe all this—then she needed to keep in mind that nothing here was going to be what she would call normal. Why was she even fighting it? What she needed to figure out was if she could live with it—at least until the "program" was over.

"All right, so you're barbarians—I'm sorry, I know you don't like that word, but you brought it up. And you say these rules that I object to are for my own protection. Why? What happens if I don't follow them?"

"You will be punished."

"You have jails for this?"

"No."

"Whipping posts?"

"Do not be silly, woman," he said sternly. "Your punishment would be mine to give, and you know I would not cause you physical pain."

She did know that. He was always mindful of his greater strength, always so careful in touching her. She sighed, leaned forward to lay her head on his chest.

"I'm beginning not to like this discussion," she said in a tired voice.

He immediately began to soothe her with his hands. "We need not finish it now, yet it is my wish that you have no more questions when we leave here."

She was all for that. She'd avoided those answers, or had had them avoided for her, too long now.

"That must have been quite a talk you had with your father," she remarked.

"How did you—?"

"Martha."

"Ah, Martha. Indeed, she was thorough in her report. My parents were together to hear it."

"I take it you're ignoring her advice to continue patience with me?"

"My patience has not assisted you to full acceptance," he said.

"Dalden, I'm *never* going to accept this fantasy. If you can't accept that—"

"Answer me this, *kerima*," he cut in. "If you did believe everything that has been told you, would it change your feelings for me?"

"No," she said without hesitation.

"This is what my father pointed out to me. Martha's predictions of doomed failure did not take into account a woman's heart, which Martha can never fully understand."

"Then why bring me out here?"

"To assist you to a full acceptance of me."

"But I—"

He put a finger to her lips. "I will endeavor to explain what I mean. The culture differences that so worried Martha are indeed real. Already you have shown an unwillingness to embrace my culture. What you have yet to realize is there is no choice in the matter, for you or for me. If this were a different country in your world that you were visiting, would you refuse to obey its laws while you were there? Would you expect immunity from those laws simply because you were not born there?"

"No, but—"

Once again he didn't let her finish. "Then why do you resist doing so here? Because here is not real to you? Is your denial, then, the true problem after all?"

"But what's that got to do with a full acceptance of you?" she demanded.

"Everything, *kerima*," he said gently. "You *will* have to obey our rules. You *will* be punished if you do not. Can you accept this, and understand that it is not something I will enjoy doing? A warrior often suffers as much, if not more, in the punishment of his woman."

She didn't snort, though the urge was there. They treated their women like children—the punishments were no doubt of the same nature. His worry, and what was beginning to worry her as well, was, could she accept *him* enforcing one of those childish punishments on her? Probably not. But she could compromise. She could follow their silly rules so that the matter would never be put to the test.

She said as much. "How 'bout I just obey the rules, so you can stop worrying about punishments you're never going to have to dish out? Will that ease your mind?"

"It pleases me greatly that you will make this effort," he said gravely.

Her brow knitted in a frown. "Then why don't you look pleased? That wasn't what you wanted to hear, was it? Do you *really* want my permission—and forgiveness—before the fact?"

"These things are not needful," he replied. "It is your understanding that I wish to assure. I have explained what can happen. I need to know that you understand why such things are necessary here."

She counted to ten before she lost it over what *wasn't* needed. She finally sighed.

"I think I'll take you up on that offer to drop the subject for now. You've given me a lot to think about. I need some time to digest it."

Having said that, she tried once again to move off his lap and out of his reach. Again, she couldn't. She narrowed her eyes on him.

"That's major advantage taking, using your strength against me like this."

"A benefit of a warrior," he said, grinning at her to show that he might be teasing, but she'd place her wager on not. "For what reason do you wish to move?"

"So I can sulk, of course," she retorted.

He shook his head at her, still grinning. "If we are done with discussing matters of importance, then it is time for—other things."

"Such as?"

"A benefit of being a woman."

It turned out to be quite a benefit that night.

Chapter 48

IT NEVER SEEMED TO CHANGE, THE COMPLETE AND utter distraction of Dalden's kisses. From the moment his mouth claimed hers, everything else was forgotten. Where they were, what they'd been discussing, her annoyance—all gone with the touch of his lips.

That was quite a power he had over her. If she didn't trust him, it might worry her, that power.

He stripped her in his lap, a task made too easy by the *chauri*. He merely placed his hands by her neck, moved them over her shoulders and down her arms in a slow caress, and the *chauri* went with them, baring her to the waist. She barely noticed because he was still kissing her, a deep "you're mine" kind of kiss that instantly ignited her passions—which was a good thing. His hands might be slowly caressing her, but the rest of him was on a much faster time schedule. A slight change in her position and she was impaled and exploding with pleasure. All within a matter of minutes. And still sitting on his lap!

Dazed, breathless, still throbbing, she barely had a chance to notice his grin before he began anew. And thus it went for most of the night. She lost count of the many different pleasures she received. Her barbarian was inexhaustible. She wasn't, but sleep wasn't on the agenda. He had only to touch her again, to start the kissing again, and she was fully awake and in need.

Overdosed on pleasure. Absolutely amazing. This was his way, she knew, of making up for all the harsh "realities" of his world that she didn't like, by reminding her of the benefits—the benefits of being a woman. What he should have said was the benefits of being *his* woman.

She was hard pressed when she finally awoke the next day to get rid of the silly grin she was wearing. It was late. They'd slept the morning away, or at least she had. He was already awake and simply holding her next to him when her eyes opened. And he seemed no more inclined than she was to start up that depressing "this is how it is" conversation again.

He fed her leftovers from the night before. He wanted to know about fishing, which she'd mentioned more than once. They apparently had fish in their lakes and streams, but no one had ever bothered to think of adding them to their list for daily consumption. She didn't buy that, but had fun whittling a fishing pole with one of his daggers, borrowing some *hataar* tail hair to braid for a line, and showing him how to use the finished product in the stream nearby.

He was impressed, but he concluded there was no challenge in hunting fish, as he put it. He preferred larger game that would provide more than just one meal. She'd already figured out that he would be doing some of that kind of hunting on this trip, and he left around midafternoon to take care of finding their dinner.

She wasn't sure why she'd thought she'd be allowed to go with him. Actually, it was probably because when she'd hunted with her brothers, they'd all done it together. But women here weren't allowed to hunt whether they knew how to or not. Nor was it open to discussion. She was ordered to stay in the tent while he was gone, to not leave it under any circumstances, and that was that.

He did pause long enough to explain that the tent was her only protection while he wasn't with her. It would be considered her home, and as long as she was in it, any warriors who might come by wouldn't intrude without permission. It was also built sturdily enough to keep out any animals, so she'd be safe as long as she stayed *in* it.

She'd had to agree to do that before he would leave. She felt he was making too much out of nothing. She'd been outside while he was there, down to the stream, around the edges of the clearing. It was a peaceful setting. She wasn't worried about being left alone there, was more annoyed at being restricted to the tent than anything else.

But he assured her he wouldn't be gone long, gave her a parting kiss to give her something else to think about, and rode off. She paced about the tent for a bit—prowled was more like it—until she finally shrugged off her annoyance and decided to grab a short nap to pass the time.

She'd no sooner laid down on the soft fur rug than she heard the *hataar* that had been grazing in the clearing run off. She didn't think much of it. If it was anything at all like a horse, even a bird flying past could spook it. The animal should have been staked. Dalden would just have to go chase it down when he got back. But then she heard other noises closer by, the sound of clicking, of something dragging on the grass, a couple of thumps.

She got slowly to her feet. She'd heard Dalden's *hataar* leave. She would have heard it return. It wasn't Dalden out there making noises around the tent edges. The sounds were too strange to be coming from a human anyway, so it was some animal investigating the tent. She still wasn't that alarmed. If it was a predator, it would have chased after the *hataar*—unless it counted the *hataar* as too big to handle.

She had no weapon other than her fishing pole, which wouldn't do her a bit of good against the two-legged kind of predator, but might scare off the four-legged kind. But she was more curious than anything else. This was an unplanned visit, so no illusions or costumes would be involved. She had a chance to see a perfectly normal-looking animal from her world, a deer maybe, or a bear, something to reinforce her version of where they were.

She just wanted a quick look. Dalden wasn't there to see her disobey his order, and she'd be back in the tent before he was. She unlatched the tent flap. The animal was on the left side of the tent. She stepped outside, moved slowly to that corner, and peeked around it—and stared wide-eyed at yet another oddity that defied belief.

It was a long, spiked tail that had been dragging on the ground. Her gasp drew slanted yellow eyes to her. She ducked back and dove back into the tent, but it used powerful legs to leap over the corner to try to stop her. It was so swift it had turned and landed in time to see where she went, and pushed its way in behind her. She didn't know that until she turned to secure the flap and saw it squatting there just inside the tent, staring at her.

She had absolutely no idea what it was. The animals she'd seen so far, though weird, still bore some resemblance to animals she knew. Not this thing. It was big, about four and a half feet tall, and fat, at least on the bottom half of it. The top half tapered to thin shoulders and a round head with pointy ears, no visible nose, those slanted yellow eyes, and a jutting jaw with lots of teeth. Its arms were misshapen and seemed too short compared to the rest of it to do anything. It maneuvered and balanced itself with the long tail and powerful, squat legs, each with three clawed toes. It was gray and hairless, its skin wrinkly. If not for all those exposed teeth, it would simply look funny.

She was nervous, but she didn't think anything that looked that weird could be dangerous. It could have just followed her out of curiosity. A lot of animals were more afraid of humans than vice versa, and this one might just need reminding of that. With that in mind, she picked up the fishing pole at her feet and thrust it forward like a sword, at the same time screeching really loudly. Nothing. It just stared at her.

Annoyed now, she poked her whittled stick at it a few more times, growling, "Get the hell out of my house. Go on. Scat! Shoo!"

One thrust actually touched it. It didn't like that, started some growling of its own, and that clicking sound again. Its teeth? The claws on its stubby arms? She couldn't tell, but decided one of them had to leave. And if *it* wouldn't . . .

She moved slowly to the front of the tent, forcing it to turn to keep its eyes on her. She hit her stick on the floor a few times, trying to get the thing to move back away from the opening that it was blocking. It did, but its growling increased. It was getting angry. It lowered its head nearly to the ground, raised it again.

She was afraid it was getting ready to rush her. She would have liked to back it farther into the corner before she exited, her hope being that if she made enough noise on that side of the tent from the outside, it would turn in that direction rather than follow her, and trap itself in the tent long enough for her to get away.

She ducked outside, screamed Dalden's name, ran her stick along the side of the tent as she raced toward the back, then ran straight for the stream. Water. A scent masker. And she'd noticed a few pockets deep enough where she could submerge if necessary. She just had to reach it while that thing was still trying to find its way out of the tent.

It landed in front of her. It had leapt an incredible distance to land right in front of her! And there was no stopping, as fast as she'd been running. She collided with it, tumbled over it, and rolled down the rest of the bank, coming to rest half in, half out of the stream.

She was dazed, but too frightened now for that to

stop her. She sat up. It was foremost in her mind that she had to get to the other side of the water. It might be afraid of the water, or at least wary enough not to cross it. That could be her only salvation.

It landed on top of her, breaking half of her rib cage, crushing one lung. There was no breath left for screaming, no breath at all. She fainted for a moment, and woke up to excruciating pain ... wet, warm, bloody. She wasn't dead yet, but wished she was. Its hands really were useless. It was dragging her out of the water with its teeth, feeling like it was ripping off half her leg in the process.

Her last thought before the pain sent her back into blessed nothing was that Dalden had brought her across the universe to be eaten by a stupid beast. He wouldn't be pleased.

Chapter 49

"*A*RE THEY REALLY THAT STUPID?" TEDRA DEMANDED of the computer link in her hand. "To declare war on a League-protected planet is to declare war on the entire Confederation."

"Not stupid," was Martha's placid reply. "Just too primitive to think that far ahead."

Tedra was furious, not over the audacity of the inhabitants of Century III who had arrived en masse, but because Challen was taking this seriously *and* looking forward to a good old-fashioned war. But there'd be nothing old-fashioned about it. The Centurians weren't planning on landing for any hands-on fighting. They'd be bombarding from space.

Jorran had apparently done a lot of crying and complaining when he got home. That he hadn't been in the best condition, left somewhat deformed by his mended injuries, had obviously enraged his relatives enough to want revenge on his behalf. You simply didn't treat a High King that way and expect to live to tell about it.

The highest High King of the lot, Cayden, head of their royal family, had confiscated every visiting ship in their star system, for a total of twenty-three ships, from common traders and swift privateers to battleships. An impressive flotilla, which was probably why Cayden had sounded so confident. He thought he had the upper hand.

Martha disagreed. "Rust buckets," she called his entire fleet, every one of them so ancient, they hadn't been converted to crysillium, much less gaali power. Which was why she wasn't the least bit concerned about this invasion. Still aboard the *Androvia*, she was just waiting for permission to blast the Centurians back to where they came from.

Challen was refusing to give that permission, which was probably a good thing. The Centura League strived to avoid war, to exercise any and all peaceful options first, resorting to war only as an absolute last measure. They expected planets under their protection to follow suit. Tedra knew that and would have been pointing it out, if she weren't taking this personally. Challen was also taking it personally, but for different reasons.

Demands had been made. If not met, war would be declared. So far they had stalled the Centurians, who were asking for Dalden's head, and his woman. Dalden wasn't around to offer it, had taken his lifemate off for some prime time alone. Even if they knew where he'd gone, it would take time to reach him. Not that Tedra had any intention of letting him know that his head was on the table for negotiation, when Dalden was known to make sacrifices in the name of honor.

It wasn't that Dalden's death and his lifemate delivered into Jorran's hands was the restitution the Centurians wanted for the insult dealt to Jorran. This wasn't even considered by Challen. No, he was seeing this from a warrior's viewpoint, not a father's.

The Centurians dared to make war on Sha-Ka'an. And there wasn't a warrior on the planet who wouldn't be insulted by this and rise up joyfully to the occasion. The planet as a whole didn't know about it yet, however. The demands had come through the Visitors' Center and were relayed directly to Challen through his link to the director of the Center. One of the Centurian ships had managed to fool the Center into gaining entry before the rest arrived. The director was in their hands, the global shield already turned off.

A lot of damage—and deaths—could result if the Centurians started laser-blasting the planet. Which was why Challen was stalling. He wanted time to get his warriors to the Center.

Tedra just wanted a little extra time to think of all the ramifications before she mentioned that it wasn't necessary to go to the Centurians, that those who had taken control of the Center could be brought to them instead, instantly Transferred, just as Cayden could be. But when Challen became warriorish, he seemed to overlook what Mock IIs in super-high-tech warships were capable of. Or perhaps he didn't overlook it, he'd just rather do it his way.

And he was about to do just that, to leave with his warriors, who had been summoned to the castle. Tedra moved quickly to block his way.

He had only to look at her stubborn expression to warn, "Do not interfere, woman."

Which meant that if she did now, she'd be in trouble. He hadn't told her to be quiet, though, and she wasn't.

"Which would be more satisfying, to have Cayden laying in a pool of blood or to have him eat crow and beg your forgiveness for coming here?"

"The man is a leader of his people," Challen replied. "I would not belittle him with humiliation, but offer him honorable death."

"But which would be more *satisfying*?" Tedra persisted.

He gave her a chagrined look. She took advantage of his moment of indecision to add, "And he's not at the Center. Only Jorran and his crew are. High King Cayden is up on the biggest of their ships, calling the shots in what he thinks is complete safety."

"Jorran isn't at the Center, either," Martha suddenly put in to Challen. "You might want to hold off doing anything, big guy. I've just been contacted by Jorran to perform an emergency Transfer to a meditech."

"For him?" Tedra asked in surprise.

"No, for your daughter-in-law."

Tedra paled. "Was it in time?"

"Undetermined yet," Martha was forced to reply. "She's lost a *lot* of blood, is barely hanging on by a thread." It was eight suspenseful seconds before Martha was able to add, "Okay, Transfer was in time; she's out of immediate danger. I hate to say it, but Jorran saved her life by contacting me. You are now officially indebted to the jerk."

Tedra swore a blue streak. Challen came to put his arms around her.

"It is doubtful his act was without self-interest," he said. "Was it, Martha?"

"No indeed. He wanted Brittany saved so he could take her home with him. Those idiots lucked out getting Transfer this time on one of their ships, but there's still not a meditech among them. He managed to find Brittany by scanning for her language. He Transferred to her location, killed the *sa'abo* that was ripping her to shreds, and knew that the only thing that could save her at that point was a meditech. And the only way for him to get her to one was through me."

"Where the hell is Dalden?"

"Scanning the surrounding area for him now," Martha answered. "But with him not talking, I'm not likely to get a fix on him. And he's guaranteed to go berserk if he shows up and finds all that blood at his camp but no Brittany. I had visual and it wasn't pretty. So I've sent Corth II there to await his return with explanations."

"Are you sure Jorran didn't Transfer him somewhere?" Tedra asked.

"He swears Dalden wasn't there when he arrived. I'm inclined to believe him. He's pretty shaken up."

"*He* is?"

"And Brittany wouldn't have tangled with a *sa'abo* herself if Dalden had been there," Martha pointed out.

That being true, the edge was taken off Tedra's fear for her son. Which left only the annoyance that they couldn't deal as harshly with Jorran now, with their gratitude getting in the way.

"What was he doing searching for them?" Tedra asked next. "Are their demands just a ploy?"

"Probables tell me Jorran neglected to tell his relatives about me and the *Androvia*. The highest king is legit. He *is* here for revenge, his house offended by our treatment of one of theirs. But Jorran knows firsthand what they're up against, and that the only way he'd get what he wants would be to sneak in and accomplish it himself while we were otherwise distracted by Cayden."

"So he brought his relatives here knowing they'd get egg on their faces? Why?"

"When I mentioned that he liked our Brittany, I didn't think it was necessary to stress just how much he liked her. All things considered, we shouldn't have crossed paths with him again, so it wasn't an issue."

Tedra frowned. "How much are we talking about?"

"He wants her for his queen, and since she'll bring him no land, status, subjects, wealth, or other queenly gains, it's a safe guess his 'want' is strictly personal."

"*Farden* hell," Tedra mumbled.

"He's given up his advantage by rescuing her and giving her back to us for mending. Had he found them alone, it's a guarantee he would have Transferred them both to his ship and would be racing for home already, using Dalden as leverage to keep us from following. And Dalden wouldn't have found the journey pleasant. That Jorran found Brittany about to die put an end to those plans. Her dire condition has probably saved Dalden from endless torture. I hope the boy takes that into account before he starts thinking about punishing her for tangling with a *sa'abo*."

"Did she have a choice?"

"That critter is too stupid to find its way inside a secured tent. Need I say more?"

"No, but near death—I'd say she's already suffered enough."

"Since when do warriors take previous suffering into account when lessons need to be taught? That only reinforces their need to assure the situation will never happen again, and we know the name of that tune."

That got Challen a glare from Tedra just on general principle. That he chuckled at his lifemate confirmed that Martha had called it right.

Chapter 50

IT WAS FORTUNATE THAT THE LID OF THE MEDITECH opened before Brittany's eyes did, or she would have thought she'd been sealed in a coffin. Not a thought far off the mark, since she had known that she was going to die. But she wasn't dead, or if she was, at least the pain that had surrounded her was now gone. Yet with Tedra standing there offering her a hand to help her up, she had to conclude she wasn't in Heaven, either.

She sat up, carefully at first, in case she was only imagining that the pain was gone. But it was. She could breathe normally now, too. And looking down at herself, she saw the evidence that she hadn't dreamed it all, her *chauri* in bloody shreds barely hanging onto her limbs. But no wounds on those limbs.

"It works from the inside out, which is why it doesn't require naked patients," Tedra remarked.

Brittany recognized *it*, the meditech that had put her back together. It sat in a small room by itself, she assumed in the castle. No one else was there, just Tedra—and Martha, if that was a computer link hooked to Tedra's belt.

"Would you like a list of the injuries that have been fixed?"

"No, I felt most of them as they occurred," Brittany said. "I don't need reminding, thank you."

Tedra winced. "You're taking this pretty calmly."

"I'm not calm," Britanny replied. "The shock hasn't worn off yet."

"Understandable. That was one of the nastier predators around here that you tangled with. *Sa'abo* bring down their prey by ripping out its neck, usually resulting in instant death. I'm glad it didn't reach yours."

"That wasn't the shock I meant. You really are his mother, aren't you?"

It must not be a computer link that was attached to Tedra's belt, or Martha would be gloating by now. Tedra merely smiled in understanding.

"It is a bit difficult to ignore being brought back from the brink by a machine, I suppose," Tedra said. "But don't try to assimilate everything you've discounted yet. You'll have plenty of time for that."

Assimilate everything? Things were rolling through Brittany's mind at high speed: the *Androvia*, all the different planets that had been mentioned, the different degrees of evolution, Sha-Ka'an on the bottom of the ladder in development, barbaric, yet amazing for all that . . .

Embarrassment began to override the shock. These people had been so patient with her, Dalden unbelievably so. She'd as much as called him a liar countless times with her continued disbelief, but he hadn't given up on her. He wasn't brainwashed, hadn't been playing a role. He was a real alien from a warrior caste of people who were barbaric in their customs and beliefs. And she was married to him, or bound to him by their equivalent of marriage—his lifemate.

"You'll want to go to your room and change clothes before Dalden is found and Transferred here," Tedra was saying, taking no pity on a mind gone haywire with the unbelievable suddenly turned real. "The less he sees of the trauma you went through, the better."

"Why? It wasn't his fault. He warned me to stay in the tent. There's no reason for him to blame himself."

That caused Dalden's mother to frown, and as if Martha had a visual of it, she proved she was present and accounted for by saying to her owner, "No need for confusion, doll. Our Brittany sees this from an Earthling's perspective, where their men have been conditioned to shoulder blame whether blame is theirs or not. She hasn't grasped yet that when a warrior's rules are obeyed, protection is guaranteed. So the only way for harm to occur is if the rules are broken. All blame is then on the rule-breaker, and the rule-giver is required to reinforce those rules with lessons guaranteed to leave lasting impressions, so the rules don't get broken a second time."

"Did you have to remind her of that, Martha?" Tedra said with a sigh.

"'Course I did," Martha replied in distinctly smirking tones. "Nothing like a big dose of reality to shake off the cobwebs that shock leaves behind."

It did take a few moments for those cobwebs to clear enough for Brittany to grasp what Martha had actually said in her long-winded way. She went very still.

"Let me get this straight. I just went through hell. If it weren't for mind-boggling inventions like Transfer and meditechs, I'd be dead right now. And you think Dalden's going to punish me on *top* of that?" No answer from either of them, which was answer enough and had Brittany shaking her head. "No way. He wouldn't."

"Let's look at the facts." Martha switched to her teacher tone. "The beast that nearly had you for dinner is about as dumb as they come. It could smell you in your secure tent. It could be certain you were in there. But it's too stupid to even think of looking for a way to get in at you. It would instead wait for you to come out. It might wait a long time, because it does smell food. But eventually it would get hungry enough to go look for food that it can actually see instead of just smell. Of course, Dalden would have returned before then and killed it with little difficulty. Warriors are good at that. So if you *had* stayed in that tent as you admitted you were told to, would you have gone through hell?"

"You're missing the point that I've already suffered enough."

"No, you're missing the point that you wouldn't have suffered at all if you had simply obeyed your warrior. And he's going to be furious that you came to harm because you didn't obey him—and make damn sure you never put yourself in that kind of danger again. Are you understanding their logic yet?"

"I understand it," Brittany mumbled. "That doesn't mean I agree with it."

A chuckle from Martha. "Warriors don't require agreement. Tedra can assure you of that."

"Leave me out of this, old girl," Tedra replied. "I happen to be getting along just fine with my warrior this week. Don't remind me why I shouldn't."

"She's exaggerating, kiddo. My Tedra gets along with her warrior all the time. She might step out of line occasionally and suffer the consequences, but she makes sure Challen makes up for it big-time."

Brittany stared at her mother-in-law. "You come from a society much more advanced than mine. I would have thought that you, more than anyone, would find these rules and laws as barbaric as I do. Ordered to stay in that tent, I fully understand now. I didn't and found out painfully why I should have. But everything else? Unneeded escorts, clothes to mark your status—why don't the rules get put on the men instead? Why aren't they told that women are to be left alone? How can you accept being treated like a child?"

"Hot damn, I'm looking forward to this answer myself," Martha said.

Tedra ignored her instigating computer to hook her arm through Brittany's. She began to escort her to her room while she explained, "I don't accept being treated like a child, but I do accept the laws of the land. No one expects you to be a model of Kan-is-Tran womanhood overnight, not even Dalden. I had an easier time adjusting because my first month here was spent in a challenge loss, which was about as close as you can get to slavery. Since I had agreed to the challenge, I had to honor the results of losing it, so I couldn't really complain about how belittling the position was. My point being, I was introduced to the way things are around here while I was on the bottom of the social scale. Which made it much easier to accept the things allowed higher up on the scale, even if most of those things grossly favor the male of the species."

"Grossly?" Brittany snorted. "How 'bout one hundred percent?"

Tedra grinned. "Face it, it's a male-dominated society, and because these males happen to come in giant-like proportions, they've had to make up a few little rules to keep themselves from hurting their women. The women raised here don't mind the rules because they've never known anything better. Are you getting that particular point yet? To them it's *not* barbaric, it's normal."

"And exceptions don't get made for visitors?" Brittany asked.

"Why should they? It's not as if a visitor from another world can be differentiated from a visitor from another country here. They don't have schools as you know them. They aren't taught about other people on their own world, much less about other worlds. They exist in black and white, and don't recognize much gray. They keep things simple, uncomplicated. If a woman doesn't have a protector, then she's up for grabs. You can't get much simpler than that. But once she has a protector, then she has to obey him to keep herself protected. You really can't get much simpler than that."

"You do realize that you've just defined childish?" Brittany said.

Tedra didn't try to deny it, at least not completely. "From an advanced perspective, certainly. But from their perspective, it's actually pretty civilized. They aren't killing each other to take what they want. They've set up laws that they all abide by, self-governed by their warrior code of honor. They are light-years beyond our own prehistoric people. They are unique, without comparison—actually, that's probably half your problem, kiddo. You need to stop comparing them to your own species."

"It's kind of hard to ignore twenty-eight years of my own upbringing."

"Because you're looking at things here while wearing modern glasses. Take off those glasses and you'll get a completely different view, one much easier to tolerate. I know that's asking a lot. It was also easier for me because I spent three years training for a career in World Discovery before I was allowed to switch to my preferred career in Security. And one little gem I learned in Discovery was that if you want to live on a world other than your own, you do so not with the intention of changing that world, but of adapting to it. These medieval worlds *must* be allowed to evolve at their own pace. It's not for us to tamper with them just because we know better ways of doing things."

"I hate to break up such an excellent lesson in how to deal with your local barbarian," Martha interjected sarcastically. "But Corth II just informed me that Dalden is now approaching his camp."

Brittany frowned. "If Dalden didn't find me and get me back here, who did?"

"Martha did."

"I thought her link got left behind."

"It was," Tedra said. "It was actually Jorran who found you, and only because he was specifically looking. He had his ship computer contact Martha for a Transfer directly to a meditech. You didn't have enough blood left for any other option."

"Specifically looking?"

"He has returned with an army for revenge—and you. Not that he'll be getting either, but because he more or less saved your life, we're having to deal with him diplomatically again. He's requested permission to speak with you and has agreed to leave afterward. Because it's a peaceful way of avoiding an outright war with Century III, we were inclined to agree. He's catching a ride here on an airobus as we speak."

"No Transfer?"

"He's used up his quota for the day—which reminds me. Corth II will be filling Dalden in on what happened, but you might want to point out to him that your meeting up with that *sa'abo* caused Jorran to change his original plan, which was to capture you both and cart you off to Century III, and Dalden probably wouldn't have survived the trip."

"Delete that," Martha said. "Jorran wouldn't have found them without her reverting to using her own language. It was what he was hoping for, the only way he could have located her. And she wouldn't have done that if she weren't alone with a *sa'abo* breathing down her throat."

"*Farden* hell, must you always get technical, Martha?" Tedra complained.

"Never mind that. Dalden wants Transfer now, and

I mean *now*. I warned you he'd go berserk when he saw all that blood."

"For stars' sake, you know how to stall someone better than anyone else. Let her at least change clothes first," Tedra said, then suggested, "Transfer him to Challen. *He* can calm him down some, if you can't."

Which made Brittany start to panic. If Dalden's mother was this worried that she was in big trouble, she was likely in some seriously big trouble.

Chapter 51

CHANGING CLOTHES WASN'T ENOUGH. BRITTANY WAS still smeared with dried blood, even though there were no wounds left to account for it. She had just enough time to drop into the sunken bath, scrub thoroughly, then drain the water—leaving a pink pool wasn't a good idea—and get into a fresh blue *chauri*. Not enough time to dry her hair completely, but that was a minor point. She wasn't trying to hide the fact that she'd been hurt, which Dalden already knew, just the visible reminder of how bad the injuries had been.

Tedra left Martha's link behind and told her to use her discretion if someone needed Transferring out of there until emotions settled down. At that point, Brittany had no idea who that someone might be, since her own emotions were getting out of hand as well.

By the time Dalden finally walked into their room she had worked herself into a fine state of nervousness. And what kept repeating in her mind was he was for real, *really* for real. He wasn't someone playing at being a barbarian, he *was* a barbarian, and how the hell did you deal with an archaic mentality that, instead of offering comfort over an injury, was going to add punishment to it as well?

He didn't look angry. But she knew him well enough by now to know that he wouldn't look it. Wrapped in his warrior's calm, you had to search for more subtle signs than the obvious, and they were there: a certain stiffness, compressed lips—no warmth in his golden eyes.

Her problem, and the reason she couldn't shake the dread building in her, was that she didn't know what to expect from him at this point. He'd said he would never cause her physical pain and she believed that, but what about mental? Just what was a barbarian's idea of punishment if it wasn't whips and chains? Dumped in some dark, dank hole for a week? A month? Solitary confinement? Her only defense was anger, and she wrapped herself securely in it.

"Remove your clothes."

She blinked, stiffened, narrowed her eyes at him. "No way."

"Remove them," he repeated as he started to cross the room to her. "I need to see that you are whole."

That should have reassured her. He just wanted to see for himself that she was okay. She would have wanted the same visual proof if he'd been the one injured. But this wasn't a normal situation.

"Forget it," she said and started backing away from him. "I'm not putting myself in a vulnerable position like that when you've got punishment on the brain. Do I look like I'm flipping out of my mind?"

She'd just given him a chance to deny it. He didn't take it. The anger wrapped more firmly around her.

"You can stop right there," she told him. "I'm fine, good as new. You *will* take my word for it. And I've already learned the lesson you think needs reinforcing, so there's no need for reinforcing it. I'll obey all future orders."

"Then obey this one. Remove your clothes!"

That was about as close as Dalden had ever come to actual shouting. Incredibly, it made her *want* to obey him, which was insane!

She shook her head at him, but dread was swiftly replacing her anger. She continued to back away. "That order has nothing to do with safety, just the opposite. And I'm warning you up front, I won't accept punishment from you. I absolutely refuse to accept it. So don't even *think* of—"

She'd run out of room for escaping, had come up against the wall behind her. Not that it mattered when his longer legs had already brought him within inches of her. And it didn't even take him two seconds to pull her away from the wall and peel that stupid *chauri* to the floor. He then turned her around, once, twice, held her arms out to the sides, and felt her limbs in a clinical manner.

Brittany bristled under the close examination, was

too indignant to be embarrassed over it. He should have taken her word for it.

She slammed her palms against his chest. A normal man would have at least been shoved back a little by it, since she put every bit of strength she had into it. Dalden wasn't budged. Her hands now hurt.

"Satisfied?" she growled. "I *told* you I was fine! Why couldn't you just believe me?"

He dropped to his knees in front of her, wrapping his arms around her. His head rested between her breasts. She was completely confounded by this, too surprised to think for a moment.

"I am sorry for my compulsion to see for myself," he told her with a great deal of feeling. "I am sorry for the pain you suffered," he added with even more feeling. "I am sorry I was not there to prevent it."

"Dalden, stop," she said, wrapping her arms around his head.

He didn't. "I am sorry you could not trust me enough to know that I would not give you an order without there being a good reason."

"Dalden, please, you're killing me with guilt here," she told him. "You have nothing to be sorry for. Look, if you must know, when I heard that animal outside the tent, I was hoping it was a normal animal. Our visit to the clearing was unplanned, and I wanted ammunition to discredit the Sha-Ka'an fantasy. And I was only going to satisfy my curiosity with a quick peek. But it saw me, and ended up proving me wrong instead."

His grip tightened on her. "I am sorry you had to nearly die before you could accept the truth."

She smiled. He didn't see it. "You and me both."

"And I am sorry that I must now make sure that you never let your curiosity interfere with an order given for your protection again."

She had begun to relax somewhat. Now all her muscles tensed again. He rose to his feet and picked her up to cradle in his arms.

"No!" she cried.

But he was set on his own path, was going to ignore anything she had to say. He didn't want to punish her, he *had* to, for her own "good." She knew that was where he was coming from, that he really did see this as being for her ultimate benefit, so nothing she said or did was going to stop it from happening.

She should just buck up and take it like a man. How bad could it be, anyway, if it wasn't going to cause her physical pain? But it was the principle of thing, damnit. She was too old to have lessons taught by way of punishment, as if she were a child.

It wasn't a law she broke, for crying out loud. That she could abide—break it and pay the fine or do the time. But a rule for her own safety should be at her discretion to decide whether to follow it or not. And the one she broke shouldn't even fall into that category. All he'd had to do was tell her that there were man-eating beasts in that woods and she would have damn well stayed in the tent.

He carried her to his bed, laid her on it, joined her there, and simply held her to him. He had to force it, she wasn't exactly laying still—until she realized that was all he was doing. He was trying to calm her first. He couldn't have missed her rigid stiffness. But there was no way she could get calm under the circumstances.

He must have finally realized that, because he began to kiss her. New alarm bells went off. She didn't think this was to calm her. How could it when his kissing had just the opposite effect? No, she was afraid he was trying to make amends beforehand, to cushion the blow for the punishment that was coming—as if anything could.

She fought what he was making her feel, desperately fought it. She couldn't let him get away with this. She had a stand to make here. But it was impossible. She'd never once been able to resist his kisses before. What made her think now would be any different?

Within moments she was kissing him back. Despite the grievance she should be feeling, and would soon be feeling, here, now, there was only him, a man she absolutely adored—when he wasn't being obnoxiously barbaric. And he certainly wasn't at the moment.

Meticulously, he brought every one of her senses to full awareness, set her pulses racing, frazzled her nerves in anticipation. So quickly, the coiled tension spread through her body. She was trembling, on fire, brought so close to the ultimate pleasure, only to have him soothe it away and start over again.

She told him in countless ways that she was ready, but he was determined to prolong the anticipation, to bring her to such a height of need that she'd probably explode the second he entered her. And then his hands were gone, the heat of his body next to her gone, too. It still took several moments for her to realize he'd actually left the bed.

Coming out of the daze, she sat up, growled, "What the hell was that all about?" But he hadn't just left the bed, he'd already left the room.

Martha was still there, however, and answered cheerfully, "You were just punished."

"How?"

"If you don't know—"

"I'm not kidding, how?"

"Sha-Ka'ani women are highly sexual. Warriors, at least those in this country, figured out long ago that the most harmless way to punish one's lifemate, if needed, was to bring her to an extreme state of desire, then leave her that way to reflect on the error of her ways. Being highly sexual themselves, they can't accomplish this without the help of *dhaya* juice, which temporarily kills their own sex drive."

Brittany began to laugh. So Dalden had been obnoxiously barbaric after all.

"You find sexual frustration funny?" Martha asked curiously.

"No, but it's not exactly something my people are unfamiliar with. In fact, we self-inflict it on ourselves all the time in the form of dating."

Martha made a snorting sound. "I have your definition of dating and it doesn't include—"

"Hold on, I meant what goes on when two people are getting to know each other. A few dates can lead to heavy petting, with the guy expecting to score, but the girl still undecided, so they both end the date frustrated. They could avoid the heavy petting, but since that's a learning-about-each-other process, too, they typically don't avoid it."

"Trust a low-tech human species to do things the hard way."

"I suppose advanced worlds have figured out easier ways?" Brittany retorted.

"Certainly. Computer-matched compatibility, works like a charm."

"We happen to have computer dating, and I promise you, it doesn't work like a charm."

"Antiquated stuff," Martha scoffed, adding, "and irrelevant to our subject. So the proven effective Kan-is-Tran punishment didn't bother you at all, eh? If that's the case, I'd say you've got such an advantage over that boy it isn't funny."

"How do you figure?"

"The fact that their idea of punishment doesn't faze you. The fact that he'll be drowning in guilt and the need to make amends every time he has to punish you. I'd say that puts you in the driver's seat."

Seeing it that way, Brittany couldn't help grinning. "You gonna tell him?"

"Me? Now, why would I do that? I happen to like pulling the wool over on these guys. It's just so priceless when their culture conflicts with logic they can't dispute. Makes my day, I tell you."

Brittany snorted this time, to which Martha just chuckled. But after a moment, Martha added, "By the way, Dalden didn't take anything to help him get through that. It's standard for a warrior to at least drink the *dhaya* juice first. He didn't. He was determined that if you had to suffer, he was going to suffer with you. And *your* body might be conditioned to shrug that kinda stuff off, but his isn't. At the moment, he's in a good deal of discomfort. He continues to impress me, that boy, with the depth of his caring. Has he told you he loves you yet?"

"No."

"He may never say the actual words, but you needn't doubt it now."

Brittany smiled to herself. No, she didn't doubt it at all.

Chapter 52

BRITTANY WASN'T SURE HOW TO DEAL WITH JORRAN, High King of Century III. She'd been briefed more thoroughly on the way to the room where he was waiting, about why he was there and what he had hoped to accomplish. He'd had every intention of more or less kidnapping her and forcing her to become his queen. He'd had every intention of killing Dalden, too, if he could have found him with her.

He'd brought a modern weapon with him this time to do it, since his razor sword hadn't been effective the last time they fought. It was what he'd killed the *sa'abo* with, without having to get close to it, and it horrified her that he could have killed Dalden just as easily with it.

He hadn't been let inside the castle with that

weapon, but he'd agreed to come unarmed into the enemy's camp, so he could speak with Brittany.

She'd been warned that he would probably try to talk her into leaving with him. She'd been warned not to trust anything he had to say, that duplicity was second nature to someone like him, who would say or do anything to accomplish his goals.

Jorran's relatives had already gone home. Martha had done no more than park the *Androvia* in the middle of their fleet of ships to make them rethink their demands. Considering that all twenty-three ships could fit inside the *Androvia*'s cargo bay, there hadn't been much to think about. The Centurians were a medieval people, and they recognized when they were outclassed and outgunned.

Challen hadn't been all that thrilled with the peaceful outcome of the "invasion." But when the Ly-San-Ters had become indebted to Jorran, that had pretty much ended any retaliatory sword practicing.

Dalden also couldn't do as he would have liked, which was to make sure Jorran never bothered them again in a more final way this time. Brittany was learning that warriors here weren't called warriors just because it sounded good. They could defend, exact retribution, and conquer just like anyone else, only they could do it in a *big* way if provoked.

She was left alone with him. Well, not really alone, since she had Martha's link with her. It had been Jorran's request, that privacy, and Martha wasn't going to reveal herself unless she had to. Dalden had refused to allow Brittany to get anywhere near Jorran *without* Martha's presence. He wasn't the least bit happy that she was being allowed to see him at all. It had taken

his father to get him to agree to it. And all because of
the debt they owed Jorran.

It was Brittany's debt, actually. She was well aware
of that. He'd saved her life. There was no getting
around the fact that she'd be dead if he hadn't found
her. So in an odd way, she could be grateful that he'd
tried to kidnap her. How weird.

She waited for him to speak first. He looked nothing like the Jorran she'd met at home. He was wearing
clothes from his own country, which included a fur-
trimmed royal cloak, a long fancy tunic, and high
boots. He looked now exactly like what he was, a medieval king, and his own clothing suited him much
better than a business suit.

He must have been thinking something along the
same lines because his first remark to her was, "Their
barbaric clothing does not suit you. I would dress you
in fine silks befitting a queen."

"I'm old enough to dress myself, thank you."

"I did not mean to insult."

She sighed. "I'm sorry, I didn't mean to give offense,
either. I owe my life to you. I am deeply grateful."

He nodded, expecting no less. "Grateful enough to
give that life into my keeping?"

"I've already given my life to another for keeping.
You know him well. He *is* my lifemate."

He waved that aside. "Their barbaric means of joining in marriage are not recognized on my world."

"Nor on mine, but in my heart I recognize it. So it's
binding for me."

He seemed surprised to hear that. "You *want* to stay
with him?"

She couldn't imagine why he might have thought

otherwise, but perhaps a little explaining was in order. "Jorran, when I said I would help you in my world I lied. I was wholeheartedly against what you were trying to accomplish. I was assisting the Sha-Ka'ani in stopping you. If you've been thinking otherwise all this time, I'm sorry."

He shrugged indifferently. "None of that matters. I saw in your eyes, on their ship, your real feelings for me."

She frowned in confusion, trying to remember that day of major shocks. "Sympathy? You mistook my compassion for something more. I didn't like it that they were denying you medical treatment, even though they assured me you weren't in pain. I wouldn't have liked seeing anyone left like that—but I see you're whole again. You must have come across a meditech between then and now."

"Only today," he replied with some bitterness. "In their Visitors' Center. We have not such things on my world."

"Then I'd say you have reason to be grateful as well, that you have no lasting scars from what happened. My people would have put you in prison for the rest of your life for what you attempted, if they'd been the ones to stop you. The Sha-Ka'ani only returned you to your own home with a few deformities they knew you could eventually fix."

"So in your mind that exonerates them?"

It was on the tip of her tongue to say that in her mind, he was the villain, but she diplomatically bit her tongue. "I'm just glad that no lasting damage was done—to anyone."

They'd been standing a good ten feet apart. He approached her now. It was all she could do not to try to keep that original distance, he made her that nervous. And as she'd feared, he touched her, though harmlessly, a mere brush of his fingers against her cheek.

"You have a strange way of looking at things," he remarked softly.

"Not strange, just different from how you view things. It doesn't mean I'm right and you're wrong, or vice versa. We just come from vastly different cultures."

Jeez, was she telling him what she should be telling herself? What Martha had tried to make her see all along? The Sha-Ka'ani weren't really barbarians, they were just different. Their way of doing things was normal for them, worked for them, so it was the right way. To compare them with other cultures, her own in particular, was ludicrous. They were unique. They'd evolve in their own way.

"You would like my culture," he said wistfully. "I would make you a queen. What can your barbarian offer you to equal that?"

There was no hesitation in her answer. "Himself, which is all I need to make me happy—because I love him deeply, with all my heart."

Chapter 53

MARTHA APOLOGIZED FOR NOT WARNING HER THAT Dalden had listened in on her conversation with Jorran, that it was the only way he would allow her to be left alone with the man. Brittany wasn't too happy about that. They hadn't spoken since he'd punished her. She had wanted to enjoy some of his amends-making before she officially forgave him, not have him hear secondhand that she still loved the heck out of him.

Not that it mattered. When she did finally see him again that day, he wasn't interested in talking. He marched her straight back to their room, where they spent the rest of the day and half of the next making sure neither of them were still suffering over that silly punishment.

She was beginning to wonder, though, if his dragging her off to places without a word of explanation was going to be a standard practice, because he did it again the next afternoon. He tossed a white cloak over her shoulders, took her hand, and pulled her behind him out of the castle, across most of the town, and through some of the park that fronted the edge of the mountain.

He stood behind her, wrapped his arms around her, and said nothing while she absorbed the incredible view before them. All of the verdant green valley that spread at the base of Mount Raik could be seen, woods and lakes beyond, and in the far distance, even a long range of other mountains which were a mere purple haze.

It took her breath away, all that beauty. And then Dalden said, "You will build our house here."

She swung around to stare at him incredulously. "*I* will?" she gasped.

"The design will be of your choice," he replied matter-of-factly, as if he weren't astounding the hell out of her. "You will keep in mind, however, that a warrior requires a good deal of space to keep from feeling confined."

She grinned at that point. "You're talking a big house, I take it?"

"Yes."

"A *really* big house?"

"Yes."

She beamed ecstatically—until she recalled that his country didn't have lumber mills. "I'm not sure I can work with the materials you have available here."

"Martha has assured me that she can obtain anything you require."

"It will take me a long time to build something of the size you're talking about," she pointed out next.

"You will have help. Kodos and his lifemate, Ruriko, would like to assist you. Corth II will be available, also. And I will rarely be far from your side, *kerima*. You are likely to have other volunteers as well, once the town sees what you are doing. Sha-Ka-Ra has stood here for centuries without change. Change is not required, but it is not discouraged, either, and there are many who regret that we have no knowledge of creating things. Kodos has shown that clearly in his desire to learn your craft."

"He actually agreed to let his lifemate work beside him, when your women have never known real jobs?"

Dalden gave her an aggrieved look. "To keep peace in his household, he was—persuaded—to agree. He made the mistake of telling her too much about your culture. She was greatly intrigued."

Brittany winced. "I'm not heading for trouble here, am I? I *really* don't want to go down in history as the instigator of the women's movement in Sha-Ka'an. Not that you don't need a women's movement, but it's been pointed out to me that you need to figure these things out for yourselves, not have them forced down your throat by other species."

He cupped her face in his hands. "Do you intend to make trouble?"

"Well—no."

"Then no trouble will occur."

"Yeah, sure," she mumbled.

He chuckled at her. "I am teasing you, *chemar*. I should tell you that I have come to a realization that has taken a burden from me. Long ago I made the decision to follow my father's ways completely, to ignore my mother's. It was a good decision at the time. It was not easy when I was young, to be so divided by such vastly different beliefs. But this left a hollowness in me, as if I were not whole. Finding you, knowing you, loving you, has shown me that—"

She squealed and threw her arms around his neck. "You said it! You said you love me!"

He set her back from him, gave her a stern look. "Do not try my patience, woman. You know very well the depth of my feelings for you."

"Well, yes." She grinned, not the least bit intimidated by that look. "But it's still nice to *hear* it occasionally."

He rolled his eyes, but drew her back against him. "What I wanted to share with you was that I am no longer divided. Half of me is Kystrani, and I can embrace that half, which comes with full knowledge of other worlds, other beliefs, other ways—including yours. Such things will no longer be ignored simply because they are unknown here."

"You're trying to tell me you've got me figured out?" she asked.

"I am telling you that you do not have to change completely just because you will live here now. I am telling you that your ways are understood, that such understanding will temper how you are dealt with. This does not mean you can ignore what you have thus far been taught of *our* ways. Until a warrior will not take for himself any woman he wants who is not obviously already claimed, you will obey our laws for your *own* protection."

"Yes, I will."

"Until our world is rid of beasts that can cause you harm, you will obey *my* orders."

"Yes, I will."

He frowned at her. "Why do you not argue with me?"

"Because this is Sha-Ka'an. These rules work here. They wouldn't work anywhere else, but here they work just fine. Besides," she added with a grin, "after the gift you've given me today, you're in my good graces big-time."

He kissed her deeply, then gently—they were a long way from any privacy. "You may build hundreds of houses, whole towns, if it will make you happy."

"I was talking about your love," she replied in a softly purring tone.

That did it: he took her hand again and started dragging her off to find some of that missing privacy.

Brittany laughed to herself. He wasn't really barbaric, her lifemate. A warrior, yes. Adamant when it came to protecting her, yes. A bit domineering, but understanding, too. And gentle. And caring.

And how the hell did she get so lucky?

Please look for
Johanna Lindsey's
newest bestseller

THE PURSUIT

Coming Spring 2002

And now enjoy an excerpt!

THE PURSUIT

KIMBERLY MACGREGOR WAVED THE LETTER IN HER hand to gain her husband's attention as he entered her sitting room. "Megan has written again," she told him. "She has invitations piling up, too many as usual, but in this case that's ideal. Let her pick and choose the best ones. She's sounding really excited about this. Want to read the letter?"

"Nay."

That answer was too abrupt and a bit disgruntled-sounding for a man of Lachlan MacGregor's easy temperament.

"You aren't having second thoughts about letting Melissa go to London, are you?"

"Aye."

"Lachlan!"

His disgruntled tone was now accompanied by

a matching look. "I dinna like asking the Duke and Duchess o' Wrothston for favors."

Kimberly relaxed. She should have known. Lachlan might get along famously with Devlin St. James when he and his wife Megan came to visit them at Kregora Castle, or vice versa, but it wasn't always that way. They had in fact met under bizarre circumstances which didn't account for Lachlan's remark about favors.

"This was Megan's idea, so there's no favor involved," she reminded him. "As soon as she heard that all of Melissa's beaux were being frightened off by my over-protective brothers, she suggested Meli come to England where the MacFearsons are unknown. You agreed it was a good idea. I agreed it was an excellent idea. And Meli is looking forward to it. So don't be having second thoughts now."

"I assumed she'd be staying at Wrothston, as we do when we visit them in England, no' in London town," he grumbled. "The lass has been tae Wrothston enough tae be comfortable and feel right at home. London's no' the same, and she'll be nervous enough—"

"Nervous?" Kimberly interrupted. "Our daughter is excited about this trip, she's not the least bit nervous. If anyone's nervous it's you, and you and I aren't even going until later in the summer.

Is that it, then? You're letting your worry for her override your better judgment?"

"Nay, I just dinna want her feeling she has tae find a husband afore she comes home. That's tae much pressure tae be putting on her at her young age. You have assured her—?"

"Yes, yes, I've assured her she can be an old maid if she'd like."

"Och, this isna funny, Kimber."

She tsked at him. "You're the one making too much out of it. Most young girls her age go through this; I did myself. Now I might have been nervous about it, but Meli really isn't. She plans to have fun, to make some new friends, to be awed by such a big town as London is, and she even figures she'll probably find a husband while she's at it. But that's not at the top of her to-do list by any means. She thought we wanted her to make a concerted effort to get affianced, but I've assured her if she does, that's fine, and if she doesn't, that's fine, too. Maybe you should tell her the same before she leaves, so she can just relax and let what happens happen. Now have we covered all your last-minute doubts?"

"Nay, 'tis still a huge undertaking tae be putting on the duchess on our behalf."

"Would you like us to go as well for the whole

summer instead of just a few weeks as we planned?"

He looked appalled. Just as she expected. "You said that wouldna be necessary."

"Nor is it. We covered Megan's willingness already. And furthermore, she isn't planning any events herself; she merely has invitations lined up that she was no doubt going to accept anyway. Besides, she adores Meli and is an old hand at this sort of thing. She sponsored me, didn't she? And had a hand in matching you and I to wedded bliss."

That made him grin. "Is that what we've been having, darlin'? Wedded bliss?"

She quirked a golden brow at him and asked, "You don't think so?"

He pulled her to her feet, then meshed her hips to his. "I'd be calling it heaven m'self."

"Would you now?" She grinned back at him, then made a face. "Bah, you're not going to get out of this subject that easily. Why are you really having doubts? And no more of these lame reasons that don't wash."

He sighed. "I had the hope remaining that our lass would end up wi' a fine Scot brave enough tae ignore the legend and trounce any o' your sixteen brothers that think tae bully him."

"What an unkind thought," she said, and smacked his shoulder before she moved away from him. "I love my brothers—"

"I know you do, Kimber, and I even tolerate them m'self, but you canna deny they deserve a trouncing or two for scaring off all o' Meli's suitors. If we didna have friends in England willing tae sponsor her for a season there, the poor lass could end up permanently unwed, and I want m' daughter tae be as happy in wedlock as I've made you."

She chuckled. "Listen to that bragging."

"True nonetheless," he said with complete confidence.

"Perhaps," she allowed with a teasing grin, but then grew serious again. "As for Meli and her future happiness, is the nationality of the man she loses her heart to really of importance to you? And before you answer, keep in mind that if you say yes, your English wife will be insulted."

He laughed. "Half English wife, though one could wish yer Scottish half didna come from the MacFearson himself."

She ignored the reference to her father this time. "Answer me."

"Nay, darlin', the hope was no' that her husband be Scottish exactly, was more that he just hail from closer tae home than England is. I'm no' looking forward tae our lass moving far away is all," he ended with another sigh.

She moved closer again to cup his cheeks in her hands. "You knew that would be possible."

"Aye."

"You also knew that her prospects in our neighborhood were very slim. We don't exactly live close to any towns up here, and the other clans nearby don't have any sons of an age appropriate for our lass. And being the MacGregor's daughter limits her choices even further."

"Aye, I ken that as well."

"So this is all just a father bemoaning the loss of his only daughter in marriage, even before she's married?" she asked in exasperation.

He nodded with a sheepish look. She decided not to scold him for such silliness but said instead, "Lach, I'll be just as unhappy to see her go, but we knew from the day she was born that she would be leaving us one day to start her own family, and even then we didn't expect her to start that family near Kregora Castle. Granted, we weren't thinking as far as England, but still—"

Kimberly amazed even herself when she suddenly burst into tears. Lachlan gathered her close and made all the soothing sounds appropriate to providing comfort. She finally pushed away from him, annoyed with herself.

"Don't ask why that happened," she mumbled.

He grinned at her. "I'm sorry, Kimber. I didna mean tae refresh all your own misgivings."

"You didn't. Unlike you, I'm delighted Meli

has this opportunity for a season in London. I just"— she paused for a sigh of her own—"just had the same hope as you still lurking, though I thought I had given up on that long ago. And it is pointless. Even those few young lads who did come to call on her live miles away, which is probably why you weren't all that displeased when my brothers ran them off."

"Miles away is no distance a' tall up here; they just didna impress me too much is all, and rightly so as it turned out. Look how quickly they turned tail when your brothers started in on them. That last one made his excuses after one wee warning from Ian Two that he'd be displeased if his niece was e'er made unhappy."

"I think it was because he had a fistful of the poor boy's shirt when he said it."

They both laughed for a moment, remembering how quickly the suitor had fled. He'd practically run for the door the moment after he'd made his excuses. The laughter eased their misgivings.

"Och, well, this trip canna be avoided I suppose," Lachlan conceded.

"No, it can't."

"Speaking o' which, is Meli done wi' her packing?"

"She's not leaving for three more days, plenty of time to finish that up. She's gone to see my father and probably will be spending the night. Actually, I think her intent was to assure my brothers that she forgave them for ruining her prospects here at home—a few of them have been quite gloomy over that if you didn't know. She was also going to assure them that when the right man for her comes along, she'll know it herself, so they needn't worry on that account."

"She actually thinks saying so will assure them of anything?"

"Well, she's hoping." Kimberly grinned. "My brothers can be reasoned with—some of the time."

Read the further adventures of a woman
brave enough to stand up to
her sixteen protective uncles in

THE PURSUIT

America Loves Lindsey!
The Timeless Romances of
The New York Times Bestselling Author

Johanna Lindsey

PRISONER OF MY DESIRE   0-380-75627-7/$7.99 US/$10.99 Can

ONCE A PRINCESS   0-380-75625-0/$7.99 US/$10.99 Can

WARRIOR'S WOMAN   0-380-75301-4/$6.99 US/$8.99 Can

MAN OF MY DREAMS   0-380-75626-9/$7.50 US/$9.99 Can

SURRENDER MY LOVE   0-380-76256-0/$7.50 US/$9.99 Can

YOU BELONG TO ME   0-380-76258-7/$7.50 US/$9.99 Can

UNTIL FOREVER   0-380-76259-5/$6.99 US/$9.99 Can

LOVE ME FOREVER   0-380-72570-3/$6.99 US/$8.99 Can

SAY YOU LOVE ME   0-380-72571-1/$6.99 US/$8.99 Can

ALL I NEED IS YOU   0-380-76260-9/$6.99 US/$8.99 Can

THE PRESENT   0-380-80438-7/$6.99 US/$9.99 Can

JOINING   0-380-79333-4/$7.50 US/$9.99 Can

THE HEIR   0-380-79334-2/$7.99 US/$10.99 Can

HOME FOR THE HOLIDAYS

   0-380-81481-1/$7.99 US/$10.99 Can

HEART OF A WARRIOR

   0-380-81479-X/$7.99 US/$10.99 Can

Coming Soon in Hardcover

THE PURSUIT
0-380-97855-5/$25.95 US/$39.50 Can

....

Available wherever books are sold or please call 1-800-331-3761
to order.   JLA 1101

Experience the Wonder of Romance

LISA KLEYPAS

SOMEONE TO WATCH OVER ME
0-380-80230-9/$6.99 US/$8.99 Can

STRANGER IN MY ARMS
0-380-78145-X/$6.99 US/$9.99 Can

MIDNIGHT ANGEL
0-380-77353-8/$6.99 US/$9.99 Can

DREAMING OF YOU
0-380-77352-X/$6.99 US/$9.99 Can

BECAUSE YOU'RE MINE
0-380-78144-1/$6.99 US/$9.99 Can

ONLY IN YOUR ARMS
0-380-76150-5/$5.99 US/$7.99 Can

ONLY WITH YOUR LOVE
0-380-76151-3/$6.50 US/$8.50 Can

THEN CAME YOU
0-380-77013-X/$6.99 US/$9.99 Can

PRINCE OF DREAMS
0-380-77355-4/$5.99 US/$7.99 Can

SOMEWHERE I'LL FIND YOU
0-380-78143-3/$6.99 US/$9.99 Can

WHERE DREAMS BEGIN
0-380-80231-7/$6.99 US/$9.99 Can

SUDDENLY YOU
0-380-80232-5/$6.99 US/$9.99 Can

Coming Soon

LADY SOPHIA'S LOVER
0-380-81106-5/$7.50 US/$9.99 Can

Available wherever books are sold or please call 1-800-331-3761
to order.   LK 1201

America Loves Lindsey!
The Timeless Romances
of #1 Bestselling Author

Johanna Lindsey

GENTLE ROGUE	0-380-75302-2/$6.99 US/$9.99 Can
DEFY NOT THE HEART	0-380-75299-9/$6.99 US/$9.99 Can
SILVER ANGEL	0-380-75294-8/$6.99 US/$8.99 Can
TENDER REBEL	0-380-75086-4/$6.99 US/$8.99 Can
SECRET FIRE	0-380-75087-2/$6.99 US/$9.99 Can
HEARTS AFLAME	0-380-89982-5/$6.99 US/$9.99 Can
A HEART SO WILD	0-380-75084-8/$6.99 US/$9.99 Can
WHEN LOVE AWAITS	0-380-89739-3/$6.99 US/$8.99 Can
LOVE ONLY ONCE	0-380-89953-1/$6.99 US/$8.99 Can
BRAVE THE WILD WIND	0-380-89284-7/$7.99 US/$10.99 Can
A GENTLE FEUDING	0-380-87155-6/$7.99 US/$10.99 Can
HEART OF THUNDER	0-380-85118-0/$6.99 US/$8.99 Can
SO SPEAKS THE HEART	0-380-81471-4/$6.99 US/$9.99 Can
GLORIOUS ANGEL	0-380-84947-X/$7.99 US/$10.99 Can
PARADISE WILD	0-380-77651-0/$6.99 US/$8.99 Can
FIRES OF WINTER	0-380-75747-8/$7.99 US/$10.99 Can
A PIRATE'S LOVE	0-380-40048-0/$6.99 US/$9.99 Can
CAPTIVE BRIDE	0-380-01697-4/$6.99 US/$8.99 Can
TENDER IS THE STORM	0-380-89693-1/$7.99 US/$10.99 Can
SAVAGE THUNDER	0-380-75300-6/$6.99 US/$8.99 Can
KEEPER OF THE HEART	0-380-77493-3/$7.99 US/$10.99 Can
THE MAGIC OF YOU	0-380-75629-3/$7.50 US/$9.99 Can
ANGEL	0-380-75628-5/$7.50 US/$9.99 Can

....

Available wherever books are sold or please call 1-800-331-3761
to order.   JLB 1101

Captivating and sensual romances
by *New York Times* bestselling author
Stephanie Laurens

A SECRET LOVE
0-380-80570-7/$6.99 US/$9.99 Can

A ROGUE'S PROPOSAL
0-380-80569-3/$6.99 US/$9.99 Can

SCANDAL'S BRIDE
0-380-80568-5/$6.99 US/$9.99 Can

A RAKE'S VOW
0-380-79457-8/$6.99 US/$9.99 Can

DEVIL'S BRIDE
0-380-79456-X/$6.99 US/$9.99 Can

CAPTAIN JACK'S WOMAN
0-380-79455-1/$6.99 US/$9.99 Can

ALL ABOUT LOVE
0-380-81201-0/$6.99 US/$9.99 Can

ALL ABOUT PASSION
0-380-81202-9/$6.99 US/$9.99 Can

And in Hardcover

THE PROMISE IN A KISS
0-06-018888-X/$18.00 US/$27.50 Can

....

Available wherever books are sold or please call 1-800-331-3761
to order.   LAU 1101

NEW YORK TIMES BESTSELLING AUTHOR

Elizabeth Lowell

"Elizabeth Lowell is great!"
Johanna Lindsey

ONLY YOU   0-380-76340-0/$6.99 US/$9.99 Can

ONLY MINE   0-380-76339-7/$6.99 US/$8.99 Can

ONLY HIS   0-380-76338-9/$6.99 US/$8.99 Can

ONLY LOVE   0-380-77256-6/$6.99 US/$9.99 Can

UNTAMED   0-380-76953-0/$6.50 US/$8.50 Can

FORBIDDEN   0-380-76954-9/$6.50 US/$8.50 Can

ENCHANTED   0-380-77257-4/$6.50 US/$8.50 Can

AUTUMN LOVER
    0-380-76955-7/$6.99 US/$9.99 Can

WINTER FIRE   0-380-77583-2/$6.99 US/$8.99 Can

Available wherever books are sold or please call 1-800-331-3761
to order.   LOW 0101

The WONDER of KATHLEEN E. WOODIWISS

A Season Beyond A Kiss
0-380-80794-7 $7.99 U.S. ($10.99 Can)

Ashes in the Wind   0-380-76984-0 $6.99 U.S. ($8.99 Can)

Come Love a Stranger
0-380-89936-1 $6.99 U.S. ($9.99 Can)

The Elusive Flame
0-380-80786-6 $7.50 U.S. ($9.99 Can)

The Flame and the Flower
0-380-00525-5 $6.99 U.S. ($9.99 Can)

Forever in Your Embrace
0-380-77246-9 $7.50 U.S. ($9.99 Can)

Petals on the River
0-380-79828-X $6.99 U.S. ($8.99 Can)

A Rose in Winter   0-380-84400-1 $6.99 U.S. ($8.99 Can)

Shanna   0-380-38588-0 $6.99 U.S. ($8.99 Can)

So Worthy My Love
0-380-76148-3 $6.99 U.S. ($9.99 Can)

The Wolf and the Dove
0-380-00778-9 $6.99 U.S. ($8.99 Can)

....

Available wherever books are sold or please call 1-800-331-3761
to order.   WDW 1200